Praise for

One Day's Tale

Betsy Randall's journey from England to Colonial Virginia is a bone-rattling, eye-opening voyage across the Atlantic to her brother's plantation—a place he described as "paradise." There, slavery forms a nightmarish counterpoint to the bonds of sisterhood that develop between Betsy and her brother's slave, Deborah. Lois Barliant is a terrifically gifted writer who knows this world to bedrock, and *One Day's Tale* is a spectacular act of the moral imagination—by turns lush and terrifying, it's a celebration of the love that liberates and an indictment of the institutional racism and misogyny that continue to haunt our present moment.

—Karen Russell, author of
Swamplandia! and *Vampires in the Lemon Grove*

Set near the beginning of the 18th century, this debut novel introduces the resilient and compassionate Betsy Randall. Aboard a ship bound for her brother Robert's tobacco farm and estate in Virginia, she is joined by her husband, Isaac, and their three young children. While she's uncertain if their trip from England is an advisable one, her trepidations are quickly replaced with horror ... Barliant is a deft, unsentimental writer, and scenes are portrayed with unflinching tenor. ... It's a complicated, engaging and ultimately moving narrative ... The writing is assured and affecting, and Barliant does fine work exploring this troubled era without becoming bogged down in its details.

—*Kirkus Reviews*

One Day's Tale is an exciting adventure novel about an English woman surviving violence and mayhem on the high seas, and arriving in the American colonies in very different circumstances than she expected. The atmosphere is charged, the details sure; Lois Barliant has meticulously researched her material. This is a captivating book.

—Elizabeth McKenzie, author of
Stop that Girl and *The Portable Veblen*

Lois Barliant is a brilliant writer. *One Day's Tale* is a compelling story with vivid details of the early 1700's. History mixed with fiction in the tradition of *Roots*. A serious chronicle of America's past, the abuse and treatment of slaves, along with the hardship the settlers encounter. With plenty of drama and romance, the novel is a captivating heart-wrenching view of how we lived.

—Syed Haider, author of
To Be with Her and *The Tumbleweed Collection*

One Day's Tale is a memorable and exciting historical novel about one English woman's journey to Colonial America. Along the way Betsy encounters pirates as ruthless as ISIS and the brute ugliness of slavery, but she maintains her courage and her commitments to other human beings. A moving, believable and beautifully researched story.

—Scott Turow, author of
Identical and *Innocent*

ONE DAY'S TALE

a novel

LOIS BARLIANT

austin
lamp
press

ONE DAY'S TALE

Copyright © 2015 Lois Barliant

This book is a work of fiction. Any references to historical events,
real people, or real locales are used fictitiously. Other names,
characters, places, and incidents are products of the author's
imagination, and any resemblance to actual events or locales
or persons, living or dead, is entirely coincidental.

Edition ISBNs
ISBN: 978-0-9862451-0-7 (paperback);
978-0-9862451-1-4 (hardback); 978-0-9862451-2-1 (e-book)

Cover design by Suzanne LaGasa
Book design by Catherine Leonardo

This edition was prepared for printing by The Editorial Department
7650 E. Broadway, #308, Tucson, Arizona 85710
www.editorialdepartment.com

Printed in the United States of America.

To Ron, Claire, and Anne.

If suffering alone taught, all the world would be wise. To suffering must be added mourning, understanding, patience, love, openness, and the willingness to remain vulnerable.

Hour of Gold, Hour of Lead: Diaries and Letters
of Anne Morrow Lindbergh, 1929-1932

One day tells its tale to another. *Psalm 19: 2*

ONE DAY'S TALE

Chapter 1

In the dark, Betsy Randall breathed in the scents of her family: the faint fragrance of pine from the oil her husband Isaac slapped on his cheeks, the sweet salt smell of the baby. In the bunk above, Mary wheezed. She'd be curled around Alice, her fingers in her sister's hair. Like Isaac, next to Betsy in the bunk, the children slept to the song of the ship, to the groaning boards and the scrape of the rigging. Since they had embarked the first of February, 1713, the baby David had slept better these four weeks on board the *Sally Dash* than he had in their home in Brompton-on-Thames. His cradle rocked above their table, a trunk that had been stuffed with stores of food, extra clothing, and shoes they were advised to bring to Virginia. Virginia. A land her brother had chosen, but he had been killed. The Randalls were going to claim the Harrington estate, but they knew almost nothing of his plantation. This time, between night and morning, she could escape the stench of the lower deck before the sunlight awakened her family, sneak out of bed without disturbing Isaac's dreams, and go up on deck for fresh air.

Betsy stuffed her pillow under Isaac's arm and rolled off the bunk. He slept so soundly that he wouldn't hear the creak of her step on a floorboard, the squeal of the cabin door, or the click when she closed it behind her. Through the dark gangway to the lower deck crammed with bails, she crept past boxes and crates, including the one Isaac had a carpenter build for their household belongings. Above this jumble, sailors snored in hammocks, some mumbling in their sleep. Betsy paused for their dreams to accommodate her presence. When they snored evenly again, she followed her favorite plank, new wood that wouldn't squeak when she tiptoed past them and the crates, to the wan light of the hatch. Rung by rung she climbed onto the deck and hid at the rail, a shadow between two coils of rope, to breathe sweet air.

The sea sprayed her face. Betsy took off her cap to let the breeze blow through her hair, sure the crew of the morning watch wouldn't see her. On deck, with stars bright in the west, she forgave Isaac's decision to move the family to her brother's plantation in Virginia. She pulled her mother's worn gray shawl tighter. Robert had been dead two years, her mother six months. She would not be home to lay flowers on her grave at Easter. Betsy rested her cheek on the cold rail, wet from the soft sea spray. Robert had lived in Virginia fourteen years, coming home twice. The first time, he'd urged Isaac and Betsy to leave England and farm with him. Isaac had scoffed at the idea; he was a merchant banker. The second time, wearing a fine jacket, Robert offered Isaac a tin of his tobacco, and promised that if he settled in Virginia, his brokering practice would prosper. Robert had returned to England a wealthy landowner seeking a wife, but sailed back to Virginia alone. The news of Robert's death struck Isaac as providential, and despite

Betsy's wish to stay in Brompton, he booked his family passage on the *Sally Dash*. Those thoughts plagued Betsy when she went on deck without Isaac's permission. The fresh air came in shivering gusts. A thin red light slit the horizon.

The pitch of the sea no longer sickened her; the rhythm of the ship's roll comforted her. Four weeks out, she knew which sailors couldn't resist a rude remark, a lewd gesture, or a quick pinch, and which would have a kind smile or a bright "Morning, missus." One sailor Betsy favored led the crew on hoisting the sails above her. Charlie's lopsided grin made Betsy feel girlish and light-footed. If she were not a woman, not married, not a mother, and on his crew, she could scramble up the rigging with the sailors and balance on the yard high over the sea. She knew some songs, but Charlie made up verses to those songs. She and Isaac would laugh at his words. "My Mandy is a sweet girl." Across the yard, she imagined herself standing with the sailors, heaving the sail. "Sweet, sweet Mandy," she sang with them and the screeching chorus of block and tackle. The white sheet jumped. "Her lips are cherry red." The sail bounced higher. They yanked each rope as easily as a mother might tie a kerchief around her daughter's waist. Charlie, his brown curls catching the sun, sang more verses. Out on the spar above the cresting waves, Betsy's skirt billowed in the wind. "My Mandy pleads." Betsy imagined herself tugging at the rope. "My Mandy begs." With a pull and a bit of a yank, Charlie flitted along the yardarm. "I lift the sheet." The sail popped open in the wind. "And she spreads her legs." Charlie grabbed the mast, hugging it as if it were a woman, and thrust his hips hard against it.

Betsy sank down. Isaac had warned her about the sailors, but Charlie Potts had never been crude.

"Sweet, sweet Mandy, my true love." The sailors continued the song, scurrying to the highest spar to raise the top gallant.

Betsy wanted to be back in the cabin before the sailors climbed down from the spar. She couldn't face Charlie Potts. She didn't want Isaac to see the shame on her face, though his bringing her on deck last night may have given Charlie the idea for his bawdy song.

After supper with Captain Mayhew, the bursar, and the first mate, Isaac had come down to the lower deck, tiptoed into the cabin, and awakened her. "Come see the moon," he said. He wouldn't even let her put on shoes, but pushed her ahead of him, in her stocking feet, wearing nothing but her shift and her mother's shawl, naked under the sailors' gaze. Last night, every rope and pulley, every board and nail, every bucket and box reflected silver light. Shadows blurred coils of rope. The sails glowed like silk. The sailors had stopped singing. The carpenter's squeezebox coughed shut. Cards flapped down on the barrel, and a man, caught mid-step in a jig, pointed to the moon and stared at Betsy. She'd drawn back, but Isaac gripped her waist tight and led her to the rail. He wanted her to see the moon's path on the sea. He didn't hear the men snickering. "How beautiful life is," he'd said. "How fickle. Your brother succeeded in everything, and then his gambling ended in a duel." He pulled her hair from her neck and kissed her. "You and I have inherited his fifteen hundred acres of rich tobacco land." Betsy hadn't answered. Robert was dead, but most of the time, she thought of him as still living in Virginia. Isaac's indifference to the sailors' laughter angered her. Back in the cabin, he'd apologized for reminding her of her brother's death, for bringing her on deck, and for waking her. "No,

Isaac, I'm glad we saw the moon and its silver path." It was she who made love to him, putting her hand over his mouth to keep from waking the girls.

Before Betsy could reach the hatch, Charlie was scrambling down the rigging. "Ahoy! A sail! Sail ho! Ship ahoy!" He jumped, landing near Betsy. "Morning, Missus." He rapped on the captain's door. "Sails. A ship to port. Probably a pink."

Betsy's shawl had snagged on a nail, and Charlie jumped to free it for her. "Sails straight west. Pretty as a rosebud."

The Dash careened into a trough, and Charlie grabbed Betsy's arm. She clenched her elbow to her side, out of his grasp, and gripping the rail, steadied herself. Down the steep rungs of the hatch, her skirt clutched around her knees with one hand, Betsy raced to be in the cabin before the sailors tumbled out of their hammocks and crowded the lower deck.

Isaac met her at the cabin door. "Don't go up alone," he said. He pulled her inside. "You're cold." He latched the door and wrapped his arms around her. Barefoot and in his shirt, he pulled her toward their berth. "The girls are asleep," he said.

"No, Isaac." She wriggled away. She would not spread her legs this morning.

"Don't parade on deck, smiling at the sailors, and then come down with 'No, Isaac.'"

She wanted to cover her cheeks, but he'd guess that she'd felt humiliated. "I don't smile at sailors." With a finger to her lips, she pointed to the girls' bunk. "Charlie sighted a ship."

He looked to the porthole as if to see the ship off the bow, and then opened the door to listen to the sailors' laughter and calls as they climbed up top. He pulled on his gray twill pants and reached for his stockings, white as table linens. "Did they call the ship's colors?"

"I didn't stay to hear." Betsy jerked a comb through knots the wind had made in her hair, each yank a small punishment for taking off her cap, for going up on deck, for being on the ship. Isaac had identified the sailors, even the carpenter and the able-bodied seamen in homespun, as pickpockets and thieves the first day out. Grabbing a fistful of hair, she plucked at a tangle, biting down hard on the thought that Charlie had known she was on deck when he led the song. The snarled hair combed smooth. She shouldn't have gone up top to watch the sunrise.

As he did every morning, Isaac polished his shoe buckles with an old wool rag. After he had buttoned his rose-colored vest and put on his jacket, he hitched the collar high on his neck, lined up the buttons on the deep cuffs, and with a fling, centered his wig to pull it in place. The long brown curls made him look older.

"You are a handsome man." Betsy put her comb on the trunk, going to nuzzle in his embrace. In Brompton-on-Thames, Isaac had been a merchant banker, and with the wig, he looked the part of the landowner he would be in Virginia, the equal of the Earl of Guilford.

He chucked her under the chin and bent to kiss her. The baby whimpered, and Isaac hugged Betsy close as if the child's plea increased Isaac's affection for her. After fetching David and pulling off the wet cloths without touching them to his jacket, he wrapped the baby in a dry blanket and handed him to Betsy. By the time she settled on the bunk with David, Isaac had left to see the approaching ship.

Chapter 2

At the door of the captain's quarters, Isaac stood tallest, the curls of his wig too heavy for the breeze to lift. He'd placed himself between Mayhew and the first mate of the *Sally Dash* to welcome the visiting captain in his elegant blue jacket, on his hat, a gray ostrich feather fluttering with every whiff of wind. Betsy pulled her waist in tight and smiled to meet the visitor. She nudged Mary and Alice forward, but Mayhew had stumbled back against Isaac. "Pirates."

The man nodded, a suggestion of a bow, and drew a pistol from inside his fine jacket. "Captain Emanuel Brickhart," he said. He aimed his pistol at Mayhew's chest, and as the first mate said, "God help us," the shot threw Mayhew backwards, his legs marching flat on the deck. Isaac had wet himself. Betsy fell against the steps to the gallery. Mayhew was dead.

The smell of gunpowder hung in the air. With the girls clinging to her skirt, and the baby in her arms, Betsy couldn't help Isaac. He had to save himself. And them. She picked up Alice to carry her and the baby. "Mary, come."

A sword blocked the escape to Mayhew's quarters. A pirate

with hair as long and thick as Isaac's wig smiled. "You're safe." He shoved her between the quarterdeck and the stairs.

Shielding Mary and Alice, Betsy quieted David and glared at her husband. The only chance they had was for Isaac to surprise the leader before his men could defend him. Isaac must grab that man's gun, disarm him, and protect his family. With the gun, he could threaten to kill this Emanuel Brickhart and force him to keep Betsy and the children safe. If Betsy put down the baby and Alice, she would wrestle the sword from her guard and run to Isaac before the other pirates came to their captain's rescue, but she couldn't leave the children.

A tall blond sailor, a muscular man, his beard a broom, had come on board with a loud laugh. He'd carried a barrel. "Our best Trinidad rum," he said. He rolled his Rs—a Swede. He handed Charlie the ladle for filling the mugs with rum before striding over to Brickhart's side. He was there to see Captain Mayhew shot. Before Mayhew stopped marching, the Swede pulled a pistol out of his vest and put it to the temple of the first mate. The man knelt. "Please," he said, his hands folded. His body bumped against Isaac's leg when he fell.

"Mama." Mary squeezed her arms around Betsy.

Betsy lowered Alice to the deck. Kneeling between the girls, with David at her shoulder, she prayed for Isaac. The Swede hung his arm around Isaac's neck and beckoned to a black man with strange scars on his cheeks. Before Mayhew was shot, the African had offered sailors pinches of tobacco, and they'd smiled, taking what they wanted.

Mary snuggled closer to Betsy when the black pirate moved to one side of Isaac while the Swede stood on the other.

At the two pistol blasts, the crew of the *Sally Dash* had recoiled. All the jigging, drinking, and laughter had stopped. The sailors stared at the bodies. That moment, when the pirate captain might have been off guard—right then—Isaac should have grabbed the pistol.

Before Isaac could move, Brickhart glanced at Betsy and wiped his gun with his handkerchief. He smiled as he shoved his pistol into his sash and buttoned his jacket over it. Turning to Isaac, he held out his hand. "Your ring, sir."

Isaac looked right into his eyes. "The ring is a gift from my wife."

That wasn't true. He'd been wearing the ring with the dark green stone the day he met Betsy, the day her brother brought Isaac Randall to her parents' home. Isaac never took it off.

A dark shadow had spread from his crotch down his legs, but standing between the Swede and the black man, close to the bodies, Isaac faced the pirate and appeared unafraid. Betsy knew the steady gaze in Isaac's gray eyes. He wasn't going to give the man his ring.

The girls understood the need to be still. Even the baby knew.

The sailors of the *Sally Dash* moved back toward the forecastle; some pirates mingled into those clusters of men. The cook, who had treated the girls to nuts and raisins, drained his rum. The bursar cowered behind the foremast. Until Isaac lied, the pirates had stayed clear of Betsy, respecting the sword that kept her in the corner. But now they nudged each other, mocking Isaac's squared shoulders and the puddle at his feet. Edging closer, a pirate swaggered toward Betsy. He smoothed his moustache, crooking his finger for Mary to come to him.

If the man slouched one step closer, coddling his crotch, Betsy would grab a handful of his filthy hair and yank his head to her feet. But the pirate keeping Betsy and the girls in the corner pointed his sword at the man and cut a swath of air as if to slice him in two. His dagger twitched in his other hand. The man stumbled back, slinking into a group of pirates and cursing Betsy's protector. "Jew. Heretic. Huguenot."

The sword swooped from rail to rail as if taking on all the pirates, some with weapons drawn. They tripped over each other backing away. Next to Isaac, Brickhart watched, amused with the swordsman's play. The tall Swede clapped and called out, "Dance on, LeBrun!"

Betsy nudged Mary. While the Huguenot displayed his sword, she could get the girls into Captain Mayhew's quarters and lock the pirates out, but LeBrun jumped back to pen her and the girls between the gallery stairs and the quarters. He'd warded off one man, but other pirate foxes eyed Mary and Alice. Betsy had to find a place for them to hide.

Perhaps watching LeBrun dance caused Brickhart to change his mind: he let Isaac keep the ring. With a show of good will, he stepped back, as if dancing a minuet, avoiding the bodies of Mayhew and the first mate. He offered Isaac his hand.

Ever cautious, Isaac studied the pirate's face and the open palm—perhaps questioning the honesty of the gesture—while the sailors cheered him on: "Be a good chap." "Take his hand, man." "We're all brothers."

His smile uncertain, Isaac shook Brickhart's hand.

Relieved, Betsy slumped against the bulkhead, hugging first Mary, then Alice. Then she started to run to Isaac, pushing LeBrun aside, but the Huguenot caught her elbow: "Attention, Madam."

Grasping Isaac's hand, the captain stepped back for the men to see their accord, and the two crews cheered.

Betsy held David close to quiet her own trembling. He'd slept through the demand for his father's ring and Brickhart's offering his hand, as if the baby knew he had nothing to fear.

With one hand cupped to the side of his mouth, the Swede announced the captain's name over the creaking of the ship. "Captain Brickhart. Captain Emanuel Brickhart. The Captain E-mann-uuu-ell Brrr-rick-haart."

The Swede's cutlass swept up over his head. It flashed in the sun before he brought the blade straight down through Isaac's wrist.

Brickhart stepped back, gripping Isaac's hand. He held it over his head like a trophy.

Isaac fell to his knees. Blood spurted from his arm.

Betsy lunged to help him, to tie her kerchief around his wrist and stop the bleeding, but LeBrun pushed her back against the girls. Mary called out, "Papa!" Alice tried to press her face into Betsy's skirt, but Betsy shoved them aside to get past LeBrun. Immediately, he slammed her into the corner. David began to cry. She couldn't get to Isaac.

Staring at the red spout where his hand should be, Isaac clasped it to his chest. Blood ran down his arm.

The men of the Dash scuffled back. The pirates cheered when Brickhart raised Isaac's hand higher for everyone to see. Mary started for Isaac, but Betsy grabbed the back of her skirt. "Stay here." Alice clutched Betsy's legs.

As a merchant banker, Isaac had stacked gold with that hand. He'd needed two hands to piece together notes when a debtor made a final payment. He needed that hand to hold the children. He needed that hand to hold her. Betsy needed that hand.

Across the deck from her, Isaac squeezed the stump to his chest, his white shirt now red. His wig slipped forward as he bent in pain in front of Brickhart, but he looked up at Betsy. Their eyes met, though LeBrun's arm had flattened her to the wall. Isaac's heavy wig had drooped to one side, and his face was the pale white of marble; Betsy saw courage in his eyes.

"Josiah." Brickhart glanced at the black man. "Stand him up." The captain strolled to the rail to flip the hand into the water. Betsy smothered David to her chest, one hand over his ear, the other pressing Alice's head to her side, but she heard the Swede call out, "Share it, fishies."

Brickhart saluted the big pirate and put the ring in his mouth to suck it clean as pirates and sailors squabbled for a place at the rail to watch Isaac's hand sink. Like a school of fish, they simultaneously turned to watch Brickhart hold up the ring so the gem caught the sun. Satisfied that the ring fit his finger, Brickhart, his pants, jacket, and boots splotched with Isaac's blood, pranced over to Betsy and stretched out his hand for her to kiss the ring. Sucked clean, it sparkled, but his nails were smeared dark red. He smelled of blood.

A roar from the base of Betsy's skull surged through her head and up over the men and the ship. The masts swirled above her, her legs jellied, and she pitched forward. David slipped from her grasp.

Her cheek against a deck plank, Betsy stared at an iron nail head three inches from her nose. Squat, solid, staunch, ready to stub a toe, it would hold no matter who kicked it.

"Mama." Alice tugged at Betsy's arm. "Mama."

Chapter 3

Betsy would not get up. She heard the little girl beg, but she didn't move. She held her breath, feeling nothing. Mary, responsible Mary, picked up her baby brother before Brickhart could reach him, but Betsy didn't move. The baby flailed, red with rage, his blanket hanging loose in Mary's grasp. His mouth opened, but he was unable to catch his breath.

Mary stamped her foot. "Mama, get up."

Betsy didn't budge.

From far away, Isaac's voice: "Elizabeth."

Betsy forced herself to her knees, to her feet, to being a mother. She took David from Mary and clutched him to her chest. There was an escape from the pirates. "Come, Mary. Bring Alice." In three steps, they would be at the rail, and Betsy would toss the baby into the waves, help the girls climb over, and then jump in herself. But LeBrun blocked her way. He slammed her into the wall. Betsy held David tight, smothering his scream, jostling him to stop crying.

Brickhart stretched out his arms for the child, but she would not let him take David. She looked at Isaac, wanting him to help. But he could do nothing. She couldn't jump overboard. She could only nestle the baby and shuffle Mary and Alice deeper into the corner. She patted David, but he threw his head back and bawled. "Shush, shush, shush, Davy, Davy, Davy." She couldn't quiet him.

Pirates and sailors from the Dash perched like crows on the yardarms to watch. As Brickhart came nearer, she whispered into David's ear: "Sorry, sorry, sorry." Hugging him tighter, Betsy crushed the girls against the wall, curling her shoulders over David. The braces and the rigging squealed, but the baby calmed at last.

"Dear lady," Brickhart said. He tugged at the baby. "I'll take care of your child." He nudged LeBrun.

The Frenchman dug his fingers down to the bone in her arm, rammed his knee into her back, and twisted her around to face Brickhart, who jerked the baby from her and ambled off. Betsy jumped to follow, but LeBrun clamped his hand over her mouth. He spoke with a French twang. "It's for the best."

Cradling David, Brickhart cooed for all the sailors to hear. "Brave little man. Mama's little sailor boy. Drops him on the deck, she does. Poor little tyke."

Mary kicked at LeBrun. Her fists pounded his back until he smacked her face with his free hand. She fell to the deck, but he'd loosened his grip enough for Betsy to wriggle free and run for David. Long strides ahead, Brickhart bounced the baby.

Betsy darted past pirates meaning to trip or grab her, intent on snatching her baby back.

The captain sidestepped as if playing tag, but she caught up. He yelled, "Torborg!" and the Swede wrapped an arm around her waist and skipped, lifting Betsy off her feet, whirling her around the deck while the sailors clapped to his steps. A pair of twins Betsy hadn't seen board the ship with the pirates shook tambourines. Sailors joined arms to dance, circling the Swede. The ship and cheering pirates spun. Betsy struggled to free herself, but Torborg whirled her back to LeBrun. "Many thanks," the Swede said, kissing her on the cheek; and then he collapsed on the bottom step of the gallery stairs.

Dizzy from flashes of blue-green sea, the tall masts, and men's laughter, Betsy staggered toward Mary and Alice. Their clinging to her helped her stay on her feet. With her eyes on the pirate parading her son, she stooped to embrace her girls. "Keep your sister here, Mary, against the wall." Betsy dashed back for David.

LeBrun grabbed her elbow, yanking her aside. "You must be brave," he said. "For your little girls, you must be quiet as a mouse." Mary bit his wrist; he winced and shook her off. "Bite me again and I'll boot you into the sea."

"She would thank you." Betsy writhed to pull herself free. "Boot me into the sea."

Alice gripped Betsy's legs at the knees with all her strength and they buckled. She couldn't touch her daughter's face because LeBrun had her elbows behind her back, pulling them together. In a soft voice, she said, "Mary, you must be kind to Mr. LeBrun." Betsy's shoulders ached from his grip, but he'd kept the pirates back.

With David in the crook of his arm, the captain strutted like a man presenting his firstborn at church. He passed the pirate twins, in green sashes, tapping their tambourines, and the balding cook of the *Sally Dash*, who delighted

Brickhart by making David laugh at his faces. When Brickhart passed the cook's boy, the lad turned away. He looked at Betsy and saw her plea for help, but he could only look down at the deck. Brickhart climbed to the farthest reach of the prow. Laughing, he tossed David up, the way Isaac would when he wanted to make the baby laugh after he'd come home in the evening.

His face gray, Isaac strained, a weakling wrestling a black giant. Not one sailor moved to save David. Charlie Potts, the sailor Betsy had once trusted, watched, an arm's length from the baby. She shouted, "Charlie, save my son!" He didn't flinch. The carpenter, a man with a cheerful "Morning, Mistress," turned away when Brickhart snuggled his face to David's neck, but he did nothing. Brickhart turned to Betsy and shook his head. The sailors, the pirates, the ship itself—all held their breath.

From behind Betsy, Mary veered out of reach and dodged LeBrun's attempt to trip her. "Give me my brother!" She ran through astonished pirates and sailors.

"Sven," LeBrun called, and the Swede galloped after Mary.

Not able to pull free, Betsy called for Mary to come back, but she paid no attention.

Torborg grabbed Mary's skirt and yanked her back. With his hands around her waist, he lifted her over his head like a sheaf of wheat.

The pirate who'd threatened Mary sprang forward, reaching up. "She's mine," he said.

The man reached for Mary, but the Swede, with Mary high in the air, booted the man between the legs, up off his feet, to drop into a group of sailors. Seeing the man writhe in pain, both crews made way for the Swede. Mary kicked to be put down, but in two steps, Torborg was at the rail, and with all his might, he threw her into the waves. He pivoted and set his face on Alice.

Betsy fell to her knees, folding Alice in her arms. "Don't. Don't take her!" But LeBrun pulled Betsy up onto her feet. She called out, "Isaac!" He could do nothing.

The Swede eyed the little girl like she was a rat gnawing at the ship. He brushed Betsy aside to rip Alice from her. With the child tucked under his arm, he drew his cutlass. Betsy grabbed for it, afraid he meant to behead Alice, but he had it to cut down anyone in his way.

Alice called "Mama!" but LeBrun held Betsy back. A weight seemed to pull Betsy through the deck, down through the hull of the ship, to the water.

Brickhart could save Alice with an order, but instead he cuddled her son and paid no attention to the Swede carrying the little girl. Pirates crowded between Torborg and the rail. "The girl's part of the prize. We should roll dice for her," a pirate said. They packed closer together.

"Yah. You're right," Torborg said. He stepped back, lifting Alice with both hands as he had done with Mary. He hurled her above the pirates' reach, over the rail, and into the sea. The Swede grabbed the shirt of the man who had challenged him and lifted him off his feet. "You want the little one? R-r-roll for her." He thrust the man to the deck and turned, punching the jaw of a pirate who hadn't jumped out of his way.

Betsy clutched LeBrun's hand. "Save the baby!" she cried. Brickhart was on the forecastle; only LeBrun could help her. "Save my son, Monsieur LeBrun. My child."

LeBrun pointed for her to watch Brickhart kissing David's forehead. With his grip on the blanket like a pouch, the captain swung David back and forth until, satisfied with the momentum, he let go. The bundle flew beyond the prow of the ship. Betsy ran, but Brickhart grabbed her before she could jump after David. The baby dropped into the dark water. Only the blanket floated back toward the ship and caught on the hull before pulling loose to be sucked under the prow.

Lebrun, having run after Betsy, dragged her back into the corner. He held her so she couldn't move. She didn't want to look at Isaac. She would not. But she did.

The African had closed his eyes, but he held his arms around Isaac's chest. Isaac held his blunt wrist under his chin. With his wig askew, his shirt and jacket bloody, and his pants and stockings splattered, Isaac leaned against the man. Isaac looked at Betsy, but she was unable to go to him.

Had she heard a splash when David fell into the sea? She should have heard a splash. She should remember it.

Chapter 4

Not a single whitecap as far as she could see. The pirates' ship was a few yards off. Under an empty sky, the rigging creaked. Waves sloughed the hull. Pirates poured rum. They laughed with the sailors of the Dash. In his thick wool jacket, LeBrun, smelling of sandalwood, had wrapped his arms around Betsy. Isaac shut his eyes. His face gray, he held his wrist against his chest in a clenched grip; it no longer bled. A black man with close-cropped hair and a necklace of ivory shells held him, keeping him on his feet.

There were no shadows on the ship. Every coil of rope, every box, every bucket and buckle sat in full sun. Every curl of Isaac's wig had its own shine. How hot the wig must be. How tired Isaac looked.

The black man cleared his throat. "Captain."

Brickhart nodded and kicked Mayhew's hand with the side of his boot. "Torborg," the captain said. It was as if they passed their names to one another. The Swede stood up from the third step on the staircase to the gallery, clapped LeBrun on the back, and whistled to three pirates lazing about the main mast. Torborg and the three pulled clothes off the dead men. Shoes, jackets, pants, and shirts were tossed toward Mayhew's quarters. The men jerked up the naked bodies by their wrists and ankles, lugged them to the gunwale, and pitched them over the side. Two bodies. Two splashes. Silence, except for the chatter of men at the mast and on the forecastle.

With a smile, Brickhart approached Betsy. "Would you say a prayer for their souls?"

LeBrun, Josiah, and the pirates who had robbed each corpse laughed. Isaac kept his eyes closed. The carpenter, a pious man who bowed his head to pray at sunrise, stared out over the waves. Asa, the cook, called out, "They've gone to the devil. Our prayers can't save 'em."

Brickhart taunted the men. "None of you grieves for your captain and his fine first mate?"

Apart from Asa, all the men of the Dash huddled closer to mates they knew, trusting familiarity. Betsy bowed her head. She felt nothing for Mayhew or the first mate who had whipped sailors for too little cause. She imagined Mary standing beside her, praying in her clear voice, "Our Father, who art in heaven …" but a high, nasal whine interrupted Mary's prayer. One of the dark twins squeezed the hideous wail from the bagpipe while the other twin beat his tambourine to the bagpipe's wheeze. They jumped and skipped in red neckerchiefs and wide green sashes as they played. Leaping to the middle of the deck, with one hand high, the Swede snapped his fingers and jigged. His shoe stamped blood prints on the deck. Asa, curtsying left and right, simpered like a girl, a flirt, and linked arms with Torborg. The pirates and most sailors clapped as the two romped around the deck.

LeBrun squeezed Betsy with a harsh "Shush." She'd been moaning. Isaac couldn't wipe tears from his cheeks without letting go of his wrist, but when Betsy said that she needed to help him, LeBrun pushed her down on a coil of rope next to the stairs.

It hurt to look at Isaac, but Betsy did. He squared his shoulders. If they were at home in Brompton, she'd straighten his wig.

"Your bonnet," Isaac said across the deck. "Put on your bonnet." The first thing he'd said to her after Brickhart took David. Her bonnet? It hung down her back. LeBrun reached down and fitted it over her cap, checking to see if it blocked the sun from her face. "Your nose is too red," LeBrun said. "Your cheeks, too." He tied the ribbon that had kept her bonnet hanging on her neck under her chin.

The pirates began shoving one man into the next, tested their strength against the sailors of the *Sally Dash*. Torborg set up a rope pull. The sailors gave a loud hurrah when Torborg's toe crossed the line. He picked up Asa, twirled the cook around to the side of the pirates, and they jerked the rope out of the sailors' grasp. "Huzz-AH!" Twisting Isaac's ring, Brickhart passed by Betsy. "Huzzah, Huzzah." His voice sounded tired. Betsy closed her eyes until his steps faded on his walk over to Isaac. As if confiding in Isaac, Brickhart pointed to men from the *Sally Dash*.

LeBrun stretched his legs out on the deck next to Betsy. "He needs men he trusts."

Isaac was watching her, and she looked back at him. She would never again feel his hand on her hip, his breath on her neck, his body next to hers. Her arms ached. Her breasts hurt.

His face calm while Brickhart chatted, Isaac looked at her. "Betsy," he said.

She'd never wanted to leave their home, to claim her brother's estate, and now she wondered if she'd be alive or dead when they threw her into the sea. It was so deep, but it could not be deep enough for her.

Brickhart put his hand gently on Isaac's shoulder. "Yes, Betsy." He shook his head at her. "What's to be done with Betsy?"

Isaac's knees buckled; he was only standing because of the black man's grip, and he moaned.

Brickhart raised his hand—Isaac's ring caught the light—and Torborg called out, "Captain Emanuel Br-r-rick-hart!" A solemn quiet left only the tinkling rattle of loose pulleys and the boards' constant groan. Brickhart stopped pacing in front of Isaac and trod over to the carpenter. "Did our passenger, this fine gentleman in his grand wig and costly jacket, treat you to any particular kindness?"

Betsy looked at the men. Would the carpenter tell of Isaac's peeling away a hard crust of cheese and tossing it to a sailor?

"Come. The man needs your defense." Brickhart scanned the sailors' faces as if he expected someone to speak up. The pirate had thrown her baby out in front of the ship, and he'd let his Swedish sailor throw first Mary and then Alice overboard. Off came his hat with its ostrich fluff. He studied the brim. "Did this gentleman who grew up eating bread with jam and sleeping in a warm bed stroll the deck with his pretty wife and children? Did he sit with the captain while the first mate whipped some scabby tar who'd slept past the hour of his watch?"

The sailors didn't answer. Some mumbled. Asa spat in Isaac's direction. Asa had no business spitting. He'd buggered Davy, the galley boy, every morning. Betsy had heard the lad's protests when she came back the first morning she'd escaped to see the dawn, but Isaac had refused to speak to Captain Mayhew. He called Asa's sin "the way of the sea." Brickhart was right: every evening after Isaac had walked with her and the girls on the narrow gallery around the stern, he'd sat with the captain to watch floggings—the captain insisted all the sailors witness the punishment. On the second night out, the first mate had bound a man's hands over a cannon and lashed him with a cat o' nine tails. Betsy never again chanced the girls being on deck to see the whip tear through a man's shirt. After that evening—and it happened often—when the first mate came out of Mayhew's quarters with the captain, she hurried the girls below deck.

Isaac looked past Brickhart. He'd never plead for his life. He stood as if in church, unafraid.

Brickhart said, "The coat, Josiah," and the black man pulled off Isaac's jacket. After he rubbed the blood off the brass cuff buttons on his pant leg, he held up the jacket to show the men. Brickhart said, "Who'll have this burgundy plum? Exquisite. Plush. Warm." He fingered the lapel and slipped his hand into the arm. "Shorten the sleeves, LeBrun. It will suit you."

LeBrun caught the prize tossed his way, and hung Isaac's jacket over his yellow-green wool, adjusting the collar. Betsy reached over to touch the sleeve, and LeBrun laid the cuff on her lap. She covered the splatters of dried blood and rocked as if holding David. In her mind, the baby tumbled in the dark water, startled but not crying. How could she have dropped him?

Brickhart yanked Isaac's lace cravat left and right until it pulled loose. He walked across the deck to offer it to a pirate with one shirtsleeve folded flat from his elbow to his shoulder. The man tied the cravat over his filthy jerkin with one hand, and the men sent up a "Huzzah."

Betsy clutched her own arm to feel it there. That pirate survived with one hand. Isaac could overcome his injury. She would help him. Betsy doubled over pressing Isaac's cuff to her lips. He had told her last night that he hoped she was expecting a child. She had said it would be better for David to be walking before they had another. She had not bled since they left Brompton in early February, but there was no hope of a baby. Mayhew had said they'd be in Virginia by the end of March. Hours. Days. Weeks. Times with no meaning.

Brickhart held up a curl of Isaac's wig. "Same color as my mother's." Pinching the curl, he said, "Silky as my mother's." He leaned over and sniffed the hair, brushing the curl over his lips. "It smells like my mother's." He looked at the sailors, his eyes wide in mock surprise. "I believe it is my mother's."

Asa called out, "Mama! Mama!" Sailors laughed.

Isaac turned his head to the side. The African gripped Isaac's shoulders and he winced. Brickhart slipped his dagger under the wig, lifting it off Isaac's head, and the mass of hair fell on the black man's arm. Brickhart told Josiah to cover his wool.

Too small for the African, the wig sat on his cropped head, and he tied the front curls under his chin like ribbons on a bonnet. When he grimaced, clowning at the men, they backed away. He had pointed teeth and he growled, ready to bite and tear. The men paled.

Unwittingly, Betsy grabbed LeBrun's hand and held it. He seemed to understand her fright at seeing fangs on the man who held her husband. The African laughed, showing Isaac his grin. He'd been delighted at scaring the men, but Isaac didn't look away.

Brickhart stepped back, appraising the wig. "You should sit on the bench, Josiah. A fine magistrate." He turned to Betsy. "Don't you agree, my lady?"

Betsy didn't look at the African flicking his tongue across the points of his teeth. She'd never seen Isaac in public without his wig. He looked like a prisoner in the dock, but handsome, courageous, alone: a prisoner with the sun shining on his short brown hair. The mass of curls must have been heavy. No pirate would see the kindness in his eyes when Isaac looked at her. He'd been without his wig when he lay next to her in the bunk and pulled her close to him. "You'll be the mistress of a great plantation." He was gentle in love. "Our home will look to distant mountains. From his plantation, Robert saw the mountains' blue ridges. Instead of the Thames, our river will be the Pamunkey." Before he drifted to sleep, he'd whispered into her hair. "Pamunkey, Pamunkey, Pamunkey." Betsy had echoed, "Pamunkey." Had the incantation signaled the pirates? Did this Josiah have ears as sharp as his teeth?

The African lifted Isaac off his feet, and one of Brickhart's twin toads pulled off his shoes and held them high for Brickhart to hawk. "Elegant shoes. Fine leather. Pure silver buckles."

They were soaked with blood and urine but they had new thick soles. Brickhart approached a cluster of sailors from the Dash. The carpenter took the shoes but immediately cut off the buckles with a small knife, and gave them to the twins who stood on either side of him. With a solid shove, the shoes disappeared in the carpenter's apron pockets. Isaac's fine shoes, the bright buckles, the sound of his steps leaving the house, his turning at the door for her good-bye—nothing was left. The two ships sat in the vast blue that stretched as far as Betsy could see. Alone in his shirt, pants, and stockings, Isaac faced the pirate. He had scoffed at Betsy's descriptions of the many blues the sea displayed. A wave with the exact blue of Mary's eyes crested before it slapped the prow. Had Isaac seen it? Did that make him shudder? He would never fear death. It wasn't in him to be afraid.

The black man picked him up and carried him like a child toward the gunwale.

Isaac didn't look at Betsy, but at the man who held him over the water. He let go of his wrist to grab the African's necklace with a good hand and a blunt wrist. He pulled himself up to the man's face. He said something, his eyes on the African's strange scars. What did he say? Isaac would not let go. The man held him over the water. And then Isaac nodded. The man dropped him straight down and he disappeared in the wave curling out from the hull.

Chapter 5

A school of small black fish planed the ship where Isaac sank into a solid blue. He would drift to the girls. The three of them would find David. The Frenchman had one hand on Betsy's shoulder and the other gripped her arm to keep her from jumping after them. He'd led her to the rail, and leaned out with her to watch Isaac sink, but he wouldn't let her jump. She said, "Isaac Randall." That was all.

LeBrun said, "Eet-zack Ran-dall."

Pirates and sailors crowded the rail, watching her husband being sucked under the hull. They'd bunched close to the black man, but he elbowed them away and they gave him room. He tore the wig from his head and pitched it out over the wrinkled water. It spread like a fleece on a wave that buoyed it past Betsy and LeBrun.

The men cursed. Several tossed out fishing lines, playing the hooks to snag the wig while the Frenchman steered Betsy back toward the corner.

The African caught up to them. "He said, 'My wife.'"

LeBrun laughed. "He didn't mean your wife." He stopped

laughing when he looked down at a long steel shaft the African aimed at his ribs: a pigsticker.

Lebrun pushed Betsy in front of the black man. "Fool. That wig would have traded for a horse."

The African smiled, his lips closed over his terrible teeth. Other pirates couldn't see the weapon hidden by his palm when he reached around Betsy. LeBrun drew in his breath to keep the point from touching him. Only Betsy heard Josiah say, "Tell Brick the lady is mine."

His? This man with scars on his face, filed teeth, and skin the color of soot claimed her? Why would Isaac say "my wife" to him?

LeBrun scoffed. "The captain decides on the prizes, but I do not object." He bowed, drawing his own dagger. "Josie, the dogs will clean you like a roast goose." He shook his head at Betsy with no more concern than he'd have for a cornered mouse.

If the man forced himself on her, she would take the blade he stuck in his belt to kill him. No. She would kill herself. But she had no time to grab his knife; he'd carried her up the steps to the gallery and to the poop deck, the small platform in front of the wheelhouse over the captain's quarters where every man on deck could see her.

"Look at the nigger!" "The black's got our prize." More shouts: "He had the lord, but we get the lady." Men cursing and damning Josiah pulled out knives, raised staves and clubs, and shoved their way closer. "Throw her to us." They rushed to the steps with a roar, but LeBrun and his sword blocked their way. The Swede stood with him. Betsy and Josiah could see every pirate as well as the crown of Brickhart's hat and the pistol he aimed at them.

A shot from the bow. Then silence. Brickhart had

changed his aim, shooting off to the east, and stuck his pistol in a breast pocket to plow with his sword drawn through the men toward the wheelhouse.

The African, Josiah, pointed a pistol at Betsy's head.

"Please." Betsy had heard the first mate say "please" before Torborg shot him.

"Fire. Please," said Betsy. A fresh breeze with the smell of the sea blew against her face. Was Isaac still falling through the water, was he walking on the ocean floor, seeking the children? Could he be thinking of her? The waves rocked the ship as they had yesterday. The gentle creaking lullaby would help David sleep. Isaac had said that one day they would sit together and watch their grandchildren play. Today he was in the sea, and she belonged to an African named Josiah. Betsy slid down the wheelhouse wall to sit facing the men.

Quick as a cat, Brickhart jumped to the top of a barrel. He shot a second pistol into the air, and traded it for another from the sash under his jacket. "To the forecastle, scum. If I fire again, it will be a man's life."

Growling, the men slouched as they moved back to the prow, shoving their weapons into their belts while Torborg and LeBrun kept their swords drawn in front of the captain's quarters. The twins somersaulted and cartwheeled the width of the deck. The grumbling pirates threw wet rags at them.

Brickhart jumped off the barrel and climbed the stairs to the wheelhouse.

Josiah aimed the pistol at him, but Brickhart came toward them anyway. "I mean you no harm, Josiah." The toe of his boot nudged Betsy's foot as it had Mayhew's hand. He pushed the pistol aside. "This dainty doesn't belong to you, Josey."

"No, Cap'n." Josiah sat on his haunches, his gaze on the pirates watching the twins. His eyes narrowed each time a pirate or sailor moved. "Her husband put a hex on me. That's why I threw off his wig. You'll see that he put a hex on anyone who touches his wife. Don't let your dogs use her. You'll get trouble. Keep her with me. Nobody gets her. The men curse me, but nobody dies." He stretched out one leg and then the other, leaning back on the wheelhouse, a foot away from Betsy but close enough for her to smell his sweat. He didn't use a perfume or scent. He grinned his pointed teeth at every man on deck who looked up at him. "Go read the charter to your new men." He uncorked a plug on the shaft of his pigsticker, and a small wooden pick dropped—he used the pick to clean his teeth. "Brick, I'm as loyal as Sven Torborg or Brun."

Brickhart put his pistol inside his jacket. "I should've shot you the day you climbed on board. I'd be rid of a runaway and this petticoat." He walked down the steps to the main deck, his ostrich feather even with the poop deck.

One arm under her head, Betsy curled like a worm. She'd eaten nothing that morning. She would never eat again. She'd convince the black man to throw her overboard like her husband. Somehow, tomorrow, she'd be with her family.

At first Betsy thought she was dreaming his words; the man spoke in a lower voice than when he talked to LeBrun or his captain. His wife had died and he'd held her, pretending she was alive to keep the slavers from throwing her off the ship. "Your husband said, 'My wife.' I understood him. Don't be afraid. I can take on the Swede." He didn't look at her, but at the sailors. "They'll have to come up the stairs one at a time, and I'll skewer any fool who stands on the shoulder of a mate to boost his way here." He looked down at the men, paying particular attention to where Brickhart happened to be, and unfolded a yellowed handkerchief from his shirt pocket. In the center of the homespun square, he had a pile of dried leaves. He chose one, which he rubbed between his thumb and forefinger before holding it under Betsy's nose. She turned from him, but he persisted in keeping it where she would smell it. Mint. Mint in the middle of the ocean. In the spring, while working in the garden, she would send Mary and later both girls to find fragrant new shoots along the path. They would skip from patches of thyme, woodruff, and rosemary, running back for Betsy to name them. "Mint," she said.

"I was a fool to look at your husband when he grabbed my cowrie shells, but I did."

Betsy had seen how earnestly Isaac gripped the necklace and his calm when he'd let it go. What made him trust the man?

Josiah pointed a finger at pirates looking up at the wheelhouse, plotting to get up on the poop deck. Hissing at them, he held his grimace wide, like an angry cat. Betsy recoiled from him, and he laughed. "I grew up in bush so thick, you couldn't leave the path. I hunted panthers on the prowl." He crouched as if to pounce on her, startling her so that she bumped her head on the mast rising above the wheelhouse. Laughing, he sat back against the bulkhead. "I shouldn't tell you, but I am leopard. Once I had a necklace of teeth, sharper than Uncle filed mine, but the slavers took 'em. I collected these cowries, and someday they'll get me back to my people." He looked out over the waves. "My mother's brother sold the village to the white slavers who set fire to the thatch and put us in irons." He fingered the shells. "I want to see Uncle soil himself."

Betsy cringed, but she was no longer afraid. Not of him, not of his teeth, not of the strange scars, the bumps in a square design on his cheeks with three short slashes under each eye. This face was the last face Isaac saw. She reached out to touch his cheek.

He pulled back. "Uncle scarred me when I became a man. He cut our village on my face. At night, I touch each hut on my face and think of my friends."

Betsy had a village, too. She knew every house and shop in Brompton. She knew every road and walk, but she would never hear the ripple of the Thames again or walk with friends to the church.

"My mates think these scars are magic, but they're only reminders of my people." He looked at Betsy. "I have magic, but not on my face." He breathed in the salt air and pulled out a dagger and his pigsticker. "My magic is on the point and the edge."

Betsy looked at the men. All of them had daggers and guns. The black man had put her where they could see her, more damned than Lot's wife looking back at Sodom and Gomorrah, forever a pillar of salt. Let the man with his pointed teeth speak of his village, crush mint under her nose, offer her a flask of rum, wipe her forehead with a cool cloth, set her bonnet to shade her face; she wouldn't forgive him or any of the pirates. He didn't know the ship had shrunk, shriveled like his mint. None of the pirates noticed how cloth and board had withered to nothing, less significant than the louse crawling on the black man's neck. As if the ship were a seashell world, she heard a sailor from the Dash in front of the forecastle ask a pirate, "You have a house in Trinidad?"

"And me cow, me wife, and me barn."

Barn? Betsy's father used the term for children. Could

the pirate have children? Did his wife cradle them? He
hadn't cried out to save David. He hadn't rescued Mary or
Alice. Maybe the man with children would claim the Randall belongings for his wife in Trinidad. That wife would
clap her hands at their good fortune. Fortune? Isaac had
fallen to his knees, thanking God for being named the heir
to the estate of Robert Harrington, the brother she'd seen
twice in fourteen years.

Brickhart took the steps halfway up to the poop deck and
fired a pistol. Betsy tried not to see sunlight sparkle on
Isaac's ring, but she did. Torborg and LeBrun cheered, and
the pirates and sailors hoorayed. Before Brickhart could fire
the second pistol, the Swede called out, "Captain E-man-u-
el Brick-hart." Each syllable a proclamation. The Rs rolled
like a drum, while the twins tumbled about. LeBrun
brought Josiah a mug of rum smelling sweet as caramel.
The men clapped and stamped. Echoing the Swede's chant,
they bellowed, "Brick-HART, Brick-HART, E-man-u-el
Brick-HART."

Josiah applauded with them. "Brick sniffs a ship and leads
us to her. Not one man dead."

Except for Mayhew and the first mate. Isaac. Betsy stopped
herself. How could the African have a Christian name? The
men of the Dash joined the pirates, singing, "We have our
goods. We have our ship. We have the sea." Their goods
included Isaac's desk, David's cradle, and the girls' dolls. How
carefully Betsy had packed treasures from their home.

Brickhart paused until the men were silent. "Who owns
the cargo in the hold?"

LeBrun swung Isaac's jacket over his head. "We do."

"Who sells our cargo?" Brickhart cupped his hand to his
ear.

Like dogs, the men barked, "We do. We do. We do." The twins hooked arms and spun around. Asa, the cook, first grabbed the bursar, who stumbled, too clumsy to follow the jig. Charlie stepped between them, pushing Asa into a pirate, who embraced the cook in a hug, and the two skipped like children while the bursar crept over the carpenter.

"Who serves our good Queen Anne?" Brickhart opened his arms to their response.

Silence.

The captain jumped from the gallery steps to the deck, his chest a foot in front of a sailor from the Dash; the man blanched to the yellow of cheese. Brickhart spit at his feet. "Crawl to the *Zephyr*." Brickhart strode over to Charlie. "Eat worms with your bread. We free men eat at one table." He pointed to the other ship. "Sail the *Zephyr*. She's yours. You'll have her papers and the log." He crossed the deck to a thin pirate hunched in talk with the carpenter and the bursar. "But before you sail, every man must tote the stock to our new bucket. The *Zephyr* will sail faster empty." Facing Asa, he said, "None of Her Majesty's ships or any privateer knows the *Sally Dash* has a new commander." He threw his arms over the shoulders of the twins. "We're able seamen, loyal to the crown, sailing a merchant ship." He scrambled up to the lowest spar of the mast, looking through Mayhew's telescope to the west. "Sweet winds will blow us straight for Carolina and welcoming inlets." He jumped down to the deck. "To it, lads!"

The pirates sprang up like puppets to grapple the ships together. Barrels rolled up the hold of the *Zephyr* and down the cargo hatch of the *Sally Dash*. They sang, "Molasses—more lasses—molasses." Sailors joined in, loud, gleeful. "Salt pork. Pickles. Ale. More rum." Bales of fragrant tobacco dropped into the hold already crammed with the cargo, including the Randalls' crate of dishes, bedding, and furniture. The men would have little space for their hammocks.

A sack of meal slipped from a pirate's grip. He was missing three fingers. Betsy looked more closely at her captors. The lid of another's left eye had been stitched shut, mended to his cheek. Piggy, the peg-leg sailor on the Dash, tried to keep pace with a pirate whose beard was hairless on one side from a burn. The carpenter had sawed off Piggy's leg because a crate had slipped from a hoist and crushed his knee. Many of Mayhew's men were scarred or maimed. Charlie Potts had a missing little finger.

With block and tackle on a boom, the two crews had a cursing competition as they heaved two large cannons onto the ship. The day had no end. No whistle piped to end the watch. Torborg sang, "Roll me a barrel of rum, roll the rum," and a cloth sling, bulging with cannonballs, swung from the *Zephyr* and thundered into the hinged boxes along the rail. "Let thunder roar, let lightning crack, no cat o' nine will lash my back." Torborg sang and the sailors echoed his words. They whistled. They jigged. They worked.

Next to her, Josiah breathed evenly, his eyes not closed, but not seeing. Without a sound, Betsy inched away from him. Her breasts ached, but they would cool fast in the sea. Josiah clamped his hand on her leg. "You're going to live." He roped her at the waist, tying her to the mizzenmast.

Where Josiah's left ear should be, he had a puffy scar almost as ugly as his teeth. Betsy had seen it soon after the pirates boarded, but she hadn't wondered about it. She closed her eyes. No one could rob her of what she'd seen that morning. No one would want the memory, but she squeezed it down to a stone and hid it under her tongue. This market was no place for Isaac. Betsy had thought she needed him, but she did not.

The sailors gripped three pigs by their hocks and lugged them toward the open shaft. Squealing, a pig wriggled free, and the men, tumbling on ropes and boxes, grabbed for it. Chickens, with one leg tied on a hemp rope, cackled and flapped to escape the flock. Men stacked sheaves of meadow grass along the rail for two sheep, bleating against being herded until they smelled the hay, and then they trotted over, happy to eat.

Mary and Alice had enjoyed feeding sheep. This time of year, they could pet new lambs and hold fat pink piglets at the market. They would lift yellow chicks, balls of fluff, to their cheeks while Betsy bought eggs from the farmwives.

A youth, his face gray under the fuzz of new whiskers, limped toward the sheep. He favored his right leg, wincing when a pirate shoved him onto the grass.

Not one man spoke to the lad. "Is he a pirate?" Betsy asked.

Josiah frowned at the edge of a boarding ax he sharpened. "They brought him from the farm, afraid he'd call out. If his leg heals, they'll sell him for a 'denture."

Brickhart sauntered over and rested his hand on the poop deck near Betsy's foot. "Sailing back on the *Zephyr*, Josiah?"

"No, Cap'n. I'd be sold 'fore we docked." He chuckled, a hard, cruel sound. "I'm guardin your prisoner." His eyes narrowed. "People buy white women? How much would she bring?" With Brickhart, Josiah made his contempt for her clear, though he spoke kindly to her when side by side, they sat alone.

Brickhart's laugh was interrupted by a cow's bellow.

On the hoist used for the cannon, in a skein, a net for oddly shaped cargo, a brown cow panted, her udders jammed into her belly, her eyes rolling in terror. She tossed her horns and bawled to set her hooves on solid ground. On deck, she charged the men, but her hooves slid, splaying her front legs. From the yard, Charlie dropped a noose over her horns and jerked her to a stop. A pirate slapped her haunch, and she whirled to butt her tormentor, scattering the crew. The carpenter and Torborg clamped their arms around her neck in a double collar, steering her toward the chute. The cow balked at going into the stink of the hold.

Making a show of unbuttoning his fly, Asa strutted before the men, jerking his thumb in Betsy's direction. "Since I can't have me lady, I'll take me Dolly." With mock gentleness, he lifted the cow's tail to one side, and yellow-green stool sprayed over him. Catapulted back, he slipped on the filth to the hoots of pirates and sailors. Cursing, Asa lurched toward a coil of rope, and then fell on his hands and knees, his face aflame, unable to regain his footing. LeBrun and Brickhart appeared next to him, cutlasses drawn. A silence gripped the crew. Brickhart commanded two pirates to strut the cook around the deck with his britches at his knees.

Betsy watched. She hated the man, but she presumed the way they treated Asa hinted at how they would deal with her.

While Torborg and the carpenter steered the cow down the ramp to the safety below deck, Asa thrashed to be free; but then he looked at the pirates parading him and he began to prance, challenging the men to compare their cocks to his. The men filled leather and wooden buckets with seawater, dousing Asa and his escorts. They applauded his jig until, having made the round, he slipped on the dung again and thudded onto his backside.

Sailors whooped. The farm boy laughed with the others but Asa, having landed directly across the deck from him, got up on all fours. "Aye. You can laugh."

The boy's face burned red and he scooted toward the rail even before the cook stood and walked toward him.

"Save him." Betsy kicked Josiah. She wanted him to look at the boy, to stop his tormentor, but Josiah kept his eyes on the blade he was sharpening and shook his head. He wasn't the only pirate unwilling to witness the crime. Brickhart and LeBrun disappeared into Mayhew's quarters while Torborg guarded the door, his head just visible from the poop deck.

Asa swaggered over to the lad, shafting his thumb and fingers over his penis. The pirates clapped with each step he took. After punching the boy's ear, Asa flipped him face-down and jerked off his pants. The boy's shrieks maddened the cheering pirates. Sailors from the Dash cheered the cook, too.

Betsy shoved Josiah's arm and the stone left the blade at an odd angle. "Help him."

Josiah held out his hand, palm down, stiff; three inches from her face and with the boarding ax he'd sharpened, he peeled his skin from below his thumb to his wrist.

Stop." Betsy turned her head.

"Feel nothing," he said. Blood oozed up, first a few dots and then a red skim that formed a thick drop.

Betsy swallowed the bile filling her throat

"Yah. Nutting." Torborg hadn't seen Josiah skin himself, but he'd heard every word.

"Why save me and not the boy?" No matter how hard

Betsy pressed her eyes to her knees and her palms to her ears, she couldn't keep from hearing the boy's cries or the grunts and cheers of the man raping him. Worse, though she rocked, she kept hearing Davy, the galley boy—where was he hiding now?—his whimper from the galley, more than one morning, when she'd crept back to Isaac in their cabin. She'd heard the cook snarl softly, the way a dog growls when claiming a bone, "What's it you want?" And Davy, still a child with a cap of copper curls, hardly older than Mary, hurried to say, "What you want, Asa. I want what you want." Davy's yelps explained his purple bruises. Looking at the crowd of men, Betsy couldn't find Davy on deck.

Having vomited over the rail, the bursar sought the protection of the carpenter who stood shoulder to shoulder with Charlie, whispering and glancing at the *Zephyr*. If Betsy weren't roped to a mast, she could jump over to the other ship. If she weren't roped to a mast, she'd be sinking in the blue water. The carpenter's shadow moved. The sun caught Davy's curls. He was shielded by Charlie and the carpenter from the pirates jostling for a turn with the farm boy.

The twins plopped down in the corner where LeBrun had first penned Betsy. The boy no longer screamed. LeBrun and Brickhart snuck out of the captain's cabin and walked over to the twins for that bit of shade, patient as cats in the sun or crows waiting for carrion.

Leering at Betsy, a pirate staggered from the crowd. He pointed at her as if, though drunk, he would follow his finger to her. He didn't wave a dagger or pistol, but LeBrun drew his sword, ready to take on Josiah or ward the pirate away from the African's knives, but Josiah booted him back down the steps to LeBrun's sword. Staring at the four inches of steel coming up through his stomach and disappearing when the surprised LeBrun yanked it free, the pirate, his face chalk-white, collapsed against the Huguenot, spitting blood down his shirt.

In front of Betsy, Josiah crouched for the next attack.

Brickhart took the man from LeBrun's embrace and lifted him up over the gunwale, dropping him into the sea. None of the pirates or sailors went to the rail, though twice the man called, "Throw me a line."

Torborg picked up the farm boy's body and tossed it off the starboard side.

Betsy rocked on her knees. "God have mercy on his soul."

Josiah lined up his pigsticker, his daggers, and his pistol. "Amen." He nodded. "Amen."

Chapter 6

Brickhart goaded sailors of the Dash to weasel off to the *Zephyr*. "You have a mainsail and plenty of salt water. Claim the pink, piss-hearted worms." Betsy wriggled to loosen the rope around her waist Josiah used to tie her to the mizzenmast. She leaned forward to make undoing the knot easier. "Let me go over," she said. On a ship named for a wind, Betsy would float free. "I can sail the *Zephyr*."

Instead of freeing her, Josiah unwound a leather cord from his wrist, tied Betsy's hands together, and dropped them into her lap.

Piggy tossed his crutch, more of a weapon than a support for walking, into the hold and dropped after it. "For me gear," he called up.

Josiah listened to peg-legged Piggy hobbling on the lower deck. "You'd sail with him?"

The bursar eyed the carpenter, who nudged Charlie, but none of them moved.

Piggy's crutch slid up from the hatch onto deck, and he popped up after it, a wooden chest the size of a church Bible tucked under his arm: Isaac's box. The family prayer books, baptismal certificates, and the papers for her brother's estate. Nodding left and right, Piggy ran to board the *Zephyr* before the pirates ungrappled it from the Dash.

LeBrun kicked the chest out of Piggy's hands, and it thunked to the deck, springing the lock. The lid fell open and silver coins, along with a few gold guineas, rolled in every direction. Isaac had counted those treasures before going to bed on Sunday, but there should have been more. The sailors gasped, ready to jump on the coins, but pirates held them back. LeBrun's sword slashed through Piggy's neck, and his head dropped facedown, cracking his nose on the deck while his body sprinted on to the rail and toppled onto the *Zephyr*. One of the twins picked up Piggy's head and held it by the hair for his brother to kick it leeward into the sea.

Betsy pulled at the bindings on her wrists with her teeth, but it only tightened the knot. She struggled to get to her knees, but the rope held her down. She stretched her hands out to Josiah. "Please let me off."

"Fool." Josiah held the flask of rum to her lips, but she clubbed it away with her arms, splashing rum on her shift and on Josiah. Laughing, he dribbled rum into his mouth and pointed at the sailors from the Dash crawling about, collecting coins, wiping them on their pants to clean off Piggy's blood, and dropping them into Isaac's box. LeBrun held it open while Torborg pointed his cutlass at sailors and pirates who had stepped on coins rolling past.

Not far from LeBrun, a gray-haired pirate jabbed his elbow into the side of a pimply youth. "We'll be off." The two pirates straddled the rails of the ships. "Farewell, Captain, and God guide you." Some of their mates spat their good-byes. Seeing them leave, one of the twins jumped from his brother's side and cleared the gunwale to land on the *Zephyr* with an easy leap. He disappeared down the hold without a farewell. Not one pirate seemed to care that he left. Not even his brother.

When Brickhart called out, "Peace be with you, Chapman," to the old pirate and his scrawny mate, and paid no attention to the twin's leaving, the carpenter, with Isaac's shoes poking out of his pockets, followed the deserters, leaving everything except what he carried in his apron on the Dash. Charlie helped the bursar over the rails, and then climbed after him. Charlie, the carpenter, and the two pirates released the grappling hooks holding the ships together. Betsy wanted to yell for them not to leave her, but Josiah clamped his hand over her mouth before she made a sound. She tried to bite his palm until she saw Davy, the cook's boy, sneaking toward the other ship. She prayed that he would succeed, but Asa saw him go and flung him back across the deck.

Davy didn't move. Striding past Asa, Brickhart picked Davy up like the father in the Prodigal Son, and Asa's face turned fish-belly white.

At the cook's side in two long steps, Torborg swung his long arm around his shoulders. Peeking at the Swede's toothy grin, Asa regained his color and watched Brickhart carry Davy into Mayhew's cabin.

As if offended with Brickhart's saving the boy or Torborg's coming to Asa's defense, the second twin sprang off to the *Zephyr*. The ships were no longer tied together and he had to make a running vault to land on its deck. Like his brother, he dropped below deck, not to be seen or taunted by his old mates, but none of them cared. Betsy pulled at Josiah's sleeve for him to take his hand away from her mouth, for him to let her leave the ship.

He only clamped his hand more tightly, turning her head so she saw the twins grab ropes from the yardarms and swing onto the Dash despite the ships drifting apart. Doing back flips and handsprings, somersaulting to their feet, they joined the pirates' "Huzzah! Huzzah!" Josiah let go of Betsy and stood to clap and stomp with the men. "Huzzah!"

Alone in front of the captain's quarters, Brickhart waved his hat and joined the cheers. His favorite monkeys lowered their britches and wiggled identical backsides, making faces at him through their legs. A circus. Betsy was a curiosity. A prize to be sold when the ship docked.

Charlie raised the sail, and the *Zephyr* bucked the waves tacking away from the Dash.

"May you rot in Hell for the nothing you left us," the bursar called out. He shouted over the din of the jeering pirates, "But better nothing than damned to Hell!"

The men were leaving her on a ship they damned.

"Give me Hell," Torborg sang out. "You keep nothing." He picked up a twin in each arm and twirled them around for the pirates to swat their bare buttocks. Pirates and sailors, imitating his brogue, sang out, "Nut-ting. You keep nut-ting."

Brickhart took the steps to the wheelhouse three at a time. "Your pardon, Josiah." He stepped over Josiah's legs onto Betsy's hem. "She's in my way." He kicked at her skirt.

Betsy pulled up her knees and tucked her skirt tight. "That boy's life is on your head."

"Muzzle her, Josiah." Brickhart stood in the center of the poop deck like the lord mayor of London with poor Betsy roped at his feet. He had no scars or cuts. His boots, oiled that morning, had splatters of blood. His fingernails, some rimmed with dried blood, had been buffed. He wore Isaac's ring. "Sailors of the *Sally Dash*, LeBrun will read our charter."

The Frenchman carried a ledger and placed it on top of a cask of rum, opening the book like a vicar reading the Lessons on Sunday morning. He bowed to Brickhart and to the men. The pirates stopped talking and faced him, their chests held high. LeBrun recited the story of Brickhart's lashing John Praxton with his own cat. He'd tossed Praxton overboard the day Brickhart, Torborg, LeBrun, and five able-bodied seamen claimed the Avalon. He chanted, "The rules as set down on April 5, 1711." He looked out over the sailors. "Officers are elected by the crew. Anyone wishing for a change of command may call for a vote."

The recruits from the Dash mimicked the reverence of the pirates. How differently the men listened to LeBrun than they had to Mayhew. They cocked their heads to hear every word. Josiah listened as if to be sure that LeBrun read the whole charter. He gestured for Betsy to pay attention, too. What difference did it make to Betsy if each man had a vote, if each would share the prize? Brickhart was entitled to two shares. Any man crippled in taking a ship would have his share and a half, but many of the crew seemed entitled, since many were maimed.

Asa raised his arm. "You lose a leg, you get your share and half of your mate's?" He scowled at LeBrun, who looked up to see who had questioned him.

LeBrun put his finger on the page. "We divide the goods on deck where everyone has a full, fair view."

When another sailor asked if the captain assigned the watch, the one-eyed pirate answered, "It's us decides who works; it's the cap'n who shoots the rat drinkin rum when the keel needs scrapin." The men of the Dash looked from one to another. None of them would mourn Mayhew. His former crew scurried to sign the charter. Men pushed to be first in line, but the pirates were giving older sailors that honor when thunder exploded to the southwest.

Less than a mile off, flames blazed. Ink-black smoke spired skyward from the *Zephyr*. Fire licked the main sail; it flashed into a square of flame. Betsy and the men on the *Sally Dash* stared at boards shooting up from the hull at a second blast of gun powder. On his feet, Josiah jumped, clapping louder than any of the sailors crowding the rail. The doomed men on the *Zephyr* must have heard his "Huz-ZAH!" Brickhart watched the ship burn through a glass and handed an extra telescope to Josiah. The twins climbed the main mast like acrobats, shouting, "That's nut-ting!" The pirates echoed their call. Sailors from the Dash stood dumb, looking from one mate to another as, fringed fiery orange, the prow of the *Zephyr* tilted skyward under a broad, smoke plume.

"The twins know their fireworks." Josiah clapped more softly, slower.

Brickhart said, "Thank Josiah for keeping you on the ship, milady. I would have given you permission to go with the carpenter."

A flame flickered on the horizon and the *Zephyr* sank. The pillar of smoke drifted off.

"Mr. Josiah, you knew?" Betsy edged away from him.

"I did."

"Did those two from your own crew know?" Betsy turned to see Brickhart's face, to see if he felt any guilt after watching the men blown up.

He shrugged. "The old man did. He sailed the *Zephyr*

and saw the twins blow up the Mercury; he couldn't stomach the farm raid." Brickhart looked at the men below on the main deck. "Why Caleb Long went with him, I don't know. Maybe he was sickened by what they did to the lad." He held out his hand for the telescope he'd given Josiah, but when the African put it in his pocket without looking at him, he didn't insist that Josiah give it back.

If Brickhart heard Betsy's "God forgive you," he ignored it, jumping down to the main deck. She yelled out over the ship, "God—"

Josiah covered her mouth, muffling "—protect them" with his palm.

When Betsy sat back, defeated, he pulled a piece of carved bone from his pocket. The carving had a long, thin face with a high forehead, shrunken cheeks, and earlobes down past the chin. The thick lips bore no expression. Like a death mask, the closed eyes saw nothing; but to Betsy, they held a secret. The thin scab on Josiah's thumb matched the length of the carving. Closing his fist over the talisman, he said, "Slavers burned the village. They caught the people running out of their huts and put them in irons." He looked at the spot where the *Zephyr* went down. "My wife, they shackled behind me. My brothers and their families were shackled, too. All of us shuffled through the bush. If I looked back, I'd see the smoke rising from our thatch. It burned all that night. I could smell it. I can still smell it. I have that smell and this." He squeezed the carving.

Betsy looked at the smoke from the *Zephyr*, thinned to a barely visible wisp. Thatch could smolder for hours. Dry thatch caught quickly and spread fast.

Josiah, his face as still as his talisman, looked out at the waves. "Sometimes I see my village. I hear the women singing while they pound cassava." He put the amulet back in his pocket. "Three days we walked to the water." Leaning back on the wheelhouse, he picked up the stone he used to sharpen his knives and pulled a dagger from a strap around his leg, the fourth blade he'd honed that morning.

"Untie me, Mr. Josiah." She should have been on the ship with the carpenter, the bursar, and Charlie. "Please."

He drew the blade across the stone. "If you call out, I'll gag you. If you try to run, I'll rope you down." He looked off in the direction where the *Zephyr* sank. "I'm keeping you here because of a promise to your husband." With one jerk, he undid the knot in the leather cord binding her wrists, wrapping it around his wrist again.

Isaac should have known that Betsy would want to be with Mary and Alice close to her. She needed the baby. Her breasts ached for him; her arms yearned for his weight. Closing her eyes to be rid of the pirates, she listened to the scritch, scritch, scritch of Josiah's blade on the stone and remembered the creak of her mother's rocker when she sang Mary to sleep. Keening to that melody, Betsy took up Mary's needlework as if she held the linen in her hands. She threaded the thought of a needle she couldn't see or touch, but the thought was all she had. It worked to hold the silk thread only she could sense. She rocked back and forth, poking her needle through the square of linen, keeping the cloth taut in Mary's hoop. Her daughters depended on each stitch being snug. The resistance of the thread pulling through the fine weave and the extra jerk to bring the silk tight separated her from the ship with the pirates' laughter and the air filled with their curses. She would embroider a protective shroud for her children. She rocked, and the ship rocked with her. Searching the wide sea for the floss she needed, she saw the exact blue she would use for the D. D for David. A clear green for Mary's M. Not like the waves. Not the color of Isaac's ring. The green of leaves. The green of grass near the garden wall. The new green of springtime for Mary. What color would make Alice smile? The yellow of a daisy's center? Violet? A flower hiding under leaves. A pink? No, a rose. The light red of petals in sunshine. Petals scented sweeter than honey for the A. But who would bring the flowers? Stitching up, down, through, up, down, through, she was alone, alone, alone, but she didn't stop the embroidery. Her nose stung from the sharp smell of earth coming from Josiah's coarse whetstone against the warm blade. He chanted strange words softly. Earlier, Betsy would have thought that he was conjuring up the devil, but now she knew that once he had a wife and that his village had been burned. He was singing for them. She didn't look away when he scowled at her.

"My mates think I sing to the devil." He laughed, scornful.

Betsy waited for him to go on, her needle so tight between her thumb and forefinger it hurt her hand.

"My mother sang one song when she planted yams." He went back to honing the blade. Josiah hummed. "She sang another song with the women while she washed clothes in the river." He unwrapped a piece of charcoal from his pocket and drew a map of his village on the deck. "My uncle painted the wall around our compound with turtles." He drew a circle, adding feet and a head. He drew around Betsy. Zigzags for snakes. "Horns of our antelope." Two spirals meeting at a point. "Uncle's drawings protected us, until he sold us to the slavers."

Betsy's prayers had not protected her family. "I'm embroidering a shroud." She looked at her work. She'd embroidered the edge with flowers even she couldn't see.

"Every man on board thinks you're doing witchcraft." Josiah patted the pocket with the talisman. "My bone protects me." He spit on his whetstone and rubbed the saliva in a circle. "I was a fool to look a dying man in the eye."

"My husband?" Had Josiah drawn the symbols around her to protect her from the men, or them from her? She stopped stitching, her needle still. Her hands fell to her lap, the linen, thread, and needle gone. She bowed her head, closed her eyes, and dropped into the deep water. To her surprise, it burned. Her hands were red from the sun.

Brickhart, his jacket slung over his shoulder, sauntered over to a grizzled pirate with one arm. The captain led him over to look up at Josiah and Betsy on the poop deck. "Wave your hands in the air, woman," Brickhart said. "Whatever evil you concoct will come to nothing." He came close enough to be sure that other pirates wouldn't hear him. "Had I known that you're a witch, I'd have tied you to the mast of the *Zephyr* and made the sign of the cross when you were blown into the air." He held up his fists and thrust his fingers toward her like the boards of the ship exploding, and then called Davy to come out of the captain's quarters.

"I stitched a shroud for my children. My husband. And the farm lad. And the men on the *Zephyr*." She looked at Josiah scraping his dagger on the stone. "None of you can see my needlework."

Scoffing, Brickhart said, "Up the steps, lad."

Davy took the steps one at a time, looking back at Brickhart to see if he had to keep going. Behind him, pushing him toward Josiah, Brickhart said, "What do you think, my son? Is the lady a witch?" He frowned at Josiah's drawings before smudging them with his boot, and beckoned the old pirate to come up the last step. "Is she a witch, Mange?"

Betsy shut her eyes, pretending to sleep.

The old pirate spoke close to Betsy. "Her husband had a ring and a fine wig." He felt the leather of Betsy's shoe. "Which the nigger cast off for no reason." He touched her earlobe. "My lady's used to more than gold earrings." When he lifted the hem of Betsy's skirt back almost to her knee, Betsy opened her eyes to watch him rub the cloth between his calloused fingers. "She's hid her finest jewelry where our mates couldn't see it."

Brickhart's eyebrows arched in mock surprise. "She didn't trust the sailors?"

The small gold earrings had been Isaac's wedding gift. Betsy saw that only a ragged edge remained of the old pirate's earlobes, not enough for earrings. He readied to rip Betsy's earrings off, but she turned away and gave them to Josiah, who dropped them into Brickhart's palm.

"Tell Josiah your name, lad." Brickhart laid a fatherly hand on Davy's shoulder and passed him the earrings. Davy stared at the gold circles and closed his fist over them. He glanced at Josiah, staring at his filed teeth, then turned to look at Betsy.

She watched his eyes go from her sunburnt face, her hair undone, to the wet patches where her milk had leaked. She looked down at the deck and let the boy stare. "His name is Davy," she said.

Not long after they sailed from Lyme Regis, Betsy had come down from the top deck as the cook's boy was making his way to the galley, and she noticed that he winced when he rounded a corner and his shirt touched his back. She'd told him she needed help with the porthole, and when he came in the cabin, she demanded to see what hurt him. She'd helped him ease the shirt away from the raw welts and long purple bruises. He pulled away from her involuntary "Father in heaven," but he let her dab his back with brandy from a bottle Isaac brought to share with Mayhew. He was too young to be away from his family, and she wondered how the boy with pretty eyelashes and full pink lips came to work on the ship. Mary had sat on the bunk, her hands in her lap, her wrists crossed, staring at him. Betsy had asked, "Will you tell Mary and me your name?" Alice sat beside her sister, clutching Mary's skirt. That was weeks ago. His welts healed. Nothing on his face showed that the cook used this boy of ten, maybe eleven, as his whore. Now, tied to the mast, Betsy didn't know what would happen to her, but she didn't want the boy to see it. "His name is Davy." Her wrists were crossed as Mary's had been that afternoon of his flogging.

"Davy, is it?" Brickhart said, his voice kind. He looked over to see the boy's face.

"They call me Davy."

"Ah, Da-vid." Stressing the first syllable, Brickhart pulled the boy's shoulders back. "Mange, old man, our young mate is named for the great king of Israel. Think of it. On board our ship." Brickhart struck a pose, waving his hand up in front of his chest and over his head, demonstrating a king's posture.

The day Betsy had dabbed Davy's back with brandy, Mary had jumped up from the bunk. "Our baby is David, too." She'd run to the cradle. "He's named for the king in the Bible." Betsy turned from Brickhart and Davy to stare at the sea. The boy had gobbled slices of dried apple she'd given him and run from the cabin the moment she moved out of his way. Now he had her earrings in his fist.

"David, my boy ..." Brickhart looked at Mange while he spoke. "Have you seen our fine lady wearing necklaces? Bracelets? A sparkling pin?"

"She didn't come on deck, sir." Instead of looking at Brickhart or her, Davy's eyes were fixed on the pigsticker Josiah twirled as if he were keeping it ready.

Betsy had stitched a gold necklace in the seams of her skirt. Her mother's garnet earrings she'd nested in the buckram piping around her neckline. How could she give them to the pirate? Once she'd thought she'd give the necklace to Mary and the earrings to Alice.

Loud enough for the sailors in the forecastle to hear, Brickhart said that Mange had ears on his fingertips; he could hear gold hidden in the widow's kerchief or stomacher. The mob crowded nearer, but Torborg and LeBrun drove them back. They couldn't see the old man's eyes fastened on Betsy's breasts or the way he licked the tips of his grimy fingers.

Josiah's thumb grazed the edge of his pigsticker, and he kicked the old man's foot. When Brickhart stepped toward him, he flipped the pigsticker and crouched, ready to attack.

"Josiah, we would never harm your lady." Brickhart held up his hands to show he was unarmed. "You have my word." He laughed and patted his jacket where his pistols bulged against the cloth.

The old pirate, stinking of rum and urine, pulled off Betsy's cap and tossed it over his shoulder for the men on the main deck, but Josiah caught it on his pigsticker and pocketed it. Mange pulled out the comb that held Betsy's braid off her neck, and her hair, mostly out of the braid already, spilled down her back. The crew stomped. Glad to be rid of the comb that pulled against her hair, she shuddered as Mange skimmed his fingertips over her scalp like spiders crawling toward her neck. His hands pressed her ribs and bruised her swollen breasts.

From the deck, a pirate yelled, "I go after Mange."

Betsy told herself not to smell the rum, but to think of Isaac and being on deck with him in the moonlight, to think of David when she first lifted him from the cradle in the morning.

Mange cut the laces of her bodice and the ties holding her stomacher—that brace that supported her back and held her stomach tight but chafed after being worn all day. Stripped to her shift, she faced the men and Davy. Mange displayed the linen dress he'd pulled away from her. "Fine piece of cloth. First-grade lawn. Ten pounds in Bermuda." He bundled the dress and stomacher and threw them beyond Betsy, where Josiah couldn't reach them. He began groping Betsy's legs under her shift, and a roar went up from the men.

Springing up next to Brickhart, Josiah held the captain's elbow and pressed a dagger only she and Mange could see between the captain's ribs. Brickhart coughed, a whisper. He had to say "Mange" twice for the old man to hear.

Betsy's tormentor spit at Josiah. "Heathen."

Brickhart smiled. He and Josiah feigned friendliness that sickened Betsy. Davy's eyes were wide, and he looked at her as if she could advise him. She shook her head and looked to the captain who would be the one to decide what would happen to her—and to the boy. Brickhart said, "Josiah Giddings. You have my word." He waved the old man away from Betsy. "She has nothing, Mange." He touched his side and showed Josiah the smudge of blood on his finger. "You cut the silk, Josiah." He took a long breath, scanning the sea, his men, and the sky to the west. Stretching out his palm toward Mange, he nodded. "Here. Now."

Mange pulled Betsy's slippers out of his pockets and handed them to Brickhart, who guided Davy down the steps, never looking back at Josiah.

Freed from the ropes Josiah had loosened for the old man to take off her dress, Betsy jumped to her feet and lunged for the rail, but he grabbed her shift and pulled her up against the stink of his sweat. "No, lady. You are as bound to this ship as me."

"What good am I to you?"

"None, but if I let you jump, every man on this ship would want a slice of me." With a four-foot lead freeing her to sit, stand, or lie down, Josiah cinched a rope around her waist. "Poor Brickhart can't admit to the crew that he wants you dead."

Betsy, roped like a monkey for the pirates, lay on her back, looking up at the evening star twenty degrees above the horizon in an azure sky. Beautiful and far away.

"S-s-t." A weasel's hiss. "S-s-s-t" again. From the main deck, LeBrun tossed Isaac's jacket over the railing onto Betsy's feet. She hugged it, shivering from the night air on her sunburned arms and face. She pressed the sleeve with its faint smell of pine to her lips and then cuddled the jacket, gently so not to cause it any pain. The soft wool against her cheek, she imagined him holding her as he had on the moonlit deck. She put the jacket arms around her.

Music and laughter drifted up from the hatch and from the men on deck. They hung lanterns from the spars, and Mange piped on a small flute. The twins jingled their tambourines. In dancing light, men jigged. Torborg bumped Asa with his shoulder, and they began twisting right and left, never quite touching, their hands clasped behind their backs. In Isaac's arms, Betsy paid them no mind. It was the children she missed.

————

The silver moon threw the shadows of masts and yards on the deck. The door of the captain's quarters shut softly. Torborg and Lebrun, their shirts hanging loose over their pants, came up the steps to the poop deck, and they walked the gallery to the stern behind the wheelhouse. The Swede sang a hymn for eventide; Betsy recognized the tune. She strained to hear but couldn't understand his words.

The wind came with a fragrance of rain. Sniffing the air, Josiah, with the velvet motion of a mink, spread a spare sail for the mizzenmast over Betsy. She threw off the musty canvas to protect the smells of Isaac's jacket. Josiah stretched out under the rejected canvas, close to Betsy. Shivering, she pressed her arms over her breasts to blunt their ache. Stinging strips of rain—fresh water—whipped her face. And then, chasing even the smallest cloud, the wind left acres of stars. Stars beyond stars. Betsy looked for the farthest, and pulled Isaac's jacket closer, her teeth chattering.

Josiah left the sail and curled himself around Betsy, clamping his hand on her knees until she stopped shaking. "I had a wife and son. Our village was far from the sea. We had no fear of slavers." Josiah spoke to the night, to the boards of the ship, to the waves, to the stars. She'd grown accustomed to his soft Rs, his stretched Ls, his occasional switching of the two sounds. "When we heard the slavers at the other huts, my wife tried to hide our son, but he rushed out of his hiding place when they threw me to the floor. Me. I was first. On the floor, in irons, they held me, and one of them raped me in front of my wife. Then they raped my son until he was as still as the farm lad. And they raped my wife." His laugh had a knife's edge. "Don't you hear their cries?"

Betsy lay like a stone with him curled around her. Why was he telling her this? Why would she want to know?

"They marched us in irons, single file. My wife bled behind me, but they would not let me carry her. A drink in the morning and no food; three days to the slavers' port."

Waves shushed the groaning ship.

He got up and walked deliberately to the rail. Grasping a rope, he leaned out over the rail and urinated into the sea. On the ship, the slavers had cut off his testicles. "Brickhart won't let the sailors sell me. In port, he chains me to a mast below deck. Even the Swede and LeBrun—especially Le-Brun—would sell me for half the price of a woman."

The last thing Betsy heard was Josiah telling her how cheaply he'd be sold. She fell asleep. Alice pulled on her apron; Mary made a mistake in her stitching. They were on the ship, and Isaac was unfolding pieces of paper. With both hands—his ring on his finger—he spread notes on the deck, wet from the rain. The papers fluttered, and Isaac tried to keep them from blowing away. David cried out in his sleep. Betsy had to leave Isaac to care for the baby. His cry came from the crow's nest high up on the main mast.

"Sails! A ship! Ship to port!"

Josiah shot up the mizzenmast and peered through the glass Brickhart had let him keep.

He jumped to the deck. "A man-o'-war."

Chapter 7

Betsy pulled a feather pillow forward so her cheek wouldn't touch the drool on the linen and pressed her arm over her ear to stop the men's voices. She curled into a ball on a mattress as thick as the bed in Brompton. Her hand hurt from gripping Isaac's jacket. Where was her mother's shawl? Where was Josiah? She remembered a man said, "She can sleep in my quarters until we arrange a cabin for her." She remembered being helped down to the long-boat—where Brickhart sat in front of two sailors. She pressed her arm harder to keep from thinking. The only voice in the cabin she recognized belonged to the captain who had taken her off the *Sally Dash*.

Davy had been in the long boat. She'd asked for him. She didn't want to see Charlie or the carpenter. They'd claimed they came to rescue her, but they did nothing to take the baby from Brickhart or stop Torborg from throwing Mary and Alice overboard.

Betsy caught a whiff of Isaac's jacket, the lining, and breathed in his smell. She wanted back into her dream. Her knees tight to her chest, she thought herself back to

Brompton. She sat at the kitchen table, braiding Mary's hair
while Alice watched, her fingers twisting three strands,
over under, over under, over under, until only the tail
remained. Mary preferred red ribbons. Alice picked yellow.
Betsy wished Isaac beside her and pulled his jacket to her
lips, remembering his morning whiskers. Home, in her own
kitchen, she'd be making breakfast. Later she and the girls
would buy cheese at market. Betsy rocked, quietly, so the
men wouldn't notice her.

The men had brought her to the captain's bunk on the
man-of-war. Isaac would have been at the table, talking to
the captain. By pressing her teeth together, she could stop
a moan in her throat, but she couldn't stop the thoughts in
her head. In her head, guns thundered, cannonballs
screamed, and wood cracked as shells burst open on the
deck. She kept seeing Torborg throw Mary over the side.
Alice. David. In the bunk, she pressed her face hard into
Isaac's jacket, and still Alice called, "Mama."

Josiah had left her bound to the mast on the poop deck
so he could help Torborg jam blocks under the cannon
wheels while Asa and Mange threw the sheep and chickens
over the rail to clear the deck. The pirates' curses drowned
the bleating and squawking. Afloat, the wooly animals
swam away from the ship; this was the last thing she saw
before Josiah leaped up the gallery steps to wrap a sail
around her. "Three layers of sail will keep shell and shrap-
nel from cutting you. If they set us on fire, we'll burn
together."

Late morning light flooded the captain's cabin. Glass
doors on bookcases reflected the sun around the cabin. A
whiff of roast beef hung in the air, and the tang of tobacco
drifted from the table. The wood cabinets, brass pulls,

knobs, and hinges had been polished to a shine. The cabin had more windows than her sitting room in Brompton-on-Thames. On the bench below the windows across the stern, Davy curled like a caterpillar under a quilt. His wheeze reminded Betsy of listening to Mary breathe while she slept. She wanted to hear only that breathing.

A fragrance of home came back to her. Tea. One of them was pouring tea, and then stirred a spoon in a cup. "We all wanted Brickhart tried and properly sentenced, Cap'n."

Betsy looked over at the captain sucking his pipe to pull the flame and light the bowl. After several breaths, a thin spiral of smoke clawed the air.

In the longboat that morning, Brickhart, splattered with blood and black from gunpowder, sat facing Betsy with a ball and chain around his ankle. His hat had probably been left in Mayhew's quarters. His hair was matted and his shirt torn. A cut above his eyebrow had stopped bleeding. He'd leaned toward her. "I'll not trouble you further." Despite manacles, before anyone could stop him, before Bennett—that was the captain's name: Bennett—before he could call out, Brickhart heaved the iron ball over the side and rolled after it. He'd dropped straight down, bubbles rising around him. Isaac's green stone found its place in the sea.

Betsy pulled the quilt up, over Isaac's jacket, to her chin. She'd been taken from the *Sally Dash* wearing only her shift. At the end of Captain Bennett's bunk, her green linen dress lay folded over her stomacher. Next to the dress, her stockings were rolled in her shoes, all cleaned. Someone had spread her mother's shawl over the quilt on the bunk. She touched it to be sure it was there and not a dream that would be gone if she moved. While the captain and his first mate—Able Carter—smoked their pipes, she whispered the names of her children, changing the order, hoping the little ones heard her; they should know she was calling them. Mary, Alice, David. Alice, Mary, David. David, Alice, Mary. Mary …

The first mate jumped to his feet. Captain Bennett walked slowly over to the bunk. "You are safe here, Mrs. Randall." He spoke softly, each word crisp. "I am Captain John Bennett, commander of the *Falconer*." He re-introduced his first mate. Rather than say that she remembered their names, she repeated the names for the children, again, but silently.

"Carter, call Dr. McNeill," Bennett said. He paced the length of the cabin after the first mate left. Then he turned to Betsy as if to reprimand her. Was she still saying the children's names out loud? Davy had stopped her from repeating them on the longboat. Bennett and his men thought Davy was her son until he explained that he and the baby had the same name.

Bennett stood next to her. "You're protected by Her Majesty's navy, Mrs. Randall."

Carter and the doctor must have been at the open door waiting to knock until Bennett finished speaking. Earlier, it had been the pock-faced McNeill in a plain black coat who led Betsy to the captain's cabin. His hands had been blood-stained, and he'd smelled of sweat. Now he saluted the captain, and his hands had been scrubbed clean. "Four marines dead. I amputated Sandler's leg at the knee." Leaning over Betsy, the doctor pulled back her eyelid. She turned toward him. When they were still on the *Sally Dash*, he'd spoken so kindly that she wanted to tell him about Mary and Alice.

"Our Dr. McNeill," Bennett said.

"Dr. McNeill." Betsy put his hand to her cheek. Her whole body hurt. Before the doctor gave her the laudanum that confused her sleep and her waking, the doctor had argued with Bennett about whether Davy was being truthful when he said that the pirates had only undressed her and never taken off her shift. "I need to nurse the baby," she said.

Shaking his head, the doctor pulled his hand free and gently covered Betsy's mouth. He'd washed with lavender soap.

"Three marines shot off the spar," Bennett said. He lit his pipe again. "Dropped straight to the sea."

The doctor shook his head. "Seven brave men lost, am I right?" He looked at Bennett.

"And a boy killed." Betsy didn't say they hadn't counted Isaac or the children. They didn't know about the farmer's son.

"Davy is here, Mrs. Randall." Bennett walked over to the boy sitting up on the bench.

Betsy knew Davy was there; she wasn't going to tell them about the other boy's death. Charlie or the carpenter should have told them. How long Davy had been awake, Betsy didn't know, but she was glad to see him scratching his copper curls. "Davy, will you sit by me?"

The boy looked at the captain who turned to the doctor. McNeill nodded. Davy came over to the bunk and let Betsy hold his hand. The night before, after the rain, Brickhart had brought Davy out on deck in a gown she'd worn for her wedding. He'd worn her shoes, the ones lying on the bunk.

Betsy sat up. "What happened to Josiah, Davy?"

The men looked at her and then the boy. He squinted, frowning at Bennett.

"Tell her, lad." Bennett put a hand on his shoulder to encourage him.

Davy pulled at a yarn tie on the quilt with his free hand. "After he covered you with the sail, he fought next to Cap'n Brickhart. Remember his long dagger and his cutlass? But when the old pirate and the skinny one came back with the redcoats, he went mad. Remember how he'd growl and show his teeth?" He turned to Bennett. "The nigger had fangs. Like a dog, all his teeth points." He touched his eyetooth as if to be sure they understood.

The first mate leaned forward to study the boy's face. "Did he bite?"

"No." Betsy wanted to hear about Josiah. She didn't want the men in the cabin to speak his name or think that they knew him.

Davy looked at her and hung his head. He nodded like he, too, had regard for Josiah. "The nigger kept the lady on the poop deck and nobody could come near. 'Cept me and Captain Brickhart and Old Mange, but all of us had to leave when they took her gown and shoes."

Betsy didn't want to hear about Old Mange. "What happened to Josiah, Davy?"

"Open a window, Carter." Bennett pointed to the window farthest from the bunk. "And set the door for a breeze. Who's Old Mange, lad?"

Davy looked up at the captain, at Carter opening the window, and then at Betsy shaking her head. She silently begged the boy not to shame her. "The old pirate Charlie shot dead before Josiah came at Charlie and the carpenter, but the redcoats cut Josiah down, lady. That's what happened to him, and then Asa pulled a pistol from the nigger's belt and tried to shoot Charlie, but he missed and the carpenter smashed the cook's head with his hammer." He looked at Betsy. "I'm glad."

She nodded and pressed Davy's hand to her cheek to thank him for telling her about Josiah and Asa. How right Josiah was to keep her from watching. She'd heard the cannons fire, the boards crack, the retort of rifles, and the blasts of muskets. It hadn't lasted long. The screams of the men hung in the air. "I'm glad Brickhart tied you next to me at the mizzenmast," she said. She shivered though she wasn't cold; the boy looked at her as if she'd betrayed him. He'd begged the pirate to let him fight. The boy got up and went back to sit on the window seat. He'd kicked when Brickhart roped Davy next to her, but the pirate said, "They'll string you up, lad." He didn't want the redcoats mistaking King David's namesake for a pirate.

Betsy wanted to ask Davy if Torborg and LeBrun were in irons on the *Sally Dash*, but her breasts ached, hot with fever. She hugged her arms hard across her chest.

The doctor came over, clasped her shoulder, and put his palm on her forehead. "Captain, Mrs. Randall should have a cube of sugar in a cup of tea."

Did he think the tea he poured would stop her aching? She wanted to turn from the men, but she didn't trust them to tell her their plans.

Bennett went to a cupboard across the cabin, opened a padlocked box, cut a cube of sugar from a block for McNeill to put in the tea. The doctor sprinkled drops from a small brown bottle into the cup. "Tincture of laudanum, Mrs. Randall. It will help you sleep." The spoon chinked the cup while he stirred in the opium.

Betsy didn't want the medicine, or the two pillows the captain put behind her back. "You didn't come in time." She wasn't blaming him, but it had to be said.

Bennett walked away from the berth to the window Carter had opened. He clasped his hands behind his back. "In time? No, though we had a good wind, but we didn't know Brickhart's whereabouts until after we picked up those who escaped." He sat next to Davy and watched the doctor hold the cup for Betsy to drink. He waited until McNeill set the cup on the table. "We would have liked to have captured Brickhart on the *Zephyr*, Mrs. Randall. You should know the men say Mr. Randall faced the pirates—and death—with courage."

Despite the sugar, the tea had tasted bitter. "Captain, do you know about the baby?"

Bennett nodded. "We were sent to hunt down Brickhart. Providence put us on course to spot the makeshift raft. The reformed pirate—I am sorry that he died—had planned the escape. He didn't know the three men would be with him, but he couldn't say enough good about Charlie Potts and the carpenter George Keyes, the man with tools to get the craft in shape. They could salvage little from the *Zephyr* before they abandoned her, knowing Brickhart would blow up the ship. Only by God's grace did we site the flag they made of Potts' shirt."

God's grace? Betsy didn't understand. She lay down, her head heavy on the pillow.

Bennett uncorked a squat black bottle he pulled from the cupboard where he kept the sugar. "A little Madeira, Doctor?" He poured the syrupy dark wine into three glasses. "After the reports, we'll salute the dead and honor those who showed valor, but before that and before congratulating the officers on the capture, why not a small glass?"

McNeill picked up Betsy's wrist. "She'll sleep 'til we wake her, her grief numbed."

Betsy lay with her eyes closed, her body a dry leaf floating on a puddle of water, listening to talk of Brickhart's cowardice in robbing them of a trial in Yorktown. Their reward for saving the cargo destined for planters and merchants would be miserly.

McNeill left to attend to the wounded. Carter walked out with him. He would row with a few men over to the *Sally Dash*, question sailors and pirates, and take an inventory of each man's gear. Sailors had returned some of the Randalls' pilfered goods, a play for clemency. Davy went with them; he'd seen what LeBrun and Torborg had hidden in Mayhew's quarters.

Betsy hoped to sleep beyond any attempt to awaken her, to drift far deeper than Brickhart's ball and chain had pulled him down.

Chapter 8

Isaac pressed Betsy's sunburned cheek to one side on the pillow. Her head ached. He caressed her leg and fingered the rock-hard lump of her breast. He kissed the nipple and licked around it, testing the edge of pain. To open her eyes to the light would be agony. She needed to be home. To be in Brompton. But she was on a ship, and Isaac was too urgent, pushing her legs apart, forcing himself into her. She twisted, but his hand gripped her shoulder while he bucked her body into the bunk. He smelled of nutmeg.

Isaac despised nutmeg; he smelled of pine. He rubbed oil of pine on his chin. His hands gave off that fragrance. He never bit Betsy's hair with his teeth. She pushed to escape from the weight on her chest and belly, the shove of the man inside her. No matter how she wriggled to get out from under him, he had her wedged tight, and now he clamped his hand over her mouth. He reeked of nutmeg. He liked that she squirmed, grunting. "Yes, yes. Just that. Yes."

Struggling to bite his hand, she raised her knee against his thigh, trying to kick him off. She called for Davy, but the captain's hand blocked her voice. He quivered and collapsed on top of her. "Thank you. Thank you, poor little mouse. How sweet you are, dear thing. I shall keep you here, but I'll have to gag you. Shush now." He propped his body up over her with an arm.

Davy, the doctor, and the first mate were gone; the door was closed.

Grabbing a fold of flesh below his ribs, Betsy dug her nails into his skin and twisted her pinch. "Get away from me." She screwed the pinch tighter, kicking him. "Josiah didn't let the pirates touch me."

Bennett grabbed her wrists and squeezed them together, keeping her from hitting him. "The more the fool." He wiped himself with a corner of the sheet. "A woman in the captain's quarters should expect to pay a fare."

She kicked the soft muscle between his rib and his hip, and he grabbed her foot. Her stockings were in shreds. "Lovely," he said and kissed her filthy arch before letting her pull her foot away. "You're none the worse for the wear, Mrs. Randall."

Betsy wanted to spit at him, but her mouth was dry. She needed Isaac, but to think of him in the captain's presence was a sin against her husband. She would not cry. "You have trampled on all that's holy between a man and a woman."

"No." He looked directly into her eyes. "No. There is more between a man and a woman than a prick thrust between your legs." He hiked up his pants and buttoned his fly. He studied himself in a mirror from a cupboard before handing her the glass, but she had no desire to see her face. He put on his jacket. "You've been drugged, dear lady. Dr. McNeill gave you laudanum, and while in its thrall, no doubt your mind tricked you with lustful impulses, part of our fallen nature." He poured Madeira into a glass and raised it to Betsy, then gulped it down. "You've had a dream. I understand your outrage." Bennett locked the bottle in the cabinet along with the box of sugar before he opened the door. "Have the boy David bring my dinner."

She could not let Davy see the shame on her face, her rumpled shift. She pulled it down over her legs, tucked her hair up into the cap she pulled from under the pillow, and turned to the wall to pretend she still slept.

"Your dinner, sir?" Davy's voice sounded uncertain. Dishes clinked and the smell of ham and turnips filled the cabin. Plates and silverware clattered.

Bennett scraped a chair away from the table and sent Davy for a clean napkin. "Will you join me for dinner, Mrs. Randall?"

Betsy pulled the quilt up to her chin.

When Davy returned, Bennett asked him to read the scripture lesson for the day.

"I can't read, sir."

The captain busied himself with the meal. "David, no matter how valiantly a man struggles to do what is right, temptation surrounds us. St. Paul warns us to be ever vigilant." He continued to chew, the only sound in the cabin other than the sound of waves coming through the windows and the voices of the sailors from beyond the closed door. "Bring the Bible from that bookcase and read to me."

Betsy moaned at the thought of Davy being near Bennett.

"How long will the lady sleep, sir?"

"The longer, the better. Sleep heals our bodies and our souls." Bennett's voice scratched from low in his throat. "In times of trouble, the letters of St. Paul comfort me. He sailed the Mediterranean—not as a sailor, but he knew the sea."

"I can't read, sir." Davy spoke so softly.

"Today, I'll read to you. The doctor is a patient teacher. He taught Ezra, my cabin boy."

Betsy slid her hand around the bed seeking Isaac's jacket, and when she came to it, she brought it to her nose to breathe the scent of pine. She'd be vigilant for a chance to join her family.

"Ephesian, chapter six, verse thirteen." Bennett cleared his throat. "'Wherefore take unto you the whole armour of God ...'" He read each word slowly and then had Davy repeat the words after he read them. He pushed his chair away from the table. Betsy felt him looking at her. "There are many evils, David. Most are not as easy to strike down as the pirate Brickhart. We strive for righteousness."

Betsy sat up and glared at the man.

"Mrs. Randall, you are awake. Would ..." Bennett belched softly. Before he could finish his sentence, there was a tap at the door and Davy ran to open it, as if he knew the duties of a cabin boy. He squared his shoulders and stood proudly. "Captain Bennett, Mr. Carter."

"Ah. Come in. I was about to ask Mrs. Randall if she would have supper."

Carter reported that Mayhew's papers had been left intact by the pirates; all the bills of sale had been filed in an orderly fashion. The Randall papers, though riffled, had been collected, and the family's belongings, including clothing, recovered. The carpenter found Mr. Randall's silver buckles on the body of a midget. Their crate hadn't been pried open, but the cradle had been pulled apart and hidden in a pirate's gear. Carter thought it best for the crate to stay on the *Sally Dash* until they docked in Yorktown, but they had carried Mrs. Randall's trunk to the *Falconer*'s lower deck.

After commending Carter for the recovery, Bennett turned to Betsy. "Mrs. Randall, your husband's papers and belongings have been salvaged from the *Sally Dash*."

The Randall papers, the crate, the cradle. Betsy looked at him and folded her hands in her lap. She intended never to speak of her family to the captain. She could feel him forcing himself on her, his tongue on her breasts. She didn't want Davy to be beholden to him. "Captain Bennett, I can teach Davy to read. In the trunk Mr. Carter brought onto your ship, my family has the book *A Pilgrim's Progress*. We also have a Bible." Davy could see how Isaac studied and wrote notes on the pages. She turned and looked out at the sea. Evenings, Mary would read Isaac what Betsy had taught her that day, and then Alice insisted on "reading" stories she made up. Betsy took a deep breath and turned to the boy. "Davy, you would enjoy John Bunyan's story."

Davy's look gladdened Betsy. She could feel how he'd take her hand when they went to read.

Bennett caught the look Betsy and Davy exchanged. "If being Mrs. Randall's pupil suits you, David, by all means take advantage of her offer."

Bennett and Carter smiled at Davy's salute, and they returned it before the captain dismissed the first mate and Davy, who quickly gathered the dishes on the tray, gave Betsy a nod, and walked through the door Carter held for him.

Betsy gathered up her clothes—her stomacher, her gown, her shoes—and held them along with Isaac's jacket.

Bennett cleared his throat. "Your husband would have rewarded Carter's efforts."

On the *Sally Dash*, Isaac took pride in peeling apples in a long, unbroken curl. What about Bennett had reminded her of that quirk in Isaac's nature? The captain seemed to think that the family's belongings mattered to Betsy. Once she'd dreaded the thought of the pirates touching anything belonging to Isaac or the girls, but those possessions had no value.

Bennett lit a pipe and pulled the papers from the *Sally Dash* in front of him. He started to read, but then got up from the table and wedged the door to his cabin open. "Shall I order your supper?"

Betsy did not answer. She had no more need of supper than she had need of the cradle.

"I'll ask the lad …"

"Davy." She said his name. Davy mattered to her.

Silent for a moment, Bennett nodded. "Yes. David. I'll have him bring your supper." He smoked the pipe. "We have a fine wind." He walked to the stern and closed the open window. "Within three days, we'll sail into the Chesapeake." At the door, he said, "I'll send the boy." He left, closing the door.

She stood by the bunk, holding the curtain for balance. Wobbly or not, she'd put on her dress, force her feet into her shoes, and go out on deck. She laced her stomacher tightly. Her breasts ached; the stiff garment held the pain in place. The skin on her forehead and cheeks burned, but she didn't know the whereabouts of her hat.

Chapter 9

Before Betsy had taken three steps on the gallery walk of the *Falconer*, a grim-faced, silent Carter ushered her back to the captain's quarters.

Bennett came in. "I'm ordering Carter to lock you in the cabin for your own safety, Mrs. Randall." His voice sounded apologetic. "The carpenter assures me a cabin with a locking door will be ready on the lower deck. Your trunk will be there for you." He wanted her moved during the first dog watch, but before then, he'd have Davy bring her dinner. Bennett left to take the helm.

Davy took care arranging her meal on Bennett's table. He held the pot with two hands, one keeping the lid in place. "Tea." He nodded as he pulled a chair out from the table for her. "The doctor wants you to drink all your tea and finish your dinner."

"Did he put drops in the tea?"

Without a second thought, he poured a little tea in the cup and tasted it. "It's just tea." He nodded and poured more into the cup. "Very nice." He looked at his arrangement of the covered plate, the cup, knife, spoon, and napkin, obviously pleased with his work. Then he put the gold earrings, the ones Brickhart had given him, next to the cup. "I saved 'em for you."

Betsy felt her earlobes. She didn't need the earrings and hid them under her palm. "They were a gift from my husband."

"Like the ring you gave him."

Betsy nodded. She didn't say Isaac had lied, but held the earrings out to him. "These were a gift from Brickhart to you."

"No, ma'am. They were part of the prize, but he didn't want me being a pirate."

She put the earrings in her pocket. Having no appetite, Betsy sat back and looked at Davy's curls, his long eyelashes, his pretty mouth, his determination to get things right. "Brickhart was cruel, Davy, but he protected you." She pushed the plate away. "Do you have brothers and sisters?"

He nodded and lifted off the overturned bowl covering the plate, sliding it back in front of her. "Doctor says you have to eat."

"How many in your family, Davy?"

He frowned. "I'm sorry about the wee one, ma'am. He had my name, you know."

Betsy turned to the window. "I imagined my husband walked into this cabin last night. Like always—his shoulders back. Tall. In his burgundy jacket." On her walk, she'd folded it over her arm, and Carter took it before leading her back to the cabin. He'd hung it on the chair.

"I don't have dreams." Davy said the captain wanted her to talk about Brickhart and the pirates on the Dash after she finished her mash and peas.

Could she eat? She had a notion that she held memories

in her mouth, and if she ate, she would lose them. To keep Davy in the cabin, she rearranged the peas. Charlie Potts, the carpenter, and the bursar had told Bennett all he needed to know about the pirates. "Davy, are the Swede and the Frenchman still alive?"

Davy walked with the stealth of a thief to the door and silently closed it. He stood next to it, listening, and then, just as quietly, walked back. "A cannon got that LeBrun. He was swabbing it out and the boat lurched. The cannon broke the rail and his foot caught in a rope and pulled him over. That cannon would'a sunk faster than a rock." Davy glanced at the door. He looked at Betsy to see if she'd heard anyone coming, but she hadn't.

"And the Swede?"

"He jumped after him. He dove in. Like this ..." Davy put his palms together above his head and bent at the waist. "That was before any of Captain Bennett's men stormed the ship. The rest of the pirates? They gave it up, but not Brickhart and the nigger. Asa tried to act like he was against the captain all along."

"I see that you are stronger, Mrs. Randall." Bennett stood at the open door.

Davy jumped to salute.

Betsy stared at the man. Was she stronger? Maybe. She'd been alone with Davy long enough to be at ease with him. She'd learned that Torborg and LeBrun were both dead. The memory of the Swede singing a quiet hymn to LeBrun bothered her. When Torborg threw Mary and Alice into the sea, LeBrun said, "You must be strong."

"Mrs. Randall ain't hungry. Do you want me to take her mash back to the galley?" His shoulders back, his face flushed, Davy ran to hold the door for Dr. McNeill, Carter, and another man Betsy didn't know. The boy hurriedly cleared the table, except for her cup of tea, and left with the tray when Bennett waved his hand.

The captain strolled over to the table and sat with Betsy on his left, his face to the door. The other men took their places, the stranger next to Bennett. He put a packet of papers on the table within their easy reach. Dr. McNeill sat across from Bennett, on Betsy's right, and Carter took the chair at the end of the table. He set up an inkpot, quills, and the logbook, ready to record what was said. Bennett introduced the bursar, Mr. Trout, who studied Betsy so closely she looked away from him to the ship's wake through the windows at the stern. She'd used Bennett's comb to braid her hair before she'd covered it with her cap. The skin on her nose was peeling. The tea smelled like it had been sweetened with molasses.

Davy slipped back into the cabin, careful not to look at her. When he stood behind Bennett, the sun made a halo of his copper curls.

Before Bennett could ask the first question, Betsy said, "Captain Mayhew had at least one sailor of the *Sally Dash* flogged every day. Even Davy." She didn't know why she said it.

Davy's chin dropped to his chest, and she wished that she could take back the words.

Bennett pushed back his chair.

Instead of following Isaac's advice to say nothing, she went on. "The first mate's favorite was late for his watch, but he punished Davy instead of his chum."

Bennett stretched his hand to stop Carter from writing. "Strike that." He turned to Betsy. "We've been told that the runaway slave kept you in front of the wheelhouse, and that you may have witnessed what took place after the carpenter and the sailors left, Mrs. Randall."

"Worse than the flogging was Captain Mayhew's meager fare, but you should ask the bursar about the sailors' poor meals. Grown men ate the crusts of cheese or apple peels Mr. Randall would drop. I asked my husband to be more careful, but he saw it differently."

Bennett pushed his chair away from the table. "How would you describe Emanuel Brickhart, Mrs. Randall?" He looked at Carter, whose pen was poised to write but not moving. Trout rubbed the side of his nose and sighed. "The night before we rescued you, the sailors we picked up told us Brickhart and his man shot Captain Mayhew and the first mate. Did you see that?"

A gunshot. And another. Two bodies, limbs jerking on the deck. Torborg and the pirates dropping them over the side. Betsy bowed her head and then looked up. "We were all on deck, Captain Bennett. My daughters and I were as close to Mayhew as I am to the bookcase. Isaac stood between the two men. Perhaps Charlie Potts told you that." He and the carpenter would have told them about unloading the *Zephyr.* "I wanted to escape, too. Davy started, but the cook held him back, and Brickhart rescued Davy from the cook. Josiah wouldn't let me go, but it didn't matter. The pirates wouldn't have let me go, either." She noticed that Carter had laid down his quill. Had the escapees told Bennett, McNeill, Trout, and Carter about the pirates stowing the farm animals—and the lad? She could not tell them that; even to think it hurt. Suddenly, she heard LeBrun reading the pirates' liturgy, and she spouted it for Bennett, as if from memory. Carter wrote as fast as he could. The bursar dipped a different quill for him each time the one he used went dry.

Betsy remembered much of it because Josiah had recited it as if in a refrain to LeBrun's reading: sailors chose their own course and had equal claim to the cargo.

Bennett's mouth hardened as he listened to the scratch of the quill. "Mr. Carter."

Carter looked up and put the quill in the inkpot.

"We all know the promises pirates make, Mrs. Randall." Bennett's voice was tired. He had probably been awake since Charlie Potts and the others came on board. He certainly hadn't slept in his bunk since the capture of the *Sally Dash*. He leaned toward her. "Have you no recollection of the goods that Brickhart loaded onto the ship from the *Zephyr*?

Betsy looked at Davy, who stared past her to the curtains pulled in front of the bunk. Did he too see the barrels and crates being hauled into the hold while Torborg led the songs? Did he see the sheep and chickens penned on the deck? Did he remember the smell of roast pig? Betsy had been drenched with rain. Was that rain before Torborg sang to LeBrun?

She folded her hands. "I packed a christening gown." Isaac's grandfather and her own children had worn it. Each child had blessed the cloth, each child's weight and need added heft to the thread, each child's sleeping and waking, a great-grandmother's prayers were part of the weave. Betsy studied her hands—the slight curve of her fingernails. Alice had that curve, too.

Bennett sighed. "We have more than enough to convict Brickhart's crew and the mutineers, but I didn't expect you to come to their defense." He stood up and walked to the window. "If we find the baptismal gown, it will be returned to you." He held out his hand to help Betsy to her feet.

A simple thing, to put her hand in his, to accept his

gallantry, but a whiff of nutmeg when he came near repulsed her. She pushed her chair from the table and turned away from him. "I need to relieve myself."

Bennett strode to the door and waved for the men to leave. Davy kept his gaze down when he passed Betsy. Carter said he'd return in half an hour to take her to her new quarters.

————

Carter went along with Betsy's wish to walk over to the gunwale, to stretch out the time on deck before being locked in the cabin below deck. "You'll be comfortable with no people comin and goin." He had a clean, pink face, blue eyes, a small chin; Betsy trusted him. He said that Bennett scheduled two marines for every watch to guard her door. With a bolt the carpenter from the Dash had for the door, she'd feel safe. Davy would bring her meals and come for his reading lesson twice a day. He'd take her on a walk for half an hour on the gallery in the afternoon—if the weather was fair.

The cabin at the stern had a porthole, a narrow bunk—not as wide as those Mayhew set up for the Randall family on the Dash—and the family's trunk crammed parallel to the bunk bed with three inches to spare. Between the door and the trunk there was a board to serve as a table or desk hinged to the wall, wide enough for a person sitting on the berth to reach comfortably. A leather flask of water hung from a hook next to that board. Under the bunk, one-inch boards held a tin chamber pot in place.

When Betsy stopped at the door, reluctant to go in, Carter put his hand at the small of her back and pushed her forward. She leaned against the table hooked to the wall while he flung a sheepskin over the horsehair pad on the bed ropes. "Not as wide as the captain's berth. Cozy." Over the sheepskin, with two quick swoops, he smoothed the fine linen sheet Bennett insisted she have. "No more whistles. No pipes. No snuff." Closing the door, he showed Betsy a small mirror. "Give it a smile," he said, smiling himself. "Bolt the door. Keep it bolted." He left.

After shoving the bolt home, Betsy stood against the door to see where she would be living. She couldn't remember ever being so alone. Only a bed and the trunk. She sat on the berth to stare at the trunk packed with her family's clothes and belongings. Isaac, Mary, Alice, and David seemed present, in the cabin, breathing the air. Betsy leaned back against the hull. She didn't want to disturb them, but overcome with fatigue, she lay down, eyeing the trunk, the empty space above it, keeping her family there. Humming a lullaby to help them sleep, she slept. In a carriage without a coachman, runaway horses galloped through a wood, hurling the carriage against trees and into deep gullies while a highwayman—Josiah—pounded on the door, his eyes wide with the fear of death. Betsy strained to unbolt the carriage door and pull him in. Rolling off the berth, thrown against the wall, she gripped the trunk to pull herself to her feet and work the bolt free. The ship righted. Betsy tumbled back onto the berth, and the ship, topsy-turvy, threw the door open. Betsy clutched a rope under the mattress to keep from being pitched to the floor.

Carter burst in. "Storm!" He wore pants and a shirt tarred to shed water, but he was soaked through. "Cap'n wants you tied down." Without waiting for Betsy's reply, he looped a rope under the sides of the bunk, over her, and set a knot, folding Betsy's hand over one end of the rope. He worked, free from fear, sure the knot would hold. "Yank it and the knot's undone." He smiled. "But not till I—" He pointed to his chest. "Me, Able Carter, says it's over. A calm can mean the worst is coming."

Through the window, Betsy saw gray-blue clouds roil over a band of fevered yellow-green light between sea and sky. "Is it morning?"

A wall of green water crashed against the stern. "Soon." Carter tested the knot. "Bennett'll steer us through this squall. Now it's 'God save us.'" He braced his legs and set the bolt up. When he jumped out, slamming the door, the bolt fell into place.

How well he did the thing. Not only had he roped her into the bunk, secured the knot so she could undo it, and fixed the bolt to slip into place, but he'd set things right for her family. Unafraid, they sat on the trunk, David in Isaac's arms, Mary and Alice on either side. Then they left. The waves dropped the ship, wrenching beams that groaned louder than thunder. Betsy screamed. She screamed to hear her own voice above the storm. "Isaac!" No one heard her.

The unceasing roll of the ship had once annoyed her. Now it rocked her like a cradle. She fell asleep. The storm passed. Alone in the cabin, she stared at the girders supporting the top deck. Carter's knots had held her in place.

Footsteps. A quick knock. "Mrs. Randall?" Carter's sure voice comforted Betsy. "Steady wind, clear sailing. Gale blew us off, but we'll be in Yorktown by week's end. Cook's serving breakfast." His heels clicked and he was gone.

When she no longer heard his steps, she yanked the rope and wriggled free. She fingered the bolt but left it in place and went to the porthole to gaze at the wake. "Yorktown?"

Chapter 10

"Smell it, ma'am." Davy leaned over the gunwale for sight of a shore. "Land."

Betsy sniffed the breeze, and, yes, a whiff of kitchen fires. More than that, trees. She clutched Davy's hand. Maybe he was right. Maybe she smelled the land itself. She took a deeper breath as if embracing a friend, clinging to an intimacy of long acquaintance, and pulled her mother's shawl tighter around her shoulders, not because she was chilled, but to wrap her longing in it.

Following Bennett's order, Carter had led them to the gallery, warning them not to be underfoot, telling them to go round the stern to the starboard side to watch how sea and sky change as the ship sails into the harbor. Gulls, glistening white flashes in the sun, swooped and soared, shrieking above the choppy water. A lacy fringe of black tufts on the horizon grew more distinct. Offshore winds ruffled bundles of yellow, pink, and reddish-brown, a welcoming of trees with new leaf buds. The breeze carried a scent of pine. Like Davy, Betsy couldn't open her eyes wide enough to see everything. She couldn't allow them to rest, not even on smoke rising like a kite string in the sky.

The neighing of a horse carried over the water, and Betsy squeezed her arm around Davy. He laughed and pulled away. "Heard it, ma'am." He filled his chest to yowl with glee. "It's you and me left, ma'am."

Betsy gripped the rail. "Yes. It is." The smooth, hard wood didn't give. Neither did Davy's words. Her nose and eyes stung; she blamed the smoke of distant wood fires, but she couldn't keep her hold on the wood. "Mary. Alice. David."

Davy squeezed her wrist. Twice.

She smiled and pulled her hand away from the rail. He wouldn't notice that she clutched her skirt in her fist. She would let go slowly, in her own time.

During the five days since the storm, Davy had come for his reading lessons once in the morning and twice in the afternoon. She'd sat at the hinged table in her cabin with him, two hours in the morning reading verses from Genesis, the Psalms, and the Sermon on the Mount, which he'd copy verse by verse on Mary's slate. In the two afternoon lessons, he learned simple arithmetic and to read a chart of England and the waters around the island that Bennett gave him to study. He learned fast, excited at discovering that he could figure out marks on paper that once meant nothing to him. How carefully he worked at writing his name, the names of his friends on the ship, and "Captain John Bennett." His skin, gray from working in the galley on the Dash, had turned a rosy tan as if he himself were made of sunlight and fresh air. He'd knock on her cabin door, bursting with stories from Potts, Carter, or Cabe—the cabin boy training him to serve the captain. Aping one of them, he showed her how to jig and taught her their songs, his voice high and sweet, like Mary's, only stronger and liable to break into laughter. Once he came in and clapped her on the back. "That's how Cabe does me." He puffed with pride at being a sailor. Bennett had ordered a smart jacket sized to fit Davy and insisted that he wear clean britches. He wore stockings and shoes, too big, but polished. His hair was trimmed and combed, his face scrubbed raw like Carter's. "Cabe reads Scripture good as the cap'n at prayers. Cap'n expects I'll take a turn soon." She'd agreed. He would do it well.

"Mrs. Randall." Davy gazed at the changing horizon; his posture suggested that she should stand ready beside him. "Cap'n Bennett says I'm meant for a life at sea." He saluted Betsy, a sharp chop from his brow to his thigh. He moved so his shoulder bumped her arm. "Did you think you'd ever see land again, ma'am?"

She'd expected to be standing with Isaac and the girls, a baby in her arms. She hadn't wanted to go to Virginia, but she was glad to see land. Side by side, she and Davy stood on the gallery walk, high as the wheelhouse above the sailors, out of their way. Ahead of the *Falconer*, the masts of the *Sally Dash* and of another ship rose above the treetops, sentinels beyond a spit of land jutting into Chesapeake Bay. Bennett had the Dash deliver cargo to a plantation ahead of the *Falconer*. He and Trout, the bursar of the *Falconer*, surrounded by shrieking seagulls, had set off in a longboat to supervise the transaction with the bursar of the Dash.

A gun shot. Startled, Davy jumped, but he didn't want Betsy's arms around him. She hugged herself. The gulls raised a shrill protest. The sailors on the *Falconer* crowded the rail on the main deck. No one could see beyond the grove of trees on the spit forming a harbor, but a stench worse than the streets of London drifted back to the *Falconer* wobbling on the waves. McNeill bounded up the steps, shaking his head at the shouts, curses, and howls from another ship. As the *Falconer* rounded the cove, a stronger reek of excrement hit Betsy. She and Davy covered their mouths and noses, but the marines and sailors went back to their tasks on deck. Abreast the Dash, a ship with yellowed sails had anchored. The paint of her boards had weathered off, leaving her hull gray. On her deck, naked black men and women packed the prow, their cries carrying back to Betsy. She reached for Davy's hand; he had squeezed against her. Josiah had been on a ship like that.

The doctor offered Betsy a kerchief that was saturated with camphor.

She took a deep whiff and gave the kerchief to Davy, who clamped it to his face but didn't take his eyes off the men and women shackled at the ankles with chains linked from their wrists to chains down their backs. Josiah had walked in irons for three days to a ship. He had scars on his ankles from the fetters. Betsy and Davy watched the men and women cower each time a bullwhip snaked over their heads and cracked like gunfire. "Down, nigger, dammit!" a white man shouted. A second white man, pistol in hand, yelled, "Nigga-rigga-wump-wump!"

"Wump?" Betsy looked for the doctor's explanation.

"Gibberish. They don't know their languages, so they mock the poor souls."

Davy shuddered against Betsy, and a shiver went through her body. They couldn't look away from the captives who had no escape from the cat o' nine tails, the bullwhip, or the men making them cringe. Betsy pushed away from the rail, from their terror and helplessness, the weight of their chains, and the stench. Instead of sympathy—no, alongside her sorrow for them—she wanted them gone. She wanted the slavers and their gruesome ship to sink.

A high wail brought every man on the *Falconer* to a stop. Two men on the slaver were dragging a woman, naked except for a yellow cloth hanging from a string at her waist, down the length of the dock to ten other captives, their wrists and ankles in irons. The woman kept looking back at the ship, her cries long and high. Those left on its deck began a low murmur of lament, a long, slow, anguished pulse, until the men brought the whips down on the heads of those who grieved. Betsy began to moan, and the doctor gripped her shoulders, steering her to the stern to go down to the main deck. "You'll want to rest before we dock."

Jerking away, Betsy took her place next to Davy, her post. "I'm staying with the woman. They're dragging her away from her children." Josiah's wife and son had been killed by slavers like these. His wife had been thrown overboard after trailing behind Josiah, chained to him for three days. "You should stay, too."

She took the doctor's small square of linen from Davy. Though warmed by his hands, the medicinal odor couldn't cover the stench of pain and horror. Betsy used the cloth to wipe her cheeks. Josiah had carried mint. Smelling the dried leaves had comforted him.

Seagulls screamed overhead, diving toward the ship.

On the main deck below, a young sailor, his face red, glared up at McNeill and Betsy. "You've seen nothing, ma'am. Blacks stacked like cordwood, layered in the hold." He pointed to the open sea where two other ships approached. "Every other ship sailing to Yorktown stops at this landing to bring slaves for the fields. The Atlantic washes over the bones of Africans." He scowled at the doctor as if blaming him.

"Captain Bennett said I own seventy-three slaves." The words sounded like an echo coming from Betsy's mouth. She felt Davy staring at her, but she couldn't look at him.

The doctor turned away. He had been in the captain's cabin when Bennett told Betsy about her brother's plantation. He'd sat at the table, a witness to Bennett's giving her Isaac's papers. While Bennett told her, the bursar folded his hands over Isaac's box where the papers had been saved. The last time Betsy had seen the box, LeBrun had kicked it out of Piggy's grip. Bennett had regretted that none of the gold and silver sovereigns were found. The captain riffled a sheaf of papers until he came to the title to her brother's estate, a large plantation called Good Hope in Virginia. "I'm not schooled in matters of law, but your husband was the sole heir, and as his widow, and the sister of Robert Harrington, you alone inherit the property until such time as you marry." The captain held the document at arm's length to read, "Seventeen hundred and fifty acres ..." He looked over at Betsy to see if she had heard him, if she understood how much land the estate entailed. The doctor and the bursar seemed to expect her to faint, but Isaac had read her the will. She'd heard about the tilled fields and woods, the two-story house, barn, stable, and farm buildings. Her father farmed, and she thought that Robert probably built similar buildings with changes to suit his ambition. Her father had only one horse, no stable. Bennett had paused in his reading, and Betsy said, "I'm listening. You said there is a brook through the meadow behind the barn and a well for the house." That Betsy understood, but she didn't understand how Isaac could have left out the part about the plantation including seventy-three African slaves. Betsy had been careful not to take her eyes off Bennett, expecting him to surprise her with something else Isaac should have told her. "Able Carter demanded Mr. Randall's ring from Brickhart," he said. "He freely gave it to Carter before he was shackled. Carter put it in the box."

Betsy hadn't wanted the box. She didn't want the papers. She'd pushed away from the table, away from the ring—which she had not given Isaac—away from her brother's Good Hope with its seventy-three slaves. Isaac had wanted the plantation. Betsy wanted to return to her cabin below deck.

What did owning seventy-three African slaves mean? Her brother must have bought his slaves for Good Hope from a slaver like the one in the harbor. "Dr. McNeill, what will happen to the woman's children?"

"I have wounded men in the hold that require my care, Mrs. Randall." McNeill may have had wounded men in the hold, but he stood as fixed on the deck as Betsy and Davy. He looked beyond the dock to six black men in homespun coming down a gravel path, two by two, past a guardhouse crouched like a bulldog on a quiet green lawn that sloped to the water's edge. A man in a plain brown suit, on an impatient bay stallion, rode behind the six. He waved at the men on the *Falconer*, a bullwhip in his hand.

McNeill waved back. "A man cannot run a plantation without slaves."

"Is that man your friend?" Davy asked.

Betsy wanted to hear the doctor's answer, but instead of responding, McNeill squinted at the plantation slaves who had begun examining twelve chained naked men from the ship, prodding their legs, poking them in their backs and stomachs, pinching their jaws. Slaves seemed to be choosing to accept or reject new arrivals. Five were singled out to shuffle back to the ship, and five replacements herded from the slaver with whips and curses.

"Who is that man?" Betsy wanted Davy's question answered.

McNeill sighed. "The overseer of Plainview. There are more slaves on this plantation alone than there are people in most towns in Scotland. He's a Scot like myself, a student of the Word, a follower of Calvin and a fellow Presbyterian." When he spoke, his mouth had a twist of contempt in keeping with his earlier hesitation to wave back at the man. He looked away from the slaves, and Betsy followed his gaze to a flock of geese wandering over the green expanse of grass. "Mrs. Randall, you'll discover that Virginia is a colony with beautiful homes and kind, accomplished people." McNeill nodded as if pleased with his comment.

The gray ship weighed anchor, unfurled its tattered sails to catch the wind, and sailed past the *Falconer* before veering back into the bay. The slavers held long-handled cups to the mouths of the slaves, dribbling water down their chins. Betsy and Davy stepped closer to McNeill, as if for protection, and watched the craft steer into the mouth of the York River.

"Look away from the slaver." The doctor himself turned so that he faced Betsy, blocking her view of the ship. Seeing the determination in his face, she turned back to the shore where Bennett and the bursar spoke to an older white gentleman on the dock next to the *Sally Dash*. Barrels from her hold—along with the brown cow—waited on the dock where the goods were matched against the ship's bill of lading. Two men, dark as the captives but dressed better than most working men in Brompton, arranged the cargo on a wagon.

"Doctor, are those slaves?" Betsy wondered if slaves at Good Hope dressed that well.

McNeill didn't answer.

"Mr. Randall and I saw blacks in Brighton." She and Isaac had seen a Negro coachman dressed in a bright pink jacket. Isaac had insisted on a trip to the sea before Mary was born. She told the doctor about a young boy with cocoa-colored skin being spoiled by his mistress.

The longboat skimmed back from the dock with Bennett, grinning broadly, at the rudder. He climbed aboard the *Falconer*, waving to them, and leaped up the steps to the gallery walk. "You've come to a land of plenty, Mrs. Randall." He put his hand on Davy's shoulder, as if he, too, should be glad for her.

McNeill looked at the sails of the slaver. "Some call Virginia the Promised Land."

Isaac had said it. He'd called Virginia Paradise, but he'd never seen a slave ship or heard the irons clink with every step the slaves took as they walked: a chain of prisoners. Betsy shook her head. "Captain Bennett, did you hear the woman wail when they dragged her away?"

Glaring at the doctor as if he'd asked the question, Bennett made a stiff salute, an about-face, and left.

Davy started after him, but McNeill caught his jacket, keeping him with Betsy on the gallery walk; the boy looked out over the stern, his back to her. The sails of the *Sally Dash* unfurled, and she followed the *Falconer* into the bay. Farther off, two other ships, with sails spread like large seabirds, seemed to glide on the waves. Betsy blinked at the shore, at brick buildings, black slate roofs, and clumps of chimneys. Sunlight reflected off windows. The doctor pointed at a church spire in the distance, blowing his nose to cover his emotion at seeing land. He put his arm around Betsy. "God's blessing on you, ma'am." She wiped her eyes with her mother's shawl. "When we dock, I'll be back to escort you to your lodging." He put his other arm around Davy's shoulder. "You stay with Mrs. Randall, laddie. She'll be needing you here." He bounded off around the stern and disappeared.

Davy saluted the doctor. He would follow the command to stay with her. "Soon you'll be in Virginia, ma'am. The captain says people will treat you kindly."

Betsy smiled but didn't have time to tell Davy that she'd never wanted to come. Carter came up onto the gallery with a jaunty salute. "We'll be in Yorktown before the next watch." He poked Davy. "Don't be thinking you'll be jolly-ing the ladies." He winked at Betsy. "Begging your pardon, ma'am. Charlie and me'll keep an eye on your lad and Cabe." With a nod, he left.

The boy stood stiff. In a week he seemed to have grown six inches. Davy had become the darling of the ship. The afternoon that Bennett had given her Isaac's papers and she'd learned about the slaves her brother had owned, Davy had come down for his reading lesson. He'd had news for her: the captain planned to present her to the governor of Virginia. He'd stressed the word governor. Imitating Bennett's stance, his manner of speaking, his gestures, Davy had said, "A damn handsome woman. An excellent match."

Later that day the doctor had explained that though she'd be traveling to Williamsburg with the captain who had business there, she'd be with other travelers. How glad Isaac would have been to have the captain of a man-of-war introduce him to the governor of Virginia. He'd purchased his wig in the expectation of that introduction as the heir of Good Hope. Betsy didn't want to travel to Williamsburg; she didn't want to meet the governor of Virginia; she didn't want anything to do with her brother's Good Hope.

At the rail, she looked down into the valley of a wave carrying the *Falconer* in with the tide. Charlie Potts and Able Carter would be in charge of the boy. She had no claim to him. "The captain is fond of you, Davy."

He nodded, quite solemn. "He says I'll stay in his house when we dock in Portsmouth. I'm like a son to him." Looking from the bowsprit, up the topgallant sail of the main mast, and back to the wake, Davy squinted at the seagulls diving and screaming, circling the ship. The day shone, beautiful and clear. "I'll have my own ship someday." He looked at Betsy. "Captain Bennett says that."

Any mother would be proud of such a son. "Does the captain say that, Davy?"

His cheeks flushed red. "David," he said. He looked up to be sure that she'd heard his name correctly. "Captain and Dr. McNeill call me David. And yes, ma'am, Captain does say that."

"On this trip, I hope he takes you to Williamsburg." The doctor had told Betsy that Bennett had business in the capital, and a cousin there as well, so he would accompany her there.

"Oh, no, Mrs. Randall. I'm staying with the ship, like Cabe." He stretched four inches taller. "I'm going to help Carter and Charlie." Davy smiled with a pride that a few days on the *Falconer* had given him.

Shrill and impertinent, gulls swooped down on the ship,

landing on the yards, rails, cannons, barrels, and coils of rope. The sailors shooed off the birds, but they flew back like children tormenting a playmate. Bouncing on the waves, ships ahead waited to ride out the high tide pushing the *Falconer* into the harbor. Over the birds' screech, sailors called, hallooing back and forth to outward-bound crews. On the main deck, Bennett's cabin boy, Caleb, sang, "O diddle lee duladay ..." and every few steps, with a straight, strong arm, he swung his full pail of water in a circle over his head without spilling a drop.

Carter's sharp whistle signaled a change of watch, and sailors scurried down the hatch to prepare for going ashore. Davy grinned. "I should be on my watch."

"Yes. Go, Davy, and God go with you." Betsy nodded, and he was off. She faced the sea with its edge of land. She was alone. A breeze blew the smells of hearth fires in from the shore. No one heard her sobbing or cared that she wiped her cheeks.

Chapter 11

The clop of a horse stopped Betsy short. In a town that seemed smaller than Brompton-on-Thames, the big horse, an English black shire like her father once had, pulled a wagon down toward the dock. It had been over a month since she'd seen a horse blinkered and harnessed to a wagon—since she'd heard that clip-clop on cobblestone.

Dr. McNeill nudged her forward. "The captain sent Trout ahead to reserve a room and order dinner for us at the Silver Goblet."

Betsy's knees wobbled on the bouncing gangway. She clung to McNeill's arm, though his step was as unsure as hers. The jolt of solid ground made the doctor laugh. His knees buckled when he hurried Betsy to one side for sailors to pass. They gripped ropes to keep a barrel from rolling away. Staggering, Betsy looked back at the *Falconer*. From the quarterdeck, Bennett watched the unloading of the ship; he saluted her and the doctor. Since the day he forced himself on her, waking her from a drugged sleep, he'd been meticulous about never being alone with her. She shielded her eyes, feigning a blinding glare from the sun to ignore him.

Church bells rang the noon hour and sailors stacking the crates stopped, pulled off their caps, and bowed their heads. Caught off guard, Betsy followed their example. The doctor said, "Amen." He stood in reverence that shamed Betsy. She wanted to walk to the town, to where the sun sparkled on windows, on the brick, clapboard, and clay plaster of buildings, on the buds and branches of the trees. The buildings and trees appeared stationary though the ground gave way with each step. Treetops bobbed as if at sea. After the first week on the Dash, Betsy had not suffered from a queasy stomach, but now a wave of nausea whirled inside her.

A woman curtsied in response to the doctor's bow. In every direction, there were women. Women in dresses and aprons, women wearing bonnets with ribbons and flowers, women pulling children along, sweeping doorsteps, carrying baskets, haggling at the stalls along the wharf. Betsy couldn't keep up with the doctor and gape at the women, women who paid her no heed as they hurried about their marketing or strolled on their husbands' arms. Betsy dragged McNeill to a stop. A black woman passed with a bundle of laundry, wide as a mattress and three feet thick, on her head. In the street climbing the hill toward the church steeple, children playing tag ran past Betsy and the doctor. He tugged at her arm. She pulled away and stumbled toward the squeals of laughter. A boy shouted, "Mary, Mary, run!"

Dr. McNeill held her against his chest, and her heartbeat slowed as he wiped her cheeks with his handkerchief. "Shush. Shush now." He drew her away from a horse and carriage rumbling by.

Again, Betsy looked back at the *Falconer*. The *Sally Dash* was docked alongside Bennett's ship at the pier. Men rolled barrels down the gangplank so fast they seemed empty. Davy waved his hat from the deck, and Betsy leaped to go back. She hadn't said good-bye.

"No, Mrs. Randall." Dr. McNeill gripped her arms. "We won't go back. He's with his mates now." Still holding her arm, he pulled off his hat and waved, as if that was her farewell. Betsy couldn't hear what Davy was shouting, but Carter was pointing to men sliding the Randall crate down the ramp. Sailors carried a stack of chairs, tables, and a cupboard: furniture from her home in Brompton. When she looked back to see Davy, he was gone. Farther down the dock, the slaver from the plantation had landed.

Across the street, a woman squealed with laughter. She slapped at a sailor who'd left his mates to put his arms around her. His friends staggered up the street, arm in arm, drunk with being on land. Free of the boatswain's whistle, they called out to every woman they saw, clutching at those who didn't veer out of their reach, reveling in their shrieks.

Every breath had the smells of home: wood fires, sawdust, horses, and houses, the stench of horse urine, ox pies, and garbage. Depending on the doctor's lead, Betsy marveled at the flowers, aching to sniff each one, to admire each pot, window box, and border alongside the taverns and shops. Oxen pulling a barrel-laden wagon plodded toward them. Instead of the squeak of rigging, wagon wheels squealed. A dog barked. Chickens clucked as they pecked between cobblestones. Birds twittered in branches where leaves whispered a greeting. Two women argued on a corner, one with fiery red cheeks. Betsy didn't care what they said; she listened to the music of their voices. A sparrow swooped away from a branch and back, as if to show how easily it was done.

"We're expected at the inn, Mrs. Randall." McNeill tried to hurry her, but Betsy stopped short.

"Mr. Randall isn't here, Doctor." Foolish, but true. She needed Isaac. She couldn't be in Virginia without her husband. She couldn't voice the names of the children. She couldn't think.

McNeill guided Betsy to the shade of a tree. "Mrs. Randall, your husband wanted to settle in Virginia, to claim your brother's plantation." On land, the doctor was small, his black coat too snug. "You have a duty to his memory and your brother's estate."

"A duty to his memory?" Betsy said what the doctor wanted to hear, though it sounded like a nonsense rhyme. "My husband wanted to meet the governor. He wanted to grow tobacco and harvest it. He wanted to own my brother's estate." Betsy tripped. She hadn't wanted to leave England.

A woman culling seeds on a stoop pointed to horse piddle in the street. She said, "Mind the mud."

No woman had spoken to Betsy since the *Sally Dash* had sailed from Lyme Regis. She wanted to sit down beside the woman, to help her push small black seeds from shriveled yellow pods, but McNeill pulled her on, past a black woman slopping water on a stone entryway to a tavern. Her head was covered with a faded rag, her sleeves rolled up, her face down. She jumped aside for Betsy and the doctor. Stumbling on a cobblestone, Betsy accidently lunged toward the woman, who raised an arm as if to ward off a blow. The knot that had twisted in Betsy's stomach when the people had been dragged from the slaver drew tighter.

"Mrs. Randall. Come." Dr. McNeill squeezed Betsy's elbow, almost lifting her up the steps of the tavern. "Our dinner is waiting." He said that he wanted to finish his meal in quiet before the crew crowded the tavern to drink. He liked the innkeeper. He liked Alex, the innkeeper's slave, who would serve them the choicest pieces of meat. Inside, blinded by the dark, the doctor and Betsy bumped into chairs until the light, eking through thick, swirled glass, revealed the welcoming tables. McNeill pulled out a chair for Betsy. "Few pleasures compare to your first meal after weeks at sea."

Suddenly chilled despite the warmth of the room, Betsy shivered. The thought of food nauseated her, but she didn't worry; in the wan light, her food would be in shadow, and McNeill wouldn't know whether she ate or not. She folded her hands and waited until her heart slowed to the swish of the broom the black man used to sweep the floor.

McNeill placed his hand on her shoulder to stop Betsy's shaking and then picked up a pitcher to pour her a glass of "sweet well water." When he bowed his head and thanked God for their being safe on land again, Betsy said, "Amen."

She tasted the water. It was sweet, but she was not thirsty.

His hands outstretched to welcome McNeill, a man in knee britches and a vest, the buttons straining around his paunch, bustled through a back door of the room. The doctor introduced Mr. Falls, the tavern owner, to Betsy. Swinging his whole arm up, Falls beckoned a woman spreading a cloth on a corner table near a small, crackling fire in the hearth. "Come. Meet our guests." His wife's cheeks and lips were smeared with thick rouge, making her smile bright red. She pulled a chair up and sat right next to Betsy, as if they were old friends. She smelled of wood smoke and wore one garland of small flowers around her neck and another on her head. "Yes, I'm Mrs. Falls," she proclaimed and stuck out her hand, pumping Betsy's hand with three firm shakes. Mrs. Falls smiled approvingly when a young black man set two bowls of beef stew, brimming with carrots and onions, on the table. "Ah, very nice, Alex."

Steam rose from the bowl in front of Betsy when Mrs. Falls took it upon herself to stir it and lift several chunks of meat to the top. She shook her head and wrapped Betsy's fingers around the handle of one of three tankards of ale Mr. Falls brought. She leaned over so the flowers in her hair brushed Betsy's cheek and spoke in a low voice. "They told us 'bout your Brickhart." Picking up a tankard of her own for a sip, she said, "We've sorrows upon sorrows." She and McNeill raised the foamy brew. She waited for Betsy to take a sip. "Drink up."

The bitterness of the ale suited Betsy. She savored the taste even after swallowing, but she didn't want another sip.

Mrs. Falls took a long drink and sighed in unison with Dr. McNeill. Sliding Betsy's bowl closer to her, she said, "Eat. We must be thankful we have breath." Using a knife, she sliced a hunk of bread off a loaf Alex had brought on a wooden plate along with a wedge of yellow cheese.

Betsy smiled. She liked Mrs. Falls, but she didn't agree about being thankful for breath.

The woman had a thousand questions and the kindness not to wait for answers. Isaac wouldn't have resisted the smells of the peppery thick stew. Like McNeill, he'd have shoveled down two bowls before Betsy lifted a carrot from the bowl and watched it fall back. She was relieved that Mrs. Falls took no notice of her shifting pieces of meat to the edge of the bowl without eating. McNeill wiped up every last globule of gravy with his bread. "Mrs. Randall, it's important that you eat."

He moved to a chair next to Betsy and took her hand. "Mrs. Randall, are you well?"

She wanted to answer him, but she couldn't open her mouth. She sat back in the chair, pulling her mother's shawl tight up to her chin, and closed her eyes.

"Mrs. Randall, are you ill?" He put his hand on her forehead.

She turned away, not wanting to open her eyes. She would not.

Betsy didn't object when Mrs. Falls led her to an attic room she could have to herself, where the innkeeper's wife insisted that Betsy drink a little broth before she slept.

Chapter 12

The carriage Bennett hired rumbled up to the inn for Betsy and her trunk an hour after dawn on a Friday morning. The Randall furniture and the crate of household belongings from the *Sally Dash* originally destined for her brother's plantation would come later by barge. Betsy's trunk and Isaac's box were wedged on the back of the carriage, heaved in place by three sailors. Bennett asked, "Did your husband pack stones from Surrey for the plantation, Mrs. Randall?"

"My husband was a careful man. He wanted a sturdy trunk so that it would arrive at Good Hope with our belongings." The contents would only remind Betsy of all that she'd lost.

She'd recovered from her fatigue, but Mrs. Falls stayed next to her, not giving up her post until Betsy rode off in the carriage. For a week, Dr. McNeill had Mrs. Falls spoon-feed Betsy beef broth and strong tea. She brought wet towels to cool Betsy's fever and covered her eyes to treat the ailment she called "the seasoning," an affliction that ended in death for many colonials. The different air and new land overcame them.

Betsy felt like a straw doll swaddled in her shawl, but its warmth reminded her of her mother's comforting embrace. Strange things had happened. Yesterday, the doctor told her that Bennett engaged a dressmaker for her the day after they landed and promised to pay the woman double if she completed her project before week's end. McNeill told Betsy that, being superstitious, the captain believed that if she had the clothing she requested, she'd be restored. Betsy couldn't recall telling any of them that she wanted to dress in mourning, but Mrs. Falls showed her a black silk gown, folded in paper and packed at the top of the trunk. McNeill said Betsy had insisted everyone wear mourning. It had seemed right that the doctor wore black. He always did. But she didn't believe that she'd called him "Josiah" like he said she had.

At the inn on Friday, when Bennett alighted from the carriage, Betsy caught a whiff of his nutmeg and turned to go back to the inn for a pillow to block the smell. Mrs. Falls stopped her and handed Betsy a nosegay of pinks. "When you're feeling poorly, sniff these. You'll be yourself again."

Betsy asked the captain if he'd seen Davy, and he smiled. "He came to visit you and, with the doctor's help, read you Psalms. You must remember, Mrs. Randall."

"Yes." On the ship, she and Davy had read together, but she didn't remember his being at the inn. "He reads well." She caught Mrs. Falls's questioning glance at the captain; she didn't want them to coddle her any longer.

Two sailors rolled up a wheelbarrow full of a fat, laughing Mr. Wicks, a merchant friend of Mr. and Mrs. Falls. He paid the sailors enough to send them off singing before he helped Betsy into the carriage—a space the size of an eggshell—and then squished her into the corner, apologizing for missing the hour.

After heaving the basket of food and drink Mrs. Falls had prepared onto the seat, Bennett seated himself opposite Mr. Wicks and Betsy. She held the pinks, glad their cinnamon fragrance protected her nose from Bennett's nutmeg and the cheese of Mr. Wicks's breakfast.

The captain rocked forward, his knees bumping Betsy, as the carriage rolled off. "A little like being at sea," he said, and Mr. Wicks agreed. Betsy turned to the window. Holding the flowers close to her cheek, she pretended to sleep, leaving the men to blather on about the cost of transporting goods from York to Williamsburg. The carriage rocked to the horses' rhythm. Each jolt said, "Alone, all alone, all alone." Mr. Wicks began to snore, and Betsy drifted off. The clack of the horses' shoes on brick pavement in Williamsburg awakened them. Fat Mr. Wicks wrenched himself out of the carriage at one end of Duke of Gloucester Street. In a cheerful voice, he said, "Good-bye, good-bye." He raised a foot with a look of disgust. "Oh, those blamed oxen." The carriage jerked on down the road. Wicks called out, "The dial's d'rectly on twelve." Betsy hadn't seen a single ox.

Bennett sat with his hands on the seat as if reclaiming his share of the carriage. "Excellent trip. Good time. I enjoy a fellow traveler who talks until he puts himself to sleep. I'm glad his snoring didn't keep you from your rest." He craned his head to see the houses along the street. "My cousin never married. He has yet to meet the woman who has all the qualities he seeks in a wife. You know the verse? 'Who can find a virtuous woman?'" He braced his arm against the frame of the carriage window to keep from bouncing into

Betsy. "He has shown great virtue in caring for his ward: a delightful, headstrong orphan. She'll win your heart as she won mine, Mrs. Randall. A child, perhaps fifteen, she'll plan your every minute in Williamsburg."

"An orphan?"

Bennett nodded. "My cousin, his sister's child. Sad story. She's done well in her uncle's care."

The street, broad as any in London, was shaded by signs hanging over the shop doors. On one side, men sat on a tavern porch between a printer's shop and a surveyor's office. On the other side, a cobbler, a barber, and a wigmaker. The noontime shadows from the signs lay like spikes on the road. Young trees in front of the shops hadn't grown enough to shade the walk at midday. The carriage rattled past a village green large enough for military maneuvers. Sunburned farmers and their wives hawking vegetables and fruit, baskets and brooms crowded the green. They worked in stalls under flimsy canopies. A young black boy restacked cheeses. Many of those shopping and selling wares were black, some alone, others following an Englishman or woman. Some people, Betsy guessed, must have been slaves dressed in livery or in maids' caps and aprons. Others wore coarse hemp britches or shifts. Betsy looked from one side of the street to the other with a vain hope of seeing a friend—Martha Adler or Nancy Finch—among the Virginians. She knew no one. She missed Mrs. Falls, the doctor, and the boy, Davy. Isaac would want to be there, to see a cleric conferring with three tall, strangely dressed men, their heads shaved except for tufts of hair tied with ribbon at the crown.

"Native Virginians," Bennett said. "Elders of the Choctaw." After squinting at them, he tried to straighten his posture even further. Two of the men dressed like Englishmen, but the oldest was draped in a blanket and had three feathers propped in his hair. They walked into a church on the corner; Betsy had wanted to look at them longer. The carriage slowed and stopped in front of a stately brick house across from the green.

A tall slave hopped down the steps of the house. Dark as Josiah, dressed in blue livery, he opened the carriage door and pulled down the carriage step for Bennett to step out. The man bowed to Betsy, his face to the ground.

Bennett climbed down, smiling, clearly glad to see the man. "Peter, how is Mr. Osborne? I hope he's about to sit down to the table." Once on the pavement, the captain extended his hand to help Betsy down from the carriage. Instead of accepting his help, she handed him the nosegay of wilted pinks and climbed down, arching her back in relief from the cramped seat.

A young woman in blue silk skipped down the steps toward Betsy and the captain. She looked like a dressmaker's drawing, with her hair pulled back with ribbons, her waist cinched, and her stomacher pushing up peach-sized breasts powdered as white as her face. She welcomed Bennett with outspread arms. He tossed the flowers down by the carriage wheels and kissed his niece's hand, and then embraced her, smiling with a look of grateful calm. Mary would have loved to see the dress, the curls, and the soft white slippers, even the painted mole below the collarbone. Behind the girl, in faded blue-and-white gingham and a simple apron and cap, a woman with skin the color of honey waited. Older than her mistress, she stood with her head bowed, her hands clasped behind her back. A smile twitched at the corners of her mouth for a moment while her mistress greeted the captain, but she didn't lift her gaze from the hem of the girl's silk dress.

"Captain Bennett, at last you are here!" The young woman slipped out of his embrace and took his hands, as if to dance. "We have you at last. Tell us every gruesome detail of capturing the pirate." She shuddered in anticipation. "It must have been frightful." She stressed frightful as if expecting a treat.

Seeing the young woman's adoration for the captain, Betsy stepped back. How could the girl endure the odor of nutmeg? He bowed like she was the queen herself. "Miss Phillipa Townsend," he said. With a kiss for each hand and a frank head-to-foot-appraisal, he didn't have to feign admiration of her beauty and charm. Though he didn't look at the woman behind Miss Townsend, Betsy sensed his awareness of her being as glad as her mistress to see him. Compared to the pretty women shimmering with joy at the captain's arrival, Betsy, in her tattered shawl and drab green linen, felt more wilted than the crushed pinks.

The captain took Betsy's arm. "Mrs. Randall"—Bennett had never been more pompous—"may I present Miss Townsend?" He smiled at the young woman. "Miss Townsend—"

Her eyes opened wide with horror and sympathy; she stepped back, crossed her arms over her heart, and curtsied. "Your pardon, Mrs. Randall." She stood and took Betsy's hands. "I haven't seen Captain Bennett for two years, but my delight at seeing him does not excuse my thoughtlessness." She scowled at the woman behind her, as if her slave had been responsible for the inappropriate exuberance; accepting the blame, the woman hung her head. She kept her head down. This slave wasn't black or brown, but a deep gold, with a figure that men and women would admire. Seeming to sense Betsy eyeing her, she took a peek up. She was accepting of people staring at her gray-green eyes, fine features, and round breasts.

Miss Townsend took Betsy's arm and led her to the stairs with the measured step of a funeral procession. Betsy marveled how easily the girl could switch from delight at seeing Bennett, fascination with the pirates, annoyance with her servant, and now solemnity as she led Betsy up the steps past her slave, whom she ignored as if she were a post.

Two steps behind Miss Townsend and Betsy, Bennett stopped next to the slave. Betsy looked back and saw him whispering in her ear, cupping his hand firmly under her seat; the slave blushed a deep rose but didn't move. Bennett grinned at Betsy and ordered Peter to help the coachman with the boxes. "You'll need an army to carry Mrs. Randall's trunk."

Miss Townsend bristled, seemingly contemptuous of Bennett's wrapping his hand over the slave's fingers. Frowning at the slave, she invited Betsy in.

Outside, behind Miss Townsend and Betsy, the slave gasped. Over her shoulder, Betsy saw Bennett pull the woman close and stick his hand deeper between her legs. Miss Townsend grimaced at the captain's familiarity. With a weak smile, she said, "Our home, Mrs. Randall."

Betsy didn't move. Her readiness to go in the house was soured by Miss Townsend fuming at the slave instead of at the captain. She didn't understand the relationship of Bennett and the two women. Still angry, Miss Townsend said, "Dee, show Peter where to bring Mrs. Randall's box at once."

Extending his leg, Bennett blocked Dee's escape up the steps. "My dearest Phillipa, Peter and the coachman are seeing to the luggage." And when Dee started to creep past his leg, he grasped her wrist and held her back.

"Captain Bennett, Uncle Osborne is waiting for you at the Four Farthings," Miss Townsend said. She looked down at him, a fifteen-year-old with the frown of a bitter old woman. "You know how irritable he gets when he hasn't eaten."

Bennett laughed. He held up a hand, a plea for patience. "I'll be seated at the table before he's finished his How-do-you-dos with every man, servant, and dog in the place." He smiled, sure she'd excuse him. "I'd like a word with Dee before I set off. I am famished, and I'm sure Mrs. Randall must be as well." He steered the slave into an anteroom at the end of the hall.

Phillipa huffed at the closing door. In a loud voice, she said, "Dee, cold meat, bread, and cheese to Mrs. Randall's room." When she took Betsy's arm, she had the pleasant face of a friend with a confidant. "Right now, I wish the captain were back on the *Falconer*. Two years ago he fathered Dee's child."

Betsy stared at the door Bennett had closed. "The captain has a wife in London."

"And he has Dee here, thanks to Uncle Osborne."

Betsy could see that Phillipa accepted the arrangement. Had Osborne offered his slave to the captain? "Your uncle?"

Phillipa ignored Betsy's question. She opened a door to a sitting room with light green silk walls and twin settees upholstered in matching damask. Tired, achy, dusty, Betsy wanted to stretch flat on the hearthrug and sleep, but she forced a smile. The rumble of carriages passing by and voices from the street came through the open window; the young woman prattled on about what good friends she and Betsy would be. Maybe, but not before she slept. She followed Phillipa through the foyer to a wide staircase. "Let's have our dinner in your room, Mrs. Randall. It will be quiet, and afterward, you can rest."

As they turned on the landing to the second floor, a church bell chimed one o'clock. Phillipa came to an abrupt halt, her finger to her lips. She stepped away from Betsy, her head bowed. The single peal of the bell hung in the air.

"What's wrong, Miss Townsend?"

Phillipa held back a window curtain floating in toward the landing. In the light, her face powder gave her skin a chalklike pallor. "Mrs. Randall, it has been three years since my mother died. At one o'clock, they say. On my twelfth birthday. The bell no longer reminds me of her death; but just now, it did." She stamped her foot like a child who has forgotten some small thing. "Uncle forbids me to be gloomy. He'd be so disappointed."

Betsy put her arm around the girl, drawing her close; she smelled of rosewater.

"Did the captain tell you that my parents died of a fever?" Phillipa didn't wait for Betsy to say that he had. "Mother died first. In Bermuda. I grew up there." She looked out the window. "Afraid I'd catch the fever, Papa put me on a sloop and had Tante Cecile take me to Uncle Osborne, Mama's brother. While we were at sea, Father died in Bermuda. And Tante Cecile died as we sailed into the harbor. They said a prayer and dropped her body overboard."

The white curtain billowed toward Betsy like the crest of a wave rolling toward the *Sally Dash*. She rocked briefly—like she was back on the ship—and reached for the banister.

"You see, I do understand," said Phillipa.

She started up the next half flight of stairs. "I'm all right now. I think of Mama before I sleep. I remember that she'd lay her palm on my cheek before she wished me pleasant dreams."

A carpet muffled their steps as they walked down the hall. Betsy thought of her daughters and their soft cheeks. Now, Mary and Alice were floating in the dark water. The breeze brushing the back of her hand might have been their hair. Phillipa led her past two doors on either side until they came to the last door on the left. In that room, a large canopy hung over a bed with a white linen spread.

"Mama used to sing me to sleep," Phillipa said. Sweeping her hand over the bedcover, she surveyed the room reflected in a tall mirror on a wide mahogany armoire that shone with the light from a window overlooking a garden. Betsy wound a loose lock of Phillipa's hair back under her ribbon. She'd lost the strands of Mary and Alice's hair from the brush she found in her trunk on the *Falconer*. She should have saved them in Isaac's box, but that would have meant opening it and seeing the ring.

Bennett's laughter rang out from the street below the bedroom window.

Phillipa ran to pull the curtain aside and looked down. "Captain Bennett is completely in Dee's power." She closed the window without a creak. "Uncle has forbidden me to talk about the men Dee traps—he says I'm naïve—but it's hard for me to be civil to Dee when men like the captain visit." She paused to check her appearance in the mirror of the dressing table. "Do you like the room?"

"It's beautiful." Betsy wished the girl would leave her

alone and let her sleep; instead, Phillipa called down the hall to Dee. "Where is Mrs. Randall's dinner?"

As quiet as a breeze, Dee came into the room with her head bowed, carrying a large tray of covered dishes. She must have been waiting at the door. "Forgive me, Miss Phillipa."

All the while Dee set out the cold ham on white bread, pickled pears, and cider, Phillipa preached about women who seduce upright men, Jezebels who think they're the Queen of Sheba. As Dee poured cider into Betsy's glass, her hand trembled; the gold stream of cider wavered.

Surprised at her thirst, Betsy thanked Dee for the sweet cider and drank a second glass before she understood the strong drink made her even drowsier. She laughed at the way Phillipa nibbled bread and ham. She laughed at Phillipa, saying that she preferred ham with sweet mustard. She laughed when Phillipa said, "You must taste the ham, Mrs. Randall. You must eat some food." When Betsy reached for the third glass of cider, Phillipa set it on the other side of the table.

Phillipa looked past Betsy to another woman, younger than Dee and darker, a bright pink ribbon on her cap, who lugged a copper bathtub into the room. An older black woman followed, carrying two buckets brimful of hot water. Phillipa told the slaves to go ahead and pour the water into the tub. The younger slave dipped a curtsy, her head bowed. "Miss Phillipa, you want more water?"

Betsy walked around the table for her glass. The cider was even better than the first two glasses, sweeter and stronger than she served in Brompton. Betsy liked the green silk on the walls of the room. She didn't understand

Phillipa's talk about the water and lemon-scented verbena. "Miss Townsend, why a tub? Are we washing clothes?"

Phillipa said, "After your ride from Yorktown and a stay at Mrs. Falls's tavern, you'll want to be rid of every little creature that attached himself to you. Besides, a bath washes away our cares." Pleased with her explanation, she began arranging the folds of her skirt. "Mrs. Randall, you can trust Charity to soothe muscle and bone." She turned to the slave who stood waiting. "You pesky tribulation. Yes, Mrs. Randall will need more water."

Betsy sat back in her chair. She buttered a thick slice of bread that would taste even better with cider. A bath? In the spring, she'd bathed in the kitchen; but here in Williamsburg, people ate in the bedroom and slaves brought the bathtub and hot water upstairs.

Charity bobbed a curtsy. "Beggin your pardon, Miss Phillipa, but I ain't no tribulation." She dipped her hand in the water and jerked it back. "I'll bring two buckets." Flicking off drops of water, she said, "You want Miss Randall to have the sandalwood soap Cap'n Bennett brought from England?"

"Yes, and Felicity, you comb olive oil through Mrs. Randall's hair before you wash it."

The cider made the prospect of a bath amusing. "Sandalwood soap will be fine." Betsy had no idea what sandalwood was, but it sounded costly. "It will be good to bathe." She nibbled a slice of the ham with pickled peach, and drained her third glass of cider before Dee, obeying Phillipa's wave, cleared the dishes onto the tray and left.

Betsy stumbled getting up from her chair, but Phillipa caught her. "Mrs. Randall, be careful drinking cider. One glass is good, but two glasses are too many."

"I enjoyed all three." Betsy could not undo a knot in the laces on her stomacher, but Charity had no trouble with it; and after Felicity helped take off Betsy's clothes, she led Betsy to the tub. The hot water felt better than a warm bed. She leaned back on a towel Felicity spread over the back of the tub, and closed her eyes. With Brompton-on-Thames far away, Betsy lay back while Felicity worked olive oil into her hair and combed out the nits. Charity pared her toenails. The fragrances of the sandalwood soap and verbena oil spiced the air. When the slave rinsed her hair with rose water, Betsy said, "You are aptly named, Felicity."

Phillipa stood up to leave. "And you are wonderfully drunk, Mrs. Randall." Maybe she didn't mean for Betsy to hear, but she had. The slaves heard her too and glanced at each other. Betsy didn't care. At least Miss Townsend had left.

The hot water turned Betsy's skin red and seeped warmth into her bones. Felicity sloshed the bath water over her back and shoulders, washing her neck and her ears with a gentle hand, lulling her toward sleep, while Charity washed each toe and rubbed a soft stone against the rough skin of her heels. Her eyes closed, Betsy gave in to indolence, drifting on the slaves' incantation: "Mama, Mama, rock me, rock me. Rock me all the way to sleep. Rock me, Mama." Felicity sang, and Charity would murmur, "That she do, that she do." Then Charity began singing about planting buttercups and daisies in a garden. Between verses, she said, "I can't remember Mama's face. For the longest time, I didn't remember the words or the melody." She rubbed olive oil into Betsy hands, concentrating on working the skin around each nail. "Dee told me not to worry about what I can't

remember, but singing those words brings Mama back."
The smells of the soaps and oils reminded Betsy of her garden, too.

Charity sang, "You ain't goin cry while I hoe the corn.
You goin to listen to the scrape of the hoe. Corn's goin
grow and we goin to eat. You ain't goin cry while I hoe."

Charity, the younger of the two slaves, ordered Felicity
to bring another bucket of hot water for the widow. After
she left, Charity said, "Miss Phillipa weeping; she lonely
and scared. I make up tunes, get the words rhymin good,
and she forgets her worst dreams. She likes baths, Miss
Phillipa does. She not waitin till her skin crawls to have her
Charity bathe her good."

Gently, Charity washed Betsy's breasts, still tender, and
lifted her arms, sloughing off dead skin with the soaped
stone. Felicity came back with hot water for Betsy and then
dipped the buckets to carry pails of now cold water from the
room. Leaving, she promised to bring warm towels, the
kind Miss Phillipa likes.

Never had Betsy been treated with this care. She let her
head loll against the pillow of towel on the rim of the tub.
She felt a fool's grin spread over her face. Charity's hands
kneaded her shoulders and back, then worked up her legs to
her thighs. Her legs tingled when Charity spread her legs
to wash the upper thigh. Betsy opened them even more
when Charity slipped her hand over the patch of hair and
glided to a spot inside with a delicate pressure. Moaning,
Betsy moved to gratify the desire the slave probed. Betsy
wanted the fondling to meet her craving for an old self-
inflicted pleasure. It was wrong to give in, but Betsy did.
Finally, she found the word: "Don't."

Saying it broke Charity's spell. The slave was licking

Betsy's nipple, her eyes closed and her fingers deep inside Betsy's body. Wriggling, gripping the tub to climb out, almost slipping back, Betsy managed to step over the side.

"Felicity." Charity scurried to the door. "Felicity, where them towels?"

The woman scurried into the room with the towels and a bowl of strawberries. She draped the towel over Betsy and the two women began to rub her dry.

"I'll dry myself." Betsy was trembling, rubbing the towel over her arms and legs, determined to stay calm. Her face burned. She'd let the woman do what shamed her now.

Careful to stay behind Betsy, out of sight, Charity rubbed her back. "I don' mean harm, Mrs. Randall. Miss Phillipa calls what I did 'soothin' her." She moved away like she expected Betsy to slap her. "You was likin it."

Felicity wiped the tops of Betsy's feet with a small cloth. "Wha's the matter, Miss Widow? Why is you cryin?"

"You know she lost her babies." Charity lifted a clean linen shift over Betsy's head.

Betsy pulled down the shift and tied the bow at her neck. She walked to the window. She didn't want to think of Mary or Alice while she was in this room. They should never know the wrong their mother had done. In the garden below the window, young fruit trees frothed with blossoms of pink and white. Virginia. Robert had chosen this place, and Isaac had chosen to claim her brother's plantation. He knew Good Hope had slaves, but he hadn't told her. "Charity. Felicity. I'm not angry." Betsy wasn't angry with the two slaves, but she was angry. At Miss Townsend. At Isaac. She had many reasons to be angry with her husband, but she was most angered that he was not with her.

Charity held out a robe of soft wool for Betsy to slip her

arms into the sleeves. Felicity brought the bowl of strawberries. Too tired to ask how they had strawberries in
March, Betsy pushed the bowl away. "You eat them."

Felicity hung her head.

Charity took the strawberries from the older slave and
set them on the table. "Can't you be happy, Mrs. Randall?"
They drew the coverlet down and plumped the pillows.
"See how you makin Felicity sad?"

With Betsy in the bed, Charity flung the blanket over
her. She smiled, giving Betsy an example of the face a grateful guest should wear, and she tucked the coverlet up to
Betsy's chin. It felt good to be treated like a child, even by
someone who had stirred poisonous desires. Betsy hadn't
wanted Mary and Alice in the room, but now she wished
they were lying on either side of her. If she weren't so tired,
she'd read to them.

Charity and Felicity were going to let her sleep in a green
room with the smell of strawberries. Betsy turned on her
side toward the window. After a moment, Charity said,
"Ain't nobody gonna know she told us to eat these berries.
Ain't nobody gonna know we ate 'em."

Chapter 13

Betsy pretended to sleep while Phillipa bounced more and more forcefully at the foot of the bed. Birdsong came through the open window. Bounce. Bounce. The leaves shone bright green in sunlight from low on the horizon. Bounce. Betsy needed the escape of sleep. "The sun isn't up."

Bounce. "It's going down." Phillipa sprang off the bed and pulled at the covers that Betsy held tight to her chin. "It's twilight. Isn't that such a lovely word?"

The table where Charity and Felicity had eaten the strawberries was set with pastries and tea. Phillipa broke off a piece of bun, held it to Betsy's nose, and then put it into her own mouth. As she chewed, Phillipa poured tea with a cube of sugar into each cup. She played a tinkling rhythm with her spoon against the edge of her teacup. "Time to dress for dinner. Governor Spotswood has invited Uncle, you, and me. His wife is charm itself." Phillipa tilted her head and smiled, mimicking false sincerity and good will.

Betsy pulled the covers over her head. She was not going to a governor's dinner. Isaac had wanted to meet the

governor, rumored to be a strict Presbyterian, and he would
have been delighted to meet his charming wife, but Betsy
wanted to be back in Brompton-on-Thames in Martha
Alder's kitchen with its wonderful afternoon light. Martha
and she would be spreading spiced meat on warm bread.
Betsy's stomach hurt from hunger sharpened by the smell
of warm bread. She'd get out of bed and dress for dinner.
For Isaac's sake. She'd be as charming as Isaac would have
her be. She sipped the tea, nibbled a slice of nut bread, and
then spooned a mound of the meat on the next bite. "Thank
you, Phillipa. I do like spiced ham." She smiled as she
accepted the small buttered cinnamon bun Phillipa offered
her. "What is the enchanting Mrs. Spotswood's name?"

Behind Phillipa, the black dress Bennett ordered for
Betsy in Yorktown had been spread on a chair as if it sat of
its own accord. "Oh. No." She backed away. "I prefer my
green linen."

"Oh, yes, you will wear the black silk." At the door, Phillipa called Dee to help Betsy dress in the elegant silk. She
turned to Betsy. "It is appropriate."

Dee slipped noiselessly up to Betsy. "It's a beautiful
gown, Mrs. Randall."

Did the gown she wore matter? Betsy would rather not
be in Williamsburg; but as long as she was, why not wear an
exquisite gown fitted for her? Dee tied Betsy's stomacher,
squeezing her ribs, and eased the dress over her shoulders.
After Dee fluffed the skirt, the hem fell evenly to the floor.
"Don't frown, Mrs. Randall. Your eyes so pretty when you
smile."

The silk whispered at the least movement, but Betsy
could quiet it if she kept her stomach taut.

"Here's something to make you sparkle." Dee opened the

clasp on a small carved box and held it out to Betsy. The gold necklaces and her mother's garnet earrings shone on the velvet lining of the box, the same red as the jewels. Stung, Betsy stepped back from Dee and put her hand to her neck. "I don't want that necklace or the earrings."

Dee picked up the gold chain. "Felicity got the sharpest eyes. She showed us stitches in the neckline of your green linen that were different from the rest. Sure enough, out comes a little necklace." Dee put the strand on Betsy's neck, slipping the hook into the link at the end.

The cold metal made Betsy shiver. Mange hadn't felt the treasure. The pirates hadn't noticed the stitches. Betsy put her gold earrings in the box to wear the garnets. Betsy's father had given them to her when Mary was born. He'd died the next year. The necklace Isaac had given her at David's christening. She touched the gold, already warm on her neck.

Betsy had hidden it deep in the piping. "Felicity?"

On her way out of the room, Dee said, "She got a sense for things. Miss Phillipa can't hide anything from her."

In a blue taffeta gown, Phillipa flounced into the room, her breasts rounded high, as if peeking over the loose knot of her neckerchief. She'd powdered her skin pure white. "Are you dressed, Mrs. Randall?"

"Miss Townsend, you are—" Betsy started to say the blue dress made her eyes an even deeper blue, but Phillipa interrupted her. "Mrs. Randall, please call me by my Christian name, Phillipa." With an impish grin, she said, "We'll be sisters."

Betsy wouldn't choose Miss Townsend for a sister. To hide her distaste, she pronounced each syllable: "Phil-li-pa." She repeated it. "Phillipa." Names mattered. Some names she could never say with sufficient care—Mary, Alice, David, Isaac. She liked the name Phillipa. It sounded Spanish. "Phillipa, that blue brings out the color of your eyes."

Phillipa pulled Betsy to the full-length mirror.

She gasped. If Isaac could see the elegance of her black dress and how her hair gleamed, he'd be so pleased. The rouge Dee rubbed on before patting white powder on Betsy's face and shoulders made her cheeks glow pink in the candlelight. The gold necklace glimmered. The purple shadows under her eyes had faded almost away. Isaac used to kiss the curls at the back of her neck when he fastened the clasp. At the governor's house, she'd think of him. She was Mrs. Isaac Randall.

———

The dinner began with a clear soup followed by fried oysters, fresh watercress, chicken in a wine sauce, beef sirloin, and thin slices of salty ham, and ended with a choice of caramel pudding or lemon cakes. The guests moved into the salon where the organist of the Burton Parish Church played several fugues on a harpsichord. Separately, Mrs. Spotswood and three other women pulled Betsy aside to confide that they each had a friend who would make an excellent husband—each was prosperous, noteworthy, and a widower. Governor Spotswood invited Betsy to walk with him in the garden where other guests enjoyed the warm spring air. The pungent boxwood hedge cleared Betsy's head of perfumes and smells of rich food and wine. Spotswood repeated his condolences and echoed the praise Phillipa's uncle had for her brother, Robert Harrington. They both knew him to be honest, generous, and hospitable, one who enjoyed the company of others and who had, in a few years, established a productive plantation. The governor cautioned Betsy about opportunists who might take advantage of a widow's grief, wooing her for the rights to the property, planning to borrow money against the estate. She should acquaint herself with her brother's holdings before ceding the title to a new husband. She should be sure her suitor was a loyal servant of the Queen.

Britain was the governor's first allegiance, but Virginia had become his home. He'd purchased a large tract of land beyond Robert Harrington's Good Hope, which he planned to establish as a German settlement, a hard-working community of Bavarians and Saxons, to extend the British rule farther west. Since his plan required a detailed map, he'd commissioned a well-respected surveyor and a small contingent of troops under the command of Lieutenant Spencer Gray to explore the territory. "You were seated beside the lieutenant's mother at the dinner; you may have seen him talking to Miss Phillipa Townsend during the recital." The Grays owned a large parcel of undeveloped land next to Good Hope, giving the lieutenant a personal interest in the expedition. He'd be a responsible escort to accompany her to the plantation. It would be in Betsy's best interest to travel under that protection.

Betsy stopped and stared at the white oyster-shell walk reflecting the weak light of the quarter moon. Stepping off that walk would mean being lost in the dark grass and shadowy trees. From the far end of the garden, the voices from the governor's mansion blended like the music of a river or the rustle of leaves. Betsy said, "This journey to Good Hope, is it a matter of a day?"

"No. The terrain is rough." He looked toward the high hedge at the back of the garden. "A week's travel, I'd wager."

During the carriage ride from the governor's mansion back to the Osborne house, Betsy sat numb, half-listening to Phillipa recite bits of gossip. On the way into the house, up the stairs, down the hall, and into the green bedroom, Phillipa chattered on about a Mrs. Taylor. "The plump matron in puce, that awful bruise-colored silk." She came Thursdays to rumple Uncle Osborne's bed. Phillipa wanted her uncle married. He'd be happier. But not to Mrs. Taylor.

Betsy had been provided with the means to reach the destination of the Randalls' voyage: after a week's travel through rough terrain, she'd arrive at Good Hope. She'd be protected by troops led by Mrs. Gray's son—another unearned prize. She intended to push Phillipa into the hall. "How dull I am, Miss Townsend—"

"Phillipa, please, Mrs. Randall."

"Phillipa. Yes. Phillipa. I am too tired to think." But she was thinking. The governor had said a road was cleared beyond Good Hope, that the troops would be blazing trees to mark a survey for a settlement for Germans. Betsy wanted to shut the door on Phillipa, on the governor's wood, on her brother's Good Hope.

Charity came in with two bowls of warm milk.

Phillipa took her cup. "Tell Dee I want her to brush my hair tonight."

"Beggin your pardon, Miss Phillipa. Cap'n Bennett just pulled Dee into his room."

Phillipa set her cup on the table and went to the doorway. "Call her, Charity. Stand in the hall and say, 'Mrs. Randall needs help taking the pins from her hair.'"

Betsy called out, "I do not need help. Thank you, Charity." Betsy hurried to close the door. She did not need a slave to remove pins from her hair. She would do that herself. Though she had the urge to run down the hall to stop Bennett from using Dee as a concubine, Betsy faced Phillipa. "I wouldn't want Captain Bennett ordering me into his room."

Charity smoothed back the bedcovers. "Me neither."

Phillipa pinched Charity's arm. She held the cup of hot milk to her chin, breathing in the steam as if she wanted her skin to soak up the milk. "Mrs. Randall, the captain doesn't order Dee. She entices him. That's how she got her child."

Charity made a show of rubbing the pinched spot and stepped away from Phillipa, who glared at her.

A skim had formed over the milk Betsy didn't want. "I'm sure the child is darling."

Phillipa took Betsy's bowl, flicked back the skim, and drank a little. "Cold." She took another sip and handed it to Charity. "Uncle couldn't have been more pleased. He gave the little girl, pink as a rose, to Mrs. Taylor for her birthday last November."

The necklace Betsy had unclasped fell to the floor. "He gave Mrs. Taylor Dee's child?"

"The Taylors don't have any children." Phillipa pointed at the necklace for Charity to pick up. "The woman dotes on Rosie. The little imp smiles at everyone."

Betsy plucked up the necklace before Charity could, angry that Phillipa expected Charity to do it for her. "Mr. Osborne, your uncle, gave Dee's baby to Mrs. Taylor? Did Dee agree?"

With Charity's help, Phillipa stepped out of her skirt. "Rosie isn't a baby. She's two years old."

Betsy sat on the bed, staring at the floor. The planks, the same width as those in the deck on the *Sally Dash*, shone gold in the candlelight. Rough terrain, Spotswood had said. A week. Betsy rubbed her face and eyes to be rid of the knowledge that Dee's child had been taken from her. The long wail from the woman pulled off the slaver came back even when Betsy held her hands over her ears. Phillipa wouldn't understand the pain Dee's loss caused Betsy. Betsy couldn't know Dee's pain.

Phillipa seemed to have chosen not to see Betsy's fatigue. She traced the curve from Charity's ear down her neck while the slave unlaced her stomacher. "Dee hopes the captain will buy her and Rosie and take them to England. Uncle would never agree, and the Taylors wouldn't part with their little monkey."

Betsy pulled on her nightcap, crawled into the bed, and curled away from the two women without saying good night. She hugged herself, trying to sense Isaac there. If he were with her, he'd rescue Dee and her little girl. With him, she wouldn't dread going with the governor's surveyor to the plantation.

Uninvited, Phillipa wriggled into bed next to Betsy, squirming closer to her, even more excited than she had been before the dinner. Betsy edged away, but Phillipa wasn't spurned. She tucked her legs up against Betsy and pressed her chin, sharper than it looked, into Betsy's shoulder. "While the governor walked you through the palace grounds, I slathered Mrs. Gray with compliments about her hair and dress. I prefer not being too forward." She tightened the arm she'd wormed over Betsy's waist. "I said nothing about her son—you know, Lieutenant Gray. He studied at Heidelberg and has just returned from recruiting farmers from Germany for the governor's colony."

Betsy lifted Phillipa's arm off her waist and wormed to escape from touching her.

"You promised to be my sister," Phillipa said. "You said you'd be my sister."

Betsy sat up in bed and stared at the curtains letting a little light into the room. "Phillipa, if we're sisters, you must never call Dee's child a monkey or an imp again. How hard it must be for Dee to have her child taken from her." Betsy shuddered. "Captain Bennett is married. He has children. His wife would never agree to his having Dee as a concubine. How horribly cruel for him to make false promises to her."

Slowly, Phillipa slid up to sit next to Betsy. "You said you would be my sister."

Betsy faced her in the dark. The white powder on her face reflected the weak light from the curtained window. Phillipa had shown no feeling about a child being given away, but now she was close to tears. Betsy took her hand. "Yes, Phillipa, you are my sister."

Leaning forward to look Betsy in the eye, Phillipa checked to see if she could trust her. "I'm sorry about Rosie. I am. But Dee goes to take care of her when Mrs. Taylor comes on Thursdays." She frowned. "Let's not think about Rosie." Then she snuggled closer. "I know we're sisters, but which of us is older?"

Exasperated, Betsy said, "I am."

"Really?" Phillipa sounded amazed. She must have guessed Betsy was ten years older.

"Yes, but I've been away so long that I no longer know how to spread butter on bread or when to curtsy." Betsy

knew how and when to curtsy, but she supposed Phillipa
would happily teach her. The lively, pretty young woman
must have many friends. Betsy wished that she had made
plans to go with Martha Alder to the market. She turned to
Phillipa. "You'll have to teach me the ways of Virginia."

Phillipa smiled and cupped Betsy's face in her hands. "I
shall. I shall teach you every little thing. First, we shall
never talk about pirates." She snuggled down between the
sheets. "We'll go to the garden and I'll show you where to
smell roses, where the creek sings a pretty song, and I know
where to swing when you're lonely." She yawned. "Oh, Mrs.
Randall, I'll introduce you to the women of Williamsburg."
She stretched her arms up above her head. "And you'll teach
me to play the dulcimer."

Betsy laughed. "Phillipa, I don't play the dulcimer." Betsy
lay flat from head to toe. Lying flat on the bed reminded her
of lying on the deck of the *Sally Dash*. She remembered back
to the day before the pirates. Mary would have liked the
word dulcimer.

Dee slipped into the room to ask if Miss Phillipa had a
task for her.

After nestling down under the quilt, in a sleepy voice,
Phillipa said, "Dee, teach Mrs. Randall to play the
dulcimer."

"Miss Phillipa, you know I don't play the dulcimer." Dee
smoothed the blankets over Phillipa and Betsy. Before she
pulled the door shut behind her, she said, "Mrs. Randall
should ask Mr. Harmon. He plays all the instruments."

Chapter 14

In the backyard of the Osborne house, alone, Betsy gazed at bricks set in the same herringbone pattern as her garden walk in Brompton-on-Thames, each brick settled and safe. After her lessons, Phillipa would eat at the home of a family hosting a scholar who taught their children and others, and Betsy could dread the journey to her brother's plantation as part of the governor's expedition without interruption. Mr. Osborne had volunteered to arrange a wagon that could be covered like a tent for Betsy's comfort while traveling. She hadn't said that a better solution would be to sell her furniture and household goods, the plantation, the slaves, and Robert's whole estate, and for her to return home to Brompton; but she would not sail for England until she could travel with another woman on board, one traveling with her family so that Betsy could go on deck with them on those long days at sea. Mrs. Spotswood had assured Betsy that she wouldn't be sailing home for several years, that very few women in the colonies risked sailing back to England.

Dee came out to the garden with a small table and placed

it in front of Betsy. Roast beef, a heavy egg pudding, mashed peas, bread, and pickles crowded a plate. "Mrs. Randall, Master Osborne says I'm to stay until you finish this food. He says if you don't eat, you won't be strong enough to travel to Good Hope."

Dee's words reminded Betsy of Davy's trying to get her to eat in Bennett's cabin. "I was thinking of a boy I knew on the *Sally Dash*. I would have liked for him to have come to Williamsburg with me, but Captain Bennett wanted to keep him on as his cabin boy when he sails back to England."

At the mention of the captain, Dee picked up the knife and began to cut the beef in tiny squares.

"You don't have to cut my food for me, Dee." Betsy gently brushed Dee's hand away and spooned up some of the peas and pudding, but she left the spoon on her plate. She didn't want Dee to watch her eat.

"You enjoy the food, Mrs. Randall, and I'll tell you a story," Dee said. Her gentle hands rubbed Betsy's shoulders and worked loose a deep ache in her back. "Take that bite, Mrs. Randall." In small circles, her fingers massaged the muscles along Betsy's spine. Dee told of a fine man with eyes the color of bluebells who came to visit Master Osborne. He had such strong hands. And a strong back. Fine black boots. She looked up to study the blossoms of fruit trees behind Betsy as if the story were in the flowers— or as if she were asking for their permission to tell her story. Osborne's guest had had Dee come into his room, and he showed her a locket with a miniature of a beautiful lady with white skin and silver hair. In the locket, the painting of the woman faced a picture of his son. Dee said, "The boy wears a white wig, but his face is pink!"

Dee paused, waiting for Betsy to continue eating. If Betsy didn't eat another bite of the beef, Dee wouldn't go on with her story. "Captain Bennett says I need a child." She poured Betsy a glass of pale gold cider. "I'm praying for a little girl."

Betsy didn't tell her that she knew about the daughter Mr. Osborne gave to his mistress.

"Boys are trouble."

"Trouble?" Betsy looked at Dee's face, and when she turned away, Betsy gripped her wrist. "Tell me."

Dee pulled her hand away. "No. I was foolin." Her laugh had none of its usual music. "You eat that bread."

"Not until you tell me." Betsy kept watching Dee's face. "I want to hear."

A person listening from inside the house wouldn't have seen Dee shake her head or the small, scornful smile that showed she didn't expect Betsy to understand. "I was remembering Master Osborne telling me that my brother Marcus had been shot." She cocked her head toward the house to be sure no one had come into the garden. "An 'accident.'"

Betsy slumped toward her. "How was it an accident?"

"Master Osborne sold Marcus to the vicar, and his daughter kept finding excuses to have him run errands and bring packages to her room. I told Marcus to be careful, and I believe he was, but the vicar had decided to sell Marcus to a planter upriver—until his wife had a tantrum: She favored having a 'fetching nigger' answer their door." Dee stacked the dishes, though Betsy hadn't finished the food, and picked up the table to return to the house. "The vicar took Marcus hunting, and the other slaves said Marcus ran." She picked up the table. "Like a deer."

Betsy watched her carrying the table, her back straight. The sun came at an angle that cast a shadow behind her as she walked. Bennett had told Betsy that Good Hope had seventy-three slaves. She'd resolved on the *Falconer*, at Mrs. Falls's inn, and during the governor's dinner that she would do her best to manage the plantation with Isaac's rigor and care. Again she thought of Isaac. What advice would he have if he knew about Josiah's wife and son—or if he heard about Dee's daughter and brother? What would he say about the expedition under the protection of Lieutenant Gray's troops through "rough terrain" to her brother's plantation? She dreaded going.

"Mrs. Randall! Mrs. Randall!" Phillipa's calls rang through the house and out the open windows.

Betsy didn't answer. She started counting slowly to rid herself of thoughts of Dee's story; she imagined stitching numbers on a sampler. She counted the stitches and told herself that she must find handiwork to keep busy. She could mend for Phillipa or her uncle.

"Mrs. Randall, your furniture is here." Phillipa grabbed Betsy's hands, pulling her to her feet, toward the house. "Come. I can't wait to see everything."

Betsy yanked free. The everything Phillipa couldn't wait to see was everything that Betsy owned. Except the plantation. Chests, cupboards, the children's bed, the bed she'd shared with Isaac, linens, carpets, dishes, the skillets and pans, the kettle, the table, the chairs, the silver from Isaac's home, her mother's favorite plates and bowls, their pillows—belongings. Isaac's and hers. None of them belonged in Virginia. Betsy walked past Phillipa. She didn't say that the boxes had no value, that she was angry with Isaac for wanting to claim her brother's estate.

"Phil-lip-a!" The door banged behind Mr. Osborne. He huffed, red-faced, down the path. "I'd like a moment alone with Mrs. Randall. Dee is bringing tea for Mrs. Randall and me." He wiped his face with his handkerchief and seemed not to notice Phillipa's scowl. "Go to your room, Phillipa. Read your Bible passage for the day, and when I see you next, recite it—without error." He pointed to the house and Phillipa stomped off, her arms crossed, her head bowed.

Winded by the rush into the garden, Mr. Osborne motioned for Betsy to sit next to him on a bench. He reached over to pat her hand. Beckoning for Dee to bring the table—the same one she'd cleared after Betsy ate—he sat back and waited for her to set it in front of him. She hadn't brought tea, but a small bottle with two tulip-shaped crystal glasses. He poured a dark, syrupy liquid into Betsy's glass. After he poured his own, he held it up to the light. "Currant. Your health."

"And yours." Phillipa's leaving and his presence calmed Betsy. She put the glass to her lips, but the fumes burned her nose. She set the glass down without taking a sip.

"My niece is my delight." He sipped the liqueur. "And my tribulation."

Betsy smiled. Phillipa had called Charity her tribulation: a strange term of endearment.

According to Mr. Osborne, Betsy had no need to worry about her furniture. It could be sent to the plantation whenever she chose, but he had visited Good Hope, and he thought she would find her brother's home quite comfortable. He also thought Betsy should take advantage of the governor's offer of a military escort to Good Hope. He emptied his glass and refilled it. "Taste it, my dear. Good for the blood."

She discovered that if she didn't breathe the fumes, she could drink from the glass. The liqueur had all the sweetness of a summer's berries pressed into thick, purple juice.

Osborne rumbled on about Betsy's brother: Bobby Harrington had been a gambler, yes; but he was also an excellent planter, with the help of an overseer who sent down properly cured tobacco. "You think this liquor is fine?" He refilled Betsy's glass and his own. "You should smell tobacco from the Harrington estate." He rubbed his fingers together in front of his nose and sniffed. He closed his eyes and smiled at the pleasant memory. "His triumph so far inland is one reason Governor Spotswood is confident that a settlement he'll call Germanna will succeed."

He savored the fragrance of his third glass. "Every Tom, Dick, and Harry will be after your hand in marriage—and Harrington's plantation and slaves." He gestured for Betsy to drink. "Plenty of us lonely men"—he stretched out the word lonely as if to exaggerate their pitiful state—"would prize Good Hope enough to promise you eternal adoration." He could arrange for her crates to be stored in DeWitt's livery. He drained his glass, set it on the table, and gripped the arm of the bench. She should choose a husband only after considering all her offers. He pulled himself up. "Mrs. Randall, take a walk on the green. There's no better cure for our ills."

He left and Betsy let the last of the brandy trickle down her throat. She would have poured herself another glass, but Phillipa scurried down the steps. She sang, "Let's go open your boxes."

"You're supposed to be memorizing a verse."

"Uncle never remembers what reading he assigns me. I either recite 'Love your neighbor as yourself' or 'Rejoice in the Lord always,' depending on what he needs to hear." She took Betsy's arm.

"I'm getting my bonnet and my shawl," Betsy said. "Your uncle suggested a walk, and that's what I'm going to do."

Hearing the jingle of the harness on a team of horses at the front door, Phillipa picked up her skirts to run after the wagon. "They're taking your furniture."

Holding her back, Betsy explained that Phillipa's uncle had arranged for it to be stored until she'd been to Good Hope, and that he thought she should take advantage of the militia's expedition to the governor's proposed settlement. She'd have the troops to escort her and the furniture would be sent later.

Phillipa's eyes opened wide. "I'm going with you." She clasped her hands tight. "We'll go together. I'm so glad that we're sisters."

"No. To your uncle, we're not sisters, and you're not going. Your uncle would never permit it, nor should he. I have no wish to go, but it's unthinkable for a young unmarried woman to travel with a militia for a week." Betsy shouldn't have blurted out Mr. Osborne's advice. "Please, Phillipa, not a word of this. I shouldn't have told you."

"Oh, but I am going." Phillipa looked about as if already making plans.

"Don't be ridiculous. Don't mention it to your uncle. He has been kind to me and will not forgive my thoughtlessness."

"Promise me you won't tell him that I'm going. Don't tell anyone. Especially not Charity. She cannot keep a secret." On her tiptoes, she hugged Betsy and then wrapped her arms around herself to twirl like a child. "When are we leaving?"

"Phillipa. *You are not going.*" Betsy had no idea when she was to leave; Mr. Osborne had spoken as if the expedition would leave in a matter of days. She'd be the sole woman on this journey, as she'd been on the *Sally Dash* and the *Falconer*. It would be good to have the company of another woman. Dee would be ideal, but Betsy couldn't protect her if Gray or the surveyor turned into a man like Captain Bennett. Betsy couldn't be responsible for Phillipa; the young woman wouldn't even heed her uncle.

Phillipa's steps crunched on the gravel with a heavy, determined tread. "First, I must talk to Lieutenant Gray. Leave that to me."

"You're ..."

"Since he's leading the expedition—he is, isn't he?—he should know that I'm going."

Betsy stopped her and looked around to be sure that no one would overhear her. "Didn't you tell me that you were glad to sit next to Mrs. Gray, the lieutenant's mother, because you find him an attractive prospect for a husband?" If the governor had arranged the seating, Phillipa's uncle must approve of the match. He would never approve of Phillipa's going with Betsy, and he wouldn't be pleased to learn that Betsy couldn't keep her own counsel. "Phillipa, imagine how Mrs. Gray ..."

"We cannot leave Charity. She must come. She'll tend to everything and help with the food. I'm not eating what those men carry in their knapsacks." She shuddered next to Betsy and then laughed. "Aren't you excited? We'll be exploring the wilderness." Phillipa was certain that, except for the Choctaw or the Pamunkey, very few women had traveled as far west as Good Hope. "You should be glad for the troops' protection."

The walk had not cured any ills, but multiplied them. To get Phillipa's full attention, Betsy took her hands and made sure they were looking into one another's eyes. "Phillipa, you're not going to Good Hope."

Phillipa nodded. "I know."

She'd agreed too readily, but Betsy wasn't going to discuss it any longer. Phillipa had said something Betsy needed to remember. She'd said that Betsy should be glad for the troops' protection. "Phillipa, the governor didn't say the journey would be dangerous. The troops have been sent because the surveyor needs the protection for their travel beyond Good Hope. He will be blazing trees to set apart land for a German colony. Good Hope isn't in the wilderness. It's a settled estate."

"It isn't *all* wilderness. It's the surveyor who requires the troops." Phillipa took off her bonnet and smiled at her reflection in the hall mirror. "*We* won't need their protection."

Chapter 15

In lavender light, Charity and Thomas crammed provisions into a wagon hitched to a team of chestnut-colored horses. The horses stamped, shaking their darker brown tails and manes, impatient to start. Benjamin, the vicar's gardener, positioned two pillows on the wagon seat.

"Pillows for the ladies," Benjamin said, as if checking off a list. He heaved cartons of boxwood onto the wagon bed and jumped up to position them close to the bench. "Miss Townsend likes sniffing box. The widow, she will too." A born horticulturist, according to the reverend, the vicar had promised Robert Harrington enough boxwood to start a hedge. He also promised that he'd send his gardener to plant them. Benjamin directed Peter to lift pear, apple, and cherry saplings bound in burlap, two of each, behind the bench. "Shade for the ladies." He wedged the saplings in one up against the next. "Best ride close to the front, little fruit trees. No topplin over."

At the sound of a quick, clipping trot, Phillipa tugged Betsy's arm. "Lieutenant Gray." She posed on the top step of the house, stretching her neck and the crown of her head high, a small arch in her back. "Pretend that I'm clever." She chatted about Dee and Captain Bennett to Betsy, ignoring the activities around them. She nudged Betsy. "If a person is witty, it is courteous to be amused, Mrs. Randall."

Phillipa's whispering tickled Betsy's ear, and she moved away from her, laughing. "You're repeating yesterday's gossip."

"I said, 'Pretend.'" Phillipa skipped down the steps to the wagon and scanned the placement of boxes and plants. "Benjamin, clear a place for Charity to sit behind us." She peeked in the baskets of food and came back to tell Betsy they had no need to be concerned: Dee and Felicity had packed excellent provisions. The whole show of being responsible for the packing seemed for the benefit of the lieutenant riding toward them.

As a shrill fife, the low rattle of a drum, and a heavy march neared, everyone looked down the street to see Gray canter up. Despite Betsy's eagerness to have the expedition underway, she struggled to hide her dread of leaving a safe, welcoming place. If Isaac were there, he'd be scrutinizing the care Benjamin, Peter, and another slave took shoving the Randall's trunk up a plank onto the wagon. They positioned it over the axle and roped it in place to even its weight. Except for her combs, brush, and personal items, Betsy hadn't taken anything from the trunk. She hadn't touched Isaac's box, which Charity had wrapped in homespun to protect it. Betsy had wanted to leave the trunk—it reminded her of Isaac and the children—but Mr. Osborne insisted she'd want to have the trunk with her when she arrived at Good Hope.

Dismounting from his black stallion, the lieutenant, young, erect, and as solemn as a church door, slowed his horse to approach the wagon. Phillipa looked with admiration at the black curls that hung down to his bright red uniform, and at his boots polished to a high sheen. A handsome slave in a blue coat and gray trousers rode behind him. Eight recruits shouldering muskets, also in red jackets and knapsacks, marched four abreast down the street to halt at a final shriek from the fife, and stood at attention for the drum roll.

Blinkered, the team of chestnuts twisted to see the parade led by the stallion. They blew through closed lips, tossing their heads. Gray's slave jumped off the rump of the horse to take the reins from his master. The lieutenant leaped from the saddle and swept his hat to the ground in front of Phillipa and Betsy. The recruits shifted their gaze to Phillipa.

She smiled. The hood of her fawn-colored traveling suit was pushed back from the straw hat shading her face, and her pale blue skirt glowed in the early dawn. Apparently satisfied with the gathering at her uncle's house, she leaned toward Betsy. "Doesn't the lieutenant look patrician? In his uniform, the Roman nose suits him."

Phillipa paid the young men on foot no more attention than they paid to Betsy in her mother's gray shawl and drab green linen. She knew her skin was gray; she'd thrown up at the prospect of starting for Good Hope that morning.

"Charity swears that the lieutenant's Saul is her brother."

Charity's skin was dark brown, her nose flat, and her lips full; she had no feature in common with Gray's good-looking slave whose skin was the color of milk mixed with molasses. He had fine features with full, pink lips. Betsy said, "They don't look alike except for their lips."

"He's younger." Phillipa let go of Betsy's arm. "I'm going

to talk to Ramses." She seemed to float to Gray's horse, petting his long neck, cooing as she combed her fingers through his mane to the delight of the recruits and Gray. The lieutenant had a look of proud ownership for both the girl and the animal; he smiled at Phillipa's affection for his stallion. According to Phillipa, every unmarried woman in Williamsburg hoped to be Mrs. Spencer Gray.

Betsy paid no heed to the lieutenant's greeting except when he spoke to her at the end. "… Shall we be off, Mrs. Randall? Our journalist expects us at his gate before seven."

On the cushions, Phillipa snuggled close to Betsy. Behind them, perched on a box between two saplings, Charity waved a Chinese fan to keep flies from pestering them. The vicar bustled over from the church to lead them in a psalm. "I will lift up my eyes …" He droned like a church organ. Dee stood behind Mr. Osborne on the steps. When Captain Bennett left for Yorktown, Dee asked Betsy to buy her from Osborne. She said he'd demand a high price, but Dee would pay her back, whatever the price, in a few years. Betsy had no money, and she had no need for a slave, but she talked to Osborne. He said he valued Dee more than his favorite horse; he'd never sell her.

Phillipa poked Betsy. The vicar intoned the last verse: "He that keepeth Israel shall neither slumber nor sleep." They all said, "Amen." Betsy said it twice. No psalm had been read for Isaac or her children. Again last night, she'd imagined drifting through dark water to them.

A tearful woman standing with two others on the green waved her kerchief at the young men marching off in the procession led by Gray on his stallion. Seated next to Benjamin on a broad seat in front of Phillipa and Betsy, Saul flicked the reins over the horses' haunches. "Giddyap." The clop, clop, clop of their hooves on the cobblestones began, down Duke of Gloucester Street, past the printer, the grocery, the apothecary, and the two taverns. Farmers and their wives steered wheelbarrows of vegetables and fruit out of the way. Most called out "Morning, all," as the wagon bumped on toward the capital.

At the end of the long street and well beyond the green, Mr. Petty, a journalist Betsy had met at the governor's dinner, tightened the cinches on a yellow mare while waiting to join the caravan. His wife wore a washed-out frock and tattered shawl. "Keep an eye on him, Miss Townsend." She ran out to clasp Phillipa's arm. "Coming home from the governor's mansion, he wandered down the wrong street."

Gray's slave had slowed the horses so the wagon creaked over the cobblestones one at a time but never stopped. Phillipa leaned down to pat Mrs. Petty's arm. "Mrs. Randall and I won't let him out of our sight."

The journalist glared, and Phillipa gave him a sympathetic smile. She smoothed her skirt, pleased to have placated his wife while irritating him. When he looked back at his wife, who jogged to keep up with the wagon, he saluted her. "*Vale.*"

"He would use his Latin." Phillipa snickered into the shawl on Betsy's shoulder. "On a spring morning."

In the middle of the street, Petty's wife wadded her apron into her mouth.

Betsy turned to Phillipa. "Why is she so afraid?"

"Because Petty is brave on paper, but in life, he's a coward. Look at his mare. Why would he purchase land in the wilderness? Some people are *not* planters."

Her brother Robert had been raised to take over their father's farm. When Isaac heard that he'd inherited Good

Hope, he bought a full wig and a fine jacket. A banker, he'd never managed land. No wonder Mrs. Petty chewed her apron while her journalist husband, neither a farmer nor a soldier, rode off with troops carrying muskets fitted with bayonets.

When the paving stones ended, the horses thudded into the soft grooves of a dirt road. Well ahead of the wagon, Gray rode into a small, partially cleared field around a shambling house and sheds. Dogs yapped at the team of chestnuts but backed off, perhaps fearing the lieutenant's black stallion. Gray called, "Harmon? Francis Harmon, are you with us?"

Betsy sat as straight as she could to see the fiddler that Dee said could play any musical instrument. Phillipa had said it was true. "Nobody fiddles like Harmon. And the native Virginians are his friends. He speaks Pamunkey and Choctaw. Even some Cherokee."

Instead of the fiddler, a girl Mary's age led a skittish sorrel, packed with provisions, out of a shed attached to the house. The child, alert and watchful, was barefoot and in a shift, her hair tangled, uncombed since she'd been in bed. "Da! They're here, Da!"

A balding man in buckskin, with long fringes on his shoulders and sleeves, ambled down the porch step, his fiddle case under his arm. He ran his hand down the neck of the mare the girl led. It nickered as if impatient at his delay. Then the fiddler tousled the girl's hair. "You've done it well, my sweet Annie."

Betsy's regrets that Mary had never bridled a horse were interrupted by Phillipa's muttering that the man had three wives.

A young woman Betsy's age with hair the same red as

Harmon's "sweet Annie" followed the fiddler from the house. Behind her, a darker woman with black hair combed back in a thick braid, and a black woman with a green kerchief tied over her head, came out. In identical light-blue shifts and long, unbleached aprons, they stood on the porch with their arms linked and frowned at the wagon, the troops, and the horses. The white woman waved when Phillipa called out, "Good to see you, Miss Polly."

When two men carrying guns and powder horns came out, the women stepped aside for them to pass. All three women bent over the dogs at the men's heels and began to tug fondly at their ears; it seemed the women's way of saying farewell to the men who ambled off the steps. When the second man picked up a child toddling after him and lifted him over his head, the child shrieked in delight.

"The sweet, sweet blond is a Prussian woodsman," Phillipa said. She added a suggestive "hmm." She'd never met the man with the neatly trimmed beard, but she would like to know him.

A crowd of children, the youngest clinging to their mother's skirts, was calling to their father; Betsy stood in the wagon to see each of them. "Look at the children, Phillipa."

How could Mr. Harmon leave his wives, these children? He petted the dogs the children brought and embraced each child, kissing all eight of them, brown-skinned girls with caps over thick curls, two lean redheaded boys, and a lanky girl with braids down her back to her waist. She held up a puppy to receive the kiss Harmon meant for her.

To keep her from climbing down to embrace the children, Phillipa clutched Betsy's skirt, forcing her to stay seated as the lieutenant brought the men to the wagon and introduced them. "Mrs. Randall, Miss Townsend, meet Mr. James Morris, our surveyor." He clapped the man on the back. "Governor Spotswood has commissioned him to plot Germanna, his new settlement. And this is Mr. Karl Reinke." According to Gray, the stocky, clean-shaven man, no taller than Betsy and wearing buckskin, knew the region from Philadelphia to the Alleghenies. The woodsman raised his felt cap and squinted up at Betsy and Phillipa. He stroked the head of his shepherd dog while the dog waved his white tail. Though the dog hadn't made a sound, the hunter said, "Quiet, Falken."

Annie waited with the sorrel near the wagon for her father. Looking to the side, she studied Phillipa, copying the tuck of her chin or the tilt of her head, until her father pulled away from the clinging children and dogs barking for his attention. She held his hand while Gray introduced him as Mr. Francis Harmon to Phillipa and Betsy. When he turned back to her, she said, "Come home tomorrow."

The fiddler picked up his sweet Annie and tickled her neck with his whiskers, but when tears came to her eyes, he wagged his finger. "None a that." He shooed her and the dogs to the house where the women stood arm in arm, silent, with their children, watching him tie the sorrel to the wagon. Morris mounted his horse and whistled for his sleek black dog to start off. Gray's horse whinnied and trotted ahead of Morris's pinto to gain the lead. The women held up their hands in a good-bye, and Phillipa waved, but Betsy couldn't raise her arm. Her eyes stung. She wished she could stay with the women surrounded by dogs and waving children.

The fiddler smiled at Betsy and climbed on the wagon seat next to Saul, twisting around to kiss Phillipa's hand and wave to Charity. He refused to take the reins from Gray's man. "Keep the wheels rollin, Saul. I'm hungry. Those Pamunkey guides will have game for Mrs. Fulton to prepare at the crossing, but if we don't get there before dusk, they'll finish off a whole buck and leave us the bones."

———————

For miles, the wagon rode past black men and women hoeing tobacco shoots in fields of waist-high stumps, stripped of their bark. Phillipa told Betsy about the citizens of Williamsburg. She thought about Brompton and what people would be doing that time of day. The shadows grew shorter and the insects buzzed louder. In the quiet, she heard Phillipa arguing with Charity about people in town. Hammers banged as they passed a clearing in the woods where children dropped their tasks to wave at the men on horseback, the ladies in the wagon and the troops marching to the fife and drum. Betsy smiled at the memory of Alice running after her sister. "Wait, Mary. Wait for me."

Petty, the reins slack in his fingers, snored as his yellow mare trudged on. With the sun on Betsy's back and the wagon rocking in and out of ruts in the road, she fell asleep while birds chirped in the wild dogwood.

Startled, Betsy awakened. Nothing was different—the road still cut through a thicket of high laurel—but Harmon sat stiff on his bench, moving the reins as if sending a whisper down the horses' backs. He murmured softly to them, or perhaps to himself. Phillipa and Charity too sat up, alarmed and wondering. Morris and Gray had slowed their horses to peer into the woods. The fiddler looked right and left as he took the reins from Saul. Jiggling them over the horses' backs, he quietly urged them to keep plodding. Phillipa had mouthed the word Seneca when Morris's horse reared. The chestnuts shied into one another. Petty's horse took off to run past the stallion that snorted at the flight. Since Petty had slept with his feet hanging free of the stirrups, he fell to the ground, and with one look at the troops, the huntsman, and the wagon, he crawled into the brush. The black stallion reared upright and came down, all four hooves on the ground but trembling. Morris grunted, and his dog, Rex, stopped growling.

A man in brown with leafy twigs in his hat and his face smeared with mud pointed a musket at Gray's chest. Across the road, a man smudged like the first trained a rifle on Morris. A third bandit, his lower face covered with his kerchief, crept out from the trees, his hat pulled down so far his eyes weren't visible. From Lieutenant Gray to Reinke at the end of the troops, the travelers were silent. Gray's hand—clenched on his saber—didn't move. Betsy gripped Phillipa's knee as if that would help keep them safe— a useless gesture, like Phillipa's fastening on Betsy's arm. From a branch arching over the road, something thumped into the wagon, grazing Betsy's back, crashing into one of the vicar's saplings and Charity. At the jolt, Betsy spun to see what hit her. A woman. A short woman, browned by the sun, in pants—dark green wool—a man's shirt and vest, smeared with dirt and splotches of green as if rubbed with leaves or grass. She ignored Betsy and shoved a pistol to the back of Phillipa's head.

Betsy waited for Gray to outwit the bandits. Morris faced the rifle pointed at him. Nobody moved. Except Saul. He bolted off the wagon and into the forest, jumping over small shrubs and dodging low branches. Charity began a high wail, and the woman kicked her. With a "whoa-whoa-whoa," Harmon quieted the horses.

How easily Saul fled. Betsy wanted to run, too, but Phillipa held her tight.

"Git down from the wagon, Miss Townsend." The woman kicked Charity again when she started up. "We're inviting you to stay with us until your uncle pays for your ransom."

Squeezing Phillipa's knee, Betsy thought *Mary, Alice, David*; the names were a prayer for Phillipa and for herself. From the corner of her eye, Betsy saw a dagger hanging from the woman's belt.

The woman's voice was low, like a man's: "Keep them boys back, lieutenant, or Willy blasts you to eternal damnation."

The barrel of the pistol against Phillipa's head glinted silver in the sunlight. Phillipa, her face white, shrank from the gun, but the woman rammed it harder, and Phillipa's hand went limp on Betsy's arm.

The bandit stamped on Charity's hand. "Stop that squalling."

The wailing stopped in time for all to hear a loud click when the bandit pulled the hammer back, driving Phillipa's head forward.

Softly Harmon said, "Molly Gage, put your gun away. Phillipa's done you no harm."

"Scare me again, Harmon, and I'll pull the trigger. Git off this wagon like that nigger. Go back to Polly and your little ones."

Betsy turned back, stunned. She wanted to see the woman clearly—her pretty face hard under the grime rubbed on her cheeks and forehead—who knew Harmon's wife. The woman saw Betsy staring at her knife. "Take your eyes off me or I'll slit your throat." Her fist smashed into Betsy's cheek.

Her head ringing from the blow, Betsy gripped the bandit's wrist—the one holding the pistol—and thrust it away from Phillipa. The gun shot into the woods. Instead of cutting Betsy's throat, the woman jerked backward with a loud ugh.

Reinke, working a bayonet like a pitchfork, lifted the woman out of the wagon. He must have crept up from behind the troops, snatched one of their bayoneted rifles, and stabbed the bandit between the ribs. The woman fell on her side, coughing a red froth from her mouth and nose. Spasms contorted her body as Reinke yanked out the bayonet.

Gray's horse reared. The lieutenant shouted, "Ramses!" and the stallion crashed down on the bandit who had a gun aimed at Gray's chest; but the rifle didn't go off. In a flash of hooves, the horse trampled him. That bandit died before Morris, in the general surprise, clubbed the butt of his gun down on his own attacker's head.

Phillipa shivered next to Betsy. "Hold me. Hold me. Hold me."

Betsy did. Shaking herself, she held Phillipa. "Forgive me," she repeated again and again. She shouldn't have agreed to let Phillipa come with her. She kept feeling the kick of the gun going off up her arm into her shoulder.

Charity righted a sapling and came up on her knees to put her strong arms around Betsy and Phillipa. She chanted, "Thank you, gentle Jesus. Thank you." She turned from Betsy and Phillipa to align branches the bandit's jump had broken. "I'm sorry she hurt you, little tree."

Betsy vomited over the side of the wagon and then wiped her mouth on her sleeve before she went back to Phillipa, who whimpered, "I wet myself."

Betsy had seen the puddle. The wagon shook from the horses' quivering in their traces, their necks twitching despite Harmon's white-knuckled grip on the reins and his "Steady there; steady now." His words lulled Betsy. Her cheek hurt, and she touched the spot. It burned. Soon it would be black and blue.

The German hunter came to her side. "Are you hurt, lady?"

He should have been asking Phillipa. Betsy took her hand from her cheek. "She hit me, but it doesn't hurt. Are they all dead, Mr. Reinke?" Blood splattered his buckskin shirt.

He nodded toward two soldiers tying the woman's body to a tree, her pants and shirt stained dark red. Her face gray, her eyes half closed, her jaw hanging open, she would rot there, a warning to other bandits. Betsy turned away.

Eager to shake Reinke's hand, each of Gray's recruits slapped his back until a rifle shot blasted the quiet around them. Morris had killed a third man who had been crawling off into the woods. The dogs barked as if they had permission. Swearing an oath, Morris told the men to search the bandits' bodies for stolen gold or silver. "Specially hers." He wanted them hung on opposite sides of the road.

Phillipa stood up and yelled into the wood. "No, Charity. Come back, now!"

Charity had slipped off the end of the wagon and fled, holding the hem of her skirt gathered up to her chest, freeing her to run on the path Saul had torn through the trees.

They all stared after her and at Phillipa waving both

arms high in the air to get Gray's attention. "She's chasing
her brother. Don't shoot. She's chasing Saul. She'll bring
him back." She sat back down next to Betsy, her face in her
hands. "Please, Charity, come back."

Betsy told Phillipa that she would, but if Betsy could run
like Charity and Saul had, she'd have fled the wagon to be
on her own too. Instead, she had vomited; and though she
didn't think anyone could tell, she was still trembling.

With a sharp whistle, Morris pointed his arm straight
out to Charity, and his dog bounded after her, leaping up to
see a path over the brush.

Harmon jumped up from his seat. "Morris, call off the
dog." He handed the reins to Benjamin and sprang off the
wagon. "Miss Townsend's right, Jim. Charity's runnin to
get Saul."

"You don't know that." Morris glared at Harmon and
then looked to Gray. At a nod from the lieutenant, Morris
whistled a long, piercing note, and his dog twisted in a leap
to half-face his master. He barked and took off after Charity again, but the surveyor called him back and he returned,
slinking down as if he'd been punished.

His face red, Gray snapped his riding crop against his
boot. "Harmon, Saul's too valuable to leave his return to a
nigger who could be running off herself." He wanted the
hound to hunt down Saul.

"I don't want that cur hunting for Charity," Phillipa said.
"Give him Saul's scent."

Reinke had started back to the rear of the wagon with his
dog at his heels, but Harmon called for him to bring his
dog—the two of them could bring Charity and Saul back.
He said precious light had been wasted, and if they were to
get to Fulton's before dark, the wagon should be rolling.

Having started after Charity, he called back from the bracken that he and Reinke would have the slaves at the crossing before Gray could march his men there.

Motioning for Morris to start ahead, the lieutenant told Benjamin to drive the wagon as fast as the horses could pull it to reach Fulton's Crossing. He ordered the troops to march double-time, giving Ramses a sharp kick to set off at a trot.

Petty crawled out of the woods and lifted his foot to the stirrup of his mare, but she pranced away as the troops marched past him.

Benjamin gave the reins to Betsy. "Hold em jus like that."

Betsy laced the reins through her fingers as her father had taught her, and the horses stepped together in the ruts while Benjamin ran back and helped Petty into the saddle. The slightest restraint on the reins slowed the chestnuts enough for Benjamin to catch up with the wagon and pull himself up onto the driver's seat. Taking the reins, he gid-dyapped the team. "You know how to drive horses, Miss Randall?" The wheels squealed on in the ruts. He sat with the reins laced as she'd held them, but his loose grip proved his comfort with the horses.

Betsy said, "My father let me drive the team while I sat next to him on his way out to a field." She leaned back on the bench, mysteriously comforted by holding the reins of the horses.

Sitting upright, Phillipa said Betsy should teach her to drive when they arrived at Good Hope, and to keep Phillipa from pestering her, Betsy agreed that she would. She listened to Benjamin hum a tune so low it seemed to come from the roots of the trees. The creak of the wagon and clop of the horses' hooves had the same music they had had that morning. The shadows had switched from east to west as if the bandits' attack had changed the light. The attack had changed the way Phillipa sat. "If we look hard enough, we'll see Charity and Saul before Harmon and Reinke find them."

If they looked in the woods like that, Betsy feared that she'd see another bandit. The trees shaded the lower branches, and she couldn't see far, but she expected to see Molly Gage either crouched on a branch or dangling on a rope. Betsy held her hands over her eyes until she could clear her mind and look without seeing the woman who'd been ready to shoot Phillipa. Betsy rubbed the spot where the bandit's fist had slammed into her cheek, and realized that Isaac had had no time to take Brickhart's gun. She'd shoved the bandit's arm because the woman hit her, acting without thinking.

The shadows grew longer. Phillipa lay with her head in Betsy's lap. "You keep looking. I need to sleep. Then it will be my turn to watch."

She slept. Betsy stared at the trees, repeating to herself Isaac, Mary, Alice, David.

Chapter 16

Benjamin pointed to a small white flag waving ahead. Guns clicked; Gray and Morris aimed rifles at the spot. Phillipa jumped up. "That's Charity. That's her cap."

Under a large oak, Charity and Saul knelt by the road. Clasping her cap in her hands high over her head, she was pleading, "Mercy."

"Where's Harmon?" Betsy stood to see into the brush. "Where's the German?"

"Everybody quiet. We all calm." Benjamin murmured to the horses, and Betsy, understanding he meant for them to sit, pulled on Phillipa's skirt.

"She's back." Phillipa sat down and hugged Betsy. "By herself. With Saul."

Charity bowed her head to Gray. "He run cause he scared. He didn't have no gun. He's here now. We ran to meet up with you."

Morris halloed for Reinke and Harmon.

Silence. Except for birds chirping. The woods were crowded with trees, low bushes, grasses, vines. Betsy couldn't see Harmon or Reinke. She couldn't see how they could find their way through the mesh of trees, though Charity and Saul had.

"Master Gray, we didn't see nobody. We didn't hear nobody." She and Saul both shook their heads. "We ran ahead to the road."

Gray hooked his thumb back toward the wagon for Charity to climb back to her place, and as soon as she stepped away, he spit in Saul's face. "From here to Fulton's, you stay ahead of Morris. Step to the right, step to the left, he shoots your arrogant ass."

Reclaiming her place between the saplings shading Phillipa and Betsy, Charity bent her head to the floor of the wagon bed. "Blessed Jesus, mercy, mercy. Miss Phillipa, I'm glad you not hurt. I'm glad that German killed that woman. I'm glad you alive as God is my redeemer. And I'm glad you is, too, Mrs. Randall."

Phillipa looked straight ahead, shaking her finger at the horses instead of her slave. "If you ever run off again, I'll … If you ever … I'll … I'll …" She jabbed her finger at the trees, not once looking at Charity. "If you hadn't come back, I swear …" Phillipa never finished a sentence.

Saul ran a few yards in front of the surveyor, who rode his horse at an even stride. Betsy couldn't see the fiddler and the hunter. Benjamin tried to assure her that they were both woodsmen and would find their way.

Charity rocked her incantation no louder than the wheels in the rutted road. "Mercy. Be merciful to Saul. Mercy. Thank you, God. Thank you, Lord. Thank you, gentle Jesus."

———

Saul ran, his pace steady, with Morris's pinto pounding the road behind him as the shadows stretched to the other side. The sun slid down past the tops of the trees and the woods ahead blurred in the evening gloom. Suddenly, the surveyor spurred his pinto, and the hooves of the brown-and-white horse thudded the ground. Saul sprinted, tripped, and fell. Charity jumped up behind Betsy and Phillipa. "Don', Master Morris. Don' shoot."

Saul rolled onto his back, his arms up to ward off a blow. Betsy clutched Phillipa to keep her from standing up. They called out in one voice, "No, Mister Morris." But he had no notion of shooting the slave. His horse barreled past Saul, who struggled to rise first to his hands and knees and then stood, unsteady, like he might fall again. Gray, who had been riding next to Morris, reined his stallion to a stop and leaned from his horse to grasp Saul's forearm. He meant for Saul to swing up behind the saddle onto Ramses, but the slave couldn't jump. His legs buckled, and the lieutenant let him collapse to the ground. Gray told Benjamin to get Saul into the wagon.

The draft horses plodded up to Saul, sweat slick on their sides, their heads hanging together, heaving gusts of air— Morris set a faster pace than they'd gone in the morning. Benjamin lifted Saul, like a child grimy with sweat and dust, onto the seat in front of Betsy and Phillipa. He winced and held his side. Betsy cringed. She'd never seen a man run almost to death. Benjamin comforted Saul with steady chatter of the fine stew Mrs. Fulton would have, and how good he'd sleep under a warm blanket on soft straw in the barn.

Glints of light shone deep through the trees. Dogs barked. A voice came from the direction of the lights. "Lieutenant Gray, that you?"

In the dusk, Gray answered. "Yes, with the wagon and troops." The barking stopped.

With her arms around Phillipa, Charity began to chant. "We there. We there. Fulton's Crossing, we is here."

Candles flickered in windows under the eaves of a sprawling clapboard house. Over a wide door, a lantern welcomed the travelers. Harmon stepped up to Betsy and offered his hand. When she leaned away, shocked to see him, he laughed and explained that after they saw Charity head Saul toward the road, they took one of Reinke's shortcuts. He pointed to a wizened man with a full white beard helping Phillipa off the wagon from the other side. "That's Zach Fulton over there."

Betsy's legs twinged from sitting on the hard bench. She stood to look down from the wagon at a gray-haired woman. "Sarah Smollett Fulton, wife of Zachary Fulton, provisioner." Mrs. Fulton, small as a sparrow with bird-bright eyes, waited to shake Betsy's hand.

The formality of the introduction and the implication that all was in order overwhelmed Betsy. She wanted to hug the woman but couldn't even respond with a proper "Elizabeth Harrington Randall" or introduce Phillipa. No words came. The old woman put an arm, skinny as a rope—strong as a rope—around Betsy, providing further assurance that she was safe. "I heard you was coming, Mrs. Randall. And I know Miss Townsend's uncle well. We go way back." She put her other arm around Phillipa. "When I see Mr. Osborne it's always to hear how proud he is …" She stepped away from Phillipa and Betsy and started toward Charity. "Well, as the Lord is good, Zach, it's our Charity." She held out her arms. "I kin see Miss Townsend spoils you." Though only tall enough for the top of her cap to brush Charity's chin, she hugged her tight, rocking side to side. They both closed their eyes, lost in the embrace. Zachary Fulton came around the wagon with a broad smile and waited for his turn to hug Charity. For a quick moment, while the old lady wiped her cheeks with her apron, he did. Then she pulled Charity away from him to wipe Charity's face. "Here now. Quit that blubbering."

Sniffing back tears, Charity said, "Mrs. Fulton, didn't Mr. Harmon tell you all that Miss Phillipa almost got killed?"

Zach Fulton took Phillipa's arm. "He didn't leave out the singlest thing. He told us all about the way you pushed the gun, Mrs. Randall. That Molly Gage. She's been botherin travelers since time began—just the people travelin through, not the settlers livin here. Them she visits with her brandy and game in exchange for what she can't rob or shoot, but she's never tried ransom before." He looked around for Harmon. The fiddler and Benjamin had Saul between them, his arms over their shoulders, his head hanging to his chest. He struggled to walk, and they gave him time for each step to the barn.

Mrs. Fulton pulled Betsy toward the house. "Don't you worry, Mrs. Randall. I'll send Daniel." She said that if anything ailed Saul, her man Daniel would make it right. "Animals, slaves, planters, he heals 'em all." She patted Charity's back. "You know Harmon'll fiddle and have him sleepin like an angel on a cloud."

Charity folded her hands at her chest. "Miss Fulton, please don' be talking about angels and Saul right now."

"Well. No." She looked down at the ground and then up at Charity. "You run ahead and open the door for these ladies."

In the dark room that appeared to be a kitchen, dining room, and parlor all in one, Charity hurried to move the candle from the window to a long table. Then she set the table with pewter bowls. Though Betsy's body still felt the rock of the wagon and the jolt of the wheels bumping the rutted road, she and Phillipa had soon finished a bowl of stew Mrs. Fulton blessed before they ate. Since Zach, Harmon, and the German hunter had set up a table in the barn where the men could belch all they wanted after eating Blackhawk's stew, the women would have some peace. Eating their carrots, turnips, and chunks of venison, they listened to the story of Charity's first owners, the Tripps, two brothers who claimed land but never cleared a tree except to build their shack and butcher honest men's livestock. "Gamblers. Slavers. Cheats—even at cards." Cecil Tripp killed himself with his own liquor, and "Silas fell in a gulley—he was chasin Charity. His own dogs ate him." Her husband found the poor little slave—she wasn't ten years old—naked and shivering like a rabbit in a trap, hiding in the barn loft. "Blessed Jesus. Saddest creature I ever saw."

"We're sisters—Mrs. Randall and me," Phillipa said.

"I kin see that, dear." Mrs. Fulton eyed Betsy and raised her eyebrows as if questioning her choosing Phillipa. "That stew will help you sleep."

Phillipa spread butter on a second slice of bread. "I won't sleep a wink."

"That so?" Mrs. Fulton spooned more stew for her.

Phillipa stopped chewing a bite of bread. "Yes, Mrs. Fulton, it's most positively so." She filled her spoon with stew and sat as straight as the queen on her throne. "Please don't ever repeat that story about Charity again. It makes her sadder than a possum."

Mrs. Fulton stirred the coals in the hearth. "The sun rises early in these parts, but there won't be any travelin for the two of you tomorrow. Stead of findin Charity and Saul, the German and Harmon found two horses staked near the path and figured those sensible creatures would lead them to the bandits' den. Sure enough, them horses went right to Molly's hideout."

Phillipa finished her second bowl of stew. "You mean they weren't looking for Charity?"

"I s'pose they saw Charity leadin Saul to the road and knew they'd fare better if the lieutenant saw they repented on their own." Mrs. Fulton said that the surveyor would be the lone man at the crossing the next day. He'd keep an eye on Saul while Gray and his men retrieved Molly's stolen horses and divided her treasure.

Later, when Betsy climbed to the loft, she found Phillipa kneeling on the floor next to the bed, combing Charity's hair. Phillipa worked her fingers through strands of hair down to Charity's scalp. She admitted she couldn't see in the candle's dim light, but feeling for the nits took her mind off the bandit's gun. She doubted if she'd ever get over the scare. Then she poked her finger at the base of Charity's skull; Charity flinched, as if she felt Molly's pistol, her eyes closed, her shoulders scrunched, waiting to be shot.

"That's wrong, Phillipa." Betsy yanked Phillipa's hand away, but Charity remained hunched, waiting.

"If I don't do it, she'll be pestilent with scratching." She drew the comb down the center of Charity's head, bent forward, and kissed the part. She doused rosewater on her hands and worked it into a section of Charity's hair that stood up stiff before braiding it as lovingly as a mother, deftly twisting the wisps of hair in tight rows from front to back. Charity reached back, her hands on Phillipa's legs, her thumb rubbing the length of her thighs.

Kneeling at the bed, Betsy said her evening prayers and tried to forget how gentle, how soothing, how insistent, Charity's hands could be.

"Mrs. Randall, you don't mind if Charity lies by me until I fall asleep, do you?"

Betsy pretended not to hear.

Phillipa tossed as if unable to snuggle comfortably in her slave's arms, and Betsy moved closer to the wall. Charity sang to Phillipa, and her voice lulled Betsy until, despite the laughter of the troops coming through the open window, Betsy slept.

A moan. Another. A quiet, repeated creak of a floorboard. The bed beside her was empty. Phillipa and Charity tussled on the floor. To see why they wrestled, Betsy rolled to the edge, careful not to squeak the bed. Naked, their shifts flung to the side, Phillipa's head was between Charity's legs. Betsy flipped back to her pillow, turning away from them to the wall, and stared at the dark. She couldn't muffle the noises of lovemaking even by pressing her pillow over her ears. Phillipa whispered threats, and then words of love.

Phillipa had said that she wouldn't sleep, but when she climbed back into the bed and curled on her side, she did. Charity did not. She lay on the floor and hummed for a while before her lullaby worked, and then Betsy listened to the dark quiet. Phillipa may be Charity's mistress, but she depended on her slave's affection. The lieutenant had demanded that Saul be brought back because replacing him would be costly; Phillipa couldn't replace Charity. She needed her. Betsy needed Isaac and her children. She listened: nothing but the old couple's snoring and the quiet of night.

Chapter 17

Sunlight flooded the kitchen and shone on the garlands of flowers carved on the backs of the chairs. Betsy hadn't seen those flowers or the eagle with widespread wings guarding the room from the top of the cupboard when they arrived. Around the rim of the bread plate, birds sang. Everywhere Betsy looked, animals, birds, flowers, and fruit had been carved into wood, oiled and polished to a glow. The smell of cocoa filled the kitchen, but Mrs. Fulton had said she'd just begun grinding the cocoa. The water wasn't near a boil. She'd thought the three women would sleep longer after the long wagon ride. She gave Betsy a gentle squeeze and told her to wander down to the garden. After being kept awake by Phillipa and Charity caressing each other, Betsy didn't want to wish either of them good morning. Going out in the fresh air suited her. The cocoa would be ready when Betsy came back.

"You tell Daniel to fill this basket for me." With a slight frown, Mrs. Fulton cocked her head and studied Betsy's face. "He's a healer. Eases the deepest sorrow, our Daniel does. The vicar's Benjamin is there now helpin him divide plants and tend to the young shoots. You'll need some for your garden at Good Hope." She led Betsy to the door. "Those two men will quiet your heart a little, too."

Outside, the leaves glistened with dew. Betsy filled Mrs. Fulton's wide basket with new peas and a few carrots that Daniel and Benjamin had thinned. Betsy liked thinning plants in her garden, leaving some to grow long, plump, and round. She gathered sprigs of parsley, mint, and thyme from the border at the gate, plus a few onions Daniel pointed out for her and a dozen small turnips. Each plant had its own smell, its own color, its own hold on the earth.

Sensing a presence at the willow garden gate, Betsy turned to see a young woman in buckskin with a long black braid. Her eyes didn't waver when Betsy stared. Unlike the plain buckskin Reinke wore, her clothes had small red, blue, and yellow beads stitched around the neck and at the hem. On her back, she carried a baby supported by a wooden board covered with more fancy beadwork. A wedge at the top of the board protected the baby from sun or rain. How long had the woman been there? Benjamin and Daniel paid no attention to her. She didn't blink when Betsy had turned to her, but held up a loosely woven grass bag that hung low. She looked from Betsy to the house. "Come with me," Betsy said. "I'm going up to the kitchen."

The woman at the gate turned and led the way. Without knocking, she walked in.

As soon as Mrs. Fulton saw her and began exclaiming over the baby, the young woman handed her the bag. She spoke a language the old woman seemed to understand though she answered the woman in English and didn't translate what she heard for Betsy. When the woman left, Mrs. Fulton said, "Matty brings us game. Her husband hunts and traps turkey, rabbit, squirrel, venison, and bear." She opened the bag on the table and lifted out a shoulder joint and a loin of venison. "What with the meat Ned brought, I'll have to pickle this." She dropped the meat in a large crock and covered it with a wooden lid. "Zachary could never hit anything worth eating. Wasted lead. We give Matty's husband ammunition and he provides meat for our table. My Zach can carve birds …" She touched the rim of the bread plate, "… but he can't shoot 'em."

She filled two bowls with porridge and brought them and two cups with cocoa to the table. When she was a little girl, before Middle Plantation became Williamsburg, the Powhatan and Choctaw lived all over Virginia, but then came the Troubles. "A terrible time." She scraped the last of her porridge from her bowl. "Not many Powhatan left in this area." She pointed to the porridge left in Betsy's bowl. "You finish that."

Phillipa brought a fragrance of rosewater and almond oil into the room. She'd combed her hair and braided it with blue ribbons that matched her dress. Betsy eased away from the arm Phillipa stretched around her. Ignoring Betsy's snub, Phillipa picked up Betsy's cup. "Good morning, Mrs. Randall. Mrs. Fulton. I trust you both slept well." She sipped the cooled cocoa. Behind Phillipa coming into the kitchen, Charity hurried to fill another cup for Betsy. Phillipa smiled at Charity. "I'm going to ask Lieutenant Gray for a pistol. And ammunition to load it."

Betsy stirred the cocoa Charity had brought her. She couldn't look at Phillipa. "Mrs. Fulton," said Betsy, "Would you like to sit next to Phillipa in a wagon while she practices loading a pistol?"

When Mrs. Fulton humphed, Phillipa laughed. She

aimed her finger at the eagle carved into the cupboard. "I could shoot the red head off a woodpecker at fifty paces."

Betsy and Phillipa were different, came from different homes, and needed different kinds of comfort. A little time with Charity had brought back Phillipa's smile. Betsy pushed her bowl of porridge to Phillipa. "Lieutenant Gray wouldn't give you a pistol without your uncle's permission. Fortunately for Mr. Woodpecker, your uncle isn't here to grant it."

"That settles that," Mrs. Fulton said.

Charity turned away to tend the hearth. And to hide her laughter. Phillipa gave Betsy a saucy look. She said, "Mrs. Fulton, we cannot sit here all day while the men plunder the bandits' hideout. You must have some needlework to do." Her look dared Betsy to contradict her request. "I'm gifted at embroidery." Holding out her collar, Phillipa had Mrs. Fulton admire a delicate ribbon sewn around the border.

Mrs. Fulton stood on tiptoe to see each stitch. "This your work?" She looked at Betsy to verify Phillipa's claim. "That's fine, Miss Townsend. Fine work indeed." She held up a hand; she had something for Betsy and Phillipa to see. Near the hearth, she pulled a many-colored basket from shelves built into the wall. Smoothing her hand over the finely woven grass, she showed them an intricate design of small triangles. "The Choctaw women make these. How they keep the grass so that it smells fresh, and where they get these deep reds and blues, I do not know." From the basket, she took a round of beeswax, a palm-sized book of felt for needles, and a flat package of unbleached hemp, which she handed to Betsy.

Standing to unwrap the packet, Betsy found a square of white lambswool. Instead of opening the square and spreading it on the table that Charity had rushed to wipe clean, Betsy held the blanket for an infant, soft as kitten's fur, to her cheek. The room swayed like the *Sally Dash* and Betsy sat down. Her arms wanted to hold David, to hug him next to her. She put the blanket to her shoulder to feel him there.

Charity stepped toward Betsy. "Mrs. Randall?"

The concern in Charity's eyes reminded Betsy that she was on her way to Good Hope and glad Phillipa and her Charity were with her. She spread the blanket on the table.

Serene and deliberate, Phillipa picked up the square. She turned it over, gauging the bias of the weave. "Charity, bring my silk." She held up the square and studied it, tipping her head first to one side and then to the other while Charity's footsteps creaked overhead. "Mrs. Fulton, should I work in white so one would have to look twice to see the design or use colored silk?"

Her hand calloused, rough, and brown from the sun, Mrs. Fulton caressed the wool. "You'll not have time, Miss Townsend. I was just showin you some fine wool."

Phillipa pulled the square away from the old lady's grasp. "I'm going to sit right here until the men return. If we leave tomorrow, I'll work as we bounce on the interminably cursed road. It will keep my mind off being attacked from all sides. You'll have it again when Lieutenant Gray leads us back to Williamsburg. But if you prefer, I can stitch a vine with a few rosebuds before we start again tomorrow."

Phillipa moved to the bottom of the narrow staircase. "If Charity ever brings my silk." She stood in the doorway so Charity could not step into the kitchen without bumping her. With a quick peek at Betsy and Mrs. Fulton, Charity brushed past her with a lacquered box, inlaid with mother-of-pearl, a scene of Chinese mountains, trees, and buildings with roofs that curled at the eaves, more elegant than any Betsy had seen. Mrs. Fulton snatched a pair of eyeglasses from a cup on the mantel and shifted the box so the mother-of-pearl shimmered in the light. She touched the lady's dress. "Slippery as silk. Feel there." She pointed for Betsy to feel the figures. "That old man's beard is bristly as Zach's. And almost as long." She looked at Phillipa with new respect. "Miss Townsend, my Zachary must see this."

The man's beard hung down past his waist, three times longer than Mr. Fulton's. The fruit on the trees had the smooth peel of peaches and plums. Some had a pink tint, others gave off a purple glow. Betsy had no idea Phillipa had brought something so precious on the expedition.

"That's the outside." Phillipa removed a small ivory pin that secured the lid, opened the box lined with cinnabar, and showed them skeins for embroidery. Black, white, and gray silk layered to look like pearls framing a rainbow of colors: blues to greens, yellows to golds, oranges, and reds deepening to dark purple—like the hours of the day from dawn to dusk and into the night.

Mrs. Fulton marched to the door and yelled toward the garden. "Daniel, tell Mr. Morris to git up to the house and bring Saul. Tell Ben to bust his trousers getting to this kitchen." She shooed Betsy and Charity, even Phillipa, from the table. "Don't nobody touch this box."

While they waited for the men, Phillipa asked if a border of flowers would be charming, and Mrs. Fulton said she'd like daffodils, roses, pansies, forget-me-nots, columbine, foxglove. And butterflies. She picked up the bread plate with the birds chirping around the rim. A sparrow herself in gray and brown, she tipped her head to one side. "How about birds? Can you make a bluebird's wing shine like it would in the sun?"

"Miss Phillipa makes flowers so pretty, they smell sweet," Charity said.

Daniel ran up with Benjamin. "Miz Fulton, you in trouble?"

Rushing into the kitchen, Morris shoved the two aside. "Sally Smollett?" Morris's eyes roved the room for a threat. He scowled at Mrs. Fulton, but she grinned back at him and pointed at the box. His face went blank. Saul had followed on the surveyor's heels, but Morris motioned for Saul to stay at the door. "You had us leave our work to gawk at a box of thread?"

"Silk thread. At least five different greens." Mrs. Fulton showed him the arc of shiny skeins from the yellow-green of corn silk to the dark-green of pine. "There hasn't been anythin like this since Joseph's coat of many colors." She slapped Morris's hand when he reached for them. "Clean hands only." Showing the box and the carving on the lid to the slaves on the step, she gave each time to marvel at the carvings and the colored thread. "Look at that blue. If that isn't the color of the night sky, I don't know what is." She looked at the surveyor. "You seen colors like this, Jim?"

"Only when the sun sets." He chided her for scaring him; he'd thought she was in trouble.

When she said that she had Daniel to take care of her when she was in trouble, he saluted, his hand to his eyebrow, and walked out. Saul followed him, no longer limping from his long run. He'd taken on the surveyor's stride.

Mrs. Fulton waved Benjamin and Daniel away. "That Jim Morris. Hard as flint and ready to spark." She set the box on the table and picked up the blanket. "Tell you what, you border this blanket with as many flowers as you can crowd on the hem. I'm giving it to you. I don't have any need for it and never will." She looked at Betsy, her lips a straight line. "I'm one of those women that wasn't meant to have children. 'Cept Zachary. And the visitors to the tavern. I love 'em as my own." She presented Phillipa the blanket with both hands. "But I want to see the garden when you're through embroiderin."

Phillipa got up from the table and kissed the old woman. As if Phillipa had kissed her, Betsy put her hand to her own cheek, remembering Mary's warm, smooth skin.

Wiping her hands on her apron, Mrs. Fulton sent Charity for water to cover the meat the Pamunkey woman had brought. With a wink at Betsy, she said, "There's talk that our lieutenant is plannin on marryin a young lady from Barbados."

Phillipa smiled. "Uncle told me I must be discreet." She put her hand on Betsy's shoulder. "He believes that you will set a good example." Her uncle had already agreed on an amount for her dowry, and he'd promised that Charity could stay with her.

When Mrs. Fulton snickered and said that men like two for the price of one, Phillipa stood up. "The lieutenant will not *touch* Charity."

"That's as may be, Miss Townsend, but if the lieutenant has any say, a smart, strong girl like Charity will have all the children she can bear."

Betsy held a turnip in one hand and a paring knife to peel it in the other. "Mrs. Fulton, that's breaking the Lord's commandment: 'Thou shalt not commit adultery.'"

Charity came into the room carrying two buckets brimming with water. If she'd heard the conversation, she didn't reveal her thoughts. After setting one bucket down near the meat in a large crock, she began to pour water over into the crock. Mrs. Fulton picked up the other bucket so the two streams of water met to form one stream until they covered the meat. Mrs. Fulton said, "It's the way of men."

"Charity, I need to walk outside." Phillipa left the blanket with the needle in a half-completed stitch, grabbed Charity's hand, and walked out the door.

"It ain't all bad, Mrs. Randall." Mrs. Fulton picked up the blanket and examined two entwining vines Phillipa had started to embroider. "It ain't all bad."

Betsy dumped the turnips and chunks of carrot into a pot of boiling water. She didn't say anything but she didn't think *it* was good.

Chapter 18

Early afternoon light stippled the trees. A wheel bumped on a stone in a rut; the horses plodded on. Every few paces one of them would blow, forcing air through its thick lips, a gentle comment. One would shake its head and the other would nod back. Betsy wished Martha Alder were there instead of Phillipa. No, she wished Martha were there in Betsy's place. Unlike Betsy, Martha liked adventures. She'd wanted to sail to the colonies—to India or Madagascar. Like Phillipa, Martha enjoyed gossip. Betsy pressed her arms against her body, trying to imagine she held David in them. Her body ached from riding in the wagon since daybreak. And from emptiness.

Holding up the blanket to admire her needlework, Phillipa said, "I'll put a small butterfly here, but I haven't decided on blue or yellow." She picked a light blue skein and cut a length of thread as long as her arm. "Mrs. Fulton said that if I have clover—and of course, I do—the flowers will attract bees if I'm not careful." She smoothed the fabric over the embroidery hoop. "That old lady talks too much."

Betsy tried to ease the muscles sore from sitting on the

wagon bench. "I wouldn't want anything that could sting a child on a blanket for a baby." When people talked about children, a longing to sleep weighed down Betsy's back and shoulders.

Charity was braiding straw. "Don' put snakes in your garden, Miss Phillipa. You don' want the baby bit!" Mrs. Fulton had given Charity a sack stuffed with straw to braid into a hat. Charity said that she was praying while she plaited each strand so whoever wore the hat would be protected from evil bandits and men like the Tripps.

Phillipa snickered. "No. No evil creatures in this garden. But we need bees for honey. Paradise has a sting, doesn't it, Mrs. Randall?"

Paradise: Isaac's word for Virginia. In every direction, trees shaded the ground. Spikes of wild pink hyacinth and small speckled lilies grew in clumps under the trees. They added sweetness to the smell of leaf mulch. Birds—red, blue, brown, gray—caught a glint of sun as they flew from tree to tree. Woodpeckers hammered like crazed carpenters. Betsy had seen a deer look up from nibbling grass to stare at them earlier that morning. She'd been glad that Reinke, Lieutenant Gray, and Morris had started ahead with the troops before Harmon and Benjamin had the plantings from Mrs. Fulton's garden and the women's boxes packed in the wagon.

The fiddler turned around and smiled at Betsy. "Let's teach our fine English lady a little music from Virginia, Miss Townsend. If I fiddle and you and Charity join Ben singing, she'll know the songs before the day is done."

Charity rose to her knees and pointed up at the sky. A thick column of smoke climbed above the trees. Benjamin's back tensed, but he kept the reins loose in his fingers. The horses trudged on. Putting his fiddle back in its case, Harmon picked up a musket he'd stored behind his seat. "Probably a kitchen fire."

Phillipa folded the blanket into a tidy square and noiselessly put it in her satchel. She leaned over, her lips close to Betsy's ear. "Don't you wish I had a rifle now?"

Benjamin shuddered at the same moment Betsy did, but he couldn't have heard Phillipa.

A raven cawed and another answered. Benjamin nodded when Harmon mouthed the words, "Wrong birds."

A shiver rippled up Betsy's spine. How could birds be wrong? She searched the trees, as Harmon seemed to be doing, for large black birds. Her mother believed that ravens foretold death, but Isaac's mother said they only heralded a carcass in a field. He scoffed when Betsy showed him the crows circling the church steeple on Good Friday.

When another raven cawed farther off, Charity reached from behind the seat to stop Betsy's leg from shaking. She kept her hand on Betsy's thigh, holding it still. From the empty blue overhead, the moon's splotchy face watched the small troop in the forest. Betsy hated the woods. She wished Mrs. Fulton hadn't told her that her husband wore a cloth cap because he'd been scalped during Bacon's Rebellion, which led to the Indian Troubles when he was a boy.

A whippoorwill cried too early in the afternoon. Betsy leaned forward to touch the fiddler's elbow. "Mr. Harmon, why would we hear a whippoorwill at this time of day?"

Harmon put the musket down at his feet. "That cawing you heard, Mrs. Randall, was Seneca thieves, maybe raiding a settlement. Gray must have surprised their party, but they run off 'fore a shot was fired. Your whippoorwill, that's our Pamunkey, Ned."

Benjamin flicked the switch over the backs of the horses. "Thas one sad bird."

Wriggling in her seat, Phillipa hugged Betsy. "We might have been massacred."

Harmon looked back at her, his face grim. "Ned's whippoorwill had too sad a note." He looked at the black cloud ahead.

"At least he sang," Phillipa said. Charity braided her straw and hummed to a quiet tune. Harmon began to play on his fiddle. Betsy looked off into the woods, thinking that her brother had lied about the native Virginians' being at peace with the British. He'd said nothing about the troubles with the Seneca raiding the colony. Except for Isaac's decision to claim Robert's plantation, Betsy had no reason to be in the wilderness. She should have sold the furniture to pay her passage back to England.

In the west, the setting sun tinted the clouds. The burning odor overcame the smell of leaf mulch and wood; it stung Betsy's nose and eyes. Someone carried a torch toward them and met the wagon at the bottom of a steep decline. Ned Parker, the Pamunkey guide, walked alongside the wagon. After talking to Harmon and Benjamin, he ran ahead and disappeared. Betsy couldn't understand his English. Neither could Phillipa or Charity. Harmon told them a cabin had been burned to cinders and a team of oxen butchered. "It stinks of Seneca."

"Are we safe, Mr. Harmon?" Betsy wanted to get down off the wagon and walk back to Williamsburg. A foolish thought. Harmon nodded and gulped from a jug of cider he'd found in the bandit's hideout.

As the wagon rolled into a clearing, Gray's troops called out their greetings. Lieutenant Gray helped Phillipa down from the wagon. "You're in time for our feast, ladies. We've roasted a hog."

———————

When Betsy heard the splash of water over rock beyond the clearing, her first thought was that she would wash the dust from the road. She'd just started toward the sound when Phillipa joined her. Phillipa looked around the clearing and told Betsy they'd be sleeping in the woods. They walked through the clearing to the charred remains of the house. Its upright blackened timbers, bronzed by the reflected light from the last rays of sun, appeared like a specter warning them of nearby danger. On a tree near the house, half the leaves had been seared brown and crinkled on the branches; on the other side, the leaves waved in a soft breeze, a deep green. Tethered to the tree, a cow chewed at clumps of grass under the tree's branches. Her calf tugged at her teat, butting her side. Phillipa pulled Betsy to the mud-daubed hearth, still intact, a monument to a family. At the hearth, six crosses marked graves dug by the soldiers. The family was buried in the ground where they'd lived. Instead of dark, newly shoveled earth, Betsy saw deep water. She thought of praying, but no words came.

Trembling, Phillipa put her arm around Betsy's waist. "Who were these people?"

Gray had walked beside Phillipa. "Of no account. Squatters. People with no title to the land. They cleared it and built a shack. Their kind has no respect for the governor's settlement with the Indians."

The notched poles supporting the house at the corners hadn't burned completely, but none of the boards connecting them remained. Though he hadn't intended any hurt, Gray's remark cut Betsy. She felt no entitlement to her brother's estate. And what was Robert's right to the land? He'd struck deeper into the wilderness than this family, and Betsy didn't see why the Seneca would respect his claim to the estate from Governor Spotswood. Hadn't he been a squatter, too?

Gray took Betsy's arm. "Don't be troubled, Mrs. Randall. The Seneca fled as we approached. I've ordered the men to unload the wagon, and Benjamin will prepare a comfortable bed off the ground for you and Miss Townsend." He took Phillipa's arm and urged Betsy to walk with them to join the others eating by the fire, but she preferred staying a little at the graveside of the family to ponder who the woman who lived there might have been. Mixed with the smell of the torched wood, the small plot had a fragrance of a newly tilled garden. At the base of the hearth, a glint, like glass, shone in the dirt. Walking around to the chimney, she pulled up a small silver spoon with a bowl shaped like a seashell. She brushed off the loose dirt. These people had left so little: the cow, her calf, the pigs, and one silver spoon. According to Harmon, there had been children. Polishing the spoon with the corner of her apron, Betsy wondered if she should leave it near the hearth, but feeling someone eyeing her, she dropped the spoon in her pocket.

In his brown waistcoat, Petty, the journalist, watched her from a stump near the burnt house, his portable desk balanced on his knees. "Mrs. Randall, our harbinger of misfortune." The journalist dipped his quill and went back to write his next line.

"How can you write in this place?"

"The light is failing. I wish I had a lantern." Petty blew

on the paper for the ink to dry. "Ah, here comes Miss Townsend." He stood to button his jacket and straighten his collar.

Phillipa frowned at Petty and clutched Betsy's arm. "Don't look at this rubble, Mrs. Randall." She pulled Betsy away. "The lieutenant, the fiddler, and the surveyor all say we're safe in this clearing."

Seated by the fire, Gray, Harmon, and Morris ate the roast pig with corn bread Mrs. Fulton had sent with them. Charity and Saul had set up a makeshift table from the backboards of the wagon. Crates served for chairs. Benjamin and a few of the troops chopped wood to keep the fire going while they slept. Phillipa put her arm around Betsy's waist and pulled her close. "I'm glad that we're here together, Mrs. Randall. No woman should be alone in these woods."

"But this woman was." Betsy was glad to feel Phillipa's arm around her. She looked back at the burnt house then sniffed the roast pig. She sniffed again; that sweet fragrance had always been a favorite.

Phillipa laughed at the change in Betsy's expression, and beckoned for Lieutenant Gray to bring them cups of cider, which Betsy gratefully accepted. She and Phillipa ate and drank before joining the others clapping and singing to Harmon's fiddle, a recruit's fife, and Benjamin's wooden spoons.

While he clapped, a thin blond recruit kept an eye on Charity, ogling her as she filled mugs with cider. Later, when she started for the creek with a lantern and a bucket, he poked a friend with ox-like shoulders next to him, and they followed her. They'd both had several mugs of the bandits' cider, and the younger man, the blond, reeled into his friend as they walked. Morris grabbed his gun and signaled for Saul to come with him after the men. He called, and the two soldiers slouched back to the fire, watching Morris and Saul amble down the steep bank after Charity. At last Betsy could wash at the creek. She'd have the light from Charity's lantern and Morris's protection. She hurried after them.

A few yards behind Morris, Betsy slid on putty-colored ground down the embankment, but she kept her footing by gripping small trees and shrubs along the path the family had worn to the creek. The ground, smooth and hard as wet marble, reflected the glow of the half moon. At the stream, Saul stretched an arm, blocking Betsy's path. "Mrs. Randall, you stay by the fire. I'll bring water."

She pushed Saul's arm aside. "Where's Charity? Where's Mr. Morris?" Betsy couldn't see either of them on the bank.

Saul looked out across the creek. "They gone."

Charity's lantern hung from a branch upstream. Betsy listened for voices, but only heard the gurgle of the falls.

"Mr. Morris don' want nobody down here." He looked upstream, as if he feared that Morris would catch him talking to Betsy, but she had no intention of going back up the slippery bank without washing her face in fresh water. She stepped around him toward the lantern light.

He spoke out loud enough for the camp to hear. "Mrs. Randall, you not s'posed to be by the creek."

Exasperated, she said, "I need to wet my kerchief." The bank was flat, the sand soaked from the stream. She stepped past Saul.

Morris and Charity had tracked the wet bank to willows growing around a small pond at the base of the waterfall.

Charity's bare foot kicked the branches. Betsy lurched to help her. Morris had Charity on the ground, grunting while she kicked the air. Betsy spun back to get Saul, but he was scrambling up the bank. Betsy didn't call for Gray or any of the men. Ashamed, angry, a coward, she trudged back up the slope.

Leaving the fire, the lieutenant walked to Betsy, puffing on a pipe. Before she could tell him that Morris was raping Charity, he scolded her about the dangers of going down to the creek—true at any time, but at twilight, bears and other predators prowled. The Seneca would seize the chance to kidnap her. If she had need of water, she should send Charity or Saul. And before Betsy could say that the night was not safe for Charity, that at this moment, Morris was taking advantage of the dark to force himself on her, Gray said, "Mrs. Randall, James Morris is a man of his word. If he follows a woman to the water, he'll bring her back." He turned away to suck on his pipe and the tobacco in the bowl burned red. "You are my concern."

He walked away, his back straight, his head high, his step sure.

Betsy didn't move. Her feet seemed glued to the ground, her body numb. She didn't protest when the fiddler came to take her arm. She said, "Mr. Morris is forcing himself on Charity."

Harmon kicked a tuft of grass until it came out of the ground by the roots. "You don't know that, Mrs. Randall."

When Betsy saw a look in his eyes that acknowledged she was telling the truth, Betsy said, "They were as close as the wagon is to us now. Fewer than ten steps away. Yes, it is dusk, but he had Charity on the ground."

"If you saw that, Mrs. Randall, you were in the wrong

place." His voice quiet, his eyes down, sadness lined his face.

"She lost her shoe," Betsy said. It had been flung a little way from the willows.

He nodded. "Ned or me. We'll find it before we leave in the morning. Benjamin will find a safe place for her to sleep tonight."

Listening for Charity to come up the hill, Betsy took one slow step at a time to the wagon. As she climbed into the bed that Charity and Benjamin had made, Phillipa whispered, "Where's Charity? I sent her for water and she is still not back."

"Ask Lieutenant Gray." Betsy didn't want to look at Phillipa, but the young woman was shaking, her knees curled to her chest. Betsy put her arms around her. Above the wagon, stars speckled the sky. Sarah Smollett Fulton wouldn't think so highly of Mr. James Morris if she'd been in the clearing that night. A sob, a little bark, came out of Phillipa's throat. "She should be here now." She grasped Betsy's hand. "Lieutenant Gray forbids me to have Charity sleep with us in the wagon."

Betsy's shame for doing nothing to protect Charity sat like a grotesque old man on her chest. Her back ached from the jostling all day in the wagon, but she hurt more from having run away without helping Charity and being too cowardly to stand up to Gray.

Chapter 19

In her dream, a fire started in Asa's galley on the *Sally Dash* and blazed toward the sleeping children. Betsy sat up. She *did* smell fire. No longer on the ship but in the clearing, she had to leave the wagon without disturbing Phillipa before the smoke from the smoldering logs made her vomit. She gripped the wagon and placed one foot on a spoke of the wheel to jump down to the ground. Ghostly quiet, she stooped and raced to the trees, hoping to get away without alerting the sentry before she threw up. If she could get far enough into the woods, hovering leaves and thick shrubs would muffle her retching. Every time she and Phillipa got off the wagon, Gray, Morris, Harmon, and Reinke would warn them, as they would warn the troops, about losing their way if they wandered into the woods. But Betsy had no choice. She'd look for markers to lead her back, and she'd listen for the waterfall to guide her return.

A lightning-scarred tree at the edge of the clearing would be her signpost of the camp. Close to it, a mottled trunk reflected the scant light. She'd remember the long leaves glistening like blades on a triangle of laurel bushes. With her hands clamped over her mouth, she took ten steps, straddled a dead tree, and skirted a clump of small bushes. No one would hear her. She no longer heard the creek, but she would have the dead tree and the laurel to guide her return.

Kneeling, doubled over, Betsy puked until her gut ached. Sitting on her heels, wiping her mouth on her sleeve, she wished she could hear the water, go down to the edge of the stream, and wash her mouth. The nausea wasn't from the fire or from her shame—it was from her body telling her she was going to have a child. She had no husband, but she would have a baby.

Faint, she grabbed a thick vine hanging from a tree, pulled herself up, and hugged it, waiting for her dizziness to pass before she retraced her steps to the camp. She came to the three laurel bushes, but instead of one tree with splotchy bark, there were two. No, three. And she hadn't come to the fallen tree. She'd never seen a bush blooming with white flowers. She hadn't noticed any pine. Sniffing for the fire, for the burnt home, she smelled the scent of moist earth in the woods. She couldn't hear the splash from the waterfall. She took three steps to the left. Silence. The trees changed again. It had been dark, but she'd been able to identify markers. Mottled bark was everywhere and most of the bushes had long, smooth leaves shining in the predawn. "Lieutenant Gray." No answer. Louder, she yelled for Reinke and Harmon. "Phillipa! Hello! Help!" Not even an echo. "Mr. Reinke, can't you hear me?" Calling, hurrying to a light that might be the fire, she tripped on a root.

The ground was soft, but twigs and bits of gravel pricked her hands. The sharp-eared surveyor or Saul would come. The troops were young and would hear the least sound.

Someone would lead her to the camp. No sooner did she call "Mr. Morris," than he grabbed her and covered her mouth.

It wasn't Morris.

The man was black but covered with whitish-gray clay. His wild hair was matted with earth that matched the brown of the trees and the ground. He wore nothing but the clay and a small cloth that hung from a string at his waist. Was he Seneca?

She screamed, but with his hand over her mouth, the clay suffocated her. Nothing came. She pushed on his arms, wriggling to be free, but he grasped her wrists in one hand, pressing it to her chest, holding her against his chest, not moving, until her heartbeat slowed. He wasn't hurting her, not pulling her arm back as the pirate LeBrun had, but steadying her. Slowly he took his hand away from her mouth and loosened his grasp, but he didn't let her go. Clay covered all but the circles of his eyes, making them more distinct. They were kind eyes.

Gently, he stepped away and waved for her to follow. Speaking a language so strange she couldn't distinguish the words, he led her as if a path were marked for him, holding back branches to keep them from slapping back into her face and scratching her. He urged for her to walk faster. Far off, an owl wooed. The rumbling waterfall splashed right next to them. They'd come around the back of the burnt house, opposite the fire and the sentries. By the time she had figured out where she stood and turned to thank him, he'd disappeared.

Morris leaped from a crouch near the wagon, his rifle aimed at Betsy.

"Mr. Morris." He wouldn't be able to see Betsy in the

shadows of the trees, but he and the sentries would recognize her voice. The clay-covered man would have been a target, but they'd never spot him.

Morris lowered his gun.

Betsy tucked loose strands of hair into her cap and walked into the clearing. "Good morning. I didn't mean to startle you." She brushed leaves and dirt from her skirt, but he grabbed her arm, squeezing down to the bone above her elbow. Betsy yelped, surprised but not afraid. He wouldn't hurt her with people sleeping a few feet away. His nails dug into her arm when Betsy twisted to get away. He smelled of sweat, horse, and tobacco; the sour stink from last night's cider hit her like a fist. "Mrs. Randall, you had no business going to the creek." Every whisker in the stubble on his chin seemed to bristle. "I whipped the boy for not keepin you back, but the fault was yours."

"I wanted your protection at the creek. I thought you went to help Charity, not force yourself on her."

"What happens with that nigger gal is between me and the man payin me." He jerked Betsy up against his side. "He wants whelps that won't whimper, and there's not a whimper in my blood. I got no appetite for Miss Townsend's whore, but I'll earn my pay."

Miss Townsend's whore? The words struck Betsy, but the strange protector in the woods had given her courage. She faced Morris. "You don't know Charity, or you couldn't speak of her like that."

"Oh, I know that gal. And I know Osborne's niece. As unnatural as her slave." Morris spat in the direction of the wagon, where, as if to prove him right, Charity climbed into the wagon to be with Phillipa. "The Lord made women for men. That's nature's order. It's in the Bible." He looked at the men around the fire, raking smoldering logs to rekindle them. "A woman such as yourself would be safer sleeping with the troops."

Betsy left him to get her shawl from the wagon. She saw Charity cuddled alongside Phillipa. Betsy sat down to stare at the fire. In a few months, others would know she was expecting a child. Isaac had no understanding of this wilderness. She sat on the ground, her knees snug to her chest.

———

With the vicar's saplings for Good Hope loaded back on the wagon and the sun inching toward the tops of the trees, Gray led the expedition out of the clearing. Next to Phillipa on the bench, Betsy braided a thin string with a little of Charity's straw. Charity had complained that her bones hurt that morning. She slept on her side between the clumps of boxwood. Betsy asked, "Miss Townsend, if Charity has a child, whose would it be?"

Phillipa pricked herself. A spot of blood plumped when she squeezed her thumb against her finger. "You said you'd call me 'Phillipa.'" She pouted and sucked the blood before she corrected her posture. "Charity isn't having a child." She licked her wound again.

The wheels of the wagon creaked along. Betsy braided straw and watched Phillipa weave green thread with some gray silk to embroider leaves shaded like those Betsy had thought would point the way to the camp that morning. "But if she did have a child?"

Phillipa stopped her work and turned to look at the trees the wagon passed. "You don't understand, Mrs. Randall. Niggers ... Africans ... Negroes. They're like children."

She sighed and tested the tightness of her stitching before she aimed the needle for the next stitch. "They'd be wild if we didn't care for them. They run off at the first chance. They don't have families like yours or mine." Phillipa held her finger away from the cloth. "People who own slaves are responsible for them. I care for Charity as best I can."

Neither Harmon nor Benjamin, who drove the team of chestnut geldings, moved, but stared straight ahead. Betsy wondered, from the way they sat, if they'd heard what she and Phillipa had said. The man in the woods must be a runaway like the black pirate Josiah, but Josiah ran off after he'd learned English. Did the man hiding in the woods coat his body with clay to keep warm or to keep from being discovered? Why didn't he dress in deerskin like Reinke and Mrs. Fulton's Pamunkey woman? He'd treated Betsy with kindness. So had Josiah, after he dumped Isaac overboard. He'd had a family, and he still grieved for them on the *Sally Dash*.

Ahead of the wagon, Gray's troops marched to the tune of the fife, and soon they were so far ahead, Betsy could no longer hear that shrill whistle. Reinke walked, his rifle cocked, next to the wagon. Behind them, Petty slumped on his mare. The third day of trees. From time to time, the wagon passed a crew of men, black and white, swinging axes and clearing land. The men sang as they worked to the rhythm, like the crew on the Dash, but the farther the wagon crawled, the fewer songs Betsy heard.

When Phillipa bumped Betsy's arm, she pretended to stay asleep. Phillipa huffed. "Tell Mrs. Randall about your plantation, Mr. Reinke."

"I have no land, Miss Townsend. I'm a wanderer."

With Charity asleep, her knees to her chin, and Betsy

pretending to sleep, Phillipa was left with no one to listen but the hunter. "Mr. Reinke, would you tell me about Bavaria?"

As if obliging a spoiled child, Reinke described the church organ in Augsburg. He spoke of the town where he was born, the baker on the corner of his street, his uncle, a blacksmith and a tenor in the choir. Though no older than five when his father bought passage to America, he remembered the music well.

Phillipa jostled against Betsy to select another thread from her satchel. "Do you pray in your Dutch or in English, Mr. Reinke?"

Poking folds in her skirt under her to add cushion to the pillow and keep her bones from pounding the seat, Betsy sat up. "Would you say the Lord's Prayer in German for us?"

Phillipa sat straighter. "Mrs. Randall, a person doesn't say a prayer to hear the sound."

Except for the wagon's squeal, the horses' shuffling, and faraway whistling of the recruits, the woods were silent. Betsy swallowed her annoyance with Phillipa. "On the contrary, the sound of prayer comforts us. Our Creator asks only that our intentions be sincere."

Behind them, Charity rolled to her knees and bowed her head. "Our Father, which art in Heaven …" Reinke joined the prayer. "… *Geheiligt werde dein Name. Dein Reich komme …*"

Phillipa lay her embroidery in her lap, took Betsy's arm, and together they prayed, "Thy will be done…'"

Chapter 20

The fence surprised Betsy. At the sight of the ugly log barrier, trunks and branches stacked in a zigzag, the lieutenant's vanguard of recruits erupted in a "Hurrah! Hurrah!" The sun sat above them unmoving. Over the course of the morning, the road had narrowed to ruts threading through brush and trees, and they'd made little progress. Whenever a steep patch made the load too heavy for the horses, Charity would jump from her seat and help Betsy and Phillipa down. They'd walk behind the wagon while the troops, Benjamin, Saul, and Charity pushed it from the sides and rear. Here the path, wider and flat along the fence, lay smooth beside a cleared field with stripped tree stumps, waist high, gray as tombstones, amid small scattered hills of loose soil ready to be planted. This field was Robert's land; Betsy was sure.

Isaac had expected a grand plantation comparable to the Earl of Guilford's estate. Mrs. Fulton's notched sticks fenced her garden more nobly than this scrubby fence at Good Hope.

"Your plantation, Mrs. Randall." Phillipa threw her

arms wide open. "As far as the eye can see." She cheered with Reinke, Harmon, and the others, but Morris clapped three deliberate times. He got off his horse and stomped up dust on the road. He began to clap faster, more boisterously. He called Harmon down from the wagon and the two men jigged. Everyone—except Betsy—clapped, shook hands, and embraced each other to celebrate having arrived at Good Hope at last. She grasped the seat to have something she trusted in hand. Isaac had sold their home in Brompton because he believed her brother had left them a plantation, not a wasteland fenced by stacked wood. He couldn't have envisioned these stumps and little hills of dull earth. Phillipa, who lived in a fine mansion in Williamsburg, must see how grim the land looked, but she joyously reached to yank Betsy to her feet. "Your tobacco, Mrs. Randall. Stand up."

"Miss Phillipa, sit down." Harmon had climbed back onto the wagon seat. "We're not at the gate." He snapped the whip above the horses' necks to start again. "Mrs. Randall has the rest of her life to see this field." He turned to wink at Betsy. "Why, in good time, she'll be buried by her brother here at Good Hope."

Betsy stared at the man's back. Buried in this wilderness? She hoped not. The wagon rolled on, and Phillipa thumped down on the seat. Scrunching her nose at the fiddler, she snuggled against Betsy. "I can't wait to see Robert Harrington's house—your home."

Having seen the fence, Betsy had no trouble imagining how squalid the house must be. She and her family had left a brick home in Brompton. She could hear the click of the key when Isaac locked the door. He'd left that key with their neighbor for a man and his wife who would live there. They'd have Betsy's white picket gate with a firm latch which had swung open to the tiny plot of land she'd tended, a garden with evenly spaced rows of carrots, turnips, radishes, and leeks. Thyme and mint gave off their fragrance along the walk inside the brick walls of her garden. In Virginia, Betsy had seen palaces along the York River, mansions twice the size of Osborne's house in Williamsburg. And she'd seen Harmon's place: a shambled collection of barns and shacks. Mrs. Fulton's clapboard house had added rooms for people stopping overnight. If Robert had built a fence like this one, his house would be a hovel.

Phillipa wriggled on her seat, muttering that Harmon should make the horses trot, chattering about the many guests and parties Betsy would have. "People will come for Christmas and stay till February." The lieutenant's plantation was a half-day's ride; his friends would stop to see Betsy, too. Playing the older, wiser sister, Phillipa put her arm around Betsy. "Stop worrying, little worm. You're home at last."

Home? Why hadn't Betsy returned to England? Bennett would have helped her find a ship that pirates wouldn't dare attack. She'd never wanted to hear the shriek of rigging or the snap of sails again, but it wasn't the fear of a voyage that had kept her in Virginia. Taking over Robert's farm had been Isaac's plan, but she'd seen how well her brother dressed, how scornfully he'd smiled at their parlor, how his back stiffened when she showed him where he would sleep in the children's room, and how he'd arranged to get an invitation to stay with the Earl of Guilford instead. She couldn't dislodge the memory of that visit. After Robert's second visit, Isaac had convinced Betsy they should give up their Brompton home. Less than a year later, they received the news of Robert's death and of his leaving his plantation to Isaac Randall, Esquire, his sister's husband. As she tried to rid herself of thoughts of her brother, he appeared, sitting on a stump in the field, laughing at her. She tried to see through him, but he was real. Very much alive. Not a ghost. This was his home. He'd tricked her into coming, to seeing how he'd chopped down trees and left stumps. Now, he was no longer sitting on a stump but in a fine walnut armchair upholstered in cordovan leather from Isaac's parental home. At Osborne's suggestion, Betsy had left that chair in Williamsburg. But Robert sat in it now, before her, with his legs crossed, amused by his sister's dismay.

She blinked and looked the other direction, across the road to the trees with thick vines hanging from their branches. Her brother Robert should have known enough to vanish before she turned back, but he stayed on in his velvet waistcoat and white stockings. Robert had crowed about finding soil that would yield a higher grade of tobacco. Phillipa's uncle had affirmed that Robert Harrington grew a superior crop; and there sat Robert, daring her to claim his land when she knew nothing about growing tobacco or harvesting it. Five years older than she, he'd never told her any of his secrets.

Another cheer went up. Robert Harrington didn't stay. He was gone when Saul opened the newly painted white gate to the graveled lane between whitewashed fences of smooth, planed boards. In a few years, the young trees planted on either side would completely shade the road to the house.

Phillipa dropped her head on Betsy's shoulder. "How charming. You must be pleased, Mrs. Randall."

The clop, clop, clop of the hooves and the crunch of the wheels on the gravel lane comforted Betsy. Red-brown cows with wide horns and brass bells grazed in a broad meadow. New calves romped in the grass. Sheep, their thick wool ready to be shorn, clustered near a brook. The smells of the meadow mixed with memories of Betsy's childhood in Surrey. Robert would have been at home here. Opposite the pasture, beyond an expanse of grass, the sun's reflection shone from four small windows on the second floor of a large clapboard house with a low-pitched roof. Two young oak trees partially shaded the proud front door. Large windows gleamed on either side. Betsy let herself slip into a fantasy in which Isaac sat beside her, instead of Phillipa. He would lift first Mary and then Alice down from the wagon. He'd even lift Betsy, as if she weighed nothing. David? David slept in his cradle in the wagon, and Betsy wasn't expecting a baby—not yet. In this waking dream, she ran to catch up with the girls and grabbed Alice by the hand. Mary kept looking back, and Betsy couldn't wait to pull her close, to kiss that soft skin of her neck. "Mimi, you wait," Alice said.

Mary stopped. "Kittens, Mama. Little kittens."

But it wasn't Mary. It was Phillipa tugging at Betsy's arm to show her a gray cat carrying a kitten into the barn.

"I see them." Betsy wiped tears from her cheeks because Mary and Alice had been there. They were gone now, but they had been happy running to the house.

An Englishman in a black straight-brimmed hat and a plain black coat marched from the house down the gravel walk to the wagon. Barrel-chested, with bushy sideburns and jowls like a bulldog, he squinted at the travelers. A whip wound in a tight circle hung from his belt.

Gray and his troops, in formation, saluted. Two setters yapped from the steps of the house. Morris's hound barked until the surveyor snapped his fingers near the dog's ear, and it slunk under the wagon.

Whoever the man in Quaker black might be, he belonged on the plantation. He scanned the group until he spotted Reinke, and then his face and shoulders softened with relief. Morris introduced the man to the lieutenant. Except for Harmon and Gray, who'd told Betsy that they'd known her brother, none of the men had said they knew anyone at Good Hope. Why hadn't she asked? During the journey from Williamsburg, Isaac would have gleaned whatever he could about the plantation. He would have sensed a moral obligation to learn about growing and selling tobacco. Isaac would have known about this man in the broad black hat.

"Mrs. Randall, may I introduce the overseer here at Good Hope." Gray extended his hand. "Martin Whitmore had the complete confidence of your brother, Robert Harrington."

The overseer removed his hat and looked up at Betsy when he heard "Robert Harrington." His hat left a red dent across his broad forehead. Making no pretense of a gentleman's finesse, he scrutinized Betsy, moving his stare slowly from her face to her hands limp in her lap, studying her as boldly as a cattle judge observes livestock at a country fair.

To cut short his stare, Betsy smiled and bent toward him, hoping to see kindness in his face. Below the red line from his hat, his skin was brown, his face round and friendly with a small, flat nose. His mouth twitched. Betsy said, "My brother spoke highly of you." If her brother had told her stories about his overseer when he last returned to England, she didn't remember any of them. She should have been more interested in the stories he'd told.

Red splotches flamed from Whitmore's neck to his brow.

He cleared his throat—twice. "Madam…" He pulled at his neckerchief. "Uh-uh-um …"

Glad he lacked the skill of hiding his reactions to others, Betsy watched him turn his hat like a platter, as if the words were printed on the wide brim. He started, "Mrs. Isaac Randall …" He peeked up at her and then back down at his wheeling hat while he talked about the grief that she must feel about her husband and children being lost at sea. Her brother, Robert Harrington, often spoke of her children. "It was 'clever Mary' and 'pretty little Alice.'" His red cheeks deepened to a dark wine. "Robert Harrington …" He hung his head. When he looked up, grief distorted his features. "Your brother, Ma'am … " He could not go on. Her brother had been dead two years, and Martin Whitmore was still mourning him.

"Me and Harry—we were Whit and Harry to each other, Ma'am—we worked shoulder to shoulder every day, blazing trees on the boundary of his property. We cleared the land, chopped wood to build pens, and put up a place to sleep. Not a day went by that we didn't saw logs, plane boards, hammer nails until we got the house and barn built." He motioned to the farmyard where chickens pecked at the gravel. "Together we worked, shovel and pick, digging to get the ground right for tobacco. We hoed soil by moonlight alongside slaves to get seedlings in the ground and harvest the first crop."

Whitmore sucked in air, filled his chest, and bowed straight from the waist. "Welcome to Good Hope." A bald spot on his crown was the size of a child's fist.

Lieutenant Gray, Phillipa, and the others turned to Betsy, expecting a reply. She pictured Isaac assuring Whitmore that just as Robert Harrington had every confidence in him, he knew he could rely on Whitmore as well. She thought of her brother sitting on that walnut chair in the field. She would let Whitmore know … know what? That he could keep running the plantation, but from this day forward, he would answer to her? She stood and gripped Phillipa's shoulder, partly for balance, partly to absorb the girl's confidence, but before she could begin, Whitmore pivoted toward the barn. He banged the handle of his bull-whip on a large brass disk.

Betsy jumped. The horses backed into the wagon, and Betsy plopped onto the seat before Harmon quieted the geldings with a soft "Whoa."

Betsy stood up again. "Thank you, Mr. Whitmore." Isaac would have thought about how he would greet the people working at Good Hope, but Betsy had not; nevertheless, if she kept Robert in mind, and his justifiable pride in his estate, and how responsibly Mr. Whitmore had cared for the property, she could find words of gratitude that would have satisfied Isaac. "I cannot thank you enough for the sympathy you have expressed." He'd said the girls' names too easily, but he couldn't know that she wanted their names sealed in her heart. "Clearly, my brother's success with this plantation owes much to your work, and it is good to be at Good Hope at last. You must have heard the cheer when we came to the field and then again at the white gate." She went on to tell him that although Robert had told her husband that he had estab-lished a bit of Surrey in the middle of Virginia, neither Mr. Randall nor she had envisioned a house and barn that surpassed her brother's descriptions. The stock looked as healthy as any cattle in England. The cleared fields pre-pared for planting proved that Mr. Whitmore had put in long hours of labor to ensure another successful tobacco crop. Her brother could expect no greater tribute than to have Good Hope continue to be cared for. Mr. Whitmore had proven to be an honest steward of the plantation and a faithful friend to her brother. Betsy had been moved by the grief the man had shown.

He nodded in agreement as she spoke, looking off at the barn and the fields, and finally stood with his hat in his hands, his head bowed.

"Amen, amen!" Gray led the chorus of travelers. He put out his hand to help Betsy down from the wagon. "You are home, Mrs. Randall."

Whitmore smiled broadly. "Yes. You are home." He hit the brass disk a second time. And again.

Betsy pressed her palm to her heart. The horses shied; Harmon jiggled the reins to quiet them. She would need to ask Whitmore not to ring that gong without warning her. The air continued to vibrate from the clang of the brass. The knell faded, deadened by the sound of trampling from the direction of the fields of a throng of dusty, sweaty, and barefoot people. Many were in tattered clothes; others were dressed in plain homespun cut to fit. They looked at the ground as they marched in threes and fours from different directions and assembled between the fields and the barn. Some carried hoes, some shovels or picks, and some walked with their arms by their sides. A few of the women had babies tied to their backs.

Slaves.

Captain Bennett had told Betsy her brother's estate included slaves, but she'd put the thought out of her mind until last night when Phillipa had asked her how many slaves worked at Good Hope, and she'd said she had no idea. She did know. The title to the property specified seventy-three African slaves. That title was dated 1711, two years ago.

The troops next to the wagon shifted closer to one another as the shadowy group—more men than women, most as black as Josiah, most carrying hoes or shovels—came even with the barn door and stopped, silent. They bowed their heads. Josiah had said his people moaned when the slavers burned their village and herded them to the ships. These people herded themselves into groups and waited. The men in homespun shirts and long pants and the women in loose smocks stood in four groups between the field and the barn. A few men yanked caps off their heads. One woman with an infant in a sling pulled the baby to her breast. From behind the house, a cluster of children followed an old woman waving a cane. One small child ran to grab the skirt of a woman. A boy scratched a dirty bandage on his calf with his other foot.

Phillipa was counting. "... Sixty-four... "

"Father in heaven," Betsy said. She couldn't imagine how her brother had collected all these people. Slaves. *Her slaves.*

"You have quite a herd," Petty said. The journalist had weaseled his way to Betsy's side. "I haven't counted all of them, but you have at least eighty."

On Betsy's left, Phillipa said, "Don't listen to him. You have almost a hundred. All well fed."

Reaching past Petty, Gray grasped Betsy's elbow. "These are your people, Mrs. Randall. Whitmore must see you claim your property."

The overseer strutted in front of the slaves like a rooster in a chicken yard. He may have seen Betsy recoil from Gray, who tightened his grip, pulling her to him. "They're watching," he said.

They were, but Betsy had nothing to say to them. She both wanted to look at each of the slaves and to turn away, to get back on the wagon and have Harmon drive her to Yorktown.

Gray's breath made her shiver. "They won't look at you, Mrs. Randall, but they're reading your thoughts."

Betsy tried to twist free, but Gray didn't let go. He raised his hand for Whitmore to proceed with his plans for the assembly. He hadn't finished advising Betsy and kept his low voice. "There's no trickster like an African. They have to believe that you keep a watchful eye even in your sleep. Your brother apparently had them believing he watched from the grave."

Unafraid of Gray or the men and women, Betsy smiled at Whitmore and at them. She kept her face tranquil though she had no idea what would happen next. Smiling at the crowd, she said softly, "Lieutenant, I'm acquainted with Africans." She nodded to the overseer, hoping he'd send the people away.

"Mrs. Randall, I'll call the boys leadin your Nig-groes so they can get back to work." He raised his hand. Three big men stepped toward the overseer. "Your brother named these men Aeneas, Castor, and Pollux." Whitmore puffed his chest. "Great warriors of antiquity." From the fourth cluster of slaves, a small, muscled man, no taller than a child, ran, head down like a charging bull, to stand with the three. He bounced next to them like a bee caught in a glass jar, his head bobbing right and left. Whitmore looked proudly at the fourth man and clasped his hands behind his back, his bullwhip looped in his fist. "Four drivers for our field teams." He stepped closer to Betsy and Gray and called out in a proud voice, "Xerxes."

The small man leaped out from the group, knelt with his head to one knee, and jumped back to his feet. Behind him, men raised their right arms, their hoes held skyward; they filed in four lines of ten each. His own hoe held like a spear, Xerxes yelled, "Hey-yah!" and shot off toward the fields, and those he'd called ran after him.

Gray clapped, a soft applause, and Betsy did the same, but she wouldn't want to be driven by Xerxes, who seemed a favorite of Whitmore. The overseer waited until the crew had left the yard to call out, "Aeneas." Whitmore told her that the team of thirty Aeneas led, men wearing loose rags and worn pants, cleared fields, kept up fences, and broke rock when the lane required gravel. They trotted back up the lane after Aeneas. Castor and Pollux came from opposite sides of the yard. Their gangs had both men and women. Several of the women had babies in slings tied securely to their backs. Half followed Castor south of the house; Pollux led his half north beyond the barn. The men behind Castor started a chant: "Master's corn growin day by day." The women sang, "Hoein in the sun, hoein in the sun." Their steps sped up as their words came faster. The group headed north after Pollux began another call-and-response that carried back to the house after they were out of sight.

Whitmore clipped his whip back on his belt and looked toward the house. The old woman and little children trudged off around to the back. From the shade of a young oak near the house, a woman, who looked English, stepped into the sun. She had the composed posture of a gentlewoman and stood taller than Betsy. Her skin had the glow of sunlight against her plain linen dress. Her white apron, trimmed with the same lace as her cap, bulged over her stomach. She seemed to be smiling at the overseer, and it was clear that she was proud for him. When Betsy faced her, though heavy with child, the woman curtsied gracefully, unhindered by her pregnancy.

Whitmore smiled at the woman. "This is Deborah. She tends the house and the garden."

Before Betsy could return the curtsy, Phillipa bumped against her, as if by accident. "Never. Never bow to a slave." Her words burned Betsy's neck. "You'll have to keep an eye on your house slave, Mrs. Randall. That Deborah looks clever."

That woman stepped aside for a little girl of eight or ten, with fair skin and light brown hair. She looked like Mary, though taller. She squinted, like Mary would, at the strangers. She had Mary's high forehead, square shoulders, and questioning frown. Her curls, tighter than Mary's, were pulled back at her neck. Her upper lip was peaked like Mary's. Betsy wanted to run to her, but she couldn't move. The girl clutched a bunch of purple and pink flowers. She wore rose-colored taffeta, a dress that Mary would have picked for herself. It had been let down—as far as possible—to mid-calf. Lace had been added to the sleeves to make them longer. When she walked, her red shoes seemed to crimp her feet. She stretched her arm out straight to give Betsy the flowers without getting too close to her. After a look to her mother, she curtsied and bobbed back up, still holding the flowers.

Instead of taking the bouquet, Betsy reached to brush the child's soft eyebrow as she would sometimes touch Mary's when the preacher's sermon threatened to last until Monday afternoon, but the girl arched away from Betsy's hand. Distrustful of strangers, as Mary would have been, she thrust the flowers farther out, impatient to be rid of them, and this time Betsy took them. She tried to thank the girl, but her voice failed.

Betsy wanted to move closer to the girl's mother, but then she saw another woman, with darker red-brown skin, holding the hand of a little boy no more than three. He pulled free and ran to hide behind Deborah's skirt. When he peeked out, she could see that he had her brother's eyes, and his brow wrinkled as Robert's once did. This second woman in rough homespun had a slight bulge under her patched apron, and Betsy wondered if Whitmore, like Morris, wanted slaves to have children who took after him.

"The flowers are lovely," Phillipa said. She pinched the soft skin above Betsy's elbow.

"Yes, they're beautiful." Betsy wanted to walk up to Deborah—she was sure the woman's children were her brother's children, her own niece and nephew—but Phillipa kept a firm hold on Betsy's skirt and tugged for her to stay back. Betsy fought her instinct to rip her skirt out of Phillipa's hands and run to the children. She looked at the overseer. "Mr. Whitmore, you haven't introduced the children."

"No. No, I have not." He grasped the bullwhip at his belt and beckoned for the woman behind Deborah to come forward. "But first, this here's Naomi. She helps Deborah keep Mr. Harrington's house and does the washing." The woman curtsied and stepped back into Deborah's shadow. Then Whitmore motioned to the girl with the flowers. She approached and stood near him, her head tipped up to smile at him. "Harry named Deborah's daughter Susannah and her boy Isaiah."

Betsy said, "Susannah, a pretty name for a pretty child." The girl stared back at her. "And Isaiah," Betsy said. She started again for the children, but Phillipa held her back.

Teasing, but tense, Phillipa said, "Mrs. Randall, you mustn't scare the children."

And Phillipa was right. She understood the children. Betsy was a stranger to them. They didn't know her. Susannah looked with longing at Phillipa's blue silk dress, and Betsy wished that she'd worn the black gown Bennett had ordered for her in Yorktown so the little girl might admire it too.

From behind his mother's skirts, the little boy watched Betsy. Yes, these were her brother's children. Her niece and nephew. Cousins Mary, Alice, and David never knew they had. Betsy wanted to hug them close to her, but before she could move, Susannah ran back to her mother. Betsy held the bouquet to her heart. Had she known these children were at Good Hope, she would have come as soon as she disembarked at Yorktown. Robert had bequeathed his estate to Isaac, his brother-in-law, when his own son had a prior right. Unable to look at the children and their mother, Betsy looked at her feet. Gravel and sparse grass. A speckled hen scratched in the dirt, clucking to herself. Betsy didn't understand how Robert's children could be slaves to Whitmore.

"Your house, ma'am." Whitmore stood at the open door. "Empty, but cared for since the day we carried your brother's body to his grave."

Betsy stepped back, almost bumping Phillipa. The two women, Susannah, and Isaiah were leaving, walking around to the back of the house.

Gray invited Whitmore to join him and the surveyor, the woodsman, and the troops for a venison delicacy that the Pamunkey guides, Ned and Nighthawk, would prepare.

Phillipa led Betsy toward the front door. "There's no

hedge, but Benjamin can plant the box here. I cannot wait to see your house."

Betsy feared going into the house. Her brother might surprise her there as he had in the field, and she didn't want Phillipa to see her fear. She frowned at the gravel walk and at Phillipa. "When did you decide there must be a hedge?"

"I'm sorry. Uncle says I must learn discretion. And something else I never remember."

"Restraint," Charity said off to the side. She carried small bags of belongings for both Phillipa and Betsy, waiting for the two women to go ahead of her into the house.

"Yes," Phillipa agreed, smiling now that she remembered, having been reminded. "Restraint. But he's wrong. Every lady practices restraint. To be a lady is to practice restraint."

At the word "restraint," Betsy thought of Deborah. The woman had mastered restraint, and Betsy could see that she intended to teach her daughter. Deborah wore her simple linen dress and a lace-trimmed apron with an elegance Betsy wished she had. Bedraggled and dusty in her old green dress and worn shawl, she walked into her brother's house. Whitmore said that it had been empty, but it smelled lived in, well kept, with waxed floors and polished furniture. A red Moorish carpet, scattered with tigers and lions hunting deer, cushioned her feet. Where had Robert found such a rug? The walls, papered in the same green that Osborne used in his home, were radiant with light from a window at the back of the foyer. To the right, through an open door, was a dining room with a long table and a sparkling chandelier. Beyond the staircase, two doors opened on either side of the hall. From a door on the right, a soft clatter of dishes and the fragrance of warm bread promised that she and Phillipa would be served tea soon. Next to the newel post, on a small oval table, a crystal vase held tiny sky-blue flowers: forget-me-nots.

"A delicate arrangement." Phillipa used her older woman's voice.

Deborah arrived from the back room with a tray. "Mr. Whitmore buys Master Harrington's favorite tea. Would you like a cup?"

"Yes, of course. Mrs. Randall and I are fond of tea." Phillipa steered Betsy into the sitting room.

Betsy smiled. What difference did it make if Phillipa answered for her?

She'd anticipated a home with Mrs. Fulton's rough-hewn plank floors and coarse plaster walls. Robert's home had fine carpets that had been freshly beaten, and the varnished woodwork shone. Betsy chose to sit on the settee upholstered with slick black horsehair. Robert had arranged seven blue-and-white vases on the mantel. Above the vases, a convex mirror caught the whole room in miniature. The curtains, which matched the silk walls, had been roped back from the windows. Two bookcases stood on the back wall. Had Robert read the books? He had asked Isaac to send books but had never written that he had a daughter. The little boy might not have been born before Robert was killed, but he could have written a letter telling them he was expecting a second child.

For once, Phillipa was quiet, and Betsy, appreciating her repose, watched Deborah stir the tea and set about to pour.

Suddenly, Phillipa jumped off the settee and walked to a harpsichord between the hearth and the foyer. "Flamed mahogany. The grain flares like a Chinese chrysanthemum." Her fingers glided over the surface of the instrument. She read from the panel above the closed keyboard. "'P. John Craxton, London, 1691.' In gold, Mrs. Randall."

Deborah watched Phillipa try to lift the lid.

"Where's the key to unlock this harpsichord?" Phillipa felt under the instrument.

Deborah uncovered a plate of cold meat and lifted a napkin that lay on top of slices of oat bread. "Master Harrington kept that key in his bureau, Miss Townsend." She brought Betsy a cup of tea and set the other on a side table.

"Have your tea, Phillipa." Betsy didn't want her rummaging for the keys in Robert's desk. She spread a piece of bread with spiced ham. While she ate, she wouldn't think about Robert, the men and women from the fields, or Lieutenant Gray and his troops—not even the niece and nephew she'd just met, this woman in the lace cap, or the key to the harpsichord.

"When you finish your tea, if you want to see your home, I'll take you from room to room." Deborah backed out of the room, her head bowed, smiling. Isaac had known about the slaves, but being a banker hadn't prepared him for managing a plantation. He had no idea of the work Robert—Harry—had done, of the calluses of farm labor. And Betsy? Good Hope had no need of her dishes, her furniture—no need of her.

To Betsy's surprise, Phillipa said she had no intention of following Betsy while Deborah showed her the house. She'd sit, quiet as a mouse, right where she was and contemplate the beauty of the room. No, she wouldn't hunt for the key to the harpsichord. If she decided to read, she'd put the books back on the shelves in exactly the same place. Betsy and Phillipa reached simultaneously for a slice of bread. They laughed and then ate in silence.

Chapter 21

Next to the forget-me-nots, Deborah waited, contemplating the tiny blue flowers, one hand on the side of her round belly; she gazed as if she saw a world in the flowers and the vase. When she heard Betsy approach, she brightened with a strained delight. The calm in her eyes remained: a shadow of whatever thought caused her to smile at the flowers. She had the kind of beauty that holds the eye. No wonder Robert had never found a wife he favored. Facing her, Betsy forced herself to be congenial for her brother's sake. Deborah had no reason to be glad that Betsy had come to claim Robert's property, but she greeted Betsy kindly. "Welcome to Master Harrington's home."

"You cared for it well."

Deborah eyed Betsy with a sharp, defensive look before repossessing her smile and averting her eyes to the floor. And Betsy would have missed the look if she hadn't been determined to watch Deborah closely—not due to Gray's callous advice or Phillipa's caution about keeping an eye on her house slave, but because Betsy had known little of her brother for many years, and Deborah may have been the last person with him, the one who closed his eyes. Deborah's smile to please shielded her feelings and protected any private thoughts that Betsy might wish to know about Robert.

"Master Harrington hoped you would visit Good Hope, Mrs. Randall." She gestured for Betsy to go through the open double doors into the dining room.

"Did he?" Robert had urged Isaac to come, to secure better trades for his tobacco. Isaac thought Robert might have planned to spend more time at cards, leaving Isaac to manage the plantation, but her brother had done well enough by himself with the help of Whitmore. He must have succeeded with either cards or tobacco to purchase the beautiful table reflecting a sparkling chandelier above it, and the twelve graceful chairs. Betsy pictured Robert sitting there with the Earl of Guilford. As if in a dream, she saw Deborah sitting at the opposite end of the table, listening to Robert describe his horses to the earl.

Softly, Deborah said, "Master Harrington believed a fine wood table makes a house a home." She asked if Mrs. Randall and Miss Townsend had enjoyed the tea. Was it flavorful? Not bitter, she hoped. Her soft voice carried an apology as if she couldn't hope to serve Betsy as well as she deserved. "Master Harrington wanted tea like he remembered having in Surrey."

Robert had never spoken of tea. Cards? Yes. Clothing and fine furniture? Definitely. He flaunted his obsession with horses and tobacco, his expertise with wine. Betsy said the tea was every bit as strong as her mother made it. She was thinking how struck her mother would have been by a Dutch stove with gleaming blue and white tiles in the dining room. Robert had bragged about buying the stove, but

Betsy hadn't known how welcoming its shine would be. "Robert told us that each tile is a Bible story." Mary would have known the stories; Alice would have made up her own.

"I never let the fire die in the winter months." Deborah held her fingers a shadow away from a tile of Abraham sacrificing Isaac. "Master Harrington didn't want the fire to burn too strong." Graceful despite her pregnancy, she leaned over to open a small, square door in the front of the stove. She stood abruptly, put her hand to her back, and grimaced as if seized by an early labor pain. Having quieted that trouble, she invited Betsy to look inside. Scoured. "Mr. Whitmore knows the horses, the field hands, and the crops, but I know the secrets of this stove."

Stepping to the china cupboard on the north wall, Deborah said, "Master Harrington had the china shipped from London. Not one cup cracked." She handed Betsy a plate with a gilt border around a red picture of a pheasant flying up from a field. Deborah would have no use for Betsy's plain white dishes with a thin blue rim. Prudence, the servant who now worked for Martha Alder, had helped Betsy pack her dishes and some from her mother's house, a few cracked and chipped, lined and marked by stories only Betsy knew.

Choosing to leave the dining room, Betsy hurried toward sunshine coming from a window in a room at the back of the house. It was as if she were running from her brother. On a windowsill in the narrow pantry Betsy entered, a bouquet of lavender hyacinth glowed in the afternoon sun. Seeing flowers that she might have had in her own kitchen, Betsy smiled and lifted one of the flowers to set it deeper down in the water of the vase. "I doubt that Robert came into this room," Betsy said to Deborah. The wide shelf with a rack of knives for carving meat and serving food, an open-shelved cupboard with dishes, and a padlocked cabinet with a wired grid door all spoke to women's work. With a key from a bunch tied on a long ribbon attached to her apron pocket, Deborah opened the cupboard to show Betsy a row of dark green liquor bottles and a wooden sugar box. She didn't offer Betsy the keys after locking the cupboard, and Betsy chose not to demand them. She guessed one of Deborah's keys would open the harpsichord.

The way Deborah kept her eyes down bothered Betsy. Why couldn't she look directly at her? Not once had her skirt come within an inch of Betsy's gown. Betsy stepped closer, smiling to herself when Deborah backed away to slip into the dining room without touching Betsy. She said, "Deborah, the overseer said the house has been empty since my brother died, but it doesn't smell empty. It smells like a home. It's not just the flowers. Why don't you and the children live here?"

Deborah's back stiffened, her chin dropped. "Nobody lives here, ma'am. We keep the house like Master might come home. He would have wanted you to feel at home." She looked out the pantry window to the west, and Betsy waited. "Mr. Whitmore lives in that house yonder." A log kitchen house stood midway between the main house and the garden. "Master Harrington lived there too, while he and Mr. Whitmore built this house." She paused and, at the sound of footsteps from above the pantry, looked up at the ceiling.

Listening to the footsteps, Betsy said, "That may be Miss Townsend exploring the upstairs." More than one person roamed upstairs. "She must have asked Charity to bring her bag up to one of the rooms."

The frown on Deborah's face eased into a smile. She looked through the pantry window to a smaller wood house. "Mr. Whitmore used to sleep by the hearth of the kitchen dependency, but he sleeps in the loft above it now." She looked at the hyacinths. "I sleep there too." She pressed her hand to the small of her back. "I lived in the dependency until Master Harrington moved up to the big house and wanted me to be where I could serve him." A flush on her cheeks made her all the more beautiful.

"Master Harrington? My brother? You lived in this house with him?" Betsy gripped the doorknob to steady herself even though she should have guessed that Robert had lived with her as man and wife. Had he told Isaac about Deborah? Betsy walked into the hall and opened the back door for fresh air. On the ground near the garden, Lieutenant Gray and his company sat eating the roast buck that Ned or Nighthawk had shot and prepared. Beyond them and the kitchen house, two rows of unpainted, windowless cabins with clay chimneys faced a narrow dirt yard and small gardens. The closest one, larger than the others, had two windows. Betsy shivered; something about the huts brought to mind Josiah's telling her of his village. "What are those huts, Mrs. ...?

"Master Harrington called me Deb'rah, Mrs. Randall." She faced the squat sheds with their small gardens but didn't look at them. "Those the quarters."

"Quarters?"

"The slaves sleep in the cabins and grow their peas and beans in small gardens. Mr. Whitmore gives them stew meat and barley." She discreetly closed the back door as if not wanting to talk about the huts with it open. "Twelve cabins for the field hands, the foremen, and their families.

If a man and woman want to live together, Master Harrington let them build a place and raise children. The house with the windows? That's the first house Master Harrington built for him and Whit—before he had slaves. Before he had the patent to own Good Hope. He lived there before he bought me. Naomi sleeps there now." With a ghost of a smile, Deborah watched Susannah, who'd changed into a loose hemp shift, hoe in the garden next to that house.

Robert's daughter—Betsy's niece, Susannah—a slave working in a tiny garden. Betsy asked, "Where do Susannah and Isaiah sleep?"

Perhaps Deborah didn't hear her. She said that she'd served her master for twelve years. "Master Harrington brought me to Good Hope after he and Whit built the kitchen dependency, the first house with a plank floor. Xerxes and a few other slaves sawed logs and planed the wood. When they had it built, he had me sleep in the loft of the dependency with him and Whit slept near the hearth. I fixed meals for him and Mr. Whitmore. I tended the fire."

"Tended the fire?" When Robert visited them in Brompton, he'd told Isaac and Betsy about his horses and breeding cattle but never mentioned Deborah or her children. His children.

"Master Harrington visited the Phelps plantation and saw I was trained to be a house slave." Deborah faced the door across from the pantry and fanned out the keys on her ribbon. She said her master and the overseer taught her to sharpen a hoe and turn a lathe, press cider, and saddle a horse. "I hoed the garden, but I told Master Harrington that working in the fields would spoil me for housework. Mrs. Phelps, my first mistress, knew how to run a fine house, and Master Harrington wanted that." She curtsied. When she stood up, her eyelids closed. She looked tired. "Before you go into Master's bureau and the bedrooms upstairs, I'd like to show you his collection of books—the pride of Good Hope, according to Master Harrington." She motioned Betsy past the vase of forget-me-nots into the sitting room.

Phillipa no longer sat at the tea table in quiet contemplation. The room was empty. Betsy didn't go to the window, but she guessed that Phillipa had decided to rest in an upstairs bedroom.

Deborah walked to the bookcases. She said, "Master ordered the books, but he had little time to read."

Many of the titles Betsy recognized because Isaac had ordered the books when Robert asked him to send books that men in London were reading. Isaac read his Bible, John Milton's *Paradise Lost*, and John Bunyan's *Pilgrim's Progress*, but he'd asked the vicar to recommend books for his brother-in-law in the colonies. Robert may not have had time to read, but these books had been read. Some spines showed more wear than others. In some books, ribbons marked pages. A small book of Dryden's poems had black threads hanging down, and when Betsy pulled it out, she noticed two small books on either side of it. One, in a dreary ivory-colored jacket, was titled *The Second Treatise of Human Understanding*. It opened to pages of small, thick print. The other book was *An Essay Concerning Human Understanding* by John Locke. On one of Robert's return visits to Brompton, he and Isaac had argued about how man is governed and the thinking of Milton and Locke. Betsy had wanted them to stop. Now, holding the book open, she sensed she was trespassing. Had Deborah read these books? She didn't look away fast enough for Betsy not to notice her distress, and Betsy put the books back. She had no interest in the two books about understanding, but later she would read the poems Robert—or Deborah—marked.

Standing at the harpsichord, Deborah looked toward the hearth. Her hand reached for the covered keyboard.

"Do you play the harpsichord, Deborah? My brother didn't, but you do, don't you?"

Deborah stepped back from the instrument. "Master Harrington enjoyed music, Mrs. Randall." She smiled at the harpsichord and flicked away a bit of dust that Betsy couldn't see—no wonder her brother was drawn to this woman. Perhaps to explain her attachment to the instrument, she said, "My last mistress insisted that Master Phelps sell me, and to make it even, my old master gave Master Harrington her harpsichord. They tied the instrument behind the saddle, and I walked with Master Robert from Glenmere to Good Hope."

The two women stood in the dimly lit room, the afternoon light giving the leaves outside the window a golden sheen. Betsy looked at Deborah and Deborah looked with longing at the harpsichord. Betsy could guess what had happened between her brother and Deborah the day Master Harrington strapped the harpsichord on his horse, but she knew Deborah would never tell her. And she wouldn't tell her that she'd learned to play by listening to Miss Cecilia Phelps practice. Deborah learned to read music and to play piano because Miss Phelps needed help with lessons. She had Deborah sit with her during the lessons, and afterwards, she'd have Deborah help her memorize what her tutor taught. Deborah pretended that sitting with the tutor was a terrible punishment. And it was: the tutor thwacked her arms with a switch whenever Cecilia made a mistake, but since she'd been given to Cecilia, Deborah endured any discipline meant for her mistress. When their breasts grew, if a neighbor had smiled at Deborah, Cecilia would have her whipped. At night when the house was dead, Deborah touched the tops of the wooden keys as light as a moth on a pillow. She heard the scales, the chords, and the arpeggios as if she actually struck the keys. Years later, she'd sat on Robert's lap while she played. He was dead, but she could still feel the muscles of his thighs.

The baby kicked, and Deborah put her hand on her stomach to quiet it.

At the sudden jump of Deborah's apron, Betsy smiled. "Your time is near."

Deborah nodded. She didn't tell the widow about Robert bringing home music by Purcell. Deborah had smelled London when she opened the book. "Master Harrington agreed to take the harpsichord for visitors to Good Hope." Her head tipped toward the harpsichord, and she averted her eyes, challenging Betsy to guess that her new master had possessed not only the harpsichord, but Deborah's body—not in the bed upstairs where they would sleep—but on the grass by the road, less than a mile from Glenmere, while his horse grazed. Later he wanted her naked in front of the kitchen hearth. After she treated him to delights Master Phelps had demanded of her, he'd lay back and let her fish the key to the harpsichord from his jacket pocket. She'd play for him. He would steal up behind her, draw her up to face him, and kiss her as a man kisses a woman, with a gentleness Whitmore could never master. Since that afternoon until he died, she served Robert Harrington willingly, knowing he found pleasure in her love. When she was alone with him, he was her Bobby.

In the foyer, Betsy noticed that the red carpet had images of men hunting with arrows and spears, along with lions and tigers. "I didn't know my brother well."

Deborah glanced at the forget-me-nots. "It's best you ask Mr. Whitmore. He and Master Robert worked like a team of horses." As she'd done with the hyacinths in the pantry, she repositioned one of the stems deeper in the water. "Master Robert bought this vase for me to have flowers here to welcome guests. Even in winter, some small bit of creation in this vase will cheer the eye." She turned the vase so the flowers faced Betsy. "Master treated me with favor."

With favor? Deborah no longer called Betsy's brother "Master Harrington," but "Master Robert." She'd had two children by him. They'd lived as man and wife. They'd eaten at the walnut table and spent evenings in the sitting room, but Deborah wasn't willing to tell that story. Betsy said, "The overseer seems devoted to Good Hope."

With one hand on her belly to quiet the child and the other on the small of her back, Deborah looked toward the window. "This is Mr. Whitmore's child."

Using keys from her apron pocket, she opened the door opposite the pantry. "Master Harrington's office." She didn't follow Betsy into the room, but stood at the door, looking at the desk, with a tenderness in her eyes. "The day he was shot, I made strong cocoa like Master preferred in the morning." She turned her head away to look through the foyer to the garden and the dependency. "Mr. Whitmore built his coffin while Naomi and I washed his body and dressed him for the Resurrection." She bowed her head. "Mr. Osborne had them rest the coffin next to the harpsichord for the funeral, and Mr. Harmon played. He can play any instrument."

The room gave off a whiff of stale smoke and dead air. No dust in the house and no dust on the desk, but dust covered the furniture and even the windowsill in Robert's office. Dust motes floated in the light from the window. Betsy, loath to go into her brother's office, held her handkerchief to her nose.

"Everything is the same as the day Master died, except the books."

"I shouldn't have kept you on your feet so long. Forgive me, Deborah. You should rest."

Deborah started to curtsy, but she stopped halfway. "This child does torment me."

Betsy watched Deborah walk, each step slow, to the kitchen dependency, her hand pressed to the small of her back. Not as graceful as in the morning, she still held her head high.

———

Out in the fresh air of the fields, Robert had sat in his comfortable chair, challenging Betsy. That strange vision had not been welcoming, but she had no fear of meeting him in the stagnant room where gray dust sprawled on the collar of a heavy green jacket hanging from a peg. The desk alone had been polished; it glowed in the late afternoon light. Three sharpened white quills waited next to the corked inkwell. From a dark brown ledger with a blue ribbon marking the page of the most recent entries, Betsy read through dates indicating when the fields had been cleared, planted, and harvested, and which teams of slaves worked in each. The dates indicating the purchase of tools and live-stock had been tallied in a careful hand. Paging back, Betsy found a page indicating what Robert had won and lost gambling, and whether it was at Good Hope or at another plantation. There was no entry for the date of the duel or for his death.

On the first page of the ledger Robert had written the words The True Record of Good Hope in large, elegant letters, as if this were the title of a book. Betsy sat down and traced the letters her brother had written all those years ago when she was living in Brompton-on-Thames with her parents, before she'd met Isaac, before her children were born. She and her mother read letters he'd sent three or four times a year. On the second page of the book, he'd drawn a map of the plantation showing three small creeks that flowed through it, and sketched areas of land to be cleared first for tobacco and others to be left as woodland. The third page showed the layout of the farmyard—not as it was, with the barn facing the house, but with the barn in back of the house where the kitchen dependency and the slave quarters were. The sketch had no slave quarters, but subsequent pages had drawings that revealed how his plans changed, with notes like "Whit's suggestion" or "DP's plan." Betsy paged on. A list of slaves: date, price, and place of purchase; births, deaths, and sales at auction or at trade. Xerxes had been won at cards in 1698 at Fulton's Crossing. Robert bought Castor and Pollux the next year for 150 pounds and a promissory note of two bales of first-grade tobacco. Aeneas came to Good Hope in 1701. On the same page, near the bottom, Betsy read *Deborah Phelps, female, 15 to 18 years. With harpsichord. Strong. Glenmere. May 10, 1703. 120 Pds.* A few lines down the ledger, Robert had written and underlined *Susannah Harrington, female, born August 7, 1704.* Robert had entered his daughter's name and recorded her birth as a slave in a ledger. Betsy sat back to ponder the dusty jacket on the wall. Robert was dead. Above the jacket, a rifle—oiled and polished—rested on hooks. A few pages on in the ledger, Robert's careful lettering changed. There were no scratches of a spent quill on the pages. Deborah had taken over writing in the book years before Robert had fought the duel. Where was the entry for Isaiah? The last entry was for two healthy male slaves shipped from Accra. Whitmore had paid four hundred pounds. The large X beside their names might mean they'd been assigned to Xerxes' crew. On the line above that entry, the quill had wavered on the letter I. Deborah had written *Isaiah Harrington, male, born Sep't 2, 1711*—three months after Betsy's brother had been shot. He'd never held the baby boy, but Deborah named her son Harrington. Betsy touched the words, felt the lines, the curves of ink on the smooth paper. She closed the book. Looking down at the jacket, she wanted to accuse him, to ask for an explanation. "Oh, Robert."

The silence was his answer, a silence she understood. If Isaac were there, she could tell him what she'd learned, but he and Robert were dead. Betsy was alone on a plantation they'd left her, and she was expecting a baby. She left the office and closed the door. She didn't have the key, but no one would want to go in that room.

Chapter 22

The forget-me-nots looked gray in the shadow of the stair. Following Deborah's example, Betsy picked up one stem and put it deeper in the vase. She closed her eyes. In the blue ledger, *The True Record of Good Hope*, Deborah had written that her own son was born a slave. Only the first letter wavered. Hands covered Betsy's eyes. Someone blew on her neck. She twisted to escape Robert's clammy hold.

The vase toppled to the floor and shattered. The short crystal stem rolled in a circle to a stop beside the scattered blue flowers.

"Oh, Mrs. Randall, look what you've done." Not the least contrite, Phillipa held her fingers to her mouth, delighted at the scare she'd given Betsy.

Before Betsy could recover from her fright and her anger at Phillipa for scaring her, before she could bend to pick up the flowers and broken crystal, Charity had run to the pantry with the larger pieces of glass and the flowers. Charity stuffed the flowers in a wine goblet and wiped up the puddle with a deft sweep of a towel. From the dining room, Naomi watched Charity dab up the last slivers of glass.

"Don't sneak up on me, Phillipa." The tremble in Betsy's voice infuriated her. "I broke Deborah's vase."

"*Your* vase." Phillipa shifted the flowers to keep them from flopping around the rim of the goblet. "I'm sorry you knocked over the flowers and that the beautiful vase broke, but aren't you glad neither of us was cut?" With the gentleness of the young for the elderly, she took Betsy's arm as if she needed support to walk. "While you dallied in the dining room and the pantry, I investigated the rooms upstairs. You and I will share the front bedroom to the southeast."

"Give me a moment's peace, Phillipa."

"Pardon me, Mrs. Randall." Phillipa dropped Betsy's arm. "Please forgive her, little flowers." She curtsied to the drooping flowers. "You mustn't mind Mrs. Randall. She'll feel better when she has seen the bedrooms."

Betsy didn't want to see any more of Robert's house, in particular, the bedroom where he'd slept with Deborah, where his children—his slaves—were born. Betsy preferred sitting on the bottom step with her eyes closed or going back to Mrs. Fulton's kitchen with wooden bluebirds on a bread plate. Better yet, Mrs. Falls's attic for sick travelers. She longed to be home in Brompton-on-Thames. She should be holding David.

Phillipa coaxed her to go up and try the featherbed. "Mr. Robert Harrington didn't spare himself comforts." According to Phillipa, Charity should unroll her pallet next to the feather bed, safe from the surveyor, and Mrs. Randall should have Morris, Harmon, and the German sleep in the barn with the lieutenant's soldiers. Before Betsy had taken one step up the stairs, Phillipa had arranged for Lieutenant

Gray and Petty—because the journalist fancied himself a gentleman—to sleep in the west room.

Rather than tell Phillipa that she herself would assign rooms for her guests, Betsy decided she'd walk down to the quarters Deborah showed her when they were in the pantry. Perhaps she'd have a moment to talk to Susannah. But before she reached the door, Gray came in with Morris. He was glad to find Betsy so he could tell her his plans to leave the next morning. Morris would survey Petty's property, and they'd explore the region Spotswood had in mind for settlers from Germany. Whitmore had heard rumors that the Seneca were raiding Pamunkey villages. Gray wanted to investigate those rumors and to report what he discovered to the governor. Ned and Nighthawk would scout for the troops. Though Petty had volunteered to remain at Good Hope, Morris insisted that he be present when his property was surveyed. Harmon and Reinke had agreed to stay with Betsy and Miss Townsend at Good Hope.

Phillipa was deciding where Betsy would sleep, and Gray was telling her his plans for the expedition. Betsy felt like a branch in changing winds, and she wondered when she herself would be deciding how she would spend the day. When she asked how long the troops would be gone, Morris guessed it would take less than a fortnight to blaze Petty's land and explore the range for the governor's settlement. Gray said the men would quickstep back to the comfort of Good Hope. Soon after their return, they'd begin the journey back to Williamsburg, and Betsy would have the plantation, with its excellent overseer and well-trained housekeeper to herself.

———

To keep out the night vapors, Phillipa closed the window and flung herself onto the bed, swooping her arms over the blue coverlet that Betsy remembered had been on her parents' bed. Betsy had been tracing the handiwork her mother had sewn when she and Bobby were children, when they still slept in the bed with their parents, when their father would lead them in the 23rd Psalm. Betsy had begun the recitation in her thoughts—her prayer before sleep. Phillipa threw back the blankets. "Susannah's quick. She'll make an excellent lady's maid." She fluffed the pillow before falling back on it. "You have Deborah to run your house and an honest overseer; you'll be able to travel to Williamsburg and other plantations whenever you choose." She turned to Betsy. "I'll help you find a husband. Lieutenant Gray and I will invite you to stay at our home from Christmas to Easter or Whitsuntide."

Before Betsy could protest that she wasn't planning to marry, Phillipa bolted from the bed. "Where's Charity?" She nabbed her dressing gown and, with an arm in one sleeve, yanked open the door.

Charity stood in the doorway, her face wet and swollen. She must have been there when Betsy was trying to say the psalm. Phillipa stumbled back, and Charity sidestepped into the room, cowering close to the wall, her eyes down. Betsy climbed out of bed to comfort her, but Phillipa, already there, slapped Charity's face hard. Then she slammed the door shut.

Charity waited with her head still turned from the slap. She didn't move.

Phillipa glared at her. "Where were you?"

"Mr. Morris cornered me in the pantry."

"Stay away from the brute." Phillipa kicked Charity's pallet toward her and it unrolled on the floor.

Betsy grabbed Phillipa, twisting her around, wanting her to take back her slap and apologize, but she stopped. Tears ran down Phillipa's face. Betsy let her go and went to the basin on the wash table to wring out a cloth. "Morris must be stopped." She wiped Charity's face, taking care on her neck where bruises had the marks of teeth. "I'll tell Gray to stop the surveyor from forcing himself on Charity. He has no right to rape guests at Good Hope."

"No!" Phillipa took the cloth from Betsy and wiped her own face. "The lieutenant must not be told." She blinked back tears and knelt beside the pallet where Charity had curled up in the far corner of the room. Phillipa cooed while she dabbed Charity's face. "Don't leave my sight. Do not leave my side."

Betsy opened the window. A breeze from the garden carried a tune from Harmon's fiddle. A high tenor voice sang "Barbara Allen." The music didn't lull Betsy's thoughts, but at least Morris would be leaving with Gray tomorrow.

Staying on the floor with Charity, Phillipa kissed her, and Betsy knew to cover her ears with her pillow. Imagining that Isaac held her in his arms, she calmed herself to sleep. In a dream, Reinke caressed her. She woke up. The dream had been more real than the blue quilt. Phillipa slept on the floor, cuddled next to Charity.

Betsy tried saying the Lord's Prayer. She recited the 23rd Psalm. Why Reinke? Pressing her head into the pillow, she started to pray, as she often did, for the souls of Isaac and the children, but instead she pictured the people coming into the yard at the clang of the gong and then following

Xerxes, Aeneas, Castor, and Pollux—all those men and women whose names her brother had written in the blue book. Deborah. How wistfully she'd looked at the harpsichord. Her child—Whitmore's child—would be born soon, perhaps while Betsy was trying to sleep.

———

In broad daylight, Betsy sat up on the featherbed. "Where's Charity?"

Next to Betsy, Phillipa lay with her hands behind her head, smiling at the ceiling. "I sent her to bring us cocoa. Don't worry, Mrs. Randall. I'll tell the lieutenant to call off Morris."

The fragrance of cocoa came through the open door, but the stairs didn't creak. Phillipa jumped out of bed. "That monster. He's grabbed her again." Pulling on her dressing gown, she ran to the door. "Where? In the pantry? We would hear them." Phillipa set her nightcap straight. "Where do you think?" She was running to the stairs.

"In the office," Betsy called after her, hurrying to dress, fitting her stomacher, her fingers fumbling with the laces. While Betsy had prepared for bed, in her own house, Morris had raped Charity. He was raping her now. And Lieutenant Gray sanctioned Morris's forcing himself on Phillipa's slave. Betsy had to confront Morris and protect Charity.

In the dining room, Petty and Harmon were eating their breakfast and arguing about the Pamunkey claim to the land the journalist had purchased along the river. No Phillipa. No Charity. Betsy didn't ask if the men had seen them. She ignored the corn mash Naomi offered her and ran to check the office. The chair had been pushed to the window, and the papers on the desk scattered, but it was empty. From the back door, Whitmore, his hat in hand, frantically beckoned for Betsy.

Before Betsy could ask if he'd seen Charity, the overseer said, "Mrs. Randall, I know that the lieutenant gave orders for me to show you the property today, but Deborah's time is here." He spoke without taking a breath, not giving Betsy a chance to ask about Charity. "Karl Reinke and the fiddler have agreed to ride with you into the fields. They know the land and the horses. The German helped me and Harry in exchange for his trapping in the spring and fall, and Harmon came to play cards." Anxious to return to Deborah in the kitchen dependency, he looked over his shoulder where the troops marched in formation to the shrill fife. He paid no heed to the soldiers disappearing around the corner of the house, but held his hat to his face to keep anyone from hearing him say that Deborah didn't want the fiddler's evil eye near her.

"Evil eye?" Betsy had heard of the superstition, but Harmon couldn't be called evil, not with the way he hugged his little children, or faced Molly Gage, giving Betsy the chance to grab her arm. At the clearing of the burnt house, he'd treated Charity and Betsy as if he were their brother.

"Mr. Whitmore, I'll help Deborah. You can show me the fields another time."

Whitmore reared back, his hat to his chest. "No, no. That won't do. Deborah wouldn't have it." He ran off, but whirled around, crushing his hat, distraught. "If you please, ma'am, Mrs. Randall, one more thing, if you have any feeling for us that loved your brother best. Deborah's scared of Miss Townsend's slave, of her powers. I wouldn't have her at Good Hope except you say so. Didn't she hex those Tripp brothers?" He got down on one knee to plead.

"Stand up, Mr. Whitmore." Betsy pulled him to his feet. "Charity is not a witch. I heard her pray the Lord's Prayer fervently from the 'Our Father' to the 'Amen.'" Whitmore must know that the words of the prayer turned to curses in the mouth of a witch. "She never faltered."

He stepped back—he feared Betsy as much as Charity. "Please, ma'am. Take her and the fiddler to the fields with you. Reinke knows. I told him which horses to take, and Naomi is fixing a basket of bread and jam." He shot off, and this time he didn't turn back but ran to Deborah in the kitchen dependency.

Beyond the dependency, at the back of the garden, Benjamin and a slave from the quarters tapped one of the vicar's saplings into a deep hole. The two men had lined up the saplings to grow between the house and the slave quarters. Off to the right, at the far edge of the herb garden, the lieutenant walked arm in arm with Phillipa in her dressing gown. Instead of leading his men, Gray whispered to Phillipa as if telling her a story. The couple strolled, no longer in sight because the kitchen house blocked Betsy's view. Once, she had walked like that with Isaac before they were married, her mother and father walking a short distance behind them.

"Mr. Harmon say I'm s'posed to go with you an him, Mrs. Randall, but Miss Phillipa's stayin here." Charity stood less than a foot behind her.

Startled, remembering what Whitmore had said about Phillipa's slave, Betsy stepped back from Charity. "You must not sneak up on a person." She looked back at the place where Gray and Phillipa had disappeared beyond the house, and then at Charity, who stood with her head bowed, her arms hanging limp, her kerchief drooping from her shoulder. Betsy lifted the kerchief back up to Charity's neck, covering new bruises.

"Mr. Morris gone off with the troops." Charity tied her kerchief, lifting it close to her ears. "Miss Phillipa's gonna punish me."

"No, Charity, she won't punish you." Exasperated at not having stopped Morris, at Phillipa's blaming Charity, and at having to ride off into the fields, Betsy put her arm around Charity's waist. "I'll talk to Miss Townsend and the lieutenant. Don't worry about Phillipa." Betsy straightened Charity's cap. "She's with Lieutenant Gray in the garden, and she wouldn't want you running after them."

At the pantry door, Naomi handed Betsy her bonnet. "Miss Randall, your horse waiting."

How long Naomi had been listening, Betsy didn't know. Like Charity, she'd come up without making a sound, carrying Betsy's bonnet and a basket of food and beer. Naomi didn't look at Charity, who stood with her head bowed, begging Betsy to let her stay with Miss Phillipa.

Betsy adjusted her own bonnet over her cap and tied the ribbon tight. "I'll tell Miss Townsend that you wanted to stay but I ordered you to come with me. Charity, I don't want to spend the morning alone with Mr. Harmon and the German hunter. Please come along." She put her arm around Charity. Whitmore was wrong, but Betsy didn't want Deborah to be fearful when giving birth. And Betsy didn't want to ride alone with the fiddler and the woodsman.

———

In the yard, Reinke helped Betsy onto a small brown mare before he climbed onto one of the chestnuts that had pulled the wagon. According to the woodsman, Betsy would have no trouble with Melinda even though he couldn't find a lady's saddle. The last time Betsy had straddled a horse like a man, she'd been twelve and riding out to the fields on the farm with Bobby. Charity sat behind Harmon on the sorrel, ready to leave the yard, when Gray sprinted out the front door of the house and mounted his horse, calling for Saul. His slave grabbed the back of the saddle and yanked himself onto Ramses's rump as the lieutenant trotted off with Petty behind them bouncing on his yellow mare.

Promising herself to ask Phillipa what Gray said about Morris, Betsy rode with the others past long, gray tobacco barns, then along fields of wheat and oats. Harmon told Betsy that her brother did a lot of roaming before he applied for the patent to the land. Harrington had looked for open land, fields the Choctaw or the Pamunkey had abandoned, fallow land cleared to plant.

"Did he buy the land from the Indians?"

"Oh, no, dear lady. Few people know of these clearings." Harmon's voice had an unkind tinge. "Claiming land at the right moment is a sign of a good planter."

Irked at Harmon's insinuations about her brother, Betsy urged the mare to trail closer to Reinke. Ahead of them, slaves sang about bringing the hoe up high and chopping down hard, deep in the ground, deep in the ground. All the hoes came down in a single chop, clinking small stones in the soil. Harmon called out, "Mornin'," and the men and women chopping around the new tobacco shoots yelled, "Yah, boss," as they continued hoeing to the rhythm of the song.

The sailors of the Dash sang when they raised the sails that morning the pirates boarded. Betsy looked up into the sky. She wondered how Davy was faring with Charlie or Bennett teaching him to be a sailor. Did the boy ever think of her? A hawk circled above the fields, one lone bird in the clear blue sky, and Betsy shuddered. She was riding Melinda on Robert's plantation, passing slaves working in fields that her brother and Whitmore—with the help of slaves like these men and women—cleared. She didn't want to be left alone at Good Hope.

When the sun reigned high over the plantation, Reinke rode ahead of Betsy, Harmon, and Charity into the farm-yard. They'd ride through the north half of the plantation in the afternoon. With the troops gone, the buildings appeared forlorn. Hens clucked in the quiet. Betsy wanted to check on Deborah. When it was time for Betsy's child to be born, she'd be alone with Whitmore, Deborah, and the slaves.

Harmon reined his horse in front of the house. "Run in, Charity, and tell them we're home and hungry." But she'd already slid off his horse by the time the words were out of his mouth and was running to the back door.

Betsy swung her leg to dismount and felt Reinke's hands on her waist. He lifted her out of the stirrup and onto the ground. Surprised by his help, she remembered her dream of making love to him. Her surprise amused him. Without a word of thanks for help she didn't need, she hurried to run through the house to the kitchen dependency.

Inside, Charity slumped on the bottom step of the stair-case, her head to her knees, shaking.

"Charity?"

When she didn't move or look up, Betsy ran upstairs.

Stretched straight out in the middle of the bed, her skirt spread flat and her hands on her stomach, Phillipa closed her eyes when Betsy came in. She wore her linen dress, a slightly darker blue than the coverlet. Her hair combed impeccably, her face, neck, and breasts powdered white, and her lips and cheeks rouged, she lay as if the bed were her bier.

"Why are you lying like this, Phillipa?" Betsy waited at the door for permission to come closer. But Phillipa ignored Betsy. Her eyelids didn't flutter. Her chest didn't move. Her calm frightened Betsy. "I saw you in the garden with the lieutenant. You made a very pretty picture."

"I shall die here." Phillipa kept her eyes closed. "But don't bury me here on your plantation." She turned her head away from Betsy's hand. "I insist that Uncle ship the coffin to Barbados. I want to be buried next to Mama."

"Phillipa, what happened?" Betsy stroked her cheek.

She closed her eyes. "You say a pretty picture? Me in my dressing gown, walking out toward the woods with the lieutenant to pick wild flowers to sketch for my embroidery. Is that your pretty picture?" She laughed. "Lieutenant Gray approves of needlework."

Betsy sat on the bed. She wasn't going to ask again for an explanation.

"I borrowed a page from Mrs. Petty's book, pretending fear for my beloved's life, and he told me the Seneca wouldn't dare attack the Virginia militia." Phillipa looked toward the window instead of at Betsy. "I know that Lieutenant Gray and his men are in no danger, but I wanted him to think that my every happiness depended on him and that, in exchange for my adoration, he'd agree to stop Morris from breeding Charity like a prize cow or sheep." She pressed her arms flat at her sides. "The lieutenant was all gentleness and tenderness of heart, until he heard Charity's name. Then his eyes burned. Black fire."

Not moving, trying not to blink, Betsy waited.

"Go out to your tobacco fields, Mrs. Randall, and keep Charity away from me."

"What reason has Gray to be angered at Charity?"

Phillipa sat bolt upright. "Charity? *Charity*? Do you care nothing for me?" She pointed to her chest. "I ... *I* ... I am debased. Vile." She folded forward on the bed, her face to her knees.

Betsy ran to close the window. "Lieutenant Gray holds you in highest regard, Phillipa. He would never insult you. He couldn't speak ill of you."

"Yes, Mrs. Randall, he could. He did. He told me it was shameful of me to parade out of doors in my dressing gown where his troops could see me." She recoiled as if struck by a blow, and hid her eyes in the crook of her arm. "It's worse than that." She sat up, and pointed for Betsy to check to be sure no one was listening on the landing. If Charity had been eavesdropping, she'd left. When Betsy closed the door, Phillipa whispered, "I must sell Charity." She wiped her nose on her sleeve. "You might think Charity would bring a better price without a big, round belly, but no, she's worth more if the buyer sees that she's going to have a child."

"Your uncle would never sell Charity. He certainly wouldn't sell her if she were expecting a child."

Phillipa said nothing.

"How has Charity offended Lieutenant Gray?"

Phillipa got down off the bed, stood behind Betsy, and mimicked Gray. "'Never mention that black whore to me. That depravity will never be part of my household." She sat on the bed, her head bowed. "Uncle gave Charity to me for my birthday. I had terrible nightmares, and he thought it would help to have her sleep in my room. I don't know if he planned for her to sleep in my bed, but I wanted her to hold me while she sang her lullabies."

Betsy sat down close to Phillipa. "Your uncle knows of your fondness for Charity."

Phillipa winced as if Betsy had pinched her. "I told Lieutenant Gray I was glad that he revealed his feeling before our engagement has been announced."

"And?" Betsy had been so wrong imagining Gray cooing to Phillipa in the garden before she and the others left for the field. Gray had mounted his horse as if returning from a conquest; Betsy thought it was of love, but it was lording his being a prospect for a husband over her. She laid her hand on Phillipa's leg, almost afraid that she'd bruise it. "And?"

"I can't stop feeling his moustache brush my cheek." Phillipa rubbed her hand over her face, harder and faster, and then opened her fingers like talons to scratch her cheeks, but Betsy grabbed Phillipa's wrists, pulling her hands away from her face.

Betsy didn't let go. "What did he say about your engagement?"

"'How important is Charity to you, my dear Miss Townsend?'" She clenched her fists to beat on either Betsy or herself, but Betsy held them together until they went limp. Tears filled Phillipa's eyes. "Can you imagine? Uncle and Gray have discussed my 'fondness' for Charity. Before he marries me, she is to be sold."

"Oh, Miss Townsend …" Betsy sat on the bed; she could offer no comfort for Phillipa.

"Oh, Mrs. Randall …" Phillipa mocked Betsy as she walked around the bed to the window and eased it open. Wiping tears from her cheeks, she looked down at the yard. "Mr. Harmon and the German are waiting with the horses." She strode back around the bed and put her hand on the doorknob, but didn't open the door. "Mrs. Randall, I told you what the lieutenant said in the garden, but to repeat what you have heard, to think of what I said, even in the deepest woods when you are completely alone, would be the greatest sin against me. What I said isn't for the amusement of the fiddler or the German."

Betsy walked to the window to check if Harmon and Reinke were saddling the horses. Melinda nuzzled Harmon's sorrel, like a girl sharing a secret. A breeze that lifted the curtain from the windowsill smelled of the meadow and the barn. About to leave, Betsy said, "I'm sorry that I left you alone with the lieutenant, Phillipa."

Tears had streaked the rouge on Phillipa's cheeks. "Wipe that foolish sorrow off your face. Go ride with my darling Charity. Laugh and sing with Harmon and that German. Learn about growing tobacco." She rubbed her cheeks with her handkerchief. "I shall forget everything I've told you by the time you reach the bottom step. If you say anything to Charity, I'll spread the most vicious rumors about you—from Charles Towne to New York."

Phillipa's attack stunned Betsy.

"That's what Lieutenant Gray promised me, but he said it with an ugly look on his face. And now I've told you, Mrs. Randall, the one person he specifically told me not to tell."

With her back to Betsy and her head bowed, Phillipa sniffed back tears. "Go. Please, Mrs. Randall." She wiped her face, and her wet eyelashes made her eyes seem larger, bluer. Gray told her he'd heard about Phillipa's unnatural feelings for her slave; but, in the past, he chose not to believe the rumors. "'Your affection for that black bitch …' Yes, he said that, Mrs. Randall." She gripped Betsy's shoulders to make sure Betsy heard every word the lieutenant had said. "'Your affection for that black bitch goes against the laws of God and man.'"

Betsy said she would tell Phillipa's uncle how important a confidant like Charity was for Phillipa.

"Poor Mrs. Randall. I have so much to teach you." She smiled at Betsy's ignorance. "You must not talk to my uncle." She smiled at the dust motes drifting in the light from the window. "You don't know my uncle." She took Betsy's hands. "You know my uncle as kind. And he is." She nodded, vehement. He had arranged for her to marry the heir to one of the largest estates in the colony, and she would never offend him or cause him to be angry. She put her hands to her hair to be sure every strand was in place, and despite her having thrown herself on the bed, her cap had remained tied and in place, as it had been when Betsy first came into the room. "There isn't a woman in Virginia who wouldn't be pleased to marry Lieutenant Spencer Gray. If you spoke to Uncle about our conversation, he'd be mortified; he'd listen politely, answer politely, and never let you enter his house again. Me? He'd have my meals served in my room or the kitchen, and I'd have to use the back stairs—that is, if he'd even let me leave the house. He wouldn't permit my shadow to be in the same room with him." She opened the door. "Don't cross Uncle on matters of family or his estate. I'm going to marry Lieutenant Gray, and Uncle will be happy with me."

In order to be Mrs. Spencer Gray, Phillipa chose to

betray Charity—to sell her—and marry into a wealthy family. Harmon and Reinke were waiting for Betsy. Soon they'd send Charity to get her.

Phillipa gripped Betsy's arms. "Mrs. Randall, did you love your husband?"

Betsy looked to the window's bright afternoon light and thought of Isaac's bringing her up on deck to see moonlight on the water. "I think of my husband often, but he isn't here. He wanted to claim Good Hope, but I'm here alone. While we rode out to the fields, I thought that he would have been proud to own the land."

Phillipa sat, her back against the headboard in the middle of the bed, and smoothed out the skirt, touched her cap to be sure the ribbons were in place, and asked Betsy to hand her the blanket she was embroidering and the Chinese box. "Say nothing to Charity." Calmly she selected a yellow spool and snipped a length of silk thread. "This is a time of trial for me."

Betsy stopped herself from saying that the trial would be much more difficult for Charity. Instead, she watched Phillipa wet the thread on her tongue and poke it through the eye of the needle, like an arrow hitting its target.

In the pantry, Charity stopped petting Reinke's dog, Falken, and rose from the floor. Naomi passed them with a tray she'd prepared for Phillipa. Betsy thought about snatching a few raisins from the plate for herself but she didn't. She hoped Charity had eaten.

Betsy asked, "How is Deborah?"

"She fine. Mister Whit sings her quiet songs."

Charity handed Betsy a slice of bread with a wedge of cheese. The two women walked together across the yard where shadows had begun creeping to the east. By the time the trees shaded the yard later that afternoon, Betsy would have seen the whole plantation. Maybe Deborah and Whitmore would be holding their baby. Phillipa would have stitched buttercups on Mrs. Fulton's blanket.

Chapter 23

"How fortunate you are, Mrs. Randall, coming in time for the birth of your slave," Harmon said.

Betsy had one foot in the stirrup to hoist herself onto Melinda. She would have slipped to the ground if Reinke hadn't caught her. The fiddler helped Charity swing up onto the back of his playful sorrel, her mane the copper-red of her coat. He settled into his saddle. "I'd pray for a boy if I were you."

Her legs squeezed into Melinda's sides, Betsy rubbed her hand down the horse's strong neck. Melinda quivered and then accepted Betsy's hand on her sleek muscles. "Mr. Harmon, Deborah and the overseer both told me the child is his."

"He's the father." Harmon flicked his reins and his horse trotted toward the fields. "His boy will be your property."

Reinke waved at Betsy, advising her to ignore the fiddler. Melinda, in apparent agreement with Reinke, waggled her head up and down as she fell in behind the chestnut, but Harmon paced his playful sorrel in step with Melinda. He

said, "If you train Whitmore's son properly, you can sell
him for twice the price of a standard black."

Betsy thought of striking Harmon with her crop to make
him quit bedeviling her about Deborah's baby, but instead
she patted Melinda, reminding herself not to jump at whatever the fiddler said. She was trapped at Robert's plantation,
caught in Isaac's plan to own an estate. Dr. McNeill, Captain Bennett, and Phillipa's uncle all preached about her
obligation to Isaac and her brother. Harmon's torment
angered her, but Isaac was at fault for getting her into this
situation of owning Whitmore's child. He'd known about
the slaves—Betsy herself knew that Robert had slaves. She
hadn't paid attention, but he had gloated about his success
at training slaves to work his tobacco fields. When he told
them, his stories had nothing to do with her home. Could
Isaac have known that slaves like Charity were bred for
sale? Her husband didn't know Robert had a daughter. Robert himself didn't know he would have a son. Isaac would
have recognized them as Betsy's niece and nephew.
Wouldn't he? Betsy let her body settle into the rhythm of
Melinda's gait. The fiddler, in no way Betsy's superior, had
no cause to trouble her when he housed his family in con-
nected sheds. "Mr. Harmon, when we left your home, you
said good-bye to three women. Which is your wife?"

Charity's laugh, a sharp bark, startled Melinda and the
sorrel; they both shied. Harmon's mare trotted down the
path while Betsy pulled back on Melinda's reins. In the distance, the repeated thwack of an ax against wood had the
rhythm of a clock. Harmon took his time riding back to the
woodsman and Betsy.

"You gave Harm a good riddle, Mrs. Randall," said
Charity. "He needlin you, and you gave him a quandary."

Charity laid her head on Harmon's back. "We're waitin for your answer, Mr. Fiddleman."

Reinke pointed to a grove of trees where Aeneas and one of his men took turns swinging axes at the trunk of a large tree, while the rest of the crew sawed off branches from another tree they had already felled. The axes chopped a steady beat, as regular as the jingle of Melinda's harness and the pad of the horses' hooves on the soft ground. Harmon said, "Polly's my wife, Mrs. Randall; but the women in my house want to be there. I don't keep 'em chained or whip 'em. I wouldn't set dogs on them if they ran off."

Melinda shivered, shaking her head from side to side. Both she and the sorrel swished their tails to drive horse-flies off. Betsy and Harmon rode side by side in silence. Charity hummed. When they came to a stretch where they could ride up to Reinke, Harmon said, "I'm not ashamed of my family, Mrs. Randall. Ashamed? I'm proud of my children. They're my joy. I don't want 'em kidnapped and sold for hire."

"I should hope not," Reinke said. "Why did Martin Whitmore work like he did for Harrington, and keep working at Good Hope after your brother died, Mrs. Randall? Because your brother paid off his indenture and promised him a place to live."

Betsy hadn't known that Reinke knew her brother, but before she could ask about Robert, Harmon said, "And now Deborah works him harder than Bobby Harrington ever did. I wouldn't put up with that Queen of Sheba. I don't care how clever she is."

He scowled at a field where Xerxes's crew worked crow-bars to pry up a large stump. "Sophie and I had two children before I had the money to buy her. One of 'em died of a cough. The four-year-old was sold to a trader from North Carolina. I've searched but I can't find him." He spit on the ground. "The child goes to the mother's master. The father has no say." With Charity wrapping her arms around his middle to stay astride the hindquarters of the quick sorrel, he prodded his horse past Reinke, well out of earshot.

The chant Xerxes used to keep his men working together faded, and Reinke and Betsy were left with the sounds of gear and the occasional snuffle of the horses. Reinke took off his hat and wiped his forehead with his handkerchief. "Yah."

Betsy looked over at him. Was he agreeing with Harmon's remark or glad for the quiet?

"Martin is scared that you'll sell Deborah."

"Sell Deborah?" She'd seen the auction in Yorktown, but the thought of her selling another person hadn't occurred to her. How could she *own* Deborah? How could she *own* Deborah's baby, simply because she owned Deborah? She owned Robert's children, her niece and nephew. Impossible. Outrageous. How horrible it must have been for Deborah to know that the baby she carried belonged to another person, was his property. "I am not the person to sell Deborah."

"No, I should think not. She runs the plantation—she has since Harrington learned how well she did when he went to England to get a wife."

With a tug on the reins, Betsy brought Melinda to a halt, and Reinke reined his horse to a stop too. Betsy stared at him. "How well did you know my brother?"

Betsy knew that Robert had returned to England, hoping to find a woman willing to marry him and to live in Virginia. She thought that he would marry one of the women he courted, but each time, he found a problem. Now Betsy could see that none of them could compare to Deborah. "I didn't know that my brother had children, but I have no doubt that he is the father of Susannah and Isaiah."

Reinke squinted through the afternoon haze at Harmon and Charity, his face red. "Mrs. Randall, according to Martin Whitmore, I am the father of Naomi's child. She didn't tell me, but when I came here, she used to come to my bed." He spurred his horse and galloped to catch up with Harmon and Charity as they rode toward the house and barn. The sun's reflection on the front windows welcomed them back from the last field. Melinda whinnied and tossed her head to gallop with the others, but Betsy pulled back on the reins, holding Melinda well behind them. Reinke had fathered Naomi's child. Had Naomi been sent by Whitmore or Deborah to the woodsman's bed? Betsy put her hand on her stomach. Aboard the *Sally Dash*, she'd hoped that she wasn't pregnant. Since vomiting that morning in the burned-out clearing, she'd prayed the child was Isaac's and not Bennett's. Her child wouldn't have a father unless she married, but she would not. She longed for Isaac. Her joy at the birth of each child had been his as well.

Reinke wheeled his horse back to Betsy. "Are you having trouble with Melinda?"

Angry that she'd dreamed of making love to him and that he'd bedded Naomi, Betsy didn't answer him but kicked Melinda's flank. The mare trotted into the farmyard to the water trough. Betsy eased her leg over the saddle and jumped to the ground. Reinke loosened the girth on his own horse and then unsaddled Melinda. Betsy asked, "What will happen to Naomi's baby?"

"The fiddler's right." Reinke jerked his head toward

Harmon, who limped to the house after the day on horse-back. "Naomi is yours. The child will be yours to keep or to sell."

At the house, Harmon went to the front door and Charity hurried around to the back. Betsy pressed a hand to her ribs. She wouldn't know whether her baby was Isaac's child or Bennett's until she saw the shape of the head, the eyes, the hands. Would the child have fan-shaped fingernails like Isaac's mother—as Mary, Alice, and David all did? She stood looking at the house. Reinke looked up to see why she waited there. She said, "The child is Naomi's, and that child should have a father. Whitmore knows he is the father of Deborah's child."

Reinke said nothing but filled his cupped hands with water from the trough, drank, and combed his wet fingers through his hair. Though he seemed annoyed, she walked with him when he led the horses into the barn to take off their saddles. She wanted him to say that he would take care of his child. He began to curry Melinda, but paused and looked her in the eye. "Do you think the only slaves in Virginia are Africans?" He slapped the horse on the rump and Melinda plodded to the pasture. "Why do you think Miss Townsend wanted to be on this expedition?" He waited for Betsy to answer, but she couldn't, being well aware that she didn't truly know Phillipa or Charity. Reinke brushed the big chestnut he had ridden. "She wants to be like the fiddler, not caring what the townspeople think, cutting her own path, but it's her Uncle Osborne who decides where she sits in church and when she smiles. She is no freer than Gray, who'd rather study philosophy in Heidelberg than march boys into territory the Seneca raid."

Betsy didn't answer him. She hadn't chosen to sail from

England. Could she choose not to stay in Virginia? Her child would need a home.

Naomi waved a towel, beckoning them from under the young oak. "The baby's here."

Betsy picked up her skirts and ran to the kitchen dependency to see the baby, the new life, a child awake to the world. Even before she reached the door, she called out, "Deborah?" The place was quiet. Betsy put her hand over her mouth to quiet her joy. She, Reinke, and Naomi, who had run after them, tiptoed to the laddered steps to the loft. Betsy, after composing herself, called up. "Deborah, may Mr. Reinke and I come up?"

"Yes, Mrs. Randall." Whitmore's voice quavered. "Come see our little girl."

The ropes of a bed creaked. In a gentle voice, Deborah said, "Mrs. Randall, come see our child."

The walls of the loft sloped sharply from the center beam of the ceiling to dark recesses on the floor. Squares of light came from windows at both ends of the room. Under a dark wool quilt, Deborah lay with the baby nestled between her breasts. The ball of her head fit the curve under Deborah's chin. Whitmore smoothed the wrinkles of the blanket.

Betsy ran to the bed and knelt to circle her arms around the mother and child, to feel the warmth of their bodies, touch the baby's silky black hair, and rest her palm on Deborah's cheek.

Her eyelids fluttered open, and she smiled at Betsy. "Tell her the name, Whit."

The overseer stood straight as if he were a soldier in a regiment. "Mary Alice." He repeated the name softly. "Mary Alice." Dropping to his knees next to Betsy, he cupped his hand under Deborah's chin. Even more softly, he said the baby's name to her.

Deborah's eyes closed. She spoke slowly. "Master Robert would say, 'Mary and Alice have hair of pure gold,' or 'Mary and Alice are sunshine itself.'"

Mary Alice. Mary Alice? Betsy walked to the window and looked down on the garden and out to the fields. Yes, her brother had played with Mary and walked around Brompton one day with Alice in his arms, but he'd spent his time with the Earl of Guilford, returning in the late afternoon to smoke a pipe of tobacco with Isaac. Mary and Alice had been sunshine, and, once, she could circle her arms around that joy. She gripped her arms around her loneliness.

When Betsy turned back to Deborah, they seemed to expect her to acknowledge the honor of a baby named for her daughters, but she couldn't talk. She hurried across the room and looked at Deborah to be sure she had permission before she picked up the baby, and then held the little girl bundled in a light-gray lambskin. Mary Alice. Betsy caressed the delicate head, and the child opened her gray-blue eyes. She stared at Betsy. How perfectly formed the round nostrils, the peaked lips, the delicate shell of the ears, the soft arch of the brows were. The eyes didn't waver from Betsy's face. "She is beautiful, Deborah. Oh, what a gift." She held the baby close and smelled her hair and the clean lambskin. Why hadn't her brother told her about the beautiful Susannah? He'd lived with Deborah but couldn't admit that love he had for her to Isaac and Betsy. He'd never acknowledged his child. Not if he'd been able to list her as a slave. How could the fiddler think of this baby, Mary Alice, as a slave?

Reinke took the baby from Betsy and brought her to Whitmore as if to show him his own child before giving the baby back to Deborah, who put her nipple in the baby's mouth. Immediately the baby sucked and her hands came out of the lambskin to reach for her mother's breast.

Seeing the baby, longing for David, Betsy felt the room tip. Having discovered on the *Sally Dash* that she needed to busy her mind with something—the headless bearskin rug with coarse black hair, Reinke's footprints across the rug, the rough table next to the bed—Betsy took a wet cloth that hung on a basin and wiped Deborah's face. Robert had bought a slave, but he must have wooed her as a man woos a wife, otherwise Deborah wouldn't speak of him with such tenderness. When Deborah smiled, Betsy leaned over the bed to kiss her forehead.

Her eyes closed, Deborah said, "I always wanted to meet Master Robert's sister."

Betsy kissed her again, and then, for the sake of Mary, Alice, and David, she gave Deborah a third, fourth, and fifth kiss. She ran to the stairs, sped down the steps, and out of the kitchen house. At the sight of the blue mountains, those distant waves, she stopped and held her breath. "Go," she said, but returning to Robert's house required careful, determined counting.

Chapter 24

"Don't stand there beholding the food," Harmon said. "Sit down. Enjoy the company." He pushed a bowl of leathery apple slices to the empty plate across from him. Three glasses of cider, cheese, and a golden round of bread. "That Phillipa Townsend." He cut himself a wedge of cheese. "The lieutenant's gone a few hours, and after being alone all day, she won't talk to Charity." He shoved the bread toward Reinke. "Gray doesn't know what he's marrying."

Betsy picked up a glass of cider. "To Mary Alice," she said. Bread, cheese, and cider in the late afternoon were a favorite delight of Isaac. She drank a little cider and took a long sniff to smell the sharp cheese and fresh bread. Deborah and the baby had been her one thought when she saw Naomi waving the towel, but she should have kept Phillipa in mind. Reinke and Harmon could have no sense of Phillipa's distress. She said, "I'll go up to Miss Townsend."

Harmon was wrong. Charity sat on a stool, darning a stocking next to the sunny window while Phillipa, enthroned on the bed, worked on her embroidery. Had Miss Townsend been there all afternoon? No, she'd been for a walk and found an herb garden, a lovers' knot. She'd read the beginning of *Pilgrim's Progress*. Did Betsy know that Christian leaves his wife to go on an adventure? Phillipa held the blanket to the light, smiled at Betsy, and sent Charity off to finish her mending in the pantry. She handed Betsy the blanket to admire the border of pink, yellow, and blue flowers. "With every flower, I'm praying that the child cuddled in this blanket will have great good fortune."

Betsy said, "Amen." The embroidered clover, tiny knots, looked like the flower itself. "And may that child have many brothers and sisters to share those blessings."

Phillipa's eyes opened wide and she yanked the blanket back. "Brothers? Sisters?" She threw the blanket on the floor. "Mrs. Randall, the lieutenant is an only child, and I'm an only child. There's no reason to have a brood." Red splotched her cheeks. She covered her face with her hands, and her whole body trembled. "I cannot sell Charity." She peeked in the mirror to pat the smudged powder on her face. "How can I have a child without Charity to care for him?"

After she picked up the blanket and laid it next to Phillipa, Betsy sat on the bed. "You know how to change your uncle's mind, Phillipa. On the return to Williamsburg, you'll do the same with the lieutenant."

Phillipa seemed uncertain of being able to trust Betsy. She sniveled and rubbed her nose. "You're right. I'll pretend to accept his terms. I'll have Charity walk with Benjamin so she's safe from Morris, and so the lieutenant knows that I understand he wants me pure. And I'll tell Charity to be careful, to stay away from me at night, but to watch Saul to see what little favors Gray likes when his food is served, how to polish his boots, how to brush his hat." She picked up the blanket and rubbed the needle in a small nub of beeswax before she threaded it again. "I'll be rude to Charity, but she'll understand; and Gray will learn, just as Uncle has, that everyone is happier with Charity in the house." She swayed on the bed as she stitched. "When Gray's off on marches, I'll manage his estates. Uncle has me help him manage my father's property in Barbados." She pulled the thread taut. "He says I make clever decisions for the estate."

She pushed Betsy a bit to the side and stood up to examine the profile of her body in the mirror. She arched her back to raise her breasts and circled her hands around the cinched waist of the blue gown. "Lieutenant Gray has the good fortune of being my betrothed. I'll make an exemplary Mrs. Spencer Gray." Lifting her chin, she tipped her head to study her reflection. "One child, yes. A boy." She began repositioning the combs holding her curls in place. "Women with too many children talk like parrots: 'Oh, we so tired. Gwumble, gwumble, gwumble.'" She made kissing sounds: "Mm'ch, mm'ch, mm'ch." Then mmm'ch, she kissed Betsy's cheek.

Betsy turned away. At the window, she tried to rub the sting from her eyes. Mary had mm'ched to keep David from crying. Betsy rested her forehead against the cool glass. The front door below her shut, and Reinke strode to the barn, his blond hair gold in the last strong rays of sun. The tan leather of his jacket clung to the muscles of his back and shoulders. Phillipa came up and lay her head on Betsy's shoulder. "Such a handsome man. So captivated by 'the widow.'"

"I'm Mrs. Isaac Randall." She glared at Phillipa.

"And he's a willing woodsman." Phillipa sashayed to the mirror. "Several widows in Williamsburg have able tradesmen they rely on to help them from time to time. Mrs. Taylor is married and yet she needs my uncle. And Uncle has Dee, when Mrs. Taylor is out of sorts."

Betsy sat on the bed. "Your uncle has Dee? You mean he uses her."

"That's crude, Mrs. Randall." Phillipa laughed and pinched her cheeks to brighten their pink. "By the by, Uncle admired Robert Harrington's cellar. You can serve his fine wine and brandies. We have a birth to celebrate, haven't we?" She twirled about the room, hugging herself. "I've put Lieutenant Gray out of my mind until he returns."

———

After a meal in celebration of the newborn and toasts to Mary Alice, after the dishes were cleared and Reinke lit a fire in the sitting room, Betsy said, "Let's tell stories." She wanted the evening to go on. She dreaded the dark, being unable to sleep and thinking about the people in the fields. She wanted no thoughts of her taking Deborah's home from her and from Robert's children.

Harmon poured glasses of port and raised his to the flickering fire. "You want us to tell stories, Mrs. Randall?"

Reinke sipped the dark red port. "The stories must be true."

"Amen." Phillipa pressed her hands together as if in prayer. She leaned against Betsy on the settee; and then Phillipa insisted that Charity, who'd brought the embroidery thread and the blanket, sit on the floor, where

Phillipa could keep an eye on her. She clapped her hands, excited as a puppy, when Harmon said that Betsy—who had only intended to listen—tell the first story. "Mrs. Randall, you have so many stories. How will you decide which to tell?"

Betsy never told stories. She had no stories except those she'd told Mary and Alice, stories her mother had told her, stories to put little girls to sleep, stories to frighten them into good behavior. She had a set of Bible stories she told on the way to church. Isaac told stories to amuse his friends. "What stories do I have, Miss Townsend?"

"From your voyage to Virginia." Phillipa moved to keep Harmon from nudging her foot.

The *Sally Dash.* Suddenly tired, Betsy said, "I don't recall a single story, true or otherwise." She did remember her mother's story about a ghost. "It was a full month after the old woman died." At the end of her story, Betsy folded her hands in her lap.

"She dropped the pitcher." Phillipa huffed. "Dreadful. A full month after she'd died." She leaned away from Betsy. "A child could tell that story, Mrs. Randall. Our woodsman said the stories should be true, not dull." Phillipa sat up to scorn Betsy. "Well, I have a story …"

Slapping his thigh, Harmon said, "Oh, I am sorry the brave lieutenant isn't here. He should hear Miss Townsend tell her story."

Phillipa slouched back on the settee, her smile gone. She waved her hand in front of her face as if bothered by a gnat. When Charity touched her knee, Phillipa slapped her hand away.

"We can skip your turn, Phillipa." Betsy didn't want Phillipa angry with Charity again.

Cocking her head to one side, Phillipa said no, they would not skip her turn. Charity would tell a story for her. She crossed her arms as if daring Harmon to challenge her. "You all know my story of the bandits; I can't tell that."

No one moved except to look at the floor until Harmon poured himself more port. "You gave us a fright, Miss Townsend. Did you see the ghost from Mrs. Randall's story?"

"Play your fiddle. Not even Mrs. Randall saw that ghost. Her mother did. If Mr Harmon told you about the ghost my mother saw, you'd be on your knees, praying." Phillipa tucked her skirt in around her legs to keep herself from Betsy. "Mrs. Randall, stop looking at me."

His fiddle under his chin, Harmon jigged as he played. Reinke added another log to the fire. The port in Betsy's glass caught the firelight like the gleam of garnet. Captain Mayhew and Isaac had held up their glasses to see that jewel-like glow. Harmon brought the bow down hard on the lower strings just as a log collapsed on the grate.

"Charity, tell my story." Phillipa sat back on the settee with her eyes closed.

"Wait." Harmon put his fiddle in its case and poured Reinke and Phillipa more port. "There's no following Charity in a storytelling contest." Betsy held her hand over her glass, which was almost full. He sipped his port. "You listen, Mrs. Randall. This cautionary tale is for you."

He'd spent a week swapping stories with Zach Fulton, who, drunk or sober, was the best storyteller in Virginia and the Carolinas, but he wasn't going to tell one of those stories. Harmon said he regretted not warning Gray about the bandits before the expedition left Williamsburg. Once on his way back from Fulton's Crossing, he'd been kidnapped by Molly Gage and her men. Molly wanted a fiddler. They didn't put a gun to his head; they poured him excellent whiskey. After he played, she insisted that he share her bed. She had a fine voice and danced like a flame on a candle. But he missed his Polly and the little ones, so he took advantage of her being soggy drunk and snuck off. On his way back, wobbly from the whiskey, he stepped in quicksand near Fulton's Creek.

He paused his storytelling, picked up his fiddle, and played furiously, as if struggling in wet sand. They waited.

He pulled the bow across discordant strings. A devil, blacker than a panther and seven feet tall, pulled him to solid ground. Left him lying there, gasping for air, too weak to walk. "Rescued this fiddle, too. Laid it next to me." He grasped the neck of the fiddle and kissed the strings. "You see, I learned that not all devils are black and not all angels are white."

"Mr. Francis Harmon, no fool would believe your story. Is there no more port?" Phillipa held up her glass, and Harmon obliged, refilling it.

Betsy watched Harmon pour port to the brim of Phillipa's glass, but she was thinking of the clay-covered man who'd led her to the clearing.

Phillipa tapped Charity with her foot. "My turn. Charity, tell my story."

Reinke stood at the hearth, a pipe in his hand. The tang of the smoke hung in the air. "Miss Townsend, may I take your place after the fiddler? There's no quicksand in my story, but just as Harmon ran away from Gage, I too ran from a woman. I'm still running."

He watched the smoke rise from his pipe. He told of a Christmas night when a neighbor near his father's farm in

Pennsylvania accused Reinke of having put his daughter in the family way. His father wanted him to marry the girl because he'd inherit a prosperous farm, but he fled to Philadelphia where a furrier, a Quaker, took him in, and he learned something of the trade. "I prefer trapping to being in a shop, and I have lived in the woods since then. Except when I bring my skins back to Philadelphia." He drew on his pipe and smiled at Betsy, as if now that he'd confessed his sin, she should forgive him.

"But did you sleep with your neighbor's daughter?" Harmon asked the question Betsy wanted Reinke to answer.

"My older brother married my accuser and farms her father's land. When Father dies, Johan will have two farms to pass to his sons." At the hearth, he knocked the ash into the fire.

Betsy wondered if he'd ever seen the child, but Phillipa kicked at Charity. "Tell my story."

"Mr. Reinke, don' you be sayin this story ain't true." Charity edged away when Phillipa kicked her again. She sat up on her heels and looked at her. "Please be careful, Miss Phillipa. The Devil's everywhere."

Charity bowed her head. "Now, when I say, 'once,' you say 'time,' that way I know you're fixin to listen."

"Good idea." Reinke sat cross-legged near the fire. He winked at Betsy, reminding her of Charlie on the *Sally Dash*, a sailor Isaac never trusted. Harmon sat at the harpsichord.

"Once," Charity said.

They waited.

"Once," she repeated, and everyone except Phillipa said, "Time." Exasperated, Phillipa said, "Of course you can't start a story like other people do."

Her eyelashes a fringe on the tops of her cheeks, Charity didn't move.

"Time," Phillipa said. She licked the rim of her glass with her tongue.

The day her mother yanked out a baby tooth, the Tripps bought Charity. "I had to pick greens and berries like my mother had showed me, but they had me doing everything." She cleaned and oiled traps, skinned rabbits and squirrels, cooked meat and made corn mush.

"You lived alone with those Tripps?" Betsy asked. Charity would have been younger than Mary. Mary couldn't keep house for grown men.

"No interruptions." Phillipa frowned and shushed Betsy.

"Maybe young Silas killed his brother. I ran out the house and they didn't ask me, but after he gone, Master Silas smoked a pipe and had a chat with Satan every night."

Phillipa shoved her shoulder. "True stories, Charity. You tell us how Satan looks."

"Don' trick me, Miss Phillipa." Charity held up her hand, fingers to the ceiling, stating what she knew to be true. "God-fearing people can' see the Devil, but they know his handiwork. When I pick feathers off the birds he shot or cleaned his fish—which I never ate—Master Silas sits talkin to nothin at all. That's how I know the Devil goes naked; he don' wear clothes."

Reinke nodded, his face set. "Yah. This is so. I've seen it too."

One night, when her master was hunting for his whip to skin her black back, she ran. The woods were darker than pitch, but she didn't care. Branches hit her face. She kept running. Stumbling, falling, getting up, and running on until an evil root grabbed her foot and down she went, mouth full of dirt, the dogs barking right behind her. Master Silas cursed behind them, his lantern bobbing up and down. "My heart's beatin like a rabbit in a trap, but I can't pull my foot free." Charity hugged her knees to her chest, rocking back and forth. She looked up at Harmon and Reinke. "Can you believe? Chop. The root is cut. Slashed so I pull free. And just like you, Harmon, the Devil himself picks me up." She looked back at Phillipa, who sat, transformed to an earnest listener.

"You said you couldn't see the Devil," Phillipa said.

"I know, but there he was." In the fire, she seemed to see the man in the woods. "He's black. I can only see his eyes. Then I see he's got horrible yellow teeth, pointy like a cat." Clasping her hands around her knees, she balled up tight. "My life was over."

"Charity, stop this story this very minute." Phillipa stamped her foot. "You never told me this story, and I don't want to hear it."

Sitting back on her heels, Charity looked to the side, considering Phillipa's accusation.

"Miss Phillipa, I never told anybody—not even Miss Fulton."

Harmon refilled Reinke's glass and his. "Miss Townsend, Charity's telling your story. Please don't interrupt yourself." He poured port into the glass Phillipa held out to him. "Time, Charity. We're all saying 'time.'"

"That black man didn't make a sound. No branches hit him. Roots don' catch him. He carries me like I weigh nothin—which I don't, cause Master Silas never wasted food on me. He lays me in a hollow, and I'm prayin, my eyes closed, hearin Master Silas's hounds bark; my heart thumpin so hard it hurts my ears. I ask myself, 'If he the Devil, how come he saved me?' He smell like smoke, that's true; and he smell like woods. I keep repeatin, 'God is my Redeemer.' He sent an African angel to save me. That's my answer." She looked around to see if any of them had a better explanation.

Betsy knew the smell. She knew the man. Betsy would never tell them about the wildman. She didn't think that he would want her to tell anyone.

Phillipa leaned down to nudge Charity again. She said, "Time, Charity. Time."

Charity cocked her head as if listening for the barking dogs or her master crashing after her. "Master Silas screamed ... Terrible, terrible scream. I almost felt bad for him. Then it was just the dogs. Howlin and growlin low." She shivered like she heard the dogs again. "Then I don' hear them, and the African's back, not sayin nothing. Jus picks me up and carries me right to Fulton's barn, right to the loft. Lays me in new cut grass like he cut it hisself and left it there for me. It smelled sweet as a meadow." She sat back with a sad look as if longing for that smell. "And you know what? That man was gone."

Her knees tight to her chest, she rocked. Betsy rocked, but not so Phillipa and the men would notice. She'd rocked on the deck when the children were gone. The anguish rocked inside her.

"He murdered your master?" Phillipa bent to study Charity's face.

Harmon stood up and kicked a log deeper into the fire. "Word was Tripp's hounds turned on him."

Reinke said, "It happens with the wrong kind of dog."

"I never said anybody murdered him. According to Mr. Fulton, only thing left was his clothes." Charity stared at Phillipa.

"You never told me that man brought you to Fulton's Crossing."

"Look at the moon." Harmon beckoned for them to follow him to the window.

The moon sat, an enormous disk, like a white gong over the roof of the barn. The gravel drive and the shingles of the barn glimmered. In the meadow, a shadow moved: a horse grazing on the dark silver grass. Harmon went to the harpsichord to tune his fiddle.

Betsy looked across the meadow to the treetops dipping in the wind, inviting her to the woods. She sat back on the settee and imagined herself in Charity's story, alone in Mrs. Fulton's loft, hunched over and afraid.

"A glass of water, Charity." Phillipa's words brought Betsy back to Good Hope and to the dancing fire; but the moment Charity closed the door, Phillipa asked Reinke if he thought the runaway who'd saved Harmon and the one who captured Charity still roamed the woods. Betsy guessed she had wanted to impress Williamsburg with her bandit story, and now she had the story of Charity's running away. Maybe she wanted her own report for the governor.

Reinke used the fireplace poker to knock the ash off the logs. "Charity told a good story for you, Miss Townsend. Silas Tripp was a wretch attacked by his own dogs or a crazed bear."

Harmon squeaked the strings of his fiddle with the low hoo-hoot of an owl. When Charity opened the door and it squealed, they laughed, and Harmon tuned his fiddle to play a jig. Phillipa jumped to her feet, stepping to the music. "Mr. Bear tips his hat, 'How-dee-do.'" She turned to Reinke. "'How-dee-do.'" Back to Betsy, she sang, "'When next we meet, bring me honey, too.'" When she repeated the verse, Harmon winked at Betsy on the word "honey" and played a suggestive slur on his fiddle.

Taking Charity's hands, Phillipa began to dance. "Watch our steps, Mrs. Randall. See how we Virginians dance." They circled the room, arm in arm, spinning toward and away from one another, equally graceful and sure of their footing, one dark and wearing blue-and-white checked calico, the other in a well-fitted blue silk with lace trim—the same height, the same age, the same delight in each other. Phillipa laughed at Betsy's watching their feet.

Harmon bumped Reinke with his elbow, tipping his head toward Betsy. To her relief, the woodsman turned away. When the fiddler bumped him the second time, Reinke couldn't pretend not to understand. He left the fire and extended his hand to Betsy. "I'm not a dancer, but if you'd like to romp around the room like Miss Townsend, I'll not step on your toes."

Betsy had good reason not to dance with the woodsman. She was in mourning, and Naomi, doing the dishes in the pantry, was pregnant with his child. But she had at last reached Good Hope; and in the firelight, Reinke's eyes shone. Betsy wanted to dance. At one point during the storytelling, she'd had an urge to fit her finger in the curls at his neck. After a glass of port—or was it two?— she put her hand in Reinke's palm, confident of the rhythm, and twirled around the room. Shadows leaped on the walls and ceiling to the rhythm of Harmon's music. Reinke put his arm around Betsy's waist and spun her to him, pressing her body with a laugh. Betsy stepped back, Mrs. Isaac Randall again, and clapped along with Reinke and Phillipa. Charity put the glasses on a tray and left the room.

"What would we have done without you, Mr. Harmon?" Betsy asked. From her head to her toes, she felt young and pretty, glad Phillipa had persuaded her to wear the black silk.

Reinke kicked at a log that shot up sparks. "We wouldn't be here. He called the bandit by her name, and then you shoved her into the bayonet." He turned to Betsy and bowed. "Guten nacht." He bowed to Harmon and Phillipa and left the room.

Betsy stared after him. She hadn't meant to push the woman into the bayonet.

When Phillipa put an arm around her, Betsy thanked her. She said she was suddenly lonely.

"Remember, Mrs. Randall, we're sisters."

Betsy smiled. She followed Phillipa up the stairs. Charity had turned down the quilt and was lying on her pallet at the foot of the bed. Soon Phillipa and Charity were breathing slowly, evenly, in unison.

Staring at moonlit clouds, Betsy listened to the fiddler playing scales, lower and lower, until the notes were lost. Betsy was Isaac's widow, but she'd liked feeling Reinke's hands on her waist. She wanted him in the bed with her. She tossed to one side but couldn't sleep. She pressed her hands up her thighs, between her thighs, over her breasts, letting her hands rove to her body's desire. And she stopped. A baby. How could Isaac's child claim a plantation when Robert's own children lived on it? Betsy ached for the girls, for David, for Isaac.

Chapter 25

Betsy pulled up her stockings, grabbed her shawl, and tiptoed across the room, clutching her shoes. She tested each step to keep the wood from creaking. On the second to the last stair, she listened. The house was silent. Harmon snored in the sitting room, perhaps asleep on the carpet. He would awaken if she bumped a wall or if the setter Whitmore kept in the house barked. Betsy reached her hand down as the dog padded over to her and rubbed against her leg. Harmon mumbled, coughed, and then snored louder. Betsy petted the dog and walked him to the door. She held his head, and his eyes shone up at her. She mouthed the word "No." Betsy gripped the brass key of the front door, gauged the pressure to release the lock, and stepped outside. Only the dog heard her leave. The wood scraped against the jamb when she pulled the door shut—a shush that wouldn't awaken the sleepers. She'd escaped.

The full moon shimmered on the grass in the pasture. It had shimmered on the wrinkled water the night she'd stood on deck with Isaac. The air was warmer than on the ship. Instead of thinking of Isaac, she should put on her shoes.

She buckled them on the bench at the front door and walked in silence across the yard. The empty wagon waited, iridescent with moon glow. Phillipa would ride back to Williamsburg, and Charity would walk. Gray and his men—Morris, Reinke, and Harmon—would be gone.

A gathering of horses, shadows in the pasture, crowded the fence. One of them nickered; others, agreeing, swished their tails. How peaceful Good Hope seemed. It smelled of sweet grass with a whiff of manure. The quiet protected Betsy. She wasn't leaving tomorrow, or the day after. She wouldn't be going back in the wagon with Phillipa. She was leaving now. Her steps on the gravel crunched a soft "Yes, yes, yes."

What Betsy needed was her mother. She needed her mother to comfort her—that and so much more. She clasped the gray shawl tight around her shoulders. Deborah knew the land and the slaves. She had her baby, Susannah, Isaiah. She had Whitmore. The kitchen house, the garden, the big house—all of it belonged to Deborah. The bed where Phillipa slept, that bed belonged to Deborah. Harmon saw her as a usurper; he'd guessed the truth. Deborah's children had stronger rights to the land, the house, and the slaves than Betsy. Their names should be on the deed. Whitmore and Deborah had worked to create Good Hope in this wilderness; their baby had a better right to the plantation than Betsy.

Shadows of trees half-hid the gravel lane. The silence came to life. Leaves murmured to one another, "Catch her, catch her." Smells of soil, weedy plants, and the trees crept up her arms and wrapped around her back. To keep from hearing her own steps, she walked on the leaf mulch at the dark edge of the lane. Moonlight on the gravel made her way clear. From a distance, she heard a forlorn hoo-hoo-hoo. From farther off, an owl answered. Betsy pictured herself, a woman in her shift, a gray shawl, and shoes, her hair flying out from under her nightcap. She stepped lightly to keep her leaving a secret. Where was she going? Another hoo-oo-oo and the distant reply. How far could she go with no food, no water, no direction? How long could she keep going? She wouldn't turn back. She'd stay on the road until she came to Fulton's Crossing. She'd walk until she could go no farther; she would not turn back. Isaac had set her on this path to her brother's plantation, and now she was returning. He'd thought he knew where they were going, but he hadn't.

Reinke's father sent his son away. His mother let her son go off alone. How could his mother give up her son for the virtue of a neighbor's daughter? A man, a young man, can run. Would a Quaker take Betsy on as an apprentice? Where could she go to escape Good Hope?

By the third hoo-oo-oo, Betsy was creeping down the main road. She could walk between the ruts and no one would hear her. To the north, a woman screamed, yowled in anger and in pain. Betsy listened, held her breath. Not moving felt safer. She didn't want to know why the woman screamed. Ahead, the road, gray in the moonlight, disappeared under the black trees. Betsy listened. Nothing. The same smells of earth and trees—night air. The earth cushioned her feet if she stepped off the road. Twiggy noises on the ground didn't frighten her. The scream came from the direction Gray's men had taken. It wasn't Deborah or Naomi. Not Charity or Phillipa. It wasn't she, though she felt a scream in her throat. Some woman in the dark woods, like the settler woman killed by the Seneca, had screamed. And she screamed again.

Betsy steeled herself to keep going.

Overhead, tree branches splotched the moonlight, shadowing the ruts. She slid her feet a few inches at a time to keep from tripping. Harmon's indignation hurt. Betsy had no intention of owning Deborah and Whitmore's baby. What did Reinke know when he said, "The fiddler's right"? The man wouldn't claim his own child. The leaves and small branches shuddered. They quaked like the men and women on the slaver docked in the Chesapeake. Worse, they pointed at her, with the sharp looks of the people following Xerxes from the fields, the slaves of Good Hope.

The road sloped downhill with loose gravel. Betsy held her arms in front, not sure the way was clear; her hands, pale moonlit ghosts, led her on. Her shoe caught on a root, and she stumbled, caught her fall, and landed on her knees. She was not afraid. She must not be afraid. Not of the dark or the black trees. The last time she'd fallen, the wild man had been there. He'd known where she would be safe, but Betsy was glad to be alone, to be where no one would find her. Next to where she knelt, she saw a bush with shiny, finger-length leaves and buds the size of a baby's fist. One had blossomed, the unlocking petals silver in moonlight. Dark wings swooped from the stumps in the cleared field and vanished in the branches overhead. The shambled fence had dismayed her when she first saw it. That fence, the soldiers' cause for cheering, had stunned her two days ago. The warped logs looked like evil haunts.

The night aroused itself. A twig cracked. Rustling. The woods had discovered her escape.

Betsy crawled on moss, leaf mold, twigs, and pebbles to the first strong tree and snuggled between two gnarled roots. She smelled dead things: old tree bark, fallen branches, spent animals, tiny voles, aged bears. In the tree's lap, she thought of her body buried in this spot. She had the alphabet. A is for Alice, *B* is for baby, *C* is for Carl ... Reinke spelled his Christian name with a *K*. Germans did. She'd come to his name before David. *I* is for Isaac. She backed against the trunk to slow her heartbeat, to quiet its thump against the tree. Roots forked beyond her feet, protecting her.

In September, her child would be in her arms. To give birth ... to deliver the child ... to have the baby command her body and push its way out, into her care. She had no one she trusted as Deborah did Martin Whitmore. The new life curled under her ribs just as she'd curled into the roots of the tree. Her breasts anticipated the child's hunger, but the child would need more than a nursing mother. Betsy couldn't live in this wilderness; she wasn't the wild man. She couldn't raise a child in the woods. She had to return to the house for the sake of her child. It had to be his—Isaac's. The Creator wouldn't punish her with Bennett's child. She'd return to Isaac's world, to Robert's plantation, to the people who worked for Good Hope, to those who knew it as home.

Betsy prayed. She squeezed a prayer for her child into her folded hands, and then placed her hands on her stomach. Isaac had promised her this child, a gift from him and God. She'd met kind people: Mrs. Fulton, Whitmore and Reinke; Phillipa and Charity. Phillipa, determined to be Mrs. Spencer Gray would keep Charity close to her. Betsy had been given lessons in courage. Dee. If Betsy bought her, she knew women who would pay Betsy to have Dee work for them for a day or a week. Betsy did talk to Osborne, but when he said he'd never sell Dee, Betsy hadn't argued. If she explained her desperation when she returned to

Williamsburg, he might be more compassionate. Together, she and Dee could live in Williamsburg. She could teach girls as she had taught Mary and Alice. And Davy. Davy had taught himself.

Braced against the gnarled trunk, Betsy inched her way up. A vole peeking out from under a leaf wouldn't have noticed. Betsy would go back. For Robert's children, she'd take possession of Good Hope, but they wouldn't be slaves on their father's plantation—on her plantation.

In the tobacco field, a stump moved. No, the shadow was too wide for the stump. Not a shadow. A man. A long, flat spike reflected a shaft of moonlight above the blunt trunk. The briefest flash of metal, and then the field was dark again. Betsy didn't move. She couldn't. Her heart thudded. The man took a step toward the fence and disappeared. Maybe she'd imagined him, as she had the woman's scream. The night had tricked her. She'd mistaken a stump, or the shadow behind it, for a man. Leaves rustled above her. She had to be calm herself or her poor child would have a mad mother. Not moving was her one protection.

On the other side of the road, a man the color of dirt stepped onto the road. His body twisted and he thrust his spear into the branches of the tree that had protected Betsy. He sprang onto the road, landing in a crouch; his dagger, as sharp as any pirate's knife, quivered in his hand. Betsy clung to the trunk of her tree. She heard a snarl and then saw a flash of dull gold. A weight dropped between the road and Betsy. A cat the size of a man bared its teeth with its claws outstretched. It writhed on the spear in its gut, breaking the shaft. When the cat lunged for her, the man plunged his knife into the cat's ribs, and the animal arched back, its jaws open to tear at him. He jerked the knife free and stuck it under the ear and cut down into the neck. Blood spurted on the road. Black in the moonlight, it flowed toward his feet. The man watched for the beast to round on him again, but except for the twitch of the back leg, it lay still.

Betsy picked up her skirt and bolted for the house. She slipped to her knees on loose gravel. Behind her, the man was binding the front paws of the cat together. He seemed not to have seen Betsy. When she got back on her feet, footsteps crunched at her side, and another man stepped into the road. Reinke, his gold hair silver in moonlight, held a rifle and her mother's shawl.

Betsy grabbed the shawl. She must have dropped it when the cat fell from the tree, but how did Reinke come to have it? Her teeth chattered. Reinke had no reason to be out on the road in the middle of the night. "Why did you follow me?"

"Go to the house." He reached for her arm. "*Bitte*."

"Why are you here?" Shivering, angry, determined not to cry, Betsy kept away from him. "Tell me."

"Quick to the house and I'll tell you." Grasping her elbow, he steered her down the road, lifting her with each step. "The cougar may have a mate in these woods."

"Cougar?" She wriggled to face Reinke. "The lion?" She was trembling. "Did you see the wild man?"

"Where were you going in your shift and a shawl?" He pulled her down the road toward the house.

"Did you see the man?"

Reinke looked ahead to the barn. "I saw your dark angel throw the spear." He pronounced angel *en-gal*. "I heard someone on the gravel near the house and came down from the barn loft in time to see you walk into the woods. I followed to see where you were going." He paused, but she said nothing. "Where were you going?" He waited, but Betsy chose not to answer. "The man saved your life."

"Did he see you?"

Reinke shrugged. "He was hunting the cat. Like me, he heard the scream, but the one he killed was closer than the one that cried."

"The woman?"

"Not a woman. The cougar was stalking you—or him."

At the house, Betsy stopped him from opening the front door. "I want to return to Yorktown." She sat on the bench where she'd put on her shoes. When he sat next to her, she was finally glad he'd come after her. "You heard the owl?"

"You're not alone, Mrs. Randall. You have friends." In the moonlight, his skin grayed to the color of stone. He turned to her. "Why is your trunk so heavy?"

Her trunk? Betsy stared at him. His eyes, his leather clothes, his boots were the same as yesterday, but why, in the middle of the night, would he ask about her trunk? She'd tried to run away, the wild man had thrown a spear and killed a giant cat that meant to pounce on her, and this woodsman was asking about her trunk. "My husband …" Betsy stopped. She wouldn't explain the great care Isaac took when he designed the trunk for their clothes and dishes. Not trusting sailors or the men on the docks, Isaac had insisted that the trunk be double-sided and sealed for him alone to open. "My husband …"

"Your husband hired a clever carpenter, Mrs. Randall." Reinke picked up a stone and threw it at the foundation of the house, just missing a mouse that ran between two bricks. "Only gold could make the trunk as heavy as it is."

"Gold?" Did the man mean pounds? Guineas? Isaac had a few gold coins in the box Piggy tried to steal, and they had disappeared when the *Falconer* captured the Dash, but Isaac said he was leaving their wealth in London. Betsy preferred thinking about Isaac when she was alone. "The few coins he packed were discovered by the pirates." Her teeth chattered again, but she closed her mouth tight to keep Reinke from noticing. She waited until she could speak without stuttering. "Captain Bennett said they couldn't find my husband's money."

Isaac would give her a few coins for the house, but he never told Betsy where he hid the money, though she knew that he had hiding places in the house, the garden, and his mother's home. He'd said he left the gold in England, but she wasn't sure that she believed him. Isaac didn't want her to ask about it. After the pirates, she hadn't cared. Sensing that Reinke was watching her, she brushed off twigs and bits of earth that had caught on her shift when she'd fallen. "My husband had the chest made in Brompton." The number of coins that rolled from the box Piggy dropped didn't match the stacks of gold Isaac counted on the first of November, All Hallows' Day, a day of reckoning, according to Isaac. Betsy looked at the barn, as if to see through the walls, to see the trunk in one of the first stalls. Whitmore assured her it would be safe since Reinke slept in the loft. It had been too heavy to carry up to the bedroom where she and Phillipa slept. "The trunk has our dishes and bedding."

"The boards are hollow." Reinke tipped his head toward the barn. "Your husband was a banker. The trunk is a vault."

Afraid the house itself might hear, Betsy whispered. "You don't know that, Mr. Reinke."

He said nothing, but turned to look at the pasture.

"Did you follow me to tell me about the trunk?"

"I followed you because you were running away and the woods are dangerous." He turned toward her. "But as for the trunk, when Ben and Saul went to move it, they needed help. Whitmore and Xerxes said the planks were too thick, a waste of wood; but knock the top planks—the boards are thick as planks on a barn floor—and the wood is solid. Knock the sides, the sound is flat. I'll wager the sides and the bottom of the trunk have coins packed with batting or sawdust to keep them from rattling." He picked up a stone, and with a flick of his wrist, flung it toward the barn. Pebbles scattered. "How did I find out? At the burned clearing, I watched the surveyor tap the trunk—the top and the sides. He walked away and looked around. He didn't see me watching him. He came back and tapped around it again. After we carried it into the barn, I tried it myself."

Reinke looked from Betsy to the pasture; and like him, Betsy gazed at the horses along the fence. The bay stood head to tail with the black mare. The brown stallion, a handsome horse that Robert must have won by gambling, faced the house. Most distant from the barn, a foal nuzzled his mother, a dark-brown mare with white stockings and a white star on her forehead. Watching them consoled her. Reinke said, "You need to break apart the trunk."

He'd said she wasn't alone, but she was, and soon she would have a child to feed and clothe, a child that would need a home. No matter what the deed said, the house at Good Hope belonged to Deborah. Susannah and Isaiah should have been named in Robert's will. Betsy said, "I'm expecting a baby."

"Is that the reason you ran away?"

"My husband wanted to take possession of my brother's

land." She walked toward the pasture. "I don't want to live here, but he would want his child to inherit Good Hope."

"He is in line for the property." He walked alongside Betsy. "I have run away. It is dangerous."

Stopping to face him, she said, "How can Mr. Harmon think that I don't understand Deborah and Whitmore's love for their child?" Pulling her mother's shawl tighter, fingering the loops of the knit, Betsy stood at the pasture fence with Reinke. "I saw a slaver, a dreadful ship. I saw a mother dragged from her child. How can Mr. Harmon think I don't know the pain of losing a child?"

One of the horses tossed its head and blew through heavy lips. Reinke said, "There are always wounded lions crouched, ready to pounce." He pointed to the stallion that had galloped off, as if frightened by gunfire; but it might have been startled by a mouse in the grass. "The fiddler fears his children will be kidnapped and sold in the Carolinas." Reinke turned to face the house. "He'd never get them back. And Morris?" He kicked a tuft of grass. "He ran from his indenture in New York. He didn't stop running until an old surveyor needed an apprentice, but he fears the man who holds his papers."

"Mr. Morris?" Betsy moved away from Reinke. The hunter had insinuated that the surveyor might be planning to steal whatever Isaac had hidden in the trunk. The woodsman knew that the brute forced himself on Charity. "Then his treatment of Charity is more reprehensible."

Trotting back to the herd, the stallion grazed with the other horses. A mare nuzzled her colt. Reinke said nothing. In the silence, the breeze carried the scent of the meadow. The horses whiffled a quiet conversation until the stallion whinnied and rose on his hind legs.

Reinke chewed a stalk of grass he pulled from near a fencepost and then spit on the ground. "My father had a slave. Two. One died. He buried him behind the barn where we buried our dogs." He looked to the back of the pasture. "Yah, that's what we did."

"With the dogs?"

"Yah." Reinke nodded. He seemed to look far beyond the meadow. "He cost my father a year's harvest and then died—no reason—before the first hard frost."

Dawn glazed the trees with pink. The horses nickered and plodded off toward the brook. Motioning for Betsy to go to the house, Reinke said, "Don't go off by yourself again."

"I had turned back." She didn't look away from him. "For the baby's sake." After glancing to the path she'd taken into the woods, she reached for the door.

Reinke pointed for her to take off her shoes before he opened the door, without making even the softest scritch. He led her to the pantry, as silent in his boots as she was in her stocking feet. He poured two glasses of cider and offered her one. Unaware of her thirst until she put the cold glass to her lips, she downed the cider and held out the glass for more. She drank a second glass.

"I'm glad you came after me, Mr. Reinke." She took his hand, and despite his look of surprise, touched it to her lips, a kiss in thanks for his telling her about the trunk. Isaac Randall would have taken the precaution of building a box with false sides to hide his gold, and kept it a secret, even from his wife.

———

Though she'd kept the ropes from squeaking when she rolled onto the bed, Phillipa turned toward her, whimpering. Betsy asked, "What is it, Phillipa?"

"Where did you go?"

"I'm here now." After the gold cat's pounce, the wild man, his spear, his dagger, his stabbing the cat's neck, Reinke's sudden appearance on the road, and their conversation, Betsy didn't want to talk to Phillipa. She didn't want to think at all.

"You went outside. You smell of night air."

Betsy's shift smelled of the tree and the forest floor. She could still smell the cat, though she didn't have that on her clothes. Betsy's mind spun, but she needed quiet. "Go to sleep, Phillipa. I won't leave."

"When I marry the lieutenant, my father's plantation will be his. Now it's in Uncle's trust. What happens to Charity isn't up to me."

When Betsy closed her eyes, the cat clawed the air and then its body hit the ground with a thud, the claws scratching for her face. Isaac hadn't known about the danger. He believed he was responsible for claiming Robert's estate. Betsy reached across the bed and took Phillipa's hand. "Men have control of the land, but we decide what is right and wrong for ourselves."

Her own words confounded her. She knew what was right for Susannah and Isaiah, but was it wise for her own child? Betsy put aside thoughts about Good Hope when Charity turned on her pallet. "How important is Charity to you, Phillipa?"

Phillipa's foot slammed into Betsy's thigh to push her off the bed. "You are a monster, Mrs. Randall." She started to kick again, but Betsy grabbed her ankle. She squirmed to pull free. "You are a worse ogre than he. You are not my sister. I've been kind to you and treated you better than a friend, but you ask me horrible things. You should have stayed in the woods."

"Yes, perhaps ... I wanted to. But I didn't have the courage." Betsy stared at the ceiling, gray in the wan light. "I didn't mean to be unkind to you. You'll find a way to keep Charity."

Phillipa didn't draw her hand away. "No, Betsy, I won't keep Charity." For the first time, she'd called Betsy by her Christian name. She'd muffled her voice in Betsy's pillow. Pulling Betsy to her, her mouth at Betsy's ear, Phillipa said, "People in Williamsburg do whisper about me and Charity." She sank back on the bed. "The lieutenant wants a wife without reproach, a wife of noble character. You know the verse from Proverbs."

"What will happen to Charity?"

"Everyone knows who treats slaves well." Phillipa brushed a wisp of hair behind Betsy's ear. "Uncle will find good people in Maryland or Delaware. He buys slaves and horses there." Phillipa turned her head to Charity's pallet on the floor. "I could be married and still love my Charity, but I couldn't marry Lieutenant Gray." She sighed. "I'll make an excellent Mrs. Spencer Gray. If I could keep Charity, I would be a happy Mrs. Spencer Gray."

"Charity knows," Betsy said.

Phillipa was quiet.

"I didn't tell her and you didn't tell her, but she knows."

Cuddling close to Betsy, Phillipa said, "I will be cold. Lieutenant Gray will be proud of me." Phillipa moved back to her own pillow. "Why did you run away?"

"I couldn't sleep." Betsy turned away from Phillipa. "It was childish. A foolish thing."

"Next time, take me with you."

"Yes, of course. Charity too."

"She'll like that. Remember her story? She ran away before." Suddenly, Phillipa grabbed Betsy's arm. "Mrs. Randall ..." She paused. "You and I are sisters. I didn't mean what I said."

"Yes, I know." Betsy let Phillipa snuggle next to her the way Mary used to curl around Alice. S is for sister. A is for alphabet. Nonsense. "Yes, we're sisters."

Phillipa slept. Long after she turned on her side, breathing evenly, Betsy said, "Charity too." The room was silent. Betsy had been cowardly to run away, but she wasn't sorry.

Chapter 26

Dogs barked. Betsy listened, puzzled. A horse whinnied. There were no dogs or horses on board. On the bunk, next to Isaac, Betsy lay still. She wasn't on the *Sally Dash*, but in Robert's big bed at Good Hope. Phillipa's rosewater scented the warm room. The horse whinnied again. Opening her eyes, with no thought of lifting her head from the pillow, Betsy lingered on the featherbed in the morning gold. Outside, below the window, hooves crunched on the gravel. A man shouted, "Tether that horse." Lieutenant Gray.

But he'd left yesterday for the march west to complete Morris's survey of the land and to blaze Petty's property and the governor's settlement. Betsy threw back the quilt and ran to the window. Morris said they'd be gone a week or longer. Betsy didn't see the surveyor.

Phillipa slept flat on the mattress, her pillow pulled to her side. Drool seeped into the sheet. Charity's pallet was rolled up next to the door. To peek out without the men seeing her, Betsy stood against the wall for a view of the lane. The men had dropped their gear to the ground and were stumbling to the well. One led Petty's horse to the corral. In rumpled, dirty jackets and pants, some of the troops with blood-soaked bandages clumped together. A young soldier with his arm in a sling helped a comrade limp to the bench by the front door. Under the trees along the lane next to the pasture, the burly soldier, his big shoulders slumped, stood in tired attention. With the bayonet of his rifle pointing to the sky, he guarded three bodies covered with blankets. Lying with his head on his paws, Jim Morris's dog whined by the blanket closest to the house.

At the fence where Reinke and Betsy had stood a few hours before, Charity vomited. She wiped her mouth on her sleeve and then retched again. Saul went to her and put a hand on her shoulder, leaning over like he was talking to her. He stayed for a moment before running to lead Ramses to the barn.

Standing near the bench where a wounded man now sat, Harmon yelled. "Git water," and Charity ran to the house.

Betsy shut the window and closed the curtain. Leaning against the wall, she wished she could close out the noise and confusion from the yard, but shutting her eyes didn't work. She laced her stomacher over her shift. A notched rim of a shell button caught on a linen thread when she buttoned her dress. After three attempts, she worried the button through. The ribbon of her cap snagged strands of hair at her neckline and pulled. Her eyes stung. She would not cry; she would help Gray and his men. After cramming her swollen feet into her shoes, damp from the dew on the grass at the pasture fence last night, she picked up her shawl and tiptoed out. The room—bed, chair, wardrobe—wobbled until she rested her head on the wall. Balancing herself as she had on the *Sally Dash*, she started down the stairs.

From the pantry doorway, Charity stared at Betsy, an empty wooden pail in each hand. In a low voice, she asked, "Mrs. Randall, why you countin?"

Taken aback, Betsy grabbed the banister. Counting? Yes, she had been counting. She was on seven. She was on the seventh step. With numbers she knew what was coming. Numbers had comforted her on the *Sally Dash* after Josiah dropped Isaac overboard. "Counting helps me work."

Charity looked off toward the pasture. "They was surprised," she said. She smelled of vomit; her teeth chattered. "Mrs. Randall, Mr. Morris dead." Charity shuddered, and one bucket knocked against the pantry door. "I didn't see the body. I don' want to see the body, but his hound won' leave his side." She squeezed her arms to her sides. "I'm shiverin cold."

Betsy wrapped her shawl around Charity and took the buckets from her. "I'll draw the water." She nodded for Charity to go out the back door. "Sometimes I say the alphabet. Letters work too." She didn't say that numbers and letters protected her, but they did. "Go wash in Deborah's kitchen where it's quiet."

Betsy walked as far from the men as possible on her way to the well.

"Where's that water?" Harmon, surprised to see Betsy with the buckets, ran to help her. "The Seneca attacked before dawn."

"I can draw water, Mr. Harmon." She handed him the bucket she'd filled to bring to the men. Betsy didn't want to help the exhausted men or see their wounds, but she could run errands for the fiddler. She stayed away from the dead, especially Morris's body. She hadn't liked the man, but his being killed sickened her. Counting fourteen steps, she set the second bucket next to Harmon and Whitmore. The overseer supported a wounded soldier on the bench while the fiddler probed his wounds. He and the other soldiers were no older than Phillipa, but in uniforms, they'd seemed like men. One moaned.

"We need bandages," Harmon said. To cut a bigger opening around the wound, Harmon edged his knife under the man's woolen pant leg.

Back in the dining room, Charity had already found a sheet of yellow homespun and begun tearing bandages. Betsy took one half of the sheet and ripped a strip the width of her hand with a count of "One, two, three." She started another. "One, two, three." Another. Charity echoed her count. When they had a mountain of bandages, Charity said, "I'm all right now, Mrs. Randall. My shakin is over." Betsy took a bundle from the top of the bandages and put them in one of the baskets Charity had brought with the sheet. Charity put the rest in the second basket, and they carried them out to Harmon.

The soldier drank from Harmon's flask. He winced and turned away.

"Charity, you leave your bandages here with Mr. Harmon. I'll bring mine to Mr. Reinke." Betsy headed to the shade of the barn where Reinke and Nighthawk had arranged a board on sawhorses and were attending to a soldier with a cut under his ribs. As she started across the yard, she noticed Mr. Petty staggering toward the fields, pulling his shirt over his head. Betsy ran to leave her bandages within Reinke's and Nighthawk's easy reach, and hurried after the journalist. He'd thrown his shirt to the ground and sat down to unbuckle his shoe. One foot bare already, he'd soon be rid of the other shoe and stocking.

Betsy picked up what he'd dropped. "Mr. Petty, please put these on. You need to sit where it's quiet. Maybe the study." When she held out his shirt, he seemed not to recognize her, and spurned her touch. She called for someone to help her get Petty into the house.

Nobody heard her. Nobody listened to Gray, either. He shouted orders but didn't finish the commands. "Clean those rifles ... Powder—cover it ... Morris's horse needs to be watered ... Ramses." He pointed to the barn. "The stables." His confused commands put the chaos of the yard into words.

Shaking free of Betsy's grip on his elbow, Petty pointed to the blankets under the tree. She tried to help him put on his shirt, but he refused until she agreed that the two of them should join Gray. The lieutenant paced back and forth, a few feet from the bodies. The surveyor's dog whimpered. The lieutenant knelt beside the hound, petting his head until he was quiet. Easing his pistol from the holster, Gray shot the dog before Betsy could look away. Its legs flung out. On one side, it quivered and then lay still.

Angry, but a coward, instead of confronting the lieutenant, Betsy turned on Petty. "You must put on your shirt. Go inside and have breakfast with the troops."

"I shall not." He took the shirt and walked to the bench where Harmon was stitching up a gash on a man's arm with a curved needle, the kind used for working leather. Whitmore held the skin together while Harmon sewed. Betsy tried to direct Petty past the bench, but he insisted on staying there. Petty pointed to Ned, the Pamunkey guide, who was carrying Morris's dog toward the pasture, and swiped his shirt against Whitmore's back. "Did you see the lieutenant shoot the dog?"

Whitmore looked up, annoyed. "A glass of cider for Jacob here, Mrs. Randall?" He held the muscle and skin of the man's leg together so Harmon could sew the wound into a thin red line. "Finish your story, Harmon. How many sisters slept with you that night?"

Betsy didn't stay to hear the answer. She left Petty to get a pitcher of cider and a mug from the kitchen house.

When she came back, Whitmore drank from the mug while he held the wound closed with the other hand. He wanted Betsy to offer the mug to Harmon, but the fiddler told her to hold it to his patient's mouth. The man's cheeks had paled to the gray of marble, the skin under his eyes faded from dark purple near the lids to the whitish-green of his cheek. He turned from the cider, but Harmon insisted that he drink. Betsy held his head to her chest and put the cup to his mouth. He looked into her eyes and drank half a cup before he turned away. He flinched. After pushing the needle through the flesh of his thigh, Harmon pulled the thread taut. Whitmore gripped the patient so he couldn't move while Harmon knotted the thread to hold the skin together.

Like a harsh gust of wind, Gray raged across the yard to where Betsy was now pouring cider for Reinke and Nighthawk. "Why is Petty stripping off his clothes?" he asked.

"Here?" Betsy thought the journalist had stayed to watch Harmon work, but he'd stacked his clothes on his shoes a few feet from where Harmon and Whitmore were doctoring their patients, and was marching, naked, toward the fields. She gave Gray the pitcher without waiting to hear him huff at her request that he serve cider. Somehow she had to get Petty into the house.

Putting down two buckets of water from the well,

Charity ran after Petty, and before Betsy was near, gently took his arm to steer him to the house. Betsy had his shoes and clothes.

"Why do you have my things?" Petty took the bundle.

Charity smiled at Betsy. "Don' worry, Mrs. Randall, he be fine. One, two, three, four. Mr. Petty and me, we goin to count."

Gray had come up beside Betsy and watched the naked man bumble off behind the house with Charity. "Phillipa's slave knows how to handle the man. She's a comfort to the troops." He looked at Harmon and Whitmore closing wounds, at the dead under the tree along the lane, and then at Reinke and Nighthawk caring for the man on the make-shift table. The sun was well above the trees, and from the distance, the song of hoeing came from the fields, as if it were an ordinary day. Gray said, "The German and Charity were the first to come to our aid."

Out the front door, in her blue linen traveling dress with a wide apron over her skirt, Phillipa, deliberate as an arrow, skimmed past Gray and Betsy, ignoring them. She'd tied her hair so that long curls spilled down her back. She looked neither right nor left on her way to Reinke, Nighthawk, and the wounded soldier.

Gray gripped Betsy's arm. "Mrs. Randall, I need your help."

Betsy jerked to pull free. "Let go of me."

Instead of letting go, he practically lifted her along, striding to catch up with Phillipa. In a loud, clear voice, he said, "Good morning, Miss Townsend."

She ignored him.

"You're hurting my arm, Lieutenant." Betsy resented his bouncing her across the yard.

Hearing Betsy, Phillipa turned. She'd picked up the pitcher Gray had set on the ground after Betsy had given it to him. "Ah, Lieutenant Gray." Her stomacher was tied so it squeezed her breasts, powdered white, to plump high on her chest. "I see you have returned unscathed." She cocked her head. "I'm glad you can report that to the governor."

Gray growled to clear his throat and started to speak, but his eyes fastened on Phillipa's breasts, giving her time to speak again. "Three Englishmen killed. How many Seneca?"

Betsy stared at her. Reinke and Nighthawk glanced up, but went back to bandaging the man on the table. Ned comforted the soldier with brandy from Harmon's flask. Everyone listened for Gray's response.

With a hard whack, he hit his leg with his riding crop. "Miss Townsend, we were attacked in our sleep, hours before dawn." Striking his leg again, he looked toward the blankets under the trees, as if the dead would rebuke Phillipa for her scolding words.

While he considered the dead, Betsy pulled free from Gray's hold. Morris and who else? Morris had no family, but several women had waved off the troops from the green that day, and those women would mourn these soldiers when they learned the solders had been killed.

After standing and staring off to the pasture, Gray spoke, his face ashen. "Morris, the best surveyor in Virginia—dead, and two recruits, not yet twenty." He gestured to the man Reinke and Nighthawk carried on the wide board toward the house. "Some might not hang onto life." He turned to the bodies under the tree. "By the grace of God, most of us returned. Our sentry, Thomas Smith, not yet sixteen, had his throat cut before he could cry out."

Thomas Smith? Betsy didn't know most of the troops, but she knew Tom Smith. She'd noticed him when he and his burly friend followed Charity but then were turned back by Morris. After that incident, he'd gone out of his way to help Betsy on and off the wagon when the road was steep. The lad had the soft beginnings of a blond mustache. He needed his ox-strong friend to guard his body. She took Gray's elbow. "His friend will miss him."

Phillipa scowled at Betsy. "Lieutenant Gray, you didn't say how many savages are dead." Confident, defiant, superior, she looked him over. "I wasn't there to fight, but rather than march around, I will dress wounds and wrap bandages."

"And I must compose my report for Governor Spotswood." He turned about face toward the house. "Ned and Nighthawk believe the Seneca have designs on the whole Pamunkey territory in Virginia, which includes the site for Spotsylvania."

Phillipa ran past Betsy, ahead of Gray, forcing him to stop abruptly. "If I were a man—"

Bowing, sweeping his hat almost to the ground, Gray stepped aside. "My dear Miss Townsend, you are, as the Book of Proverbs says, a woman 'more precious than rubies.'" He turned to Betsy. "Don't you agree, Mrs. Randall?"

"Do not ask Mrs. Randall. She knows nothing about rubies! I'm off to aid Mr. Harmon." She sashayed over to the fiddler. He told her she could help him walk the man with the bandaged leg into the house for his breakfast. The soldier tottered between the fiddler and Phillipa.

As the three walked away from the bench, Gray snapped his riding crop against his palm and smiled at Betsy, offering her his arm to go into the house. "There are those who speak ill of her, Mrs. Randall, but her audacity makes her a prize worth winning."

Instead of going with Gray, Betsy went to Charity, who beckoned to her from the corner of the house. She seemed close to tears. Mr. Petty had told Charity he wanted to read in the sitting room, but when she went to invite him to eat, she found his clothes folded on the settee. She picked up the bundle and Petty's shoes to continue her search. Betsy told her that she'd find the journalist, that Charity should go down to the kitchen house for her own breakfast. She looked first in Robert's study, but Gray sat at the desk, writing his report. No Petty in the dining room where Harmon and Phillipa listened to soldiers' stories. The men ate, their eyes on Phillipa's face, her neck, her white breasts.

Through the window of the back door, Betsy saw Petty seated on the ground at the end of the garden, facing the distant blue mountains. She understood the journalist's distress, even his leaving his clothes behind. No one found peace at Good Hope. When Betsy touched his bony shoulder, he flinched and told her to go away. "James Morris, the best surveyor in Virginia, is dead," he said.

"You must dress." Betsy held his shirt for him to put his arms through the sleeves.

"I'm sick of sleeping on the ground." He rolled to his side instead. When Betsy eased his arm into his sleeve, he sat up, pulled on his pants and stockings, and stuck his feet in his shoes.

Betsy rubbed his back, but he brushed away her hand and pointed to the mountains. "Those distant peaks look peaceful, but no; those mountains are dark, even in the strongest light." He said that Morris had mimicked his snoring, and that soon all the troops were snoring—snorting and snickering—all around him. "Not the lieutenant or the Pamunkey guides, mind you." He'd moved from the clearing to sleep in peace. And he'd slept like the dead—until the first scream. "A shriek and then howls of demons. The dark danced; the night had wings and a thousand heads." He closed his eyes. "An ogre—my fear—held me in place." He raised his arm to protect himself from the vision frightening him.

One of the soldiers from the front of the house yelled, "Mother." Or was it "Murder"?

Petty grabbed Betsy's arm. "Did you hear it?"

"Yes, someone screamed 'mother.'" She put her arm around him. Alice called "Mama" in dreams; but, not being able to answer Alice when she'd called, Betsy would wake up and sleep would be gone.

Petty showed her how he'd crimped his blanket over his head to see if the Seneca would leave anyone alive. Nighthawk, the Pamunkey, seemed to dance with his hatchet, invisible to the Seneca. "Gray too. They couldn't see him either. He swung his gun like a club. Deadly." Petty had heard the crunch of Jim Morris's skull. He kept hearing it. Did Betsy? Ned's tomahawk had cracked the neck of the warrior who killed the surveyor, toppling him onto Morris. "Gray scalped Jim's killer and laced the bloody pelt inside Jim's jacket." Petty held his hand to his chest. "He wanted it over Jim's heart."

Petty looked to the mountains. "Peter West leaped over men tangled in blankets and sleep, swinging his saber left and right; the savages ran, but one of our recruits fired his musket and hit West in the groin. Bent him double. Another

Seneca finished him. Thus Peter West, dead too." Petty turned from Betsy. "Horrible. Horrible."

Betsy pressed her tongue to the roof of her mouth as if that might keep her from hearing Petty's story. The serene blue peaks in the distance hid wildcats and terrifying men.

Petty walked past the trees Benjamin had planted and into the scruff beyond the quarters to retch. Nothing came of his spasms, and he wiped his mouth on his handkerchief. When he came back, he kept his eyes down. "I pretended I was dead. Not because I was afraid. Not of the Seneca. They'd disappeared, and they spirited away the bodies of their dead. No, I couldn't face the troops' contempt." He frowned at the trees. "I stayed under my blanket until Gray kicked my ribs." He rubbed his side. "Can you imagine his scorn when he told the others I'd slept through the attack?"

Taking his arm, Betsy led him to the kitchen house, letting him set the pace. No matter how slowly he walked, it wouldn't be slow enough for her to clear her mind of what he'd told her or to erase the wounds she'd seen that morning. The yard was empty except for the buzz of insects. Betsy would let Phillipa preside at the fine walnut table; she liked Deborah's kitchen better. "You need breakfast, Mr. Petty," she said.

Petty bowed his head. "My throat is full of blood. I try to vomit, but it's stuck."

The house would be glutted with soldiers. Like her, Petty would be happier in Deborah's kitchen. "When you see Susannah holding her little sister, you'll be yourself again." Closer to the house, she said that neither of them needed to sit at a table with the lieutenant.

The women in the kitchen hushed when Betsy walked in with the journalist. Charity and Naomi jumped up. Deborah, at the table with the baby at her breast, stood without troubling the child. Betsy told them to finish their food; she'd get Petty a plate. Petty stared at the newborn nursing. From across the table, Susannah gawked at him, a man in a room full of women.

When Deborah told Susannah to pour Mr. Petty's chocolate, she jumped up to serve. The smell of brandy wafted past Betsy. Somehow Susannah knew to add a drop to his drink.

Naomi brought plates of ham, greens, and light yellow cornbread for Betsy and the journalist. Betsy bowed her head in thanksgiving for the women welcoming her and Petty, for the food, for a moment to sit in quiet.

"Mrs. Randall brought me here." Petty apologized to Deborah and to Naomi, who drizzled dark honey over his hot bread, and then passed the crock to Betsy. Glad for the taste of honey, Betsy smiled, took a little, and passed the crock to Charity, who had a small piece of cornbread on her plate. But Charity didn't take any. She handed the crock back to Susannah.

When Susannah dipped the spoon to put honey on her cornbread, Deborah said, "What we eat today we won't have tomorrow." Paying no attention to the pout on Susannah's face, she lifted the baby to her shoulder and patted her back.

Charity took Susannah's hand. "Let me tell you 'bout the time the vicar and the mayor took Dee's brother to get honey from a tree the mayor had seen when they was huntin."

Petty clapped. "That's a story I want to hear. I've heard the vicar's account and the mayor's story. Now I'll have the truth."

Charity took her time looking around the table. "When I say 'once'—"

Before she could finish, Deborah, Naomi, and Susannah said, "Time!"

"You know I'm partial to Saul," Charity said, "but Dee's brother was the most beautiful of all God's creatures."

Betsy listened, half-asleep. She couldn't draw her eyes away from Susannah: the way she listened with her head to one side, the way she brushed her hair out of her eyes, and the way her finger slipped into the baby's palm until Mary Alice gripped it tight.

Chapter 27

Betsy slipped out of the kitchen house to see why Harmon was beckoning her. A small gold ring with a clear red stone nestled in his palm. "From Morris's kit."

The ring, a thin gold band with a clear red gem like stained glass, fit Betsy's middle finger. How different from Isaac's green stone. That gem absorbed light. Harmon didn't know the story of Brickhart showing her Isaac's ring and how she'd dropped David; Betsy never told anyone. Her hand closed over the ring. "I'll give it to Charity."

He squinted at her. "Yes, or I could give it to my Polly. She likes red, but where would I find two other rings for Sadie and Patch?" His hand on her arm, he motioned her farther from the door. "Mrs. Randall, we have another death."

Not wanting to hear of another death, Betsy fumbled for his hand. "Please not!" It would be the recruit Reinke and Nighthawk had tended. "I thought the lad would live," she said. His color had come back. He seemed strong." He'd been in pain, but he'd slept. "I thought he'd recover, that he'd have a terrible scar to show his grandchildren, but he would live."

"Recover?" Harmon seemed to have no understanding of what she was saying. "The dead man isn't one of Gray's men, Mrs. Randall. You don't know the man in the barn."

"The man in the barn? There's a dead man in the barn?"

Some movement caught his eye, and he waved for Betsy to walk farther off, away from the kitchen house. "A blue jay hopped out the door." He scowled. "The bird's a terrible chatter."

"Where?" Betsy looked for the jay, but it was Petty, thanking Deborah for a fine breakfast.

Harmon pretended to doff a hat ceremoniously to Petty. "I see that you're yourself again. Lieutenant Gray said that you were doing poorly." Harmon smirked. "Mrs. Randall, you have brought our pamphleteer back from the dead. And just in time, Petty. The lieutenant is eager for your report of the attack."

Sputtering that he had nothing to tell the lieutenant, Petty blanched. He narrowed his eyes at Betsy, as if accusing her of betraying him, and she felt that she had. Harmon meant to belittle the man, and she glared at the fiddler. Unfazed, Harmon watched Petty walk off, kicking stones on the way to the big house. Lieutenant Gray would be the last person Petty wanted to see, but Harmon never hid his feelings. At the moment, he had only contempt for the journalist's suffering. Betsy said, "Who died? Why is the body in the barn? Why shouldn't Mr. Petty know?"

A banging came from the other side of the houses—coffins for Morris and the two soldiers.

"If I wanted every sparrow and wren to know what I'm about to tell you, I'd have rung that brass gong to tell one

and all. I'm telling you, Mrs. Randall. Nighthawk sent me."
He told her the Pamunkey guides found a body of a black
man and laid it out in the barn. "They're not telling Gray,
and Petty would run with the news to the lieutenant."

"Does Mr. Whitmore know? Shouldn't Ned or Nighthawk tell the overseer?" Betsy shrank from seeing a dead
body in the barn, but she went with Harmon. The pounding grew louder as they neared the sawhorses where Reinke,
Benjamin, and Tom Smith's friend worked. Fatigue weighed
down the hammers, slowing each swing, as the men
pounded nails into the wood. Reinke had started the morning sewing up a hole in a man's stomach, and now he
worked, making coffins in the sun. Nearby, Gray's soldiers
sawed and planed planks of wood. Betsy took Harmon's
arm. "The overseer should be told."

"The dead man was never a slave at Good Hope."

Saul was sanding a board with a brick. Slaves were wash-
ing the bodies close to the well. Reinke, Benjamin, and Saul
looked up, surprised to see Betsy. From the front door,
Lieutenant Gray, his dark hair tied back and his red coat
brushed, strode toward her. He sucked a pipe, his eyes on
Harmon and Betsy. Behind him, Petty tried to swagger.
Harmon muttered to Betsy that Nighthawk didn't want
Gray to know about the body.

Betsy had to think of a reason Harmon would be taking
her to the barn. She told Gray that Mr. Harmon was telling
her what fine stalls the barn had. "And I have not seen them
yet."

Scorning her explanation, Gray studied Harmon, who
looked back at him, his face blank; but not one to hide his
feelings, he had no practice in feigning innocence.

"If you'll pardon my blunt words, Mrs. Randall,

appraising your property when we are mourning three valiant men seems a cold disregard for their sacrifice. But if you must ..." He insisted Betsy take his arm. "Mr. Petty and I will join you."

The fiddler would have to come up with some good reason to tell the Pamunkey guides why she brought Gray and the journalist into the barn. To her surprise, the barn was larger than it seemed from outside. The lofts under the open rafters gave off the smell of hay. The barn had wide entryways on the front and back, one to let the horses into the yard and another for both horses and cows to wander out into the pasture. Rather than open the large doors, Lieutenant Gray led Betsy through a regular door set inside the larger one. The smaller door admitted a thin rectangle of light from the north, but when Gray closed the door, perhaps to muffle the sounds of woodworking, they saw nothing but a square of light from the opening to the pasture. Sunlight gave the rough planks a soft sheen.

The barn was empty. No guides. No body.

————

The air smelled of leather saddles and harnesses, and the sweet pungency of cows and horses. Along the dark, unpainted sides of the barn were eight stalls for horses on the right side and eight stanchions for milk cows on the left. In some, the small shuttered window let in dim light. The stalls for milking had mangers, in shadow because the shutters were closed. A horse—Gray's Ramses—stomped as Betsy passed, startling her.

The black stallion blocked the light from the open window behind him. He whiffled for the attention of the lieutenant, who was walking next to Betsy. She didn't want to be surprised again. "The barn is large enough and well planned, wouldn't you say, Lieutenant? Let's go in to remember the dead." She wanted out of the barn and back in the sun.

"Now that we're here, Mrs. Randall, let's walk through to the pasture." Gray signaled Petty and Harmon.

Since she couldn't get him to leave the barn, Betsy steered him away from the stalls with stacked rifles and long bayonets, the soldiers' gear. She guessed the body would be laid out in a stall.

Gray's horse nickered, but Gray paid no attention to his steed. Through the door open to the meadow, dust motes drifted in the sunlight like a screen of golden gauze.

The farther she walked into the barn, the more Betsy enjoyed the fragrance of sweet hay and grain, even the smells of manure, smells that reminded her of her child-hood—and of Robert. Isaac had sold that farm after her mother died. "You were right, Lieutenant, this is not a time for reviewing property. Mr. Whitmore can show me the barn and pasture tomorrow."

The time would come when everyone who traveled with her would return to Williamsburg, and Betsy would be alone. That would be after the bodies had been buried. Was there one hidden in the barn? Gray wasn't to know. Did he sense her anxiety? "Lieutenant, we should honor the dead. Let's return to the house."

Aping Gray's gentlemanly gestures, Harmon offered Betsy his arm. "Yes, yes. We're all grieving." But when they turned, close to the small door, someone stepped back into the shadows near the stall where Gray's horse stamped his hoof again and again. Harmon whistled a short chirp, and

Betsy, uncertain of who might have stepped into a stall near Ramses, guessed that the fiddler signaled either Ned or Nighthawk to stay out of sight.

Petty, meandering in and out of stalls alone on his own exploration of her property, walked into one milk stall after another until he was well beyond the middle of the barn. He suddenly backed out of a stall. "Lieutenant. Lieutenant Gray. Come."

Betsy lengthened her steps to keep up with Gray, holding onto his arm as if she needed it for support, trying to slow him down. She didn't want him seeing Petty's find before her. Harmon trotted ahead of them to see what transfixed the man.

The back of the stall was a dusky gold. A pelt had been stretched on a web of branches and wedged upright against the manger. On the floor, the cat's head lay on its chin, the mouth and eyes shut. The paws reached from wall to wall, the tail tied to a hind leg. No wonder Gray's horse wanted out with the other horses; he smelled a predator.

The wild man wouldn't have stretched his skin here. Only Reinke could have stolen it. Betsy ran out to the infernal pounding, her fists balled to control her anger. The sun blinded her. She shaded her eyes to see Reinke's guilt when she accused him. "How could you steal the lion's skin?"

A light yellow curl of wood, the color of his hair, spiraled from the plane Reinke shoved down a board. He didn't look up or pause until he came to the end of the plank and smoothed his hand along the side.

"Mr. Reinke." Betsy wanted to shake him.

Without a word, he set the plane on a sawhorse and walked past Betsy into the barn.

Step for step, she kept up with him, past the gathering of

men, straight into the stall where he stopped and studied the skin. He reached out to touch it. Half fearful that the cat would spring to life, Betsy watched. Reinke's hand skimmed the pelt, a sad caress along the front leg, the flank, the back. He paid no heed to Gray, who leaned on the stall, watching. The woodsman felt for the puncture the spear made in the skin. Because he knew where to look, Reinke found the stitched closure, and crooked his finger for her to come closer and see that the gash on the neck had been sewn closed. "You cannot see the cut."

Betsy didn't answer when Gray asked if she'd seen the pelt before.

Reinke said, "This is the cougar, Mrs. Randall." His voice was low and sad, like gravel under a heavy wheel. "How did this skin get here?"

"How indeed?" Gray turned to Betsy. "You accused Mr. Reinke of stealing the skin? Why did you think he had, Mrs. Randall?"

Betsy had no idea how the skin came to be in the barn, but now that she'd seen it, she knew whose body Harmon meant to show her. How the man died and who would have brought him to the barn, she didn't know, but his death saddened her. Harmon hadn't known about the skin. He didn't know that the wild man had saved her from the cougar. Betsy's blaming Reinke had been unkind and she owed him an apology, but she didn't want Gray to know that she'd run away, and the two of them had seen the cat killed. She looked toward the pasture and the blue sky above it. A shift of light meant someone stepped back into the pasture. From both ends of the barn, the guides watched and listened. Betsy looked at the fiddler to see if he'd noticed that shift of light, if he knew they were being watched. He placed his hand across his mouth and chin, a signal for her not to call attention to the presence Betsy guessed lurked by the door.

The lieutenant cleared his throat. Again. "Who brought this pelt here, Mrs. Randall?" He smiled as if he were questioning a clever child whose statement would amuse him.

Instead of answering, Betsy listened again to the thud of the cougar when it fell to the ground. She saw it clawing at her. Moments before the cat fell, the man had hurled the spear, saving her life. Gray's feigned deference brought back Brickhart's false gentility when he'd questioned Isaac. Her husband had reason to fear the pirate, but he'd shown courage. Betsy decided she would be as tranquil as the dust motes floating in front of her. Her steps whispered on the wide planks when she walked to the green calm of the pasture. Careful not to look in the stalls, she stepped toward the light from the pasture. In the meadow, a doe and her fawn nibbled grass. They grazed beside cows and horses. Sadness washed over her. The wild man had saved her life twice.

Mr. Petty repeated Gray's question. "Who brought this skin here, Mrs. Randall?"

"That I don't know." Betsy wasn't prepared to face Gray or Petty. She hadn't seen the dead man, and she preferred being alone with Harmon when she saw his body. She had an obligation to him. Already mourning his death, she sought the peace of the meadow. Small yellow birds flew from branch to branch. "I saw the cat killed." She spoke softly, but despite the hammering on the coffins, the men could hear her. "It hadn't been skinned."

"You saw the cat killed?" Gray walked toward her, his steps echoing. Halfway between Betsy and the woodsman, he stopped. "Were you and Mr. Reinke out for a breath of night air?"

Gray's suggestive comment turned her thoughts from the wild man. If he chose, the lieutenant could see on her face that she would answer him, but in her own time. She'd keep her flight from her brother's plantation to herself. Reinke wouldn't betray her. "As Mr. Harmon and Mr. Reinke know, after dinner last night, we entertained ourselves with stories. When we had all retired, I found that I couldn't sleep and decided to walk to the gate." Betsy told them about the terrifying scream and deciding to turn back, but "right down from a tree in front of me, closer to me than you are now, Lieutenant Gray, the lion—with a spear in his side—landed on the road. You can imagine my fright. And a man—he seemed wild—sprang to the snarling animal, pulled his spear out of its side, and cut its neck. Before the man could get up, I ran back."

When Gray started to interrupt her, Betsy said, "Mr. Reinke had heard me leave the house and followed me, believing I might be in danger, but I wasn't aware that he had until I turned around. He watched the man kill the cougar. It was Mr. Reinke who told me this animal is called a 'cougar.'"

"A man, Mrs. Randall?" Gray expected Petty and Harmon to agree that she had poor judgment. "A man you describe as wild hunts on your property and you say nothing?" He knocked the ash out of his pipe. "Reinke, why didn't you report this runaway?"

Silent and unperturbed, Reinke looked back at Gray.

"Didn't you have your rifle? A man with a spear is dangerous. We must hunt him down."

"No need, Lieutenant. The man is here." Harmon moved next to Reinke.

Gray stepped back. "You have him here?"

"No, Lieutenant." Harmon challenged Gray but then he looked down at the floor. "His body is in the last stall."

"Impossible," Petty set off to see for himself, but Gray outpaced him, and Harmon caught Betsy's arm to let Gray and Petty go first. At the last stall, near the pasture, the lieutenant wheeled around to look at Harmon. "Are you responsible for this outrage?"

Petty hung his head. He seemed about to crumple to the floor.

"What outrage?" Betsy hoped his body hadn't been mutilated. She ran ahead of Harmon to the stall. A swath of sunlight from the open window spread over the dead man. The face and body had been washed, the clay mask cleared away. His closed eyes and mouth gave the corpse a distant serenity, an indifference to her and the others. His eyes had been kind, but now flies busied themselves crawling over the eyelids. And over his lips and the wounds on his chest and thigh. Betsy wanted to shoo the flies away, but not if she would disturb the corpse. She knelt. "Who killed this man?"

Petty looked up. "We all know who killed the man."

Gray pinched Petty's arm until he cringed. "Petty, what do you know of this black?"

Wincing, Petty stuttered. "I've n-n-never seen the man before."

Rubbing his arm when Gray let go, Petty's lips twitched. "Mrs. Randall, are you sure that this is the man you saw last night?"

Angry at Gray's bullying Petty and the journalist's cowardice, Betsy said nothing. She'd seen that silence made Reinke stronger.

"Petty," Gray made a show of being patient, "be so good

as to let me ask my own questions." He walked into the stall and circled the corpse, bending over it to see what hurt had been done to it. Finally, he approached Betsy. "Is this the man who killed the cougar, Mrs. Randall?"

Betsy looked him in the eye. He knew her answer. She said nothing.

At the other end of the barn, Ramses reared in his stall and crashed down on the gate, his hoofs striking the wood with a splintering thud, kicking as if to break out.

Gray twisted around. "Ramses!" The horse snorted, but the lieutenant, who had started to run to the stallion, stopped mid-step, and then, as if he'd seen an apparition, backed into Petty, who had scuttled out of his way.

From the shadows of the first stall, Nighthawk stepped into the light from the small door Betsy had left open when she went for Reinke. Wrapped in a blanket with one corner swung over his shoulder, he stood outlined in light, his features obscured—a solid shadow.

"N-Nighthawk?" The lieutenant stammered. "What? How long have you been here?" Gray wheeled around, his eyes accusing Betsy of betrayal, but he could read the innocence of the guide's presence on her face. Only Harmon had known the Pamunkey guide was in the barn, and when Harmon nodded to him, the guide pointed to the pasture door.

They all turned toward the square of light from the pasture, less than six feet from them. Fear gripped Betsy. When she watched the doe and her fawn, Ned had been an arm's length from her. Like Nighthawk, light framed his face, hiding his features in shadow. His voice came from that shadow. "We brought the body here."

His hands clasped behind his back, Reinke faced Gray.

"Lieutenant, the coffins must be built while there is light. I'm going to finish my work." As he passed Nighthawk, he tipped his head toward the stall where the cat's pelt had been hidden and asked if they had brought the skin.

Nighthawk crossed to the stall and then looked back at Reinke. "Soldiers did. While you took care of the man's wound, they came through the pasture."

Reinke bowed his head to Gray and Betsy and left the barn. Betsy watched him leave, listening to the crunch of his footsteps on the gravel outside. Betsy said, "Lieutenant, you let me accuse the woodsman of having stolen the skin, knowing it wasn't he."

Ignoring Betsy, Gray turned on Harmon. "Coward. Why tell Mrs. Randall that this runaway's body is in the barn? She knows nothing of the ways of Virginia."

Betsy stepped in front of Gray. "Sir, you are right. I do not know the ways of Virginia, but I know that a hunter isn't killed for skinning an animal he himself has slain."

"The man wasn't killed for skinning the lion, Mrs. Randall." Gray spat out the words. He looked like he wanted to spit at Betsy, but after looking from Nighthawk to Ned, he stood at attention, saying nothing, staring at the stall until Ramses stamped a hoof. Gray turned to Betsy. "Our Pamunkey guides and Mr. Petty witnessed this fugitive being killed for running when commanded to stop." He paced the width of the barn, looking from the stall when his stallion nickered to the stall with the corpse. "A few miles from your Good Hope, Lister caught a glimpse of something moving. Worn from the march and thinking the man might be Seneca, he went to kill him. I called out, but instead of surrendering, the man leaped to escape." Gray stopped pacing. "The savage left the pelt. I commanded him to come back, but he ran on." He appealed to Night-hawk. "When commanded to stop, he fled. Lister fired his rifle, but he stumbled on despite being hit in the thigh. When Davies and I caught up to him, he attacked, but I had the advantage of a bayonet."

Betsy walked back to the body of the man who had saved her life. At the clearing, when he'd led her back, he hadn't wanted to be seen, and when he killed the cougar, he acted as if he were invisible.

Gray walked up next to her. "Rather than let us attend to his wound, the man—but can you call a creature that rolls in mud a man?—fought us." Gray waved toward the stall with the skin. "I told Lister that since he was first to catch sight of the pelt, it was his." He kicked the foot of the corpse.

Ned flinched. He stepped forward, and his shadow covered the man's feet as if protecting him.

Turning to Ned, Gray stood as if listening to the hammering. "You saw this man flee. You saw him fight Lister rather than yield. You saw that I had no choice but to stop him with my bayonet." Gray turned to Betsy. "We left his body in the wilderness, where he chose to dwell, Mrs. Randall." The lieutenant started to leave the barn but came to a halt when his stallion tramped in his stall.

Betsy caught up with him. "Lieutenant Gray, this man is to be buried with the others."

He turned to her. "No, Mrs. Randall, he shall not be buried with the others." He tried to step around her, but she blocked his way.

Petty watched from a seat on a barrel near the barn door, a few feet from where Nighthawk had been hiding. The journalist stood to leave with Gray. He said, "The governor will want to know that there are African fugitives in the woods near his German settlement."

"I shall give the governor a complete report, Mr. Petty," Gray said. "You will not need to embellish it." Again, Gray tried to brush past Betsy. "Mrs. Randall, I don't care if you bury this renegade in the pasture or the pigsty or in the graveyard for slaves, but he is not to be buried in the cemetery with Christian men who bled and died for the Queen and the colony of Virginia."

In his fine red jacket and his polished black boots, Gray seemed the right man to honor Morris and the two young men who had been killed. Betsy remembered the first time she saw him in Williamsburg. How straight his young men had stood, ready to march into the wilderness, a wilderness where bandits, Seneca, wild men, and cougars lived in shadows. She said, "Lieutenant, I do not object to Mr. James Morris, Mr. Thomas Smith, and Mr. Peter West being buried at Good Hope—as long as this man is buried here too." To stop Gray from interrupting her, she held up her hand. "You may take their bodies to Fulton's Crossing or to Williamsburg, but if they are to be buried on this estate, their graves will be in the same cemetery as my brother and this man."

Gray's cheeks paled. "A heathen should not desecrate ground hallowed for Christians."

Outside, the hammers pounded on the coffins, and in the barn, Ramses stamped on the barn floor. Petty came closer to hear Gray and Betsy argue, and Harmon did too. The fiddler had said almost nothing since telling Betsy about the body. Whenever their eyes met, she saw that he sympathized with her, but Harmon had let Gray call him a coward without challenging the man. He didn't tell Gray why he cared about the burial of the fugitive or why he'd told Betsy about the body. She looked to the Pamunkey guides and then at the floor. "I wasn't out for a bit of air last night, Lieutenant, but on my way to Fulton's Crossing, or to Yorktown or to England." She looked directly at Gray. Could he understand her desperation? "Grief has its own madness. I stopped my flight because I didn't have the courage to go on. I heard a woman scream, and the second time she screamed, I hid beside the road. Later, Reinke told me the scream is the call of a cougar." Betsy paused. How frightened she'd been when the man stepped from behind the stump. "When I started back, this man killed the cougar as it sprang to attack me." She looked toward the meadow to see the grass and the trees, the light. "That Providence directed him to that spot at that time, I cannot question, but that it would lead to his death ..." Betsy saw that Gray listened, skeptical. "The cat's cry and the force of his jump, the thud when his body landed on the road, those are sounds I won't forget, just as I'm sure you won't forget the Seneca attack." She turned toward the stall with the body. "This man saved me from certain death. I may not know the ways of people in Virginia, but I understand the debt we owe to those who save our lives."

Gray turned and started for the door.

"Hear, hear." The fiddler stepped to Betsy's side. "You called me a coward, Lieutenant, and I am, many times over." He too looked toward the stall where the wild man lay. "This black pulled me from quicksand more than three years ago. When Ned showed me the body, I told him, but I didn't tell you." He spoke as if apologizing to Gray. "He may be a runaway, but he lived free for years. The Choctaw and Pamunkey knew him well. They shared their fires with him, as they did Jim Morris when he ran from his indenture, and as they do me when I feel a need to wander."

Behind them, Ramses snorted. Without a word, the lieutenant went to stroke his stallion's neck, and comb his long fingers through the mane. The horse nuzzled Gray's shoulder as if they were in private conversation. The lieutenant smoothed his hand over a saddle blanket draped on the gate. Lifting the heavy blanket folded in thirds, the span of Gray's arm, he held the unbleached wool out in front of him, and shook it as if the loosened dust floating off freed him from the trouble of the man's death. After folding the blanket, he gave it to Nighthawk. "Would you like to cover the body?"

Gray watched Harmon help Nighthawk spread the blanket from the man's feet to over his head. "He'll need a coffin."

Betsy took Gray's arm. "Yes, Lieutenant, he will." Through the window, sunlight gave a radiance to the blanket covering the corpse.

Chapter 28

From the bedroom window, Betsy watched Reinke and Benjamin join the corner of a coffin while Saul and a soldier sanded a lid. They'd propped a finished coffin against the barn. Shadows of trees stretched toward the barn and house. Before Betsy went upstairs to calm her mind, Whitmore came, insisting that the cougar's pelt be carried to a tobacco shed; the smell of the skin would frighten cows being milked. The wild man's body wouldn't bother the animals, since he'd laid out slaves in the barn before. The wild man haunted Betsy; as his body approached, he changed into Josiah, the pirate runaway. According to Davy, after Josiah had slashed into a hive of Bennett's marines with his cutlass, he'd been knocked to the deck, and a redcoat plunged a bayonet into his chest. As Davy had described that attack, she'd thought of Josiah's telling her about slavers raping his wife and son.

When Betsy first saw the sheep grazing with the cows on lush grass three days earlier, the plantation had reminded her of Surrey and Brompton-on-Thames. Now, Gray rode his black stallion in the pasture, circling the meadow while other horses and cattle grazed. Despite having been awake much of the night, she couldn't rest.

In another bedroom, the windows faced fields, not coffins. Whitmore, on a dappled gelding, rode toward a crew—men and women preparing a field for tobacco. They hacked the weeds, their hoes rising up and chopping down in unison. Their song didn't reach the open window, but Betsy knew from the ride through the plantation what the crews sang as they worked. Spurring his horse, Whitmore galloped to a woman behind the rest, raised a whip, and flailed her back. She sank to her knees, raising her arm to ward off the next blow. When it didn't come, she leaned on the hoe to stand. Her stomach was almost as round as Deborah's had been. Chop, chop, chop. Running and stumbling, she hoed faster. Not one slave looked back. Betsy cried, "No!" Her cry clouded the window. In the field, Whitmore cracked the whip above the slave's head again—then he slouched back in his saddle, coiling the whip to hook it onto his belt.

The man who'd wept at his daughter's birth had whipped an expectant mother, and now he was cantering off to the next field, to a group of slaves who worked—hoes up, hoes down—like soldiers. Betsy shut the curtain so she wouldn't see Whitmore whip an old man far behind other slaves weeding a patch of beans.

How could he whip a woman with child? Flog an old man? As she rushed down the steps, Betsy planned: Reinke or Saul would saddle Melinda for her. She'd ride out to Whitmore and demand that he stop.

———

"Now?" Reinke scowled at the board he'd grooved to fit over the one Benjamin held for him. "We have one coffin done, two finished except for a final sanding, but the fourth we have yet to nail together. It's almost dusk. Harmon has gone to see the graves dug. None of us can ride now, Mrs. Randall." He picked up a hammer and tapped the board in place.

Betsy didn't want to say that Whitmore had whipped a pregnant slave in front of Benjamin and the recruit helping Reinke. "After Saul saddles Melinda, I'll ride alone. I want to ask Mr. Whitmore about the work in the tobacco fields."

Reinke brought the hammer down with a bang that left a dent in the wood. He arched back, his hands on his hips. "Tobacco fields? Talk to Deborah. She decides which fields to plant, when to plant, and which slaves will do the work." He took up his hammer. "She tells him which slaves get an extra ration of corn because they worked the hardest, and which he should whip."

Deborah? Yes. Deborah would understand the overseer shouldn't whip the woman.

Rounding the corner of the kitchen dependency, Betsy came upon Naomi, her head turned away from a washtub giving off the odor of lye. She pummeled the steaming linens with a thick staff and sang of being washed in the blood of the Lamb: "Whiter than snow. Whiter than snow." Near Naomi, at a small tub, Susannah scrubbed blood from a soldier's shirt. She sang with Naomi. Neither looked up to see Betsy, and she had no time to ask when they'd seen snow. The woman in the field might be in labor by now. Her home would be one of the quarters surrounding the tubs, a cabin no better than a chicken coop. At the farthest cabin, far from the stink of the soap, children braided straw into rope near an old woman weaving a basket. Brown hens scratched the dirt and pecked at gravel. Everyone at Good Hope worked except Isaiah, who, tied to a tree with a leather strap, played with wooden blocks in the dirt.

Betsy knocked on the open back door to the kitchen. Deborah stopped humming and trickling cider broth over a side of venison. Cuddled in a wide homespun sling tied across Deborah's back, Mary Alice slept. "Mrs. Randall, aren't you resting for dinner?" Deborah pulled a chair from the table for Betsy. "My first mistress insisted on an afternoon nap to keep her skin smooth." She reached for the teapot above the hearth. "Would you like tea?"

"No, thank you. I don't need tea." Betsy squared the chair to the table. "At the bedroom window, I looked out on the fields and saw Mr. Whitmore gallop up to a field hand and whip her with such force that she fell to her knees."

Deborah's back stiffened. The baby whimpered. Deborah tightened the sling and jostled the child. "Mr. Whitmore is the overseer, Mrs. Randall."

"A woman should not be whipped. I wouldn't whip a dog like that."

Deborah swirled the pan of broth with a whisk. "How do you want me to help? Mr. Whitmore's fair. He whips slaves for good reason."

"And what good reason would he have to ride up on a woman hoeing in a field of stumps and bring down his whip so she falls to her knees?" Betsy's face burned.

"An overseer is obliged to keep slaves at their task. I told Whit that." Deborah whisked the sauce into a froth. "Master Robert said, 'Whip slaves, and they work.'"

Nothing in Deborah's manner showed any concern for the slave. Admiration for her master? Yes. She took pride in his knowing how to run slaves. "Master Robert could snap that bullwhip and cut through a man's shirt. If he didn't speed up, he'd feel that whip again. And again. Those slaves never slowed down when Master Robert might ride up."

"Would my brother whip a woman expecting a child?" Robert could be cruel, but Betsy thought he was a Christian. Picturing him riding up on a slave and whipping her shamed Betsy.

Deborah's arm jerked, spilling broth on the floor. A log collapsed in the hearth and a live spark caught on Deborah's apron. She smacked it out. "A child?" Deborah ran to the door and yelled for Susannah. "Whit knows better." She looked outside. "Susannah!"

"Don't call Susannah. Mr. Reinke said to tell you ..." But Betsy hadn't told him about the whipping. She should have run to the field.

Deborah had loosened the wrap to hold the baby to her shoulder. She patted Mary Alice to quiet her. "Mrs. Randall, I need to get Louise in from the field. She could drop that baby. We might lose it. Susannah is fast and ..."

"Mama?" Susannah stood at the door, one bare foot hooked behind the other.

With the baby in her arms, Deborah squatted to look into Susannah's eyes. "You fly—you understand me?—fly to Pollux weeding the patch by the creek, and you tell him Mrs. Randall says to have Jason and Cressy walk Louise back to her house. If she's fine." She grabbed Susannah's arm. "If she's in trouble, you tell Pole to have Jason carry her here." Deborah paused, her eyes narrowed. "And then you bring Mr. Whitmore to the house. Mrs. Randall wants a word with him." She studied Susannah's face. "Now, faster than fat catches flame, tell me what I said."

Susannah's eyes flicked blame at Betsy, but she focused on her mother's face while she spoke. "Louise. I run to Pollux and tell him Jason and Cressy s'posed to bring Louise to her house—if she fine. If she can't walk …" Susannah looked at the baby her mother held, her eyes suddenly fearful. "If she can't walk, Jason's s'posed to carry her." She faced her mother. "I find Mr. Whitmore and say Mrs. Randall wants a word with him." The moment her mother nodded, she sped off.

Betsy watched Susannah run, each step a leap, like a bird taking flight. Had Betsy run like Susannah last night, she'd have arrived in Yorktown in an hour. Susannah would get help for the woman who'd collapsed in the field faster than Betsy could have reached her.

"Louise is strong, Mrs. Randall." Deborah knelt, the baby in one arm, to wipe up the splattered broth. "Grandma Jump helped her birth two children. She knows how to hold a child." She stood, patting her baby. "Grandma Jump will keep an eye on Louise. She'll call me if Louise needs help. Whit's best at bringing babies into the world. And Mr. Harmon and the German are good as any doctor."

"I'll help Louise." Betsy knew about childbirth and she'd tended Davy after his whipping.

Deborah flung the rag to the rim of a bucket. Smiling, she walked to a corner protected from the heat to gently lay the baby in the cradle. "Good Hope can't afford to lose a baby." Back at the hearth, she cranked the roast to brown a different side. "Master Robert always said, 'Keep your stock fed and your slaves strong—only horses are worth more.'"

Betsy crossed the kitchen to stand where she could see Deborah's face. "Did you say my brother taught his overseer to ride up on people working in fields and whip them?"

Keeping her eyes on the roast, Deborah drizzled a quivering stream of broth, thin as a ribbon. "Master Robert taught Whit to keep the crews working." She frowned and slowly refilled the ladle. "Whit grieved Master Robert's death, Mrs. Randall. He'd ride out and the slaves would be shuffling to pitiful songs. 'Master Robert dead—gone, gone, gone.' Whit didn't see they'd slacked off in the fields." She dipped the ladle in the broth. "Li'l Xerxes told me, 'Slaves gotta work, Deb'rah. Me and the other drivers need Master Whit drivin the hands." Deborah's smile died. "Li'l Xerx. He felt Master Robert's lash. Oh, yes, but he told me, 'Slaves gotta eat, Deb'rah. You gotta eat, Mister Whitmore gotta eat.' And I understood. If we don't get a crop, nobody eats. Hunger, Whit understands." She splashed broth on the side of the meat. "Whit knows hunger. Master Robert too." Her face quiet, she gazed at the fire. "I've been whipped. Master Phelps had me tied to the post more than once." The chain of the hearth clinked when she pulled the gear to rotate the spit. "Whipping tears you, inside and out, but Master Robert and Whit worked too hard, night and day, building Good Hope, one field at a time, for me to watch it fall to ruin." She tipped her head toward the cabins beyond the garden. "It won't do to have lazy field hands, eating, sleeping, and planning mischief. No, Mrs. Randall, by the time you came, if Whit didn't whip those laggards— that's what Master Robert called them, laggards—half the slaves would run off and nobody'd work the fields. House and barn would be shambles. I told Whit, 'You keep Good Hope in good order.'"

The roast glistened from the broth, and the smell of browning meat grew stronger. Deborah was as sure that slaves must be whipped as she was that meat must be basted.

Betsy wanted to tell Whitmore not to whip the slaves, but she knew nothing about growing tobacco. She sat on the chair that Deborah had offered her. When she'd seen Mr. Whitmore riding up on the old man, she'd turned from the window. "Is it right that the weak, sick, and old are the ones to suffer?"

With a watchful eye, Deborah spooned drippings from her pan. "Whit's supposed to use his judgment. If the work isn't done, we can't feed our people. Simple as that." Deborah wiped her hands on her apron. "Two, three times a day, Whit rides out. Master said not every field every time. Whit rides Simon because slaves don't hear his hooves on the ground." She tossed salt on the venison. "Li'l Xerxes says, 'If you don' know when de Massa comin, but you gonna feel de strap if you a step behin, you keeps up.'"

Tired of doing nothing, weary from hearing how her brother trained slaves, Betsy went to the window where she'd seen the wild hyacinths and took a willow basket of peas from the shelf. She liked shelling peas, popping them open, and tossing the pods aside. "You and Mr. Whitmore didn't know when someone would come to claim Good Hope."

"No, we didn't." Deborah gave Betsy a white bowl for the shelled peas. "Old Master Osborne said a Randall heir would come from England. We knew the fields had to be tilled. Tobacco takes care, Mrs. Randall." She scowled at the way Betsy lined the empty pods on the shelf. "The German sent word that you'd left Williamsburg."

Betsy picked a plump pod with four fat bumps. She pulled the stem and the string, and pushed the peas into the bowl. She ate a tiny pea hiding close to the end. "For two years you ran the plantation not knowing who would come."

Deborah smiled. "You're here now, and the plantation is in order."

Betsy had never been hungry and she'd never been whipped. Her father hired laborers, and if he found fault with their work, the family was sent off with whatever belongings they could carry or pile onto a wheelbarrow if they had one. The quarters weren't so different from the huts her father provided. She'd been in a few of those huts when she went with her mother to tend to someone ill or giving birth. Betsy watched Naomi lug two buckets of water to a tub. Betsy turned to Deborah. "Shouldn't Susannah be back?"

"She'll ride back on Simon with Whit. You wanted to talk to him, and he'll come soon as she finds him." She put a plate over the bowl of peas. "You're worried about Louise. I am, too, but don't trouble yourself. Cressy works in that crew; she'd never let Louise come to harm." Deborah swept the shells Betsy discarded into her apron. "I've taught Susannah to be a faithful messenger." She emptied her apron into a bucket. "Hogs love pods."

"No one in the field looked back when she struggled to get up."

The fire popped and hissed as the logs crunched into one another; gold and orange flames licked the roast. Deborah splashed broth onto the side of venison, and Betsy watched the fat and meat juices drip into a pan set to catch the runoff.

Hearing a soft knock, Betsy jumped to open the door for Susannah, who gasped, surprised to see Betsy. She dipped a curtsy but kept her eyes down.

Betsy took Susannah's hand for her to come in the kitchen. "How's Louise?"

"She fine." Susannah kept her eyes on the floor. "Cressy was working by her side. After I told Pollux what Mama said, he told Louise to go in, but she said no, she's better working."

Betsy had filled the dipper with water. When Susannah drank it, the look she gave Betsy over the brim of the dipper was one Robert had when he liked something she'd said or done. Betsy touched Susannah's shoulder. It was the closest she'd come to embracing her brother's child. "Don't run, Susannah, but go back to the field and tell Mr. Pollux to have Jason and Cressy walk Louise to her house. She needs to rest."

Deborah came over and wiped Susannah's face with a kerchief, and turned Susannah toward the door. "Mrs. Randall, Naomi knows a good herb tea for Louise."

Whitmore came huffing to the step, wiping sweat from his face. "Mrs. Randall, I looked for you in the house. Susannah said you were in the kitchen, but I thought you'd have gone to be with Miss Phillipa and the lieutenant." Anxious and eager to do what she asked, he walked in, his hands clasped behind his back, his whip clinched to his belt.

Betsy understood Robert's having trusted the man. "Deborah has told me how steadfast you are. Good Hope has prospered." She put her arm around Susannah's shoulders to walk her out. As the child passed Whitmore, she brushed against him, and his face softened, acknowledging her sympathy. Betsy closed the door behind Susannah, glad the girl had kind feelings for the overseer. The man had to know how wrong riding up on the slave had been. "I wanted to talk to you about whipping a woman expecting a child."

The hammers pounded in the distance. The fire in the hearth crackled. Betsy wanted to sit down. She didn't want to talk to Whitmore or even look at the way his head dropped. Maybe Louise hadn't been hurt by her fall. Maybe she had insisted on working. "Mr. Whitmore, you must have known she was expecting. She fell to her knees and you didn't help her up."

"Louise." He nodded. "She leaned on her hoe to get up. I scared her." He was frowning, worried—for himself, not for the poor woman. He looked at Betsy. "Louise doesn't think about chopping weeds; she looks for shiny stones and keeps them in her pockets. She hoes and hoes but doesn't git a single weed." He looked away from Deborah to the cradle. It was as if he could see the baby sleeping there. "I was wrong to bring the whip down on her back. I should've snapped it over her, like I did the second time."

Deborah had said that he knew better than to whip an expectant mother. As if contempt kept her from looking at Whitmore, Deborah turned to the hearth to baste the roast. Poor Whitmore. He loved a woman with no patience for poor judgment, for jeopardizing property. Betsy waited for Deborah to splash the meat before she spoke to Whitmore. "I left the window when I saw you riding up on the old man."

"Lazarus? He'll tell you my whip is more crack than bite where he's concerned."

"Mr. Whitmore, which is more valuable? A man or a horse?"

Whitmore stepped to his right where he could see his wife, try to read her thoughts, though her back was to him. He looked about the room as if Betsy had asked a riddle, as if he'd thought the answer must be close by. His eyes traveled from the hearth, to the cupboards, and in the end, settled on the cradle. His face grew calm, and he looked back at Betsy. "A good horse will bring more at the market."

"The same is true in England. Woe betide the man who causes a horse to break a leg. Ships are worth more than the men who sail them."

He bowed and opened the door, taking her comment as a dismissal. Outside, Naomi's song rose over the men pounding hammers. Whitmore stopped and wheeled his hat full circle. "We don't make coffins for horses."

"No, we don't." Betsy thought of the man Ned and Nighthawk had covered with Gray's horse blanket. He was to be buried with the others in the morning. "Mr. Whitmore, after the funeral, I want you to tell me more about the plantation; but until we talk, stop whipping the slaves, no matter how strong."

He looked dismayed, disbelieving. "Stop whipping them?" He glanced at Deborah. "Don't I whip the laggards?"

"No, not even the laggards. Keep your whip for the horses or cattle." Betsy walked him to the door because he seemed reluctant to leave, struck by her words. She closed the door, careful to shut it with a lift, to keep from making a sound.

She turned in time to see Deborah hurl the pan of hot fat at the hearth. It banged against the brick and bounced back across the room, dripping grease in a long arc over the floor. Flames leaped on the spray and danced in spurts of fire between her and Deborah. Before Betsy could call out, Deborah leaped back, grabbed a bucket from next to the hearth, and flung ash in an arc, smothering the fires before the flames reached her skirt.

Betsy ran to the water bucket by the table and doused

smoldering patches of grime. She tossed the bucket back under the table. "Why?" she blurted out, but Deborah, the empty bucket in her hand, stood, staring over the long swirl of wet ash at the cradle. The fires were out and Deborah's skirt wasn't even scorched. Betsy ran over the ash and hugged Deborah, clinging to her, afraid, even though the fires on the floor were out.

Her arms straight as posts at her sides, her back a board, Deborah's anger, or hatred, stiffened, hard like iron, against Betsy's embrace. She seemed bewitched, but Betsy didn't let go. The flames were staunched, but Deborah's throwing the pan and then, just as quickly, quenching the fire frightened Betsy. She held onto Deborah for her own safety. She held tight, though Deborah didn't struggle. Betsy sensed her fury at being held, but she didn't let go. The fire blazed behind them, the roast sizzling; the grit of the ash scratched the soles of Betsy's shoes. Deborah didn't move. Naomi's song about being washed whiter than snow came through the open window. Betsy's fear eased its grip. Outside, Susannah was singing along with Naomi. Gradually, Deborah's body softened. Her arms went around Betsy and squeezed her to her chest. She smelled of almonds—not the grease, not the roast, not the ash she'd thrown on the floor. Betsy must have imagined the smell.

Deborah trembled.

At first, Betsy didn't understand that she was sobbing, but once she knew Deborah was weeping, Betsy rocked her as she would have comforted Mary or Alice. Deborah moaned like the woman who'd been taken from her children on the slave ship. It was the anguish at the loss of a child. Deeper. Her sorrow gripped Betsy and they clung together. Deborah struggled to stop the sobs, sniffing to hold back the grief. "You can't ..." She gasped. "You can't ..." She pulled free, wiping her face with her apron. "Good Hope ..." She spoke to the fire in the hearth. "Slaves have to work. Whit has to ride them hard." Having spoken, she hung her head, and Betsy strained to hear her next words. She said, "Slaves can't think they're free."

Betsy had no answer. She walked to the window. Near Naomi, singing as she hung soldiers' shirts on the line, Susannah pinned linen bandages in the sun and breeze. Robert's own daughter believed she was a slave. Naomi stopped singing to tell Susannah to take Isaiah away from the clean clothes. Betsy said, "I want Susannah to walk with me to the burial." She turned back to Deborah. "There's no reason for her to come to the funeral for the surveyor and the soldiers, but when we walk to the cemetery, I want her to come with me. To visit my brother's grave."

Silence.

"I should have gone to my brother's grave when I first came."

"Why would you want that, Mrs. Randall?" Deborah edged along the wall to close the window as if the breeze were too strong. Maybe she feared that Susannah would hear them. She looked out the window toward her daughter. "The dead, they want the living." She centered the hyacinths on the windowsill. "Before Susannah could walk, Master Robert carried her on his shoulder out to the fields. She toddled after him everywhere, in the house, the yard, the barn. She sat on his lap when he ate. If she goes to his grave, he'll want to keep her there."

Betsy went to the hearth, grabbed a towel to wipe the pan that had rolled on the floor, and set it in place for the drippings. She had to quiet the fear on Deborah's face. "I won't let go of Susannah's hand, but I want her with me at her father's grave. We'll pray that his soul will find peace." In Brompton-on-Thames, Betsy had walked with her mother and the little girls to her family's graves and she told them stories. She didn't know what she'd tell Susannah. Maybe the time Bobby found their way home after they were lost at the Brompton Cattle Fair. She hoped Susannah would tell her about the man who'd carried her to the fields, and something more Betsy hadn't yet heard about her brother, the man who'd written Susannah's name in the ledger. "When I stand at my brother's grave, it will be good to have Susannah with me."

Deborah bowed her head, accepting but not agreeing, solemn. "She'll wear her pink dress and good shoes."

Chapter 29

In the southwest, the moon hung above the small grassy cemetery. Two lanterns hung from a low branch on a lone oak in the grove of young ash. The sun wasn't up, but a gentle dawn lit the faces of Reinke, Harmon, Ned, and Nighthawk as Betsy and Charity walked to them. A few feet from the grave of the wild man, Betsy clasped her hands, as if praying, and crept closer to Charity. While Ned and Nighthawk sprinkled corn into the open coffin, they chanted the name Mbadugah. They knew the wild man's name. Waving a smoldering torch with a fragrance of tobacco and pine, Harmon shuffled beside Reinke after the Pamunkey, who was chanting Mba, Mba, Mba, drawing out the name like it was a sentence. Ned spoke Pamunkey as he raised his arms to the light in the east. Betsy bowed her head. Reinke muttered in German, and then Harmon asked the Creator to guide Mba's spirit back over the ocean to his people. When Charity began to sing, "Guide me across the water, guide me home, guide me home," she elbowed Betsy to sing with her, but Betsy didn't know the song and had no will to sing. The man had lived alone. He'd been forced

from his home like Josiah, and he'd run into the wild. Betsy
had run, but she'd stayed on the road. She had no fear of
being caught and whipped. She had no answer to Deborah's
saying that whipping kept the slow slaves working. She'd
fled the plantation because she'd never belong there as Deborah did.

When Harmon had asked Betsy if she wanted to be at the
burial, he said the guides wanted a Pamunkey ceremony, and
she should bring something for Mbadugah, something for
his spirit. Nighthawk had found the man's spear and a recruit
had given Harmon the dagger he'd found close to the body.
Betsy could have given Isaac's ring, but she thought of it as
belonging to her child. She should give him the pelt, but
Gray had given that to the soldier. She'd chosen three ribbons, one red and two blue, praying for the man's soul as she
braided them. Ned dropped in a twist of tobacco bound with
three feathers and bits of fur. Reinke knelt. He'd brought
three bullets for the man though Betsy never saw him with a
gun. Harmon gave a tin whistle. On her knees, Charity dan-
gled a cowrie shell on a black string over the grave. Before
she let it drop, she said, "Find my mama." Instead of rising,
she hunkered over. Betsy bent to comfort her and saw Charity pull Morris's ring with the red stone from her pocket and
let it fall into a fold of the blanket around the body. Betsy's
circle of ribbons landed near the fold. She prayed that God,
the Creator and Redeemer, would guide Mba to his celestial
home as the man had led her to safety. She stepped back
when the men began shoveling earth into the grave.

"Miss Phillipa be askin where I been," Charity said.

"I'll walk with you." Betsy wanted to leave the place
where her brother was buried. In the half dark as she'd
approached the grave of Mba, she'd seen a stone marker that

must have been for Robert. She would go to his grave later, in the full light of day, with Susannah. To keep pace with Charity, Betsy hooked her arm through Charity's elbow and picked up her skirts to take long fast steps.

"Mrs. Randall, if Miss Phillipa wakes up and I ain't there, ain't nobody can save me. She'll have Whitmore tie me up and whip me to the bone."

Betsy asked why Charity hadn't stayed with the Fultons.

Charity came to an abrupt stop. She was glad the Fultons sold her to Master Osborne. "Miss Phillipa need her own girl, her own age. The master don' beat slaves. We dress good."

"You said that Phillipa would have you whipped to the bone."

Seeing the fright on Charity's face, Betsy waved for her to run. Up ahead, Whitmore ducked into the woods, and Betsy hurried after Charity to that spot.

Sidewise against a tree, Whitmore nestled a large brown rooster in his arm. Both glared at Betsy, who looked from the chicken to the overseer. "Good morning, Mr. Whitmore. What are you doing with the rooster?"

Whitmore stroked the sleek blue-brown feathers of the rooster's neck, calming the bird. "Don't accuse me, Mrs. Randall. Deborah knows spirits. She fears Bob Harrington will haunt our little Mary Alice. She's wrong to think ill of her master or his poor spirit, but who can tell with the dead?"

Betsy stared at him, then at the cock with its bright red comb, eyeing Betsy from the crook of Whitmore's arm. She looked back toward the cemetery. The trees blocked her view of the men filling Mr. Mba's grave. "Why a rooster?"

"Ma'am, your brother shouldn't punish Deborah for being a wife to me. I never touched her while he was alive." Pale gray lids closed over the rooster's eyes as if soothed by Whitmore's words. "I served him, blood and bone. He can't fault me." His hand covered the rooster's head. "She told me to sprinkle fresh blood on the grave at sunrise."

Deborah feared the dead. Why not? Hadn't Robert been sitting in the field, his legs crossed, when Betsy and the expedition approached the plantation? Hadn't Betsy expected his ghost to be in his office? Hadn't she felt a chill when she first saw his grave that morning? Deborah wanted a rooster killed, a blood sacrifice, to keep Betsy's brother from claiming Susannah or harming her new baby. Hadn't Betsy herself dreaded having Morris buried on the plantation? Hadn't she hoped that Mba, buried close by, would protect the land from the surveyor? She'd dropped a braid of ribbon into a grave. Was sprinkling blood so different? In England it was witchcraft, but the Old Testament required animal sacrifice. The bird clucked next to Whitmore's chest, shaking its beak and red wattles at Betsy.

"Mr. Whitmore, my brother didn't tell my husband and me about Deborah or his children. If she believes a ritual will protect Mary Alice, sacrifice the chicken—such a brave rooster—but hurry; the sun is clearing the trees."

Men's voices saying farewell carried from the cemetery through the quiet woods and startled Whitmore. "I'm Christian, same as you, Mrs. Randall."

"I know that you loved my brother." Betsy petted the smooth iridescent feathers. She'd promised to hold Susannah's hand at the burial that afternoon. "Go kill your rooster."

He tucked the chicken into his jacket, a bulge he seemed

to think Reinke and Harmon wouldn't notice. Betsy watched him stride off toward the cemetery, stepping to the side and lifting his hat for the fiddler and his friend, the hunter, to pass. When they came abreast of Betsy, she walked with them in silence. "You're very quiet, Mrs. Randall," the fiddler said. "Not one word at the funeral."

She had been praying all through the ceremony and thinking that the wild man—Mba—would have liked the quiet. Morning light shone on the fresh green leaves of early spring. "Mr. Harmon, could you live alone in the woods year in, year out?"

"Better than being whipped." Harmon spoke at the same time Reinke said, "Better than being a slave."

Their words reminded Betsy of the song Torborg taught the sailors on the *Sally Dash*. Deborah was right: the dead torment the living. In the quiet woods, she sensed Emanuel Brickhart smiling at her from his seat in the longboat. He said he'd not trouble her again before he rolled into the sea with his ball and chain, but he was in her thoughts now. "The sailors of the *Sally Dash* cheered when the pirate captain tossed the cat o' nine tails off the side."

"Brickhart?" Harmon stared at her. Reinke too. "The pirate captain?"

Betsy didn't say how the men raced, working together to unload the ship. She wasn't going to think more about the pirates. Her mind went from Brickhart's cruelty to Whitmore's riding up on the old man in the field. When she asked if all slave-owners whipped their slaves, Harmon said Mrs. Fulton wouldn't allow it, that she treated slaves like they were family.

Betsy slowed her steps, looking down at pebbles, twigs, and the footprints of those who'd trudged out to the burial.

She picked up a rose-colored stone flecked with silver and black, and closed her fist over it. She must think of her child.

Reinke took her arm. "Mrs. Randall, the slaves at Good Hope respected your brother. They saw him as a decent man—hard on them and Martin Whitmore, but also hard on himself."

Harmon agreed: "He was well loved. I'm sorry you never saw him with his slaves. He would have introduced them as his friends. Bob Harrington never hesitated to grab an axe to help Aeneas fell a tree. Many plantations have crews, but Li'l Xerxes, Aeneas, Castor, and Pollux work with their teams the way Harrington taught them. Deborah is the only slave I know who sat at dinner with her master, and no one dared object."

Betsy squeezed the stone. "She ate at the table with him?" No wonder Deborah threw the pot of grease. She believed Betsy would destroy her beloved Good Hope with its walnut table, sparkling chandelier, and forget-me-nots. Betsy asked Reinke if it was true.

Reinke frowned at Harmon. "Yes, Deborah ate with him. And once they built the big house, Martin ate in the dependency, alone." He glanced at her fist. "Why the rock?"

"It's something I can grasp." Betsy remembered Josiah's knuckles turning white when he squeezed his carving. Her stone was for Good Hope and what it had been for her brother. The first time Robert returned to Brompton from Virginia, he'd stayed in Betsy's home, and took Mary, who was a tot at the time, wherever he went. He'd urged Isaac to settle in Virginia. The second time, he was the guest of the Earl of Guilford, and though Isaac wanted to join them for dinner, he was never invited. On both visits, he looked for a wife, but no woman suited him. A good thing, since the woman would have sensed, as Betsy had, that the home belonged to Deborah.

Betsy stopped.

Reinke took her arm. "Mrs. Randall, we must return to the house. They will have breakfast ready."

Reinke was right. She hadn't eaten. Deborah had said, "A house should be lived in or it will go to shambles." The sun shone over the trees and on the house in the distance. "Mr. Harmon, if you managed a plantation, would you whip the slaves?"

Harmon pulled off his cap and scratched his head. He pulled a small tin box out of his jacket pocket and offered Reinke a pinch of snuff before he took one himself. "It is the way of tobacco." He sniffed, gasping when the tobacco went up his nose. Then he smiled, satisfied, and took three more quick, short sniffs. "You have to train slaves. Good Hope is known for its tobacco." He pocketed the box and patted it, pleased. "Being a planter means forcing others to work the fields, to coddle the plants and pick the leaves." After spitting to the side of the path, he looked ahead toward the house. "Robert Harrington bought fine rugs. A harpsichord. Deborah. No good planter injures a slave when he whips him. Instead, he keeps them strong and drives them hard so Englishmen can stuff their pipes with tobacco."

Harmon motioned for her to walk on, but Betsy didn't. "But if a slave can't keep up—"

"The whip comes down." Reinke finished her sentence.

Harmon laughed, a joyless bark. "Or you're sold to a man who treats slaves like mules."

Betsy couldn't tell from his face what he thought of

trading people. "Is it right? If they can't work, is it right to sell the poor souls?"

A flock of birds flew overhead and turned like a giant hand, beckoning them toward the house. After gazing at the black flecks in the blue, Harmon squinted at Betsy with a look of disgust. "See." He pointed at the birds. "They fly to some command we don't hear or see. They know the way to breakfast." Over his shoulder as he left, he said, "You have to fly with your own kind, Mrs. Randall."

Before she could question him about how he could call himself an Englishman and keep three wives, he trotted off to the house. She didn't understand his relationship to the women, but they'd seemed content. Deborah seemed content, but Josiah and Mba rejected the world of master and slave. The pirates with their charter rejected the world of master and servant.

Reinke, his face set, had watched Harmon go. When Betsy stared after him, Reinke said, "He's right."

"My husband wanted to own this plantation, but it belongs to Deborah."

"Deborah belongs to you," Reinke said. Wind and sun had leathered his skin.

"Deborah lived as my brother's wife." She and Reinke were close enough to the house to hear Phillipa's laughter. Betsy said, "She had his children."

"Her children belong to you."

"They're my niece and nephew; I'm responsible for them, but I don't own them." She looked at the rock and then clenched it tighter in her fist. "I will not own them."

He shrugged and walked to the house. At the sounds of cutlery and Gray talking about his family's plantation, Betsy signaled Reinke that she wasn't going in but walking around to the back. "I need to talk to Deborah." She didn't say that she preferred breakfast in the dependency, Deborah's kitchen. "I'll join everyone in the sitting room for the funeral service."

He listened to the voices and the breakfast clatter. "You're not alone, Mrs. Randall."

She nodded and hurried around the corner of the house. Reinke was wrong. She was alone and she would be alone at the birth of her child. On her right, she had the house, on the left, the fields of Good Hope. She had no one she could trust as she had Martha Adler or Nancy Finch. Isaac had been with her for the birth of Mary, Alice, and David. He'd held the little ones and loved them as she did. She leaned against the house to rest. Her ribs drawn in, clamping her chest. In the west, jagged blue mountains sprawled, serene in the distance, but they were wild. A flock of birds overhead darkened the sky. The ache in Betsy's chest lifted, and for a moment, she did nothing but look at the mountains, trying to spot the farthest peaks. Isaac had a survey of the property. After the capture of the *Sally Dash*, she'd seen it in a dream, but long before that dream, before her family left Brompton-on-Thames, she'd seen Isaac studying a plan of the Harrington land that Dunn brought with him when he told them of Robert's death. Isaac had described his vision of Good Hope, but it was more beautiful than he'd imagined, and part of the beauty was the wilderness he thought was tamed. Isaac knew about the slaves. With pride, he would have lorded his position over Whitmore and commanded the beautiful Deborah. Betsy had known about the slaves, but she hadn't understood what inheriting a plantation with seventy-three slaves meant. Fool, she'd imagined laborers like those on the farms around Brompton-on-Thames, free to run off to London if they chose.

She slowed her step, squeezing the rock, looking at the blue mountains on her way to the kitchen dependency. Robert should have deeded his land to Deborah for as long as she lived. He should have provided for his own children. Good Hope should go to Isaiah when he reached maturity. Betsy should have visited her brother's grave; she should have walked to the cemetery with her niece.

At the kitchen window, in warm sunlight, Deborah dabbed the beaten egg over rounds of dough. She seemed to have seen Betsy but busied herself with her task. Without a word, Betsy put the rock in her pocket and walked to the table in the middle of the room. She poured herself a cup of lukewarm chocolate and cut a thick slice of bread. "I've come from the burial of a man that Lieutenant Gray claims was a runaway slave."

Deborah didn't look up. "I dare say, Mrs. Randall, if he was a black in the woods, he was a runaway." She shifted the table, protecting the loaves from the breeze, but she'd moved it like a barricade between Betsy and her.

"The fiddler and the hunter said the man would rather live in the wild than be a slave." Betsy stirred her chocolate; she didn't drink it.

Covering the rounds of dough with a towel, Deborah fidgeted, careful not to look at Betsy, muttering as she worked. When Betsy asked her to repeat what she'd mumbled, Deborah said she wouldn't trust the fiddler. She looked through the windows at the slave quarters.

Betsy sipped the chocolate, more bitter than she'd expected. "On the *Sally Dash*, the first mate whipped sailors." Though she was hungry, Betsy couldn't get herself to taste the bread. "The men hated the first mate of the Dash."

"Slaves must obey the master, not love him." Deborah washed the bread bowl and wooden spoon with a great deal of splashing. "Keeping watch over slaves without a whip is like hunting without a gun—there'll be no meat on the table." Deborah looked out at the quarters as she dried the dishes.

Betsy wanted to challenge Deborah, but she didn't know a way to make slaves work without a whip. The Fultons did it, but their place was small; they could treat their slaves like family. She lifted the skim from her chocolate and dropped it onto the saucer. She told Deborah that the lieutenant savored every bite of the roast venison at supper, pouring on so much gravy that he had to have more bread. "I thought I might save a piece of the tart for tea after the burial, but not one crumb remained on the plate. No one went to sleep hungry."

Deborah moved the worktable back to its place in front to the window. She set a small crock of pickled ham in front of Betsy, who smeared a thin coat of the ham on her bread. "I'm worried about Good Hope, Mistress."

Betsy cut the slice of bread into six pieces and arranged them around the rim of the plate.

In the quiet of the kitchen, the water dripping from a string of perch into a tub of water made its own music—until the baby whimpered in her cradle. Before she could whine again—and before Deborah dropped the fish back in the tub—Betsy rushed to lift the baby to her shoulder. Betsy held her close, cuddling the baby to keep her quiet.

Soon enough, she'd have to give her to Deborah, but for the moment, she could hold the child.

Bundled in a lambskin, the newborn calmed Betsy's mind. She nestled Mary Alice in the crook of her arm. "Small as a loaf of bread," she said. The soft spot on top of her head pulsed. Betsy touched her cheek to the feathery hair and kissed the baby's forehead. When she fit her little finger in the baby's palm, the baby tugged. "Strong hands." Kissing the tiny fist, Betsy said, "Susannah favors you, Deborah."

Deborah paused from cutting open a perch to look at the hyacinths on the windowsill. "Master Robert said she did. He called her 'darling.' 'Your darling favors you.' Mr. Whitmore says Susannah took after him. He said it again yesterday." With her thumb, she gutted the fish.

If Betsy had a miniature of her mother, she could show Deborah how much Susannah resembled Robert's mother. Raising the baby back to her shoulder, Betsy patted her. "Susannah is charming. Such a pretty voice." The hurt formed a stone at the back of Betsy's mouth. "My Mary often sang." She walked around the room with Mary Alice until the baby's eyes fastened on the fire in the hearth. Would Good Hope prosper if Betsy insisted that Whitmore stop whipping slaves? Isaac would have agreed with Deborah and Li'l Xerxes about whipping slaves. Would he have spared an old man? Betsy didn't know. If no one forced slaves to work, would they stay? Where would they go? Could they all live like the wild man? Mary Alice sucked on her fist. Betsy sang, "Sweet, sweet baby, pretty little flower."

At the window, Deborah took an egg from a wicker basket and cracked it against a bowl with a flick of her wrist. "She's lazy as her father and just as hungry."

With Mary Alice on her shoulder, Betsy moved to watch Deborah. A yolk, a gold-orange eye, looked up from a blue bowl. Crack. Another egg dropped in the bowl. "Whit can't do sums to save his soul, but Master Robert always said, 'Hitch him to a plow and you got a field.' It's true."

Betsy watched her whisk the eggs. "Who steers the plow?"

Deborah sprinkled cornmeal on a plate near the bowl of egg froth. "Who steers the plow?" She scraped the scales from a fish. "You don't mean Castor or Pollux?" When all of the fish were scaled, she said, "Before Master Robert went to England to find a wife the first time, he taught me to keep the books." She looked out the window toward the quarters. Her gaze seemed to go beyond the mountains. "I can hear his voice. 'First the day, then the date: Tuesday, September 30, 1703.'" She rolled each fish in the egg and then in cornmeal. "'Who sold the seed? What did we trade for the ox?' I wrote who bought tobacco, corn, or flax; how much, how many, the cost. I copied his letters so no man living could tell the difference." Deborah spooned drippings onto a flat frying pan. "Not even Master Robert his own self. I'd watched the way he held the quill and the one-two-three of the letters he wrote." She turned her face from the flame as she fried the perch in the bacon fat. "When Master died ..." She flipped one of the fish. "When Master Harrington died, Old Osborne couldn't tell when I had begun keeping the accounts. He told the men from Williamsburg to leave Whit in charge, but he pulled me aside." She arranged the fish on a pewter platter. "He warned me that if Good Hope wasn't maintained, I'd be sold at auction."

"He'd blame you?"

"I'd be to blame, Mrs. Randall. I didn't blink. I was grieving Master Robert, and Old Osborne felt sorry for me; but if the yield failed, Whit and I wouldn't be here today. We kept working for Master Robert." She covered the platter with a shallow bowl to keep the fish warm. "Whit's smarter than people think. He knows the land, he knows the stock, and he knows his tobacco. Nobody cures it sweeter."

"And he whips the slaves."

Deborah looked over at the hearth and then down at the smudged traces of grease fire and ash on the floor. "Two new tobacco fields and two fine yields. Whit kept the crews working. We finished the bedrooms with the paper Master Robert brought from England. Whit rose early and I woke in the middle of the night to keep the books."

Betsy wondered how often Robert had watched Deborah fry fish. In the middle of the night, she'd written the day's account in Robert's ledger, the blue ledger in his office. Now she left the overseer in Robert's bed to keep a record for Good Hope. In Betsy's arms, Mary Alice squirmed and her chin wrinkled. Soon she'd insist on being fed. Betsy lifted Mary Alice to her shoulder and jostled her, catching her cry before it came. "Mr. Harmon said that when my brother had guests, you sat at the table with them."

Deborah pulled a rag from a basket under the table and wrapped it under her breasts. Her milk must have come at the baby's snuffling and started to seep through her shift. She chose a knife to slice cold corn pudding. "Mrs. Randall, please don't trust that fiddler."

"Mr. Reinke said it was true. He said Mr. Whitmore ate alone in the dependency."

Betsy had meant to catch Deborah off guard, but when

she dropped her knife and stood with her arms stiff at her sides, Betsy wasn't sure what to do. She brought Mary Alice to Deborah and picked up the knife. "I'll slice the pudding and fry it. You feed Mary Alice."

Deborah stared at Betsy as if Betsy had struck her. "Mrs. Randall, Master Robert ..." She rocked the baby in one arm and reached for the knife. "It's not for me to sit while you fry corn pudding. That fire will scorch your face faster than paper."

"I know how to keep my face and skirt away from the fire just as you do, Mrs. Whitmore." Betsy put the baby in Deborah's arms. "You sit with your back to the fire. This baby girl needs you." She pulled a chair from the table for Deborah, and when she was rocking and cuddling the baby, Betsy sliced the lump of pudding, satisfied with the even pieces. "Mr. Harmon told me that children born to a slave are the property of the master."

Too late, Deborah pressed her hand over the baby's ear. In a dead voice, Deborah said, "The fiddler's right." She rocked. "I am your property." She paused to watch the baby knead her breast. "My children too." Her face had a sadness, a tenderness that seemed to give off its own soft light.

With each scratch of the turner, a few more bits of corn-meal fell into the fire. Betsy said, "Can one person own another? Can a person buy a child? Isn't Mary Alice a gift of God?"

Deborah stopped rocking, shifting her back to Betsy. "No one can own another's soul. You own the body." She switched the baby to nurse her other breast. "Your place is to care for the plantation and all that pertains to it. The planter is bound to make men work."

Order pleased Betsy: the rising and setting of the sun,

morning and night. The seasons. In her own life, the order
of preparing a meal pleased her. Betsy needed to know what
each hour required. She fit the slices of pudding in the pan
and gauged the time to fry them without thought or quandary. Arranging the fried pudding on a plate was a matter
of design with no right or wrong. Tending the fire, adding
a log so the others would set it ablaze, gave her purpose. But
a woman whipped to her knees and a man eating alone
when his friend served others at a fine table threw the gentle lavender of the hyacinths, the serenity of the trees, or
the blue of the sky out of joint. Betsy covered the plate of
corn pudding.

Deborah cuddled the baby. "These fine farms, Mrs.
Randall. Phelps's place, Glenmere. Good Hope. Slaves
work those fields." She walked toward the cradle. "I have to
bring that fish to the house."

But she didn't because Susannah stood at the door. How
she'd opened it without either Betsy or Deborah hearing
her, Betsy didn't know; but the girl stood, silent, as Betsy
had when she was a girl. Without a word, Betsy put the fish
and corn pudding on the tray Susannah brought and laid a
towel over it to keep the food warm. After a quick curtsy,
Susannah set off.

Betsy sat down to eat the bread with spiced ham and
drink her cold chocolate. The rock in her pocket might sat-
isfy her need to hold something, but it changed nothing.
Gray had said he'd start back the next day. With Phillipa
and Charity riding in the wagon, Gray, Harmon, and Petty
would make their way to Williamsburg. Deborah and the
overseer would sleep in the dependency; Betsy would be
alone in the big house. She took a piece of bread with

minced ham after pulling a chair from the table for Deborah. "How long have you lived at Good Hope?"

Quietly, Deborah sat down and stared at the plate of bread Betsy had offered her.

Betsy ate another bite of bread. "My husband and I didn't know my brother had children. Mr. Randall would have liked Good Hope, but he never envisioned the wilderness." She swirled the chocolate in her cup and drank it. "I see how fortunate my brother was to have you and Martin Whitmore help him." Betsy took one of the four remaining bits of ham and bread. "My brother lived with you as his wife, and that is why none of the women he courted in England pleased him."

Deborah looked at the bread but didn't try a piece. "Bobby named Susannah. I wanted her named Anne, after the Queen, but he said the queen was no beauty and Susannah would be. Isaiah was born after the duel." She nibbled a bit of bread.

Betsy chewed on ham gristle. "When did you marry Mr. Whitmore?"

"Nobody marries slaves, Mrs. Randall." Deborah sat back from the table. "Slaves don't eat at the master's table." She seemed to wonder if Betsy was truly her master's sister. "Mr. Harmon said I ate at the table with Master Robert. I did. I wore a beautiful deep rose dress—Mr. Osborne took it when he saw no record of it in the ledger with all the furniture, silverware, dishes, and books. He said Master Harrington bought it for a wife, and since he never married, it should go to a lady in Williamsburg." She stared at the fire.

Betsy guessed the woman was Mrs. Taylor. "How could he take your dress?"

"Mrs. Randall, I ate at the table, but those men saw me as Master Robert's toy. I poured wine, laughed at their jollying me, and smiled at Master Robert." She stood up from the table. "When he died, I wouldn't let Martin Whitmore come to his bed. Whit knew how I hurt, but after Isaiah was born, he said he had a right." She smiled, but with no expectation that Betsy would understand. "He said I would be his wife but I told him that if he said, 'Deborah Phelps, I take you for my wife,' three times, and I said, 'I take you for my husband, Martin Whitmore,' three times, in front of the Dutch stove, I would sleep with him." She looked at the cradle. "Nobody knows but him and me."

"And me." Betsy smoothed her apron. She needed to dress for the funeral.

"And you," Deborah took a broom from next to the hearth.

"I'm expecting a baby."

No dust rose as Deborah swept toward the hearth. She angled the broom to collect bits of litter and soot. "If you've had a child, you know when a woman has one on the way."

"Yes. Our bodies betray us." Betsy peeked in the cradle. "Your Mary Alice and my child will be born in the same year."

Deborah began to sweep. "Mrs. Randall, you'll love Good Hope as the master did."

Betsy wanted to tell Deborah how it hurt to discover that Robert had children he thought of as slaves on the plantation he'd been so proud to possess, but she didn't know how to tell Deborah this without tarnishing her image of him. "This plantation is not my land."

Deborah braced the broom in its corner next to the

hearth but couldn't be quite satisfied with making it stand upright. "Old Osborne said Good Hope belonged to Master Harrington's next of kin. He knew Master Harrington had a sister and that you had children. We all did. Osborne said Master Harrington's nephew would inherit the plantation. It belongs to your child."

Rocking the cradle to a lullaby she'd once sung for David, Betsy thought about Osborne believing her son should be Robert's heir; she knew he was wrong. She wouldn't argue with Deborah, but she'd arrange for her brother's children to inherit his land. From the door, she looked back at Deborah. "Lieutenant Gray wants to start the march to Williamsburg tomorrow. I'm going with him." The words were said almost before Betsy knew she was saying them. She watched Deborah's surprise change to relief before she could hide her feelings. When Deborah didn't respond, Betsy said, "I have clothes in the trunk you can give to the people who live in the quarters. I'm going to stay in Williamsburg for the present." She looked down at the baby sleeping peacefully, at the drool on the lambskin. Betsy looked at Deborah. "You must move up to the big house. A house should be lived in or it will go to shambles." Betsy chose words Deborah had used.

With an urgency Betsy hadn't seen before, Deborah ran to her and dropped to her knees. "Take Susannah with you. She can cook, clean, wash clothes, mend, card, spin, and bleach wool. You've seen how good she is with Mary Alice. She'll care for your baby."

Betsy stepped back. She grabbed Deborah's hand to pull her to her feet, but Deborah refused to rise. "Deborah, I'm not taking your daughter from you. She'll never be my slave."

Up from her knees, Deborah held Betsy's hand between her own. "Not for my sake, Mrs. Randall." She looked up, pleading. "Do it for Master Robert. She is Master Robert's child, not a Phelps. She's my child, but I trained her to be a slave. You say she favors me, but she's a Harrington; her features are yours, not mine." She bowed her head. "I was born to Master Phelps. All Glenmere-born slaves are Phelps people. I've been bought and sold." She paused. "I've taught Susannah all I know. She'll be a good slave for you."

"Bought and sold?"

"I was traded for three bales of top-grade tobacco because Mistress Phelps didn't want me in the old master's presence. Old Phelps threw in the harpsichord because he was angry with his wife. There was a lot of anger in that house, Mrs. Randall, but not here at Good Hope. Teach Susannah your ways. When you come back to Good Hope, you'll see it's a pleasant place to grow tobacco and raise your child."

"I don't know when I'll return to Good Hope, but you and Mr. Whitmore will be the ones to maintain the plantation. I won't take Susannah with me to Williamsburg, but I want you to teach Susannah and Isaiah to be planters, as their father was. They are not slaves. They're my niece and nephew." Betsy waited for Deborah to say something, to acknowledge that she'd heard what was said, but her face was still. "Deborah, have I made myself clear?"

She nodded, but Betsy couldn't tell if she agreed.

Betsy stepped out onto the porch and looked to the distant mountains. In England, she'd never understood the Psalm about lifting her eyes to the mountains, but here in Virginia, pondering them assured her. Three days ago, she hadn't known about Deborah and her children. She'd known her brother had owned slaves, but she hadn't known that he'd had them whipped. When they were children, he wrestled Samuel Fuller, a boy bigger than he, to the ground because the boy had pulled the legs off a frog. Yet as a man, he'd listed his daughter as a slave in a book with accounts of livestock and crops. Robert must have seen the purple mountains to the west when he planned where he'd build the house and where the quarters Betsy faced now would be. The land didn't belong to her. The slaves at Good Hope weren't her property either. They rightfully belonged to Robert's children, to Susannah and Isaiah. Betsy wanted nothing to do with Robert's estate. Deborah should be charged with the trust of the children's estate.

She flung the door open. It banged against the wall, and Betsy strode back into the kitchen dependency. "I am telling Mr. Osborne to turn the deed over to you until Susannah and Isaiah are of age."

Deborah hadn't moved from where she'd stood, as if she had been considering what Betsy had told her. After a pause, time for Betsy to understand what she would be denying her child, time for her to change her mind if she needed to do that, Deborah stepped around her and closed the door without a click or scrape. She picked up Mary Alice who had awakened with a cry. Shushing the baby, Deborah tipped her head toward the table for Betsy to sit down. "Mrs. Randall, Mr. Osborne will never agree to that change in the deed. The law won't allow it." She wiped the baby's chin with a corner of her kerchief. "The funeral will start soon. You must go. Naomi will have Susannah dressed to walk to the cemetery with you."

"There's a way for Robert's children to have his land, and I'll find it."

Deborah bowed her head. "You must adopt the children. Osborne will understand when you say they are your brother's children. He knew Bobby well, and he knew Susannah was his child. He was looking for a white woman, and Osborne knew it. He knew that I managed Good Hope, but it will be hard to convince him the land should go to Susannah and Isaiah."

Betsy placed her hand on Deborah's arm. After three days in the wagon, Betsy's skin was darker. She said, "Please ask Susannah to wait at the front door. I'll meet her there after the service to walk to the burial."

Chapter 30

Three open graves.

A breeze brushed Betsy's face. It smelled of the woods around the cemetery instead of the sea air she remembered from the *Sally Dash*. David would be buried in his father's arms, Mary on her father's right, and Alice on his left. He'd carried her perched above his heart. The graves smelled of soil, rich and moldy with last year's leaves. Betsy said, "Amen." So be it.

Standing there, she wasn't "Aunt Betsy" to Susannah, though she held her hand. Betsy guessed the girl's calm masked misgivings. Perhaps she feared Betsy, Mistress Randall, the woman who had taken their home. The girl didn't seem frightened of being in the cemetery. She looked up at Betsy and shifted her weight. Her arm brushed Betsy's side.

Though Susannah was taller than Mary, Betsy's palm fit the round, hard shoulder as if she were hugging her own daughter on the *Sally Dash*. She pointed for Susannah to look up at the white moon in the patch of blue sky above the small cemetery. Instead of walking to where those mourning Morris and the two soldiers were, and watching the coffins being waggled into the graves, Betsy led Susannah to Robert's burial plot, a rectangle covered with oyster shell marked with a slab of soft stone.

Susannah held a bouquet of trout lilies and bluebells for her father's grave. She moved a brittle clump of yellowed lace from the base of the stone off to the side. Since the burial that morning, someone, perhaps Whitmore, had placed a wreath of woodbine on the grave. As if she'd done it many times, Susannah centered her flowers in the wreath on the grave, bowed her head, and folded her hands.

Six arcs of small brown spots, three to the right and three to the left, crisscrossed the front of the soft stone. A hard rain might wash the rooster blood off the name "*Harrington*." Betsy scattered flowers from her basket over the layer of broken oyster shell. Susannah traced the chiseled letters with her finger and read "Robert Harrington August 1711." After a pause, she said, "Papa died after the duel 'cause he played cards."

"Yes. I know." Though Betsy had never been with Robert when he gambled, she pictured him at the table studying his hand. It had been two years since he died. Susannah cocked her head. "Papa laughed when I read long words. He called me a parrot."

She called Robert "Papa." Betsy hoped she would call her "Aunt." She stooped to hear her.

"Papa said I would play with Mary and take care of little Alice when you came," Susannah said. "He was glad Mama's baby would be a friend for Alice. He didn't know Isaiah would be a boy."

Betsy knelt, hugging Susannah, hoping the girl wouldn't pull away. She'd seemed to distrust Betsy the day she came to Good Hope. Betsy said, "But my brother didn't know we would come."

Sure of her memory, Susannah looked at Betsy, surprised. "Yes, he did." She seemed to wonder if Betsy was testing her. "He said if we made Good Hope beautiful, your family would want to live here."

"My husband never told me that." Her brother had tried to convince Isaac to come to Virginia, but no plans had been made. Until Robert returned to England the second time, Isaac had scoffed at the idea of settling in the colonies.

"Papa said Mr. Whitmore would help him build another big house for you, but first you'd sleep in his house—in the bedroom where the sun comes in the window. He said you liked the sun to wake you up in the morning."

Betsy smiled at Susannah. "I do like waking to the sun." She may not have known Robert as well as she thought, but he knew the sunrise was important to her. Did he know that she wouldn't want slaves whipped? That she would be troubled by treating people worse than animals? She wished she could challenge him to come up with a way to get the work done without lashing those who couldn't keep up. He'd wanted Isaac to help him buy more land around Good Hope and to broker the sale of tobacco. Harmon and Reinke praised Robert for working alongside the overseer and the slaves, but maybe he wanted her family to come so that he'd have time to gamble. "Susannah … "

Phillipa touched Betsy. "It's time for the service."

Betsy stood up and walked Susannah to the graves. She'd wanted to ask Susannah if she knew she was her aunt. How much of their conversation had Phillipa heard? Very little. Betsy had bent to hear Susannah's soft voice.

With her finger to her lips, Susannah pointed to a lady-bug marching around the rim on the basket. Betsy nodded. She'd be careful not to frighten off the little creature.

————

In the cadence of a vicar, Gray led the service from his Book of Common Prayer. Betsy followed, holding her prayer book so Susannah could read with her, but she was thinking about Susannah calling Robert "Papa." If she and Isaac had come when he first urged them to settle in Virginia, would he have continued to live with Deborah as his wife? He'd told Susannah that she could be Mary's playmate, but had he said that Betsy's children were her cousins?

After the amens, after Betsy and Phillipa dropped flowers onto the lids of the coffins, after Gray, Harmon, Reinke, and Petty shoveled earth into Morris's grave, and the troops filled the graves of their comrades, Phillipa put her head on Betsy's shoulder. "You choose to think sad thoughts, Mrs. Randall." She pointed to Susannah who was making a crown of wild flowers. "You should learn from her."

Learn from Susannah? Deborah had taught her daughter to be a slave. Betsy could learn about running a plantation from Deborah, but she didn't agree with having people live in shacks, dress in rags, and be subject to whippings. Betsy could learn from Phillipa, who'd spent a day in distress because of Gray's judgment against Charity and her, but challenged the way he'd led his men. At supper, Phillipa had toasted his safe return. She'd taken his arm for the procession to the cemetery. Betsy wanted to be still and dwell on the thought that, in a strange way, the three graves were for

her family. It was as if they'd been laid to rest in the cemetery, and now she had a place to think of them.

Betsy hoped Phillipa would go back to the house with
Gray. Instead, she whispered, "Last night, the lieutenant
said he hoped we'd be married this summer. Uncle will be
delighted."

Betsy wanted to think of her own family, of Robert, and
of Susannah—her niece. She didn't want to think about
Miss Townsend and the lieutenant, but Phillipa would
persist until Betsy answered. Phillipa wanted to be Mrs.
Spencer Gray. She wasn't asking Betsy if the man was an
acceptable husband. Perhaps while Phillipa had reigned
over the dinner table, playing hostess until Betsy joined
them, she'd refashioned her view of Gray. Betsy looked
over at the lieutenant talking to Petty while the soldiers
shoveled soil into the graves. Gray had been generous
when he commended Charity's care of the soldiers before
the encounter with Ned and Nighthawk in the barn. Betsy
looked back at Phillipa. "This summer? What about his
threat to spread rumors about you? His demand that you
sell Charity?"

Standing erect, her chin tucked, Phillipa frowned at
Betsy like she was a misbehaving child. "Mrs. Randall, I
forgave him without his apology. I'm sure he regrets his
unkind words." According to Phillipa, Gray admired Charity for inspiring Petty to act like a man.

"Like a man?" Remembering Petty's story about the
Seneca attack and his being a coward, Betsy considered
Phillipa's generosity in forgiving Gray. He had accepted
Petty as his equal at the graves. "Charity seems to have
worked magic on both men."

Phillipa put a silencing finger to her lips. "And Charity

paid Deborah for magic to stop Morris from raping her. Now he's dead and she's afraid he'll haunt her."

After checking to see that Susannah was safe, but not close enough to hear, Betsy prodded Phillipa to notice that Petty was looking at them. To escape Petty, Betsy led Phillipa to Robert's grave. "You're accusing Deborah and Charity of witchcraft."

"Exactly." Phillipa exaggerated a shudder. "Don't worry. Your Deborah concocted a spell on some flowers to quiet Morris's ghost, and I dropped those flowers into his grave."

Betsy gripped Phillipa's arm to keep her from saying more. She looked from the spots of blood on Robert's tombstone to Phillipa, her dress the blue of the sky. "Morris died from a blow that would have killed Goliath. His death had nothing to do with Charity's wish or Deborah's magic." The court in Williamsburg would show no mercy to a slave casting spells. As they stared at the oyster shell of Robert's grave, Betsy told Phillipa that a few years after she was born, her mother's midwife had been drowned by people who accused her of witchery, of causing the death of a newborn. "Unless you want Charity tried for witchcraft, don't repeat this nonsense. And warn Charity never to speak of it."

Phillipa rearranged the knot of her kerchief, glancing back at the men tapping the soil above the graves with the backs of their shovels, their work almost done. She said, "They shall not try Charity." Phillipa nestled up to Betsy so they stood side by side. "Uncle is right: I should be more discreet."

Suddenly, Phillipa's face brightened and she curtsied to Susannah, who had crowned herself with flowers. Betsy curtsied too, as if to a queen. Susannah smiled and skipped off to another cluster of flowers. Phillipa put her arm around Betsy. "Are you my sister?"

The flowers Betsy had scattered over Robert's grave had lost their color. She hadn't known her brother. Deborah should be her sister-in-law, but he'd never married her. "Yes, Phillipa, I'm your sister. You have been, and are, a sister to me."

When the lieutenant came up humming "As I Walked Forth," a tune a soldier piped on a tin whistle during the procession with the coffins, he had a sprightly step. He'd come to escort her to the house.

Beckoning to Susannah, Betsy told them she wanted to pray at her brother's grave.

As Phillipa and Gray watched Susannah skip toward them, he said, "What a charming child she is." Phillipa agreed. "Like her mother."

"She reminds me of my brother, her smile, the shape of her eyebrows. The way she squints at a question. Watch when she comes up, you'll see a look that I remember on his face." According to Deborah, Betsy might have to adopt Robert's children, since they were his true heirs; but Gray and Phillipa wouldn't be the best people to advise her.

Gray did watch Susannah approach, and when Betsy took her hand, he reached over and lifted the little girl's chin to study her face. She didn't expect kindness. She looked right back at him, judging him as he judged her.

The lieutenant smiled. "I hadn't seen the resemblance before." He looked from Betsy's face to Susannah, and then back at Betsy. "If I had a mirror, you'd see her resemblance to you."

"She has Deborah's ears." Phillipa lifted Susannah's wavy hair back to prove her point.

After pushing Phillipa's hand away, Betsy put her arm around her brother's daughter. "Will you stay with me here, Susannah?" Betsy had promised Deborah not to let go of Susannah's hand, but she'd let her wander off to make the crown. "Will your mother worry?"

"If you want, I can stay." She looked at the couple, as if wondering if they'd stay too.

Gray took Phillipa's arm. "We'll tell Deborah that you'll return soon, Mrs. Randall. With Susannah." He gave Betsy a quizzical look. "You bear a great resemblance to your brother. I hadn't noticed that resemblance until we spoke in the barn."

Perhaps the sense that Susannah's hand fit in hers was something she shared with Robert. She waited until Gray and Phillipa left before she walked with her to the three graves. "Let's listen." The voices of those leaving wafted back like the ripples of a stream, and then they heard the drone of the insects and an occasional chirping of a bird. Susannah's head fell against Betsy's arm. "You don't look like Papa." She had a sadness in her voice.

From the edge of the clearing, Reinke stepped toward them. He'd surprised her on the path in the middle of the night and now he surprised her again. He said, "Shall I sing a hymn?"

"Yes." Betsy wanted to be alone with her niece, but a hymn for Isaac and the children—and for her brother— would be right.

Reinke sang in a clear tenor. "Jesus bleibet meine Freude ... " He sang several verses, and Betsy didn't understand a word. As he sang, Susannah huddled against her, her body strong in Betsy's embrace. When Reinke stopped singing and they had only the sounds of woods, Betsy said, "Isaac. Mary. Alice. David."

"I'll get them flowers." Susannah started to leave Betsy.

"Yes, but not yet. Please stand here with me a moment longer." Betsy wanted to put flowers on the graves for her family, but holding Susannah helped her believe that her family was present for her. She bowed her head. Insects hummed. When she had a clear picture of a peaceful sea, of quiet water, she walked with Susannah to where Reinke was picking small blue bell-shaped flowers with a dawn-pink tinge on each petal. As they gathered flowers to fill Betsy's basket, Susannah began to hum, and soon she was singing a little song about finding posies in the woods, pink and blue and white. Alice had sung aimless ditties to her own melodies. The three of them scattered flowers over the loose earth covering the graves with blankets of soft color. The baby's quilt Phillipa embroidered with her Chinese silk would have lasting flowers, but the fleeting nature of the flowers they'd thrown on the graves was part of their beauty. Morris had told Mrs. Fulton that every sunrise had more colors than Phillipa's thread. Now the ring with the red stone he'd carried in his pack was in the wild man's grave.

Betsy took Susannah to the grave of the man Gray identified as a runaway, Mbadugah to the guides, and told her niece and Reinke about Josiah saving her from the pirates. "I don't know why he saved my life, but he did." She scattered the rest of her flowers on his grave. "These are for the man who lived in the woods and for Josiah."

Susannah held a small bouquet. She asked, "Did he have a family?"

"The wild man?" Until then, Betsy hadn't thought about

the possibility of Mba having a family before he'd been captured.

"No. The man who saved you." She had the same skeptical frown between her eyebrows that Mary used to have. Not angry, but curious. "Did he have a family?"

"Yes, he had a wife and son." Betsy doubted that the pirates knew that Josiah's wife and son had been killed. Betsy wouldn't tell Susannah that story. Maybe on another day. "They died in Africa."

"These flowers are for them." Susannah put the bouquet on the mound of soil over Mba's grave, paused for a moment to bow her head, and came back to Betsy. "Mistress, Mama told me not to stay in the cemetery."

"Your mother is right. We must not stay here." Glad for the quiet of the trees surrounding the cemetery and the solemnity with which Susannah left the bouquet for Josiah, Betsy took Susannah's hand. "Please call me 'Aunt Betsy.' I'm your father's sister and your aunt." She smiled, ready to start back. "Tomorrow I'm going with the others to Williamsburg. You and your family will return to the house your father built for you."

She smiled at Reinke. She was sure he was right about Isaac having built the crate to be a vault. Betsy should have known that her husband would keep his wealth safe from thieves. "Me? I'll rent a small house." As they walked, Betsy pictured living in Williamsburg. It wasn't so different from Brompton-on-Thames. Even if the crate had no treasure, Betsy could fend for herself. She'd find a way to care for her child. On Bennett's *Falconer* she'd taught David, and Isaac had packed many books. Osborne would help her find a small house with a room where she could open a school. If

Isaac had hidden enough money, perhaps Betsy could convince Osborne to let her buy Dee. She'd said she could earn the price of her freedom. Perhaps she'd help Betsy care for the schoolchildren and she'd have a place to live while she worked to repay Betsy.

When they passed the barn and saw the house, Betsy let go of Susannah's hand. "Run to your mother." She reached out her arms to embrace her niece.

Susannah clinched her arms around Betsy's waist as Mary had. She said, "I'm glad you came." Betsy hugged her tight. "Call me Aunt Betsy." Softly her niece said, "Aunt Betsy," and she sped off.

As Betsy watched the little girl round the corner of the house to the kitchen dependency, Phillipa stepped out the front door and waved toward Betsy and Reinke.

He touched Betsy's arm. "I'll leave you to the lieutenant's bright butterfly."

"Help me get the trunk back to Williamsburg."

"Yes. We'll get it to Osborne's house." He nodded to Phillipa on his way back.

Betsy waited, calm and eager to return to Williamsburg, glad for a moment alone before Phillipa would be at her side. How different the plantation seemed than when Betsy first came to Good Hope. Now she'd seen the slave quarters—those shabby gray houses, the kitchen dependency, and the garden. She'd been in the barn with its wide doors and fine stalls. She looked to the broad pasture where the horses, cows, and sheep ranged as they pleased. She looked between the pasture and the road she'd taken in the dead of night and the trees that had shaded the bodies. Isaac had wanted to live on this estate, but Betsy was surrendering it. On her return to Williamsburg, she'd adopt her brother's children, if that was the way to deed Good Hope to them.

Phillipa walked up and took Betsy's arm. "You're keeping a secret."

"And I'm not telling you." But Betsy did. She told Phillipa that she was expecting a child and that it had been Isaac's hope the morning of the pirate attack.

For once, Phillipa was quiet.

Betsy's throat constricted her voice to a whisper. "I'm not going to live at Good Hope, Phillipa. I'm going back to Williamsburg with you." She said she'd rent a small house, and when Phillipa protested that her uncle would insist that Betsy live with them, she explained that she needed her own home and garden.

Phillipa looked at the house and the fields. "When the child is born, you'll be back."

At the brave front door Robert had built for his home, Betsy put her hand on her belly. Someday she'd bring her child here, and they'd walk with Susannah and Isaiah to her brother's grave. The property would belong to his children. She and the children, her child and Robert's son and daughter, would scatter flowers on the graves. Betsy would tell them stories of Isaac Randall, and of Mary, Alice, and David.

~ FIN ~

Acknowledgments

I want first to acknowledge my indebtedness to the late Pepper Furey, a writing friend and wonderful reader, who was among the first to read the opening scene and who believed in the story. Such friends are invaluable, and I miss him.

Colonial Williamsburg, while not the inspiration for the novel, provided dependable information and a chance to observe life in eighteenth-century Colonial Virginia. The townspeople and craftsmen, the wait staff, servants, farmers, housewives, and slaves patiently answered questions with detail and enthusiasm. The backyards, meadows, greens, churches, inns, governor's mansion, and armory gave me a place to wander and see the plants, animals, and streets my characters knew. The website for Colonial Williamsburg provided more information—including what a trip from England to the colonies entailed. Any errors in the descriptions of the world Betsy knew are entirely mine.

This novel is better for having chapters critiqued at the Off Campus Writers' Workshop, the University of Iowa

Summer Writing Festival workshop, the Iowa Writers' Summer Workshop, the New York State Summer Writers Institute at Skidmore, the Taos Summer Writers' Conference, and the Tin House Summer Writers' Workshop. I am particularly grateful to Amy Whalen's thorough reading of the complete novel at the New York Writers Institute. Janet Bailey made important, discerning suggestions, as did the editors at the Kirkus Reviews.

Anna Hozian, Natalia Nebel, and Syed Haider met at the Perfect Cup on Chicago's north side to work on editing the *Chicago Quarterly Review* and critique our novels. I learned from their superb writing and their comments on what I had submitted for their scrutiny. Syed has continued to be a valuable reader, editor of *CQR*, and a dear friend.

The importance of Fred Shafer's insightful criticism in his novel workshop cannot be overstated. Over the past ten years, the writers in Fred's workshop, including Sue Gilbert, Bill Kennedy, David Pelzer, Mary Hutchings Reed, and Joyce Zeiss, have contributed important considerations for the novel.

Immeasurable gratitude goes to Linda Keane and Lois Roelofs, The Tuesday Writers who, along with Pepper Furey, read countless drafts of chapters and then read through the entire novel to check for consistency and pacing. Their own writing inspired me to keep writing and revising.

Finally, I owe most to my daughters, Claire, an art critic and editor, and Anne, a film editor, for their support and willingness to read and critique three or four "final" drafts, and to my husband, Ron Barliant, whose unfailing encouragement and confidence has always mattered most in writing this novel and in all things.

LOIS BARLIANT has published an essay in *Out of Line* and short stories in *The Clothes Line Review*, *The Heartland Review*, and *The Chicago Quarterly*, where she served as an editor. She has been a teacher in Liberia, Great Britain, and Spain, and taught high school English and Creative Writing in the Chicago Public Schools. She lives in Chicago with her husband, Ron. *One Day's Tale* is her first novel.

CPSIA information can be obtained at www.ICGtesting.com
Printed in the USA
LVOW10s2250100516

487649LV00003B/144/P